BLOODED

"You're going to cry like a baby when I don't come back."

"You're coming back," she said, finally tilting her head up to meet my gaze. Her eyes were clear, but I could sense her emotion.

"How can you be so sure? You have no idea what's in store for me. Serene could rip my skin to shreds with her bullwhip, or she could stab my heart with her metal Wolverine claws." Sounded like something the sadistic bitch would have. "There are a million ways she could kill me, and you know it. We're just sidestepping the main issue—this might be our last tender goodbye forever." I didn't want to admit it, but I was a little nervous I wouldn't see her—or anyone—again. All jokes aside, I was betting on me, but I had no idea how things were going to turn out in the end.

"Let me tell you something." She motioned me to lean over further with a curl of her finger, and I obliged. Very softly, right next to my ear, she said, "I know you're going to survive, because I'm witchy and I know a thing or two about the future. And guess what?"

"What?" I whispered.

"Chicken butt."

By Amanda Carlson:

Full Blooded
Hot Blooded

HOT BLOODED

Jessica McClain:
Book Two

AMANDA CARLSON

orbit

www.orbitbooks.net

ORBIT

First published in Great Britain in 2013 by Orbit

Copyright © 2013 by Amanda Carlson

Excerpt from *The Shambling Guide to New York City*
Copyright © 2013 by Mary Lafferty

The moral right of the author has been asserted.

A CIP catalogue record for this book
is available from the British Library.

ISBN 978-0-356-50128-4

Printed and bound by CPI Group (UK) Ltd, Croydon CR0 4YY

Papers used by Orbit are from well-managed forests
and other responsible sources.

MIX

For Daryl and Koppy.
The best two parents a girl could ask for.

The knife pressed against my neck was pissing me off. "You're kidding me, right?" I couldn't see what was behind me, but it smelled faintly of eggs. Half a beat later its Otherness began to creep along my skin like an unwanted caress. My fingers curled around the door handle of my car.

I didn't have time for this.

It hissed a few inches from my ear. "Shut up, bitch. You're going to pay for what you did—"

I brought my elbow up hard, faster than any human could follow, and cracked my attacker neatly in the face as I spun around. Without hesitation, I grabbed him by the neck and slammed him onto the hood of the car next to me. Crap, that was going to leave a dent. I glanced around. Luckily there were no bystanders nearby. "What's your problem?" I snarled. "Doesn't look like you want a piece of me now."

The rheumy eyes of a stunned imp stared back at me, blinking once. An imp, by definition, was half human, half demon—and this one was heavy on the human, which was why he hadn't triggered any of my new senses. A supe this weak had to be in close proximity to give off any Otherness. He wasn't a danger to me—more like a pesky mosquito—and to my credit he stank like a dirty bum more than any kind of demon. I examined him, not surprised to find he resembled the imp I'd killed last week. But this one was a lot weaker than Drake, so maybe a distant relation gunning for revenge?

Demons got off on revenge.

"So it's..." he gasped through a very diminished airway, "...true..."

"What's true?" I relaxed my grip on his neck so he could answer. When he failed to do so, I hauled him up by the shirt, turned him around, and pushed him against the side of my car. "I'm running a little short on time. Care to expound further?" I shook him for emphasis, letting him know there was really no other choice.

A glint of surprise along with a creepy smile full of stained, slightly pointy teeth slowly spread over his features. I jammed him back against my car, locking my forearm across his neck again, hoping to convince him to spit out an answer before things had to get any uglier. "Look," I said when he remained silent. "I've had a rough few days and I'm in no mood to be attacked by yet another supe. This is not going to end well for you if you don't answer my question, so I'll ask it again. What's true?" His greasy brown hair swung limply over his shoulders as I jostled him into a better position. What was it with imps? Not showering must be a union order.

"I didn't know you were *her*," he finally spat, his metallic breath pinging my nose like a tarnished penny. I eased my arm off his jugular. "I came to avenge my cousin. But I can smell you now. I know who you are. There have been rumors, but you won't be able to hide from us. We will find you."

Find me? My wolf shot to the surface, sensing the real threat behind his words. I wasn't hiding from anyone, especially not the imps. My secret had come out, and for all I knew the entire planet was well aware I'd become the only female werewolf on earth. It wasn't ideal, but nobody had asked me.

My nails elongated to vicious points in the span of a heartbeat. "What do you think you know about me?" I edged in closer, inhaling his repugnant scent. The possibility this moron knew more about me than I did tested my compassion on every level. "Imp, you have three seconds before my wolf comes out, and I can guarantee you're not going to like what she has to say." She growled her agreement in my mind and I echoed it out loud for effect.

Instead of answering, the imp lunged forward, trying to break out of my grasp. His movement surprised me, forcing me to take a small step backward to steady myself. But my hold didn't break, because he was weak and the muscles in my arms had already coalesced together like two giant anvils waiting to bring the hammer down on his greasy, uncombed head. "I've had enough of this crap, demon boy." I shook him. "You're going to talk whether you want to or not." I dug my nails into his neck to accentuate my point. "You can either spill it here with me, or you can face my Alpha, who is a lot less patient than me."

"You will not rule us... *bitch*," he sputtered, blood slowly leaking out of the wounds in his neck. "We are stronger. We will never follow you! Your filth cannot touch us."

Rule? "What in the *hell* are you talking about?" He wasn't talking about ruling the humans. I rocked him back on the edge of his heels, my irises flashing an angry violet. "Listen clearly to what I'm telling you now. I want nothing to do with your demon race—not now and certainly not in the future. Ruling you doesn't even make sense. I'm a wolf, and demons live in the Underworld." A place nobody in their right mind would volunteer to go willingly. "And believe me, imp, my plans aren't about to change. There's absolutely nothing about your kind that appeals to me." Stinky, unwashed cretins.

He opened his mouth, his stained teeth and coppery breath assaulting me on so many levels. "We will strike you down before you place a foot on the throne of Astaroth! The Prophecy will not stand. Your death is *imminent*," he sneered through the choke hold. "You will not best the powers of the Underworld. We are coming—"

I slammed my fist into the side of his head and he crumpled to the ground like a worthless marionette. "Yeah? Well, you're going to have to get in line, buddy, because everybody around here seems to want something from me and I'm late for a meeting."

I opened my car door and tossed him in the backseat. He was still breathing, but it would take him a while to recover. Unwanted attacks were getting old, but at least this one didn't have a foaming muzzle and three-inch canines. I slid into the driver's seat.

Now I just had to figure out why everyone in the entire supernatural race seemed to know more about me than I did.

"What did you just say?" I stood so quickly, my chair spun back and clattered against the wall. "The Second Coming of *what*? And who exactly was the *first*?"

Devon tossed a panicked look at my father, Callum McClain, Pack Alpha of the U.S. Northern Territories. The three of us had been sitting at the conference table in my office; my father had his hands folded neatly in front of him, looking calm and in charge. He nodded to Devon to continue as I stalked around the table. The fear leaking out of the Pack's computer whiz made my wolf edgy.

Devon spoke again, clearing his voice once before he started. "Um, well, according to what it says here..." I stopped behind his chair, leaning over his shoulder to read the words for myself. The text on the screen appeared to be taken from a copy of a photograph, and not a very clear one. The original parchment background looked broken and old, like the ink had rubbed off before they'd snapped a good shot of it. It read:

THE PROPHECY OF THE TRUE LYCAN:

One shall walk again; above all others she is born;
Within her the beast shall lie, well hidden in True Form;
And from this day forth, the Children of the Night shall pay;
By her supreme rule, her righteous hand will slay;
Justice to all, as none are her equal;
The True Lycan will Vanquish all Evil.

I turned away and started to pace. "What it states there doesn't make any sense. Why wouldn't we have our own record of this if it were true? Anyone could've made this stuff up—it's on the *Internet* for chrissake. That could easily be the rantings of a sixteen-year-old sci-fi nerd who fabricated a story about a female werewolf who took over the world. He probably saw a graphic novel about a hot chick who turned into a wolf and his libido shot into overdrive."

I made it back and forth twice before anyone spoke.

"Well." Devon paused. "This isn't the only place I found this information...exactly."

I spun around to face him. "What? Are you telling me what's

written there is actually a *possibility*?" The pulse of change began to twitch just below the surface of my skin, my arms and legs tightening in anticipation.

Major emotion was hard on wolves.

It triggered everything inside us, like holding a lit match in front of a can of butane. Since these sensations were brand-new to me, I was clearly having a hard time containing myself. Being overtired and worried about finding Rourke did nothing to help the situation either. There was also the slight problem of harboring a deadly spell in my veins, a gift from a deranged goddess who was trying to kill me.

"I believe it might be more than a possibility," Devon replied. "What we are seeing here is likely a loose interpretation of the original Prophecy, since the real one would be so old it would have gone through numerous retellings in numerous languages before now." He nodded toward the text on the screen. "I've cross-referenced 'True Lycan' in some of our oldest books and there are several indications in Pack history of a 'stranger who will walk again' who is 'unique from all others' and will 'dole out justice' with a supreme rule. It never specifies a female, per se, but I think all these things make it a strong possibility none-theless." He pointed in front of him. "This website went live less than twelve hours ago and the link was sent directly to me. I've been unable to trace any of the digital signatures. I don't even know what country it originated from. But there's enough correct wording, even though I can't officially authenticate any of it from the Rights of Laws, that makes me believe what we're reading here could hold truth, or at least a version of the truth, to your identity."

The werewolf Rights of Laws, our bible of sorts, had entries missing and others were charred beyond recognition. It had been destroyed in a fire long before it had been entrusted to my father. If there'd been any kind of werewolf Prophecy, it would've likely been inside those pages. Since "Lycans" were our ancestors, they were commonly referenced in our books.

I glanced at my father. "I'm not going with 'truth' just yet. We're still seeing this on the Internet for the first time and it's too similar to the Cain Myth to be a coincidence. Whoever sent this link to Devon had to have been behind sending the first Myth to the Compound all those years ago."

"Agreed." My father nodded. "But the Cain Myth was obviously changed to target our race alone. To instill hatred of you from the very beginning."

"But why would someone do that?" I asked. It seemed too complicated.

"Fear. Whoever is behind all this was worried you'd grow up to be too powerful, which you are proving to be. At the time you were an infant. There was no way to reach you. What better way to see your end than to make sure the wolves wanted you dead from the very beginning? The Cain Myth did its job effectively. The wolves have grown irrationally fearful of you, coupling you with the end of our race. If they had their way, you wouldn't have lived to see your sixteenth birthday."

I could recite the Cain Myth in my sleep.

*As a Female in Wolf Skin rises, the unborn Daughter of
  Cain is born;
In her the beast shall lie, well hidden in True Form;
And from this day forth, the Wolves of the Night shall pay;
Blood and flesh of their bones, her mighty hand shall slay;
The end of the race will be close at hand;
When the Daughter of Evil rules the land.*

I arched an eyebrow at my father. "If we already had information about a 'True Lycan' in our history, why haven't we put the pieces together before now?"

My father's irises jumped, sparking violet. His emotion tingled quickly through my veins, the blood we'd shared during the oath rearing up in my body, sending a flood of sensations through me, and at the forefront was love. "Rumors of a strong one, *Y Gwir Lycae*, the True Lycan, the one above all others who would someday rise again, have been around for as long as I can remember. Those were the tall tales the elders told around the hearth at the end of the day, a cup of mead in hand. Did I think those old stories might be connected in any way to my daughter? Never. The thought didn't even enter my mind. We are a male race, dominated by strength. Your birth was an anomaly, something I have always considered special. I thought fate had smiled on us by introducing a female line, because without them, our race will eventually die out. There are very few human women left in the world who can carry our offspring. Despite the Cain Myth and all the trouble it caused, I held fast to the hope you were here for a reason and eventually the wolves would accept you and see you as I did—as an asset to this race. It seems you are indeed here for a reason, but it's not quite the one I'd been hoping for."

"No," I said. "I don't think this is what any of us had hoped for—certainly not me."

"With that said, I believe this is not the time to lament fate," he stated firmly. "In order to move forward, we need to arm ourselves with as much information as we can gather. I agree with Devon. This is only a version of the real Prophecy. I want more answers as soon as possible." He turned to Devon. "When I return, I want a full report, even if you have to travel to the Old Country to obtain the information you need." We had an ancestral estate in Scotland. It was an old, beautiful castle filled with antiques and a library as big as a football field. "Cross-check with every entry you can find about *Y Gwir Lycae*. There should be a fair amount of texts to draw from. When you're done, I want a cohesive outline of what we are looking at here."

Devon nodded once. "Yes, sir."

I sighed, rubbing my temples. "I'm not sure what to believe. The reasoning that these old tales were actually about a female is thin. I don't have to remind you now is not a good time to find out I'm some reincarnate of an all-powerful she-wolf who is supposed to dole out justice to the supernatural world." Was there a *good* time to hear something like that? "Among other things, I have an angry police detective tied up in the other room I might actually have to kill." I slid my fingertips to the bridge of my nose and shook my head. "This is all so insane."

I was more rattled hearing this news than I cared to admit. During my first few days as the only full-blooded female were-wolf in the world I'd been ruthlessly attacked in my own home, turned on by my own kind, bound by a goddess who had stolen my mate—who was a werecat of unknown origin—and taken prisoner by a cranky Vampire Queen—whom I'd sworn an oath to that could get me killed. If this so-called Prophecy was true, it was going to stir up a maelstrom once it spread through the preternatural grapevine—if it hadn't already. Who knew who already possessed this information? We could've been the last to receive it on purpose. It didn't bode well that the stinky imp this morning had hinted about it. And if that little asshole knew, there was a chance they all knew.

"Jessica," my father said as he stood. "We will handle this. It's not ideal, but we will persevere as we always have. We are wolves. And wolves fight. We will win."

"I'm leaving town in less than five hours." I glanced at my

wrist, even though I hadn't worn a watch in years. I gazed across the room and met my father's eyes, my blood jumping with his anxiety, mixed with a hefty dose of my own. "I can't even begin to process everything this quickly. I'm going to need more time."

"Well," Devon interrupted, "there may be an upside to all this after all." He swiped a bead of sweat off his forehead. "It's much better than finding out the Cain Myth is true. At least with you being the True Lycan, we know you're not the *real* Daughter of Cain. I mean, right there, that should calm down some of the wolves, don't you think?" He raised his eyebrows and nodded. "Right?"

I shot him a dangerous glare. Devon wasn't a wolf. He was a human Essential to the Pack, brought in for his technical savvy. He was a nice guy and completely loyal to Pack, but I wasn't interested. "Yes," I answered. "Because my new job of *vanquishing all evil* is much better. The demons already seem incredibly fond of me, and the Vamp Queen can't wait to get me back in her grasp. My life is bound to improve now that my *righteous hand* is cocked and ready to kill anyone up to no good, which pretty much describes just about everyone in the entire supernatural race."

2

"Devon," my father ordered. "Leave us now."

Devon jumped out of his seat, grabbing his computer and knocking over an empty coffee cup in his haste. The clatter as as it fell to the ground mimicked how my brain felt inside. My wolf gave a low growl. *I know. This is a lot and we need to get moving.* She yipped her agreement.

When the door shut behind him I let out the long sigh I'd been holding. "When did you suspect I was different?" I asked my father quietly. "Once I changed, you had to have some idea I was not like the others."

My father turned and walked around the table to a bank of high windows that ran across the conference room wall. He raked one of his hands through his dark hair, his arm flexing tightly, straining his blue work shirt taut. "I didn't know for sure until the night you fought the rogue. Before then I only suspected."

I dropped my tired body into a chair. My mind felt like a

crowded elevator, unable to squeeze in one more piece of information. The weight of Rourke's absence pushed down on me, crushing something vital inside. I craved him in a way I couldn't adequately express. In a way that tested the boundaries of attachment. I had enough to worry about. There was no extra space for fantastical stories about my true freakish identity.

But instead of a tirade, I said nothing and waited for my father to continue. I needed to hear his side.

"When the Cain Myth was first delivered to the Compound, there was an uprising," he began. "You have to understand the safety concerns, Jessica, if nothing else. You were only an infant. I quelled it quickly and with extreme force. I made a vow to protect you. I vowed it to myself and to your mother, rest her soul." My mother had died in childbirth. Delivering one wolf was tricky, but twins was impossible. I'd been told it'd been amazing she'd been able to carry my brother and me to term. Annie McClain had been a fighter until the end. "To be clear, I never believed for a single second the Cain Myth to be true. You were my daughter, my own flesh and blood. But convincing the wolves had been much harder than I'd ever expected. Fear overwhelmed any rational explanations when it came to you. As you grew up, you were a constant reminder to them that something was wrong." He turned to me. "I desperately wanted you to stay human. I knew if you ever shifted into a wolf, it would be something that would turn the supernatural community inside out. You're my daughter and all I've ever wanted was to protect you."

I lifted my head and stared at my father. Our irises each glowed a matching violet, bonding us like nothing else in this world could. This was the parent who had raised me, who'd given me unconditional love. I couldn't argue with that. "I understand what you're saying," I said slowly, feeling more resolved. "I know all the decisions you made were made out of love and all of those events have led us here. But if you believe the Prophecy to be true, it has to be founded in something concrete. I need to understand as much as I can before I leave and I only have a little time left." I refrained from looking at my nonexistent watch for a second time.

He exhaled and stared at the ground. When he lifted his head I caught a glimpse of his true age. It lingered in the creases of his tired eyes, but it was gone in the next blink. "When you shifted the first time, I knew something was different. When your wolf signaled your change, alerting us with her beacon, it was a call made by your wolf to *aid* you. That has never happened in over five centuries of my rule. A normal wolf alert is primal and wild. Yours was not. It carried intelligence. In our oldest writings they talk of our Lycan ancestors being able to cohabitate with their wolves peacefully, that each side cooperated with the other to become one perfect supernatural—strong, powerful, and unparalleled. Then you blocked me repeatedly and could hold your suspended form, something no other wolf can do, and it became very clear you were something else. After reading the lines of the Prophecy and remembering the hearth tales about the *Y Gwir Lycae,* I realized it fit. You're more than just one of our ancestors, Jessica. I can feel it in my bones and see it with my own eyes. There's a reason a female was born to us. Fate does not get such things wrong."

Emotion rushed to the surface.

The rawness of it was new. The texture of it tugged against my skin, making me feel itchy. My wolf started to pace in my mind. This was the most honest exchange I'd ever shared with my father. For the first time, we were engaged in a conversation as two adults. He wasn't trying to protect me. It was just the two of us here in this room, almost as if the rest of the world had ceased to exist.

My father was so sure of what he was saying. His certainty poured through our connection, but it was a lot to wrap my brain around. "The Prophecy still doesn't make any sense to me," I finally said, "because I still feel like...*me*. I don't feel overly powerful or qualified to dole out justice to anyone, much less to the supernatural race. I feel like myself, only now with a cranky wolf in my head." To accent my point, my wolf snapped her jaws. *I know I'm physically different, but I still feel normal. I haven't suddenly forgotten who I am or where I came from. It doesn't work that way.*

"Jessica, I know this is a shock. It's shocking to me, and I'm an Alpha werewolf. Who and what you are is unprecedented. But before we decide how to move forward, we need to gather more information, as I've said before. In light of this discovery, I'm elated you're leaving town. That's exactly where I want you—out of sight with adequate protection."

My mind shot to Rourke. "That's good, because I'm ready to go. When I get back, we'll have a chance to regroup and figure out what all this stuff means."

"I don't want to scare you." His voice held a raw note that rang through the air. It held dread and anger. "But you have no idea what the impact of this news will have on the supernatural community. Each Sect is more wary and powerful than the next. There will be massive reactive fear in every race. This is not something we will be able to quell or explain away. This is something we have to *fight*. Fight until they fear our power, and when they stop fearing us, we fight again to prove we are the strongest. It's the only way they will back down. The only way to lessen the attacks that will come your way."

I knew he was right; it was just hard to hear it. I'd spent my entire life hoping and praying the wolves would never go to war because of me, that I wouldn't be the catalyst to end our race like the Cain Myth stated. It seemed now there would be fighting, but the irony was that the wolves wouldn't be fighting against me; they were going to be fighting to protect me. That is, if they chose to believe the Prophecy over the Myth, which wasn't a for sure by any means. "I'm willing to do whatever's necessary," I said with resignation. "I have no other choice. I can't go into hiding and I can't become something else." Though that sounded awfully good at the moment. "If we have to fight, I will follow your lead."

My father nodded his head decisively, weariness lining his features. Finding out your daughter was about to become the most wanted female in existence was not on any father's to-do list. But bemoaning things had never been my style. Nor was arguing a moot point. There was no other way out of this but to keep moving forward.

"Once you return," he said, "we'll formulate a plan and take our advantages wherever we can. When we're more educated about this Prophecy, we can determine your strengths and figure out a solid defense."

"I'm assuming you've come up with a short-term plan in the meantime?" I asked. My father would not have come into this meeting cold when he had information his daughter might be the *Y Gwir Lycae*.

"Yes." My father strode from the windows to the table and sat. Even though his stress showed, he didn't look a day over thirty-five. He was handsome, with a full head of jet-black hair. He leaned over and gave me a small smile. "James and I worked out some of the logistics last night. The very beginnings of a plan to ensure we have a fighting chance once this news spreads. Defeating the threats against you will take every wolf we have. As much as the other Sects will present a problem to us in the future—and the stakes will be high—they are not my first priority. The wolves who recently broke apart from both U.S. Packs have tossed us all into chaos. We don't stand a chance of defending you from any attack until we can pull ourselves together and unite once again. Infighting will thin us out, make us weak." He paused, looking down at his hands for a moment, then he glanced back up at me. "The short-term plan involves me doing something unprecedented."

I stared at him, assessing. Being head of Pack wasn't easy, but I knew whatever he had in mind would be a calculated move in the right direction. "I'm sure whatever it is, it's the best step."

"After we finish with this meeting," he said, "I'm heading down into the Southern Territories to meet with Redman."

"In person?" I asked, somewhat surprised. Visiting an Alpha you were feuding with was not the norm by any standards. From all the stories I'd heard in my lifetime about Red Martin, Alpha of the U.S. Southern Territories, he was a brutal sonofabitch who ruled his wolves with an iron fist. "How big is his Pack these days?"

"He leads fifty-nine wolves," my father said, contempt lacing his voice. "Thirty-seven wolves thinner than it was twenty years ago. I don't know where they've gone, since only a few have come to my Pack. They aren't listed as rogue either. I'm assuming they have assimilated into new Packs around the world—either that, or they are the wolves who began the fracture and Red has kept it quiet on purpose. Whatever the reason, I'm about to find out."

Two hundred years ago, Redman Martin was responsible for the breakup of the U.S. Pack, becoming Alpha of the Southern Territories. As ruling Alpha, my father could've easily ended his life. Instead he chose to let Red form a new Pack, because restless wolves were a hindrance to everyone. Red's nasty influence had already rent a hole in the existing Pack, so there had been no other choice. The wolves who left to run under Red's directive were of a particular *flavor*.

My father had not been sorry to see them go.

"Do you think Redman could be behind the whole fracture?" I said. "It's something he'd be capable of doing, from what I've heard about him over the years."

"I can't rule that out, but the only reason he's agreed to let me come down is to prove to me he's not behind any of this," my father answered. "He knows he has a war on his hands and once we start fighting, the north would wipe them out. His Pack has dwindled to almost nothing. He's eager to prove he's not harboring the traitors. But they have to be somewhere, and he has to answer for his missing wolves. The fracture group has to have a home base in the U.S. and it has to be close enough for them to act when they need to."

"They can't possibly be stationed in the north," I said.

"Damn right, they're not in the north. They wouldn't dare settle in my territory. If there's a brain cell between any of them, which is doubtful, they would be in the farthest reaches of the Southern Territories' borders. My best guess would be somewhere in the swamplands of Florida or the high mountains of Mexico. If they attack, they'll attack the south first, and try to amass wolves and move forward from there. They will need more than their ragtag group to go up against my wolves and they know it. Redman either sides with us, or he sides with them. He's selfish to the core, but I'm guessing he will take the easy way out. Fighting me will be a fatal decision on his part."

"He's had a taste of power for too long," I agreed. "He won't fight you and risk his status and power. If Redman is not responsible for the fracture in the Packs, who is?" I'd been running it over in my mind since I'd left New Orleans and nothing made much sense. "Stuart Lauder acted like he was in charge that night in the clearing, but there was no way he could be behind the entire operation. He couldn't have amassed such a large following on his own. He wasn't smart enough." My irises sparked remembering the fight. "But his father was." Hank Lauder, one of my biggest opponents growing up, was still at large. I'd killed his only son and he would be after me to exact his retribution; it was just a matter of time.

"I have two of my best trackers on Hank. He's still somewhere in the Ozarks, likely holed up mourning his loss. They haven't found him yet, but he will answer for his son's misdeeds; make no mistake. When they bring him in we will find out everything he knew, but I doubt it was much. Hank was loud and ornery, but he was loyal to this Pack. His biggest mistake was overindulgence. He gave that boy everything he ever asked for." And it had made him nasty as hell. "Wolves get restless, which I understand," my father continued, shaking his head, "but the fracture feels too organized. My guess is it's coming from the outside."

"Another Sect?"

"Yes."

I bit my lip. It was highly unusual for any supernatural to pair with another. Each Sect was untrusting of the other, bordering on pathological mistrust. "From what the Vamp Queen indicated, the fracture wolves had already struck a deal with the vampires." There was no way to know how binding it had been. Eudoxia, the powerful Vampire Queen—and current bane of my existence—certainly had something up her sleeve. Had she been orchestrating some kind of coup since my birth? It was a possibility. "If Eudoxia had prior knowledge of the Prophecy, she could've sown doubt over time, made the younger wolves wary with a few carefully placed spies. She said the wolves were willing and eager to swear fealty to her."

"Wolves don't swear oaths to vamps," my father growled as he arched his eyebrow at me to punctuate the statement. "Before you, it's never been done."

I had indeed broken the golden rule about swearing oaths to vampires, but I'd done it to save my mate. And I'd do it again. But that little tidbit didn't need to be announced out loud. "So where does all of this leave us?"

My father leaned forward. "I really don't know, Jessica. I'm not going to pretend to know."

Thinking about all the various implications of the Prophecy made my head spin. "I don't feel Alpha inclined," I said honestly. "I realize I'm strong, but my wolf has made it clear it's not our job to run Pack. I have to believe that won't change."

"I don't feel a threat from you. If anything, it's the opposite, which is a blessed relief."

My wolf yipped at me. We needed to get moving. I slid my chair back to stand. "Are you heading south now?"

"Yes, I'm leaving shortly and I'm taking a dozen wolves with me. We'll be gone as long as it takes." He placed both hands on the table in front of him. "Jessica, I want you to know if you encounter a severe emergency while you're gone, I *will* find you." I had no doubt he would. "I will also be in touch with you as often as I can."

There was one more loose end I had to deal with before I left town.

And it came in the form of one very angry police detective.

"What are we going to do about Ray?" I asked. Raymond Hart had unwittingly uncovered our secret and now presented a threat to our race. He'd been brought over from the Safe

House early this morning so I could have a chat with him—meaning kill him if I had to—and was currently being held under guard down the hall.

My father gave me a hard look.

I didn't want to kill him. "You know, there are other ways we can deal with this," I said. "Exterminating every human being who finds out about us doesn't have to be our normal moving forward. Plus, killing him after he's been so intent on me, has my break-in case open on his desk, and was last seen at my apartment building—his car is *still* parked there—and with Jeff Arnold, my building super, dead and all the recent calls about noise and various disturbances, it will be easy for them to piece together the coincidences. If they haven't already. I will be their prime suspect."

"I cannot, in good conscience, leave a threat to our existence in the form of a police detective running around after what he's seen. I know our ways are not easy for you, Jessica, but someone like Raymond Hart poses a serious problem. He is not someone who would assimilate as an Essential into our Pack, which is the only option left to him other than death."

He was right. Ray would never assimilate willingly. But I still didn't want to kill him. If I killed Ray, which would be relatively easy because he'd been a constant headache of mine for years, each human after him would be less of an issue.

I didn't want killing to ever be easy.

If I didn't try to change Ray's mind, no other headstrong human would ever have a chance of escaping this fate. So why not start with Ray? "What if I can get him to assimilate? You have to admit he would be a great asset to Pack. He's been a police detective for almost twenty years. We'd have someone on the inside, and as a bonus, he could make all the issues of my case vanish in one day."

My father arched a critical eye at me. "He doesn't leave this building unless I'm satisfied."

Short of a lobotomy, there was no way I could change Ray's mind that fast. "How about if..." I hemmed. "If I can't get him to swear in the next half hour"—What in the *hell* was I going to do with him if he didn't swear? He was *so* not going to swear—"I take him...with me?" *Not a good plan, Jessica.* My wolf growled and snapped her muzzle, telling me exactly what she thought of my ingenious idea.

"*With you?*" my father echoed.

Ray had a death sentence if I left him behind.

"Yep. I'll take the asshole with me if I have to."

3

"Hello, Ray." I smiled pleasantly as I entered the small suite located across the hall from our offices. It didn't technically belong to Hannon & Michaels, but since it hadn't been leased in years we'd taken it over, using it mostly for storage. "Looks like you fared okay last night." I nodded my head, acknowledging the two other guys in the room.

"Good morning." Danny winked, his cheerful English accent bringing levity to a stressful situation. "Just so you know, your man and I are getting along splendidly. We had a real *Hart*-to-heart last night. Didn't we, mate?"

Ray's eyes narrowed. I was certain his night with Danny had been less than pleasant. For a police officer, very little would suck worse than being held hostage. After all the training, a cop would know the chances were slim to none of making it out alive. "Very funny, Danny," I said. "No need to harass the prisoner any more than necessary."

"You know, humor is the hallmark of a brilliant mind."

He tapped the outside of his head and gave me a toothy grin. "Without it, we'd suffer the days away in endless monotony."

As well as being the resident jokester, Danny was strikingly handsome. He had high cheekbones, a strong chin, and brown locks that fell perfectly into his blue-green eyes, making your fingers itch to brush it out. Accompany that with the body of a pro athlete and it was a wicked combination for any woman.

It was a good thing I'd always preferred my men rough around the edges.

Extremely rough.

Rourke roared into my mind with his hard, taut body, jet-black tattoos, honey-colored hair, and a perfect layer of stubble running along his strong jawline. My wolf growled. *I know. I know. But we have to be careful or Danny will think those smells are for him, so keep a lid on it.*

I glanced at the other wolf in the room, pulling myself together with effort.

I'd never met him before. He stood on the other side of Ray, who was currently tied to a folding chair. Ray had thankfully lost my pantyhose gag from the night before, but had what appeared to be a white dish towel tied around his mouth. It might be time to invest in some quality interrogation supplies; the ordinary household supplies were looking a little ragtag. "Hi, I'm Jessica." I reached my hand out to the unknown wolf.

Hesitation lit in his eyes for a few beats before he extended his hand back to me. Selling myself as friendly to these guys was going to be a huge battle after so many years of fear.

"Tom Bailey," he replied, dropping my hand.

"Good to meet you, Tom. If you could, I'd like you to wait outside."

He glanced at Danny, who gave him a curt nod, and then left without looking back.

"One of your guys?" I asked as the door clicked shut behind him.

"Yes. He's one of the best, and can be trusted."

"He stared at me like I was a space alien."

"He was likely just admiring your beauty. You do look splendid, as usual." Danny swept a careless gaze over me, eyeing me from top to bottom like we were having a casual chat instead of being the possible harbingers of death to a human. "You were made for skinny jeans. They absolutely adore you."

I stifled a smile, and instead turned my attention to my immediate concern, Raymond Hart. "Okay, Ray. It's time for us to settle this." I lifted a folding chair and set it squarely in front of him, straddling it. "It seems you've finally uncovered what you've been dying to find out for years. Why I could track criminals so quickly, why I was so fast on my feet, why I had the best instincts on the force. But, as you can plainly see, I'm not a crackhead." I spread my arms wide in front of me and leaned forward—part intimidation, partly because I could. "The truth is, I was born into a family of wolves. Yes, real-life wolves. And recently I've become one. But, honestly, if we're playing fair, none of this was any of your business to find out. You should've left well enough alone. But you didn't. And now you're in so deep you have only one choice left. If you choose not to take it, your life ends here." I swept my finger down toward the floor. Interrogation took mad dramatic skills. None of which Ray was buying. He was completely unimpressed.

His eyes narrowed and his scent changed, going from steady fear to an acidic flare of anger in the space of a heartbeat.

The man had gigantic balls.

His normal steel-colored flattop had drooped and there were dark bags under his eyes. It was doubtful he'd slept a wink last night. No surprises there. You'd think after all he'd seen and gone through in the last forty-eight hours, he'd be ready to acquiesce. Anything to try and get out of this mess. Instead he was ready for a fight.

And I was just the gal to give him one.

I leaned into his space to accentuate my control. I had to make him believe he had only one option left, and not to take it meant his death. "The solitary choice you have remaining, after everything you've seen, is to join us," I stated calmly. "Do you understand what I'm saying? There's a place in my world for humans. But you have to be willing to come on your own. There's no in-between."

Ray spat something from between his gag. It was muddled, but I heard it clear enough.

"It doesn't matter if you think I'm a bitch, Ray. We're way beyond that. What we're here to discuss is you keeping your life. My awesome personality traits are not on the table."

Danny slid his chair a little closer to the action, scraping it along the worn linoleum, grinning like he'd just won front-row tickets to a WWE match. He perched on the edge of his seat, elbows resting comfortably on his knees. After a moment he said, "This is a nice twist, isn't it? And here, Mr. Hart, I didn't think you had a chance of seeing another sunrise. Listen to the nice lady, because she's not making this bit up. Even though we enjoyed our chat last night, I won't hesitate to kill you today. That's how it works. It's nothing personal, you understand. It's purely business."

Ray thrashed for a moment in his seat.

I wasn't interested in watching his struggle, so I reached over and yanked the towel off his mouth in one motion. "Hannon," he gasped immediately, taking in a big breath. "You're never going to get away with this!" He'd only ever known me as Molly Hannon, my alias for the past seven years. "You can't kill me. Everyone on the force will know—"

"Ray," I interrupted. "Don't delude yourself. We'll get away with anything we want. We excel in covering things up we don't want anyone else to see." He didn't have to know that my killing him would lead to more headaches than it was worth. "After hundreds of years of experience, you kind of nail it down."

"If anything happens to me, they will track it back to you. Your case is all over my desk." His face was beet red from all the strain and anger. "If you kill me, a second grader with a finger up his ass could figure it out. And you'll end up paying for this with life behind bars."

"I won't be paying for anything, Ray." I leaned in closer, my face inches from his, my voice dropping to just above a whisper. "And when we're done with you there will be no trace. There will be nothing left to identify. It will be like you disappeared into thin air." I snapped my fingers right next to his ear. Had to keep the show going.

He froze. "They'll find my body," he stammered. "I'm a police detective, for chrissake. They won't stop until the case is solved."

A slow smile spread across my lips. "Will they?" He was going to make me do it the hard way, naturally. My irises sparked violet. It wasn't a hard thing to do, since I still had more than enough emotion flowing through my veins from this morning. My wolf was at the edge and she was tired of waiting.

He gasped and started thrashing again, struggling against his bonds.

"Think about it, Ray," I continued as if nothing was amiss. "If we actually exist, what else do you think is out there? You can't believe we're the *only* ones. Joining us will give you a huge advantage. Imagine all the crazy shit you'll be able to learn and how many crimes you can solve with our help."

Ray was intelligent enough to follow what I was saying.

He stopped moving.

"That's right, Ray. Vamps, witches, demons, goblins, you name it—all true. Fairy tales exist. Think of all the things you can learn, all the cases that were never solved because they were *Other*. You'll make chief with our help. But if you don't accept my proposal now, I'll be forced to have my pal spell your body. That means you won't be you. Well, that is, until you're in the ground and buried. But before the spell wears off, you're John Fucking Doe and nobody will ever know what happened to Raymond Hart. No physical body, no evidence, no case. End of story." I had absolutely no idea if Marcy, who happened to be my secretary, a witch, and best pal, could even do something like that—but it sounded good so I was going with it. I ended with a dramatic hand slash toward the floor.

Ray didn't so much as blink.

Danny reached over and cuffed his shoulder so hard the chair nearly upended. "Spells are a backup plan for me, mate. Not the route I'd go. See, I'm more of a concrete blocks and heavy weights guy. Or maybe a nice wood chipper. I've never had the pleasure of using one before, but they look fairly interesting and easy to operate, and my garden could use a good fertilizing this time of year."

Ray's face turned a coronary red. "I don't believe you," he said. "Everything you're saying can't possibly be true. You're making this up because you want me to join your crazy-ass cult, but I'm not drinking the goddamn Kool-Aid! Do you hear me? I'm not drinking it!"

I closed my eyes, but refrained from pinching the bridge of

my nose. I spoke quietly. "Ray, you saw Danny for yourself. How do you explain away a human shifting into a wolf right before your very eyes? You weren't on any Kool-Aid then—or were you? I didn't peg you as a user, but maybe I'm wrong. Were you high when you saw Danny shift?"

"*What?*" Ray shouted with enough outrage infused in his voice to make a small child cry real tears. "I've never taken a drug in my life!" Then he shuddered. It was the first real fear he'd shown thus far. "When he...changed...that...that was just some sort of trick you played on me. He caught me by surprise, fooled me somehow." He stammered some more. This was a typical human reaction to something they couldn't explain away. Finally. Ray, it seemed, had already filed it into a neat place in his mind, coming up with a justifiable story his brain could handle. He sputtered, "I came in...and there was a strange animal...and it shocked me, so I fainted..."

I glanced at Danny and asked, "Did you happen to show him anything more last night when you two were alone?"

"Nope," Danny answered. "I threatened his life repeatedly, but I had no idea you wanted him to accept us. I figured the less he knew before we killed him the better."

Ray shot us both a searing look. If he had his gun, he would've shot us without hesitation. "It doesn't matter what you try to show me. I'm not buying it. You've been goofy for years, Hannon, but monsters don't exist and I'm not joining your cult."

I narrowed my eyes, letting them spark deeply. "I know you believe it deep down, Ray, you know why? Because I can smell it." I took in a deep breath to accentuate my point. "You're just being stubborn and making this excruciatingly hard on all of us." I sighed. "Unfortunately I don't have the time for hard. If you can believe it, I don't want to kill you. I really don't. You're all kinds of painful, but I believe you deserve to live.

The pledge I took to protect when I joined the police force was sincere. But time is running out. My conditions for not killing you are as follows—and they're nonnegotiable." He glared at me, but remained quiet. "One: you will swear a Blood Oath of fealty to our Pack. This binds you to us. If you betray the oath, you die. Once you do this, you become an Essential to our Pack—you bring value by your position on the force and we protect you. It's a fair trade. Two: you take a voluntary year hiatus to assimilate to our ways, starting immediately. Your excuse will be stress related, and everyone will buy it. After a year in the north woods recuperating in peace, you'll be good as new and no one will be the wiser."

Rage vibrated off of Ray in short, angry waves. "I don't care what you say. I'm not swearing some kind of ritual oath to anyone. You and your little cult of misfits can—"

I reached over and yanked his gag back up quicker than he could track. It shocked him into silence.

He was such a thorn in my ass.

"Looks like he's not willing to compromise, then," Danny said. "Though, it was a rather sweet deal if you bothered to ask me. I would've agreed to it in a heartbeat."

Ray started to struggle and, in a moment of weakness, I considered killing him. It would be so much easier. But unfortunately easy had never been my style. "Dammit, Ray, why are you such a stubborn idiot!" I shot off my seat and kicked my folding chair. The wall exploded and the chair clattered to the ground in pieces, accompanied by a snowfall of white dust.

"Listen, Jess." Danny stood in front of me. "You can't beat yourself up about this." He placed his hands carefully on my shoulders, glancing at me quickly before averting his eyes. My status was above his and prolonged eye contact in a stressful situation was hard. "I can see the mortality decisions are going to bloody tear you apart, because you're still seeing the world as a human does. But I can assure you this bloke isn't worth your frustration." He gestured idly at Ray, who'd shut up and stopped moving after my tirade. "We've much more important things on the agenda tonight, like setting out to find your cat." Danny was joining me as a Selective on this trip, which basically meant he was my muscle-for-hire, along with my twin brother, Tyler. "Dusk will be here shortly. I know you haven't had much experience killing yet, so I'll be happy to finish this up for you. It can be over and done with in a jiffy."

"Yet" was the operative word in that sentence. Killing innocent people shouldn't be a snap. Just because I was a wolf now was no excuse. I'd spent twenty-six years as a human. I couldn't kill the bastard that easily.

He was going to have to work for it.

"We're not killing him, Danny."

"Come again?" He cocked his head in question.

"He lives. For now."

I glanced down at Ray, and his eyes narrowed, sensing a trick.

This was the point where he was hoping to gloat while I admitted this was just a weird cult after all. But unfortunately for him there was no Kool-Aid to dispense. This was the real deal. "That's right, Ray." I exhaled a long, tired breath. "You're going to live to see another day. You're a complete fool, but I guess you're my fool now."

"Um, Jessica?" Danny asked. "I don't think your father is going to be quite as willing to let him—"

"It's already settled. If I couldn't convince Ray to swallow the quiet pill and swear a Blood Oath, I had to take ownership of him. If he stays here without me, he dies. Nobody in Pack is willing to babysit him." I could've asked Marcy or Nick to do it, but it was too risky. If Ray somehow escaped and exposed us, they would end up paying for it with their lives. "I'm choosing to decide his fate. He's mine."

Danny's face showed his confusion as he tried in vain to process my foolish ways. "Yours?"

"He's coming with us," I assured him.

"You must be joking." Danny laughed, his face incredulous. "Surely we'll be trekking where no human can follow. He's bound to end up killed or worse. Not that there's actually anything worse than dead, but it could definitely hurt more."

I shrugged. "Then he'll die. But I'm not killing him right here in cold blood."

Danny's expression switched to a sardonic grin in an instant. "Whatever you say. You're the boss."

I took a sharp breath. "You have to be careful, Danny," I scolded. "Why do you always tread so close to the hairy edge? Someday your mouth is going to spin you into trouble and no amount of sweet talking is going to get you out." Referring to me like that so boldly could cause waves where none should be, especially when the real boss was still in the building.

He didn't pretend to misunderstand. "It's an addiction, naturally. What fun is the world when everything is so safe and tidy? Everything in its proper place?"

He had a point.

I moved toward the door. "Take Ray to his house and pack a bag. If his house is under any surveillance, regroup. Meet me back at my apartment when you're done. We'll be out at full dark; the vamps will be there shortly after. Be ready."

As I left, I heard Danny say to Ray, "No need to look so glum, Detective Hart. The vampires won't kill you instantly.

They like to play with their prey first. That means you and I will have a lot more happy fun time together. Won't that be smashing?"

I headed back into the main offices of Hannon & Michaels, the P.I. firm I shared with my partner, Nick Michaels. Nick was a werefox who'd been raised on the Compound with me, my father having taken him in as a child. Because male werewolves don't play well with others, we'd been fast friends ever since.

Marcy, our fearless secretary and resident spell caster, stood from her desk as I walked in, reading me accurately with her sharp eyes. Marcy was a sassy, curvy, redheaded witch whom I secretly adored. She hated overt emotional interactions, so I tended to heap it on whenever possible.

"What's up?" she asked. "Cop chat didn't go well? You look a little haggard."

"I feel haggard. Do we have any food left?"

"Nope, you and your compadres scarfed everything down an hour ago, and there were at least twenty takeout bags in the lunchroom. What is it with you guys? Who can possibly keep up with all these constant hunger demands? It's unnatural."

"What can I say? Wolves like to eat." I chuckled to myself. Eating massive amounts of food in order to feed my new, faster metabolism was becoming a serious adjustment.

My stomach grumbled to punctuate my point.

"*Like* to eat?" Marcy said. "Your eyes roll back in your head every time food comes through that door. It's like watching a puppy dig into its breakfast bowl."

I couldn't exactly argue. Food tasted amazing with my new, enhanced senses, and just imagining a cheeseburger could induce orgasmic thoughts.

Marcy read my face. "I can order you more food, Godzilla, but it'll take a few minutes to get here."

"Never mind. I'm heading home in about two minutes anyway. Is my dad still here?"

"Yep, he's in your office making some calls."

"Did they get rid of the imp?"

"The greasy unconscious guy?"

"That's the one."

"Gone. A couple of big fellas took him away. You guys don't screw around in the breeding department. The boys who hauled him out of here were huge."

"What about Nick?"

"He's out on a call, but he said he'd swing by your apartment before you left. You're supposed to wait for him before you leave town. His orders."

"Is he still pissed he's not going?"

"Pissed wouldn't be the description I'd use." Marcy tapped a perfectly manicured nail on the table. "Try brokenhearted or severely devastated."

"He can't come."

"I know."

"Someone needs to stay here."

"Because I'm clearly inept at running things."

I arched a brow. "What if he gets hurt?" Nick was like a brother to me, but he wasn't as strong as a wolf. In our world, your animal matched your strength. A fox would be at a serious disadvantage against a powerful goddess. I wasn't willing to take the risk. Plus, someone had to stay behind to keep the business running. I had no idea how long I'd be gone—or if I'd even be *coming* back.

"He's a big boy. He can take being left behind," Marcy

declared as she sat down and started shuffling papers, avoiding me and the emotional conversation we both knew was next. "He'll get over it. Eventually."

I walked over and braced my knuckles on her smooth wooden desk. "You're a frustrating witch, you know that?"

"I know." She wouldn't meet my eyes as she continued to stack her notes.

"You're going to cry like a baby when I don't come back."

"You're coming back," she said, finally tilting her head up to meet my gaze. Her eyes were clear, but I could sense her emotion.

"How can you be so sure? You have no idea what's in store for me. Selene could rip my skin to shreds with her bullwhip, or she could shred my heart with her metal Wolverine claws." Sounded like something the sadistic bitch would have. "There are a million ways she could kill me, and you know it. We're just sidestepping the main issue—this might be our last tender goodbye forever." I didn't want to admit it, but I was a little nervous I wouldn't see her—or anyone—again. All jokes aside, I was betting on me, but I had no idea how things were going to turn out in the end.

"Let me tell you something." She motioned me to lean over further with a curl of her finger, and I obliged. Very softly, right next to my ear, she said, "I know you're going to survive, because I'm witchy and I know a thing or two about the future. And guess what?"

"What?" I whispered.

"Chicken butt."

4

I crept down my apartment hallway like a burglar.

I hadn't had the balls to confess to my neighbor, and unlikely new pal, Juanita, I was leaving again for an undisclosed amount of time. She was an extremely intelligent woman and at some point she was going to start questioning me and my new revolving posse of extra-large men, and begin to reevaluate the misplaced loyalty she'd somehow invested in me. Plus, I'd already inadvertently put her in harm's way when I'd asked her to keep an eye on my place, and I wasn't planning on doing it again.

Keeping her at arm's length was the safest for everyone.

My wolf snapped her jaws at me, urging me to move faster. *I'm going. It's just easier if we don't have to deal with the neighbors. This is what humans call* finesse. *See me* finessing *my way through the hallway instead of barreling down it like you'd prefer? My way makes us invisible; your way brings people out to investigate.* She bit the air in front of her.

My wolf was past agitation and on to full frustration. Her

number one priority was reaching Rourke. Nothing else mattered to her. But my human obligations made it impossible to drop everything and run after him. Not to mention we had no idea where to start the search until the vamps arrived. Getting their help locating Colin Rourke, the werecat who happened to be my mate, was the no-no deal I'd struck with the Vamp Queen. I'd sworn an oath to her, against my father's wishes, to return to New Orleans very soon, in exchange for vampire aid. The vamps in question had been out scouting since last evening, and after they awoke tonight, they were supposed to magically arrive on my doorstep. They were our quickest way to Selene, the Lunar Goddess we were tracking, and I'd sacrificed a lot to make that deal.

It had been only thirty-six hours since we'd left the Queen, but it felt like an eternity.

We're leaving soon. Hang tight. She growled, but finally settled down.

In the very brief time I'd spent with Rourke something had changed inside me. His clear, pale eyes, ringed in the thinnest emerald, were still at the forefront of my mind. His scent was etched like an intricate pattern into every part of my soul in painful detail—the rich, dark cloves mixed with sweet molasses—almost as if I smelled him right now. The images of him fighting for me, protecting me, kissing me, were overwhelming, and they played over and over in my mind like a broken movie projector.

I had to find him. When my thoughts drifted to Selene harming him in any way, my nails shot to sharp points before I could stop them. I wasn't just going to kill her—I was going to *annihilate* her. The anticipation that filled me was delicious. My wolf barked sharply in agreement, opening her jaws and twisting her head like she was about to snap a neck. *You got that right. She doesn't stand a chance against us.* She gave a decisive bite. *I know you've been patient and if it had been up to you, we would've left right away. But staying was the right choice. We have to wait for the vamps. Without them, we lose too much valuable time. You have to trust me on this.*

The logistics of who was in control and how often was still an uncertainty between us. I'd slammed a barrier down in my mind after our first real fight for Dominion and it still held. But I'd found quickly that I could relinquish control to my wolf when I needed to, and when the crisis was averted, she was back on the right side. In light of the scary-Prophecy-from-hell, my wolf and I were going to have to start working together as a team, learning to share both power and knowledge fluidly. I wasn't going to survive this mess without her, and she didn't stand a chance without me. There was a common place in the middle—it was the next natural step—but I wasn't ready to merge us yet. She still had a lot to learn about the human decision-making processes. I had to be the boss in this world, and as of right now, she wasn't buying it. If I switched control to her this minute, we'd be bounding out the nearest window after Rourke.

A sharp laugh punctuated the silence at the end of my hallway. I'd been lost in thought, but it brought me back quickly.

It was coming from my apartment and it was female.

There was a distinct, unmistakable ring to it. *So much for sneaking under the radar.* My wolf gave a yip of irritation.

I walked up to my door and pushed it open, resigned to my fate.

"*Hola*, Chica!" Juanita wooted as I walked in, waving at me from inside my open kitchen. "Look what I brought for you! I bring you deenar! Jour brother, Tyler—" She pointed at my brother, who was on the other side of the kitchen, sidled comfortably up to my breakfast bar on what looked like a borrowed stool. "He let me in and says you are both leaving soon. Es jour grandmother sick again?" That was the excuse we'd used last time I'd gone away unexpectedly.

I met my twin brother's amused expression as he shoveled in a big spoonful of something that looked and smelled delicious. I tried to keep the impatience out of my voice. "Yes. Unfortunately she's come down with something else. We got a call this morning and we're going to have to make another trip to see...our beloved Gram." I shut my door and walked across my empty apartment toward the pair. My entire living room was still free of furniture since my wolf had trashed it when we'd made our first change. "Juanita, you didn't have to cook for us again. That was extremely nice of you, but we don't want to keep putting you out." She'd happily fed Danny while we were away. If this was going to become a thing, I was in trouble. Having her drop in on a regular basis would not be ideal for her health.

She clicked out of the kitchen and over to me in her high heels, reaching up to embrace me. I hugged her back, because what else was I going to do? My eyes watered as her floral perfume snuck up my nose. But under all that manufactured smell, I took in her real scent and smiled in spite of myself. Eucalyptus and lime fit her perfectly. Fierce and sassy bundled together in one compact five-foot package.

Before I could draw away, she planted a huge kiss on my cheek. I caught Tyler out of the corner of my eye, delight written all over his face. I smirked and mouthed *just you wait*. He shoveled another mouthful of food into his maw to cover up his laughter.

"Oh, es no problem to do the cooking," she purred next to my ear. "I am happy to help you get back on jour feet. Jour life es complicated, no?" She gestured around my bare apartment. "It looks like bad luck has come to stay, but I weel help you. Es what I do best. Come eat."

"Um, okay," I said as my stomach betrayed me like the traitor it was. "Thank you, Juanita. It does smell delicious." The aroma was amazing, even though I had no time for company. If I was going to be completely honest, I never had time for company. I glanced out the window. It was still light out. My stomach protested again. I could spare a few minutes to eat—as if I actually had a choice in the matter.

"Come on, Chica. Don' be shy. The saliva, I see it drips down jour chin. The chicken es my specialty. No other compares. You must taste for jourself." She was remarkably strong as she half ushered, half dragged me to the counter and the giant pan full of chicken legs, sausage, and shrimp all spread on a bed of aromatic rice. A blast of saffron sent my salivary glands into overdrive. *Jesus.* My stomach gave another long, low growl. "Sit and eat. You work too hard, never taking enough breaks. You are losing too much weight lately. See, the men, dey like meat on the bone. It gives them someteen to grab on to." She tossed her head back and laughed as she pulled out another stool. Both chairs were painted in bright colors and were obviously from her place. She'd brought furniture and food. This woman had successfully barreled her way into my life and it looked like she was here to stay. I found I wasn't super against the idea, which was a little startling.

Tyler was coughing so hard at her last comment he had to rap on his own chest.

"Better be careful, bro." I grinned as I sat down. "Chicken bones can be mighty dangerous if they go down the wrong tube."

I picked up a plate without further prodding and dove in.

After the first bite my eyes rolled back in their sockets. Dammit, why did Marcy always have to be right? Stinky witch. "Juanita, this is delicious," I said between mouthfuls. "I mean, it's really, really good."

"Es no problem, Chica. When you get back, I cook for you again."

I got lost in a few more heavenly bites, then glanced at the clock in my kitchen. My fork clanked down onto the plate. "Oh, goodness!" I said in what I hoped sounded like mock surprise. I felt bad kicking her out so quickly, but there was no other choice. I had to get moving. "I didn't realize it was so late. Tyler." I nodded my head toward Juanita. "If we don't leave soon, we'll miss the plane and Gram will be alone tonight." How did you go about getting rid of someone who just cooked you a wonderful meal without looking like a chump? You didn't really.

My brother put his fork down and stood. "Yep, we better get a move on." He walked over to Juanita and playfully hooked his arm around her waist and planted a kiss on her cheek, all while ushering her toward the door. "Juanita, that was a truly fantastic meal. I haven't had anything home cooked in a long time. When we get back, we'll be sure to return the favor. It'll be our turn to bring something by your place."

"Oh, you are too much!" she twittered, looking up at my brother in adoration. "But I weel still do the cooking. Next time, I weel bring a feast!"

"That sounds perfect, Juanita," my brother told her with a genuine dimpled grin. "We'll be sure to let you know when we get home. And can you do me a favor? If you see anything out of the ordinary coming from this apartment, I want you to call this number." He handed her a card from his wallet. "But— and I can't stress this enough—please don't try to act on your own. In fact, don't even open your door. Okay, Juanita? If you hear anything, stay in your apartment and call me."

She glanced down at the card and then back at Tyler with a wide smile. He had a fan for life. "*Sí*, I weel do this for you, Tyler." It came out like *Teeler*. "But, for me, you must promise to take good care of jour sister. Do you hear what I am saying to you? Lots of bad theengs, they happen lately, and they weel happen again. *Familia* looks out for *familia*. Don' let her out of jour sight. Swear this to me."

"I understand completely, Juanita. I swear I will look after Jess. I promise not to take my eyes off her."

My heart gave a twist. Letting Tyler and Danny accompany me might not be entirely the right choice. As Selectives they wouldn't be allowed to change into their true forms. It was forbidden under a sworn oath to my father, our Alpha. If they broke that vow, they would be severely punished. And the risk and danger, especially facing someone as powerful as Selene, would be immense. But I knew my brother would never see reason, so there was no use trying.

I just had to make sure nothing happened to either of them.

"Goodbye, Chica. I weel take care of things here for you, don' worry." She waved and blew me a kiss. I waved back. "And be safe on your travels. Jour grandmother needs you, I am certain. If the road is rocky, jus' pick jourself up. That's what my *abuela* always taught me."

"Thanks, Juanita," I called. "I'll remember that."

Tyler turned and closed the door, an amused expression still lingering on his face. He shook his head. "They don't make humans like that very often. That woman has balls, and she's fiercely loyal to you. Did you smell her strength?"

"I did, but just barely. My nose was struggling to get through all the Freesia perfume. And who knew you were such a rake?

You got her out the door in one swoop. That was a talented maneuver."

"I have a way with all the ladies." Tyler grinned. "Even your elderly neighbor."

"She's not that old!" I laughed. "I think she's in her fifties, but she could pass for late thirties on a good day. What do you think she meant about the bad things that are supposed to happen again?"

Tyler scratched his head. "I don't know. She was probably talking about all your recent 'coincidences,' like your break-in and your ailing grandmother." He smirked. "Your life has been a whirlwind since you made your first shift. Humans who are close to you would be foolish not to notice."

I guess it was a good thing I didn't know many humans. Juanita and Ray were plenty. I didn't want any other human to end up on the wrong side of us like Ray had. If that happened to Juanita I'd be crushed.

"And, Jess, if you're going to be a good wolf, you have to learn to parcel away scents efficiently. It's a relatively easy thing to learn. Once you take in a new smell, you file it away and then you open up your senses to the next layer. If you don't, you're going to be at a severe disadvantage. You'll never be able to identify or track anyone accurately."

I stood, finishing the last bite off my plate as I headed to the sink, so I answered him in my mind. *I have a lot to learn about being a wolf, don't I?*

Yep, he replied. Speaking like this felt like a feather brushing up against my consciousness, each word a soft tickle. *And you're damn lucky I'm a good teacher and have the time and patience to work with someone as inept as yourself.*

I chuckled, covering my mouth with the back of my hand.

I don't think "inept" is the word you're looking for. I'm thinking "destined for greatness" or "unbelievably rockin'" are better choices. I refrained from licking my plate and rinsed it under the running water.

Tyler had followed me into the kitchen and now was as good a time as any to fill him in on my day. My father and I had decided I'd be the one to tell Tyler what we'd uncovered today. Even though Devon had found the Prophecy on the Internet, it didn't mean any of the other wolves had discovered the news. In fact, it likely meant most hadn't. Wolves and technology, other than in the form of an Xbox and a giant flat-screen TV, didn't mix well. But Tyler needed to know. He had the right to know. I just didn't want to actually tell him.

Is everything ready to go? I asked instead.

Yep. The vehicle's packed and waiting. He gathered the empty pan from the bar, one of those throwaway foils, and he pitched it into the garbage can before tying the bag and pulling it out.

I leaned my back against the countertop and crossed my arms. *There's something I need to tell you before we go.* Telling him in my mind seemed easier, less harsh than spoken words.

He turned from shutting the fridge and set the garbage bag down on the kitchen floor. *That sounds serious.* He rested his body against the doorjamb.

Devon got a mysterious e-mail yesterday with a link that contained some interesting news. No use belaboring it. *And from that he was able to cross-reference some things together about me. It has to do with who or what I might be.*

Where did it come from?

It was on the Internet, of all places, but he doesn't know who actually sent it to him. But, more important, Dad was there and confirmed it. I still don't know what I think of all of it.

Dad knows what you are? Hesitation lingered in his voice.

Yes. I shuffled my feet. *He believes I might be some sort of female reincarnate from something called the Prophecy of the True Lycan. Apparently it was predicted that a powerful wolf would rise again, or some such thing. To tell you the truth, I don't get it and I'm not necessarily buying it either. Reading something on the Internet doesn't equal fact. But Dad has heard stories of the* Y Gwir Lycae, *and because there are several accounts that point to someone "unique," he thinks it might fit. For now.*

The Y Gwir Lycae? *You?*

You've heard the tales?

Some. When Dad holds the annual Council meetings there's always drinking and reminiscing with the older wolves. I've heard some things over the years. Why would they think a female could be the Y Gwir Lycae?

Apparently this Prophecy has similar phrasing as some of the old tales. I have no idea. According to what I read, it seemed there was a female long ago and her job was to "vanquish" evil from the supernatural world. I don't know if she was the first one or if she just shows up once a millennium to shake things up.

He ran a hand through his hair and blew air out of his mouth. *What do you think it means?*

I think it's a stretch, to say the least. I told Dad I don't feel any different. I don't feel like someone else. I just feel like me.

He pushed away from the doorway and strode into my empty living room. I followed. "I think it means you're strong," Tyler said out loud. "And you can hold your Lycan form and fight, which we already knew. That means, whether or not you're the actual *Y Gwir Lycae*—you're still *a* Lycan."

"I guess," I responded slowly.

"Jess, we're *all* descendants of Lycans. They were the first shape-shifters on earth. We carry their DNA. I think you just happened to get the whole shebang. Dad's line must be strong, with deep ties to the old ones."

"Okay." I didn't know where this was heading, but I was thankful he wasn't storming out of my apartment in a rage. A strong alpha-born wolf, who was ahead of me in Pack status, couldn't like hearing his sister was powerful, whether I was blood-kin or not. "I get that we all have latent Lycan genes, and mine just decided to come to the forefront. That makes sense. But it still doesn't explain away everything else."

"What else did this Prophecy say?" he asked.

"It said I'm supposed to be some sort of justice giver to the supernatural race."

"What's a 'justice giver' supposed to do exactly?"

I laughed. "I have no idea. That's why we're having this conversation. But just so *you* know, Dad and I both don't think this has anything to do with me being the next Alpha. I'm not a threat to your direct status." Tyler was on track to be the next Alpha leader, and every wolf in the Pack knew it. There was a distinct difference between being alpha-born and Alpha. Alphas were leaders, meant to be head of Pack—alphas were dominant wolves with aggressive natures.

"I know."

My jaw unhinged a bit. "What do you mean, *you know*?"

"That smell thing I was just telling you about?"

"Yeah."

"I'm really good at it."

"So?"

"If you were supposed to be the Alpha, I'd already know it."

"What? How does smell have anything to do with being a leader of Pack?"

"Dad and James both have the same particular scent under-lay. It took me a long time to figure out what it meant. It isn't something I can explain in words. Scents are complex and strange, with millions of delicate layers. But I knew what it was when..." He stopped.

"What?" I urged.

"When I scented it on myself."

"Wow. That's crazy," I said. "Do you think being able to smell other people's auras is a special gift of some kind?" Many supes had additional powers, something enhanced beyond the scope of what was normal for their supernatural Sect. My brother could run twice as fast as any other wolf, which was considered a "gift."

"No." He reached up and rubbed the back of his neck and paced in a circle before answering. Just like our Dad. "I think I've just paid extra attention to it over the years and honed what was already there—what every wolf is capable of doing. We underutilize our noses because we rely too heavily on our strength."

That was the truth. "So let me get this straight. You're saying I don't smell like a leader? What exactly do I smell like then?"

"I didn't say that. I said you don't smell like an *Alpha*. There's a difference."

"Less than a week ago you told me I smelled like a yucky girl."

"You do... You have a very distinct smell. At first I thought it was because you were female, but now I'm not quite sure what it is. But your 'aura,' or whatever you want to call it, is totally unique. I've never smelled it on anyone, human or supe."

"Maybe it's the Lycan marker?"

"That's a possibility." He seemed deep in thought for a minute.

My eyes caught the light—or rather absence of light—out my window.

I must have appeared shocked, because Tyler turned to look out the window too. "What?" he asked as I turned and ran without so much as another word.

"It's full fucking dark!" I yelled as I raced into my bedroom.

5

I ripped a duffel out of my closet and tossed it onto my bed. Then I yanked every shirt and jean combination I had in my drawers and threw them into the bag, finishing with various undergarments. My kick-ass gear, made of spandex with reinforcements, and my stash of weapons went in after.

Luckily, most of my throwing knives were packed together in a modest-sized carrying case. My dirks, made for quick slashing, were wrapped in safety sheaths. I threw them on the very top and zipped it all up. Once I got outside, I'd grab my palm-sized handgun out of my car. I owned a 9mm Glock that shot silver hollow-point bullets, each filled with a gram of silver shavings at the tip, for those pesky hard-to-kill beasties. Guns were considered a pansy alternative for wolves, but I was willing to use whatever it took to defeat Selene.

Pansy-assed or not.

I dropped the bag outside my bathroom door and opened a few vanity drawers, grabbing essentials and shoving them into the side pockets lining the duffel. Then I pulled my long, dark hair into a ponytail for ease of travel. For combat, I'd secure it in a bun and hope like hell it stayed there.

I was back in the living room in less than seven minutes.

Tyler stood by the door waiting for me.

"Where's your stuff?" I asked.

"It's already down in the vehicle."

"Which car are we taking?" I slung the duffel over my shoulder. "Oh, and in case I forgot to mention it before, Ray's coming with us."

"Ray?" Tyler's face showed his confusion. "You're not talking about the cop, are you?" He read my expression. "Come on, Jess! We can't possibly bring someone like that with us. Not only is he going to be under our feet the entire time, he's an epic fucking asshole. Why would you possibly want to do something like that?"

He was right on all counts. But instead of answering right away, I reached around him and yanked the front door open. "I'm doing it because I refuse to kill him for no other reason than he found us out. At the very least he deserves a chance to come around, and it was either he came with us or he died. I picked alive."

"I could give you twenty good reasons to pick dead," Tyler muttered behind me.

"I bet you could give me a hundred in under a minute, but it doesn't matter. I've made up my mind." I stepped into the hallway. "Turn out the lights, will you?"

"Your electric bill is the least of your worries."

"I'm all about the environment."

"You rented a *Humvee*?" The vehicle parked at the end of my lot was not only a monstrosity, it was a canary-yellow monstrosity.

"What's wrong with it?" Tyler grumbled.

"I don't know. I could start with the color, but why go with the obvious? How about its sheer girth and notice-ability? Was the Batmobile taken? Bruce Wayne's car is the only other car in the history of the universe more noticeable than this beast of a thing."

Danny came up behind Tyler and slapped him on the back. "See. I told you yellow was too flashy for the ladies. They tend to enjoy the blacks and beiges."

Tyler calmly placed his hand on the hood. "For your information, I didn't rent it. I bought it. I found this guy two hours away who details old army vehicles. This one was available and I wasn't in a position to be picky. It's reinforced and ready to roll, so I paid the man and drove away." He arched an eyebrow at me, which I could see clearly despite the deepening darkness. "I wasn't under the impression we were going for stealth. I was under the impression we needed space and strength to achieve our goal."

"A pairing of the two would've been nice," I said. "An inconspicuous Jeep Cherokee would've sufficed. Riding around in this is like painting a gigantic yellow X on our foreheads. And in light of the recent news, the entire supernatural community is going to be interested in my whereabouts very quickly. We just gave them a huge beacon to follow." I felt like kicking one of the enormous tires in frustration. My emotions began to roil and a soft coating of fur erupted on my arms.

"Jess, you need to calm down," my brother said in a quiet tone. "I had no idea news about you was going to break. We've been home for less than two days. In the future I will be sure to couple stealth into *all* of our plans. Until then, no one is here to see us leave, nobody is watching. We will be fine."

"I realize I'm being slightly irrational." I took a step away from the vehicle. "But, honestly, a yellow monster truck was the plan you felt most confident going with?"

"This yellow monster is armored, has sixteen-inch chassy clearance, two gas tanks, a backup battery, an exhaust snorkel, foam-filled tires, bulletproof glass, and it's geared to go a hundred miles per hour."

I crossed my arms in front of me, grudging respect creeping in. My brother had planned for a missile attack and I wanted a Jeep Cherokee. He was right. "Fine." I sighed. "You win. It was the right choice, but we have to leave immediately. No more lingering by Big Bird."

My brother cracked a grin and bowed. It wasn't very often I conceded the argument. "We are ready to roll, just waiting on the vamps."

"And can I just ask, why is the whole world after you now?" Danny added. "Well, other than you're the only female of our kind, of course."

"I'll explain later. We'll have plenty of time for discussions on the road." Going into this now with Danny was not on the agenda. I walked around to the back of the beast. "Where's Ray?"

Danny pointed inside the Humvee. "He's all ready to go, just one giant teddy bear, that one."

"Except when he wakes up and bites off a finger." If Ray somehow managed to get away, we'd find him, but it would be a complication we didn't need, and it certainly wouldn't help his cause with my father. "Also, please tell me there are plans in place to investigate Jeff the Super while we're gone?" My building super, Jeff Arnold, a wereweasel shifter, had been caught trying to break into my apartment for some unknown reason.

We had to find out whom he was working for and why he'd been there in the first place.

"Yes. I gave a full report to your father this morning. He's assigned a few wolves to investigate. We should have more answers when we return."

"Excellent." Footsteps echoed on the pavement at the other end of the parking lot. I turned to see Nick and James approaching as I lifted my duffel on top of a bed of coolers, tents, sleeping bags, and supplies. My brother was indeed prepared.

While I arranged it, I glanced into the interior at Ray's silhouette. He sat slumped to the side in the backseat. The ends of his gag were visible and I heard breathing, but he was out cold. He must have given Danny some trouble.

Nick reached me first. "Is that Ray Hart I smell?" He peered into the backseat and took a few more sniffs to be sure.

"Yes. It's not ideal, but I couldn't kill him," I said. "It might be my weak human side talking, but my dad says if he can assimilate, he lives. I know he's dogged me for years, but other than his being a hard ass, I can't find any real reason to end his life."

"You're not weak," Nick replied, his voice filled with confidence. "I view your humanness as a gift. In our world compassion is rare. I admire it." Nick slipped off the backpack he was wearing and set it on the ground. "I took the liberty of gathering some things I thought would be useful. At Tyler's request, I bought these." He pulled out a small black box with a sturdy handle. There was a main lever on the side and a bunch of metal buttons across the top. "There are four satellite phones in here"—he pointed to the backpack—"along with this docking kit. They're all wired with remote GPS, fully charged and ready to use." He set the box on the ground, then unzipped the front pouch and pulled out a soft black cloth tied with a thick satin ribbon. "I also procured several throwing darts, loaded with various spells. There're a few for sleep and a couple freezers—no kills, just in case they happen to land in the wrong target." He untied the ribbon, carefully unrolling the concoctions. The spells were in thick glass vials attached to sharp metal tips, hooked in the carrying case by two elastic bands apiece, each potion shining a different vibrant color. "Marcy and I didn't think her spells would be strong enough for a goddess, so we paid Tally for them. Well, Marcy did anyway, with funds from the firm. She said, because she was family, she was able to get us a two percent discount." He chuckled. Witches never gave away anything; everything had a cost. It was how their system worked.

"Wow." I reached out to take the bundle Nick was offering. I cradled the package carefully in my hands. Spells on the whole were incredibly expensive, and Tally's spells would break the bank, but they would also be super powerful. "I don't want to know how much you spent, because I'm grateful as hell and I don't want to ruin my happiness high knowing we won't have two nickels to rub together when I get home." We used potion darts on a regular basis, because supes were wild and unpredictable and getting them down was half the battle. Marcy did most of ours for the firm, and they worked fine, but she was only a minor witch. Tallulah Talbot, her aunt, was another story. Tally ran the supernatural community here—and by "ran" I mean *ruled*. I'd never laid eyes on her, but we were extremely lucky Marcy worked for us, because Tally didn't sell her power to just anyone. Having a witch of that magnitude in our corner was like having the Terminator as backup.

I rolled up the cloth and handed it back to Nick. He placed it back in the pack along with the phone kit and lifted it all carefully into the trunk.

When he was done, I reached over for a goodbye hug. My eyes misted without my permission, an unfamiliar experience for me. I hadn't had many goodbyes since I'd left the Compound seven years ago. "The spells will be invaluable. Thank you," I said as I wrapped my arms around him. "I'll be in touch when I can."

"There are a few other little surprises inside the bag too," Nick said as he gripped my back hard. "Please, just do me one favor and don't get killed, okay? I don't think I can handle the world without you in it."

"I promise I'll do my best." I pulled back, breaking our contact. "I love you."

He nodded and stepped out of the way to make way for my next goodbye. "I love you too, Jess. Stay safe."

"Hello, Jessica." James came up and planted a chaste kiss on my cheek. "I came to see you off and wish you well on your quest."

I hadn't seen him since we'd gotten back from New Orleans. "Thank you, James. But we both know the real reason you came—so you could report back that all looked well and good." My father and I had said our goodbyes privately before I'd left the office. If he'd shown up here and had a last-minute change of heart and didn't want me to go, it would've been too hard. We'd both agreed it was better for him not to come.

As stated, emotion and wolves didn't mix.

James laughed, his Irish lilt affecting it ever so slightly. "You've got me there, but I do wish you well. I hope you're adequately protected. From what I can see here, Tyler and Danny have it well covered." James was one of the tallest wolves in the Pack; he was all brawn and incredibly sexy, with short dark hair and mossy green eyes. He wore his usual black T-shirt and cargo pants. I angled my head toward him for a moment. Our wolves had engaged in a brief interaction, and my wolf barked now acknowledging him, but other than that there was nothing else of note. Life would've been so much easier if fate had given me a wolf for a mate. My wolf growled. *I know. I get it. We don't do easy.*

"Tell my father I'm in good hands," I said. "We're as prepared as we can be." As I finished the sentence there was a loud *swoosh* behind me, and then another. I glanced over my shoulder.

The vamps had arrived.

6

Eamon and Naomi, the brother and sister vamp pair, stood statuesque on the small hill behind the parking lot, their enamel features shining brightly in the darkness.

They started forward at the same time, appearing both confident and wary. I wasn't aware vamps could look wary, but they definitely achieved it with their identical drawn eyebrows, both faces pensive and lined with small frowns. Being required to do their Queen's bidding like good little vamp soldiers had to chafe, especially being forced to interact with wolves. But they had no choice. It was either follow orders or die a permanent death via some horrible means, most likely involving gnashing, cutting, and a whole lot of blood.

As they came forward, James stiffened beside me. Danny, Tyler, and Nick moved in to form a semicircle around my back. It went against our natures to collaborate with each other. Vamps and wolves were enemies of ages old, going back to prerecorded history. If the Vampire Queen hadn't wanted something from me so desperately, there wasn't a chance we would all be standing here tonight.

As they continued forward, my wolf's unease changed to agitation. *They are not the enemy today. We have to do it this way. There's no other choice.* She swatted her tail and kept a steady growl. I guess it didn't hurt to be on the lookout for trouble. *Remember, they are bound by their Queen. They won't risk her displeasure—unless, of course, we force them to by being rude.*

She wasn't convinced.

I'm not sure I was either.

The siblings were clad in jeans and matching dark knit tops, which beat the French period outfits they'd worn when I'd seen them last. I didn't know which outfit was more ominous—looking appropriately dressed for the Renaissance or looking deadly normal.

What I knew about vampires could fill one sheet of paper—if I wrote with a big crayon. The old mythologies appeared to be true for the most part, from what I could tell from my brief interactions with them. I knew they could fly—hard to keep that one under wraps—but how they did it was still a mystery. They were rumored to have some mesmerizing abilities over humans. Their hearts didn't beat. I knew that because I'd just been surrounded by a roomful of them and there'd been nary a beat. They slept during the day and drank blood. They could be killed by beheading, like we could. That's how my father had always brought them true death. I didn't know if fire could end them or not. They also had individual "gifts" like we did. These two could apparently track and sense better than other vamps, which is why their Queen had sent them.

Other than that, they were a complete mystery. I wasn't surprised they guarded their secrets like every Sect. The more we shared about ourselves, the more vulnerable we became.

"Hello." Naomi came to a stop in front of me, her voice laced in soft French undertones. What came out sounded like *'Ello*. "We have arrived."

"Yes, that was quite an entrance. I'm Jessica." I didn't hold out my hand. I was pretty sure vampires didn't like to be touched, and actually, the thought of touching their cold, creepy skin was a little unappealing. "This is my team." I gestured to the boys behind me.

"The Goddess we search for resides north," Eamon declared stoically, coming shoulder to shoulder with his sister. They were remarkably similar. Both had sharply defined cheekbones, large wide eyes, and the same chestnut-colored hair. Eamon wore his shoulder length; Naomi's flowed freely down her back. Maybe being frozen in death in their twenties had honed their similar porcelain features over time.

"Okay, north it is." I nodded at the pair. "That sounds easy enough." North of Minnesota meant Canada. He could've said the Congo, so this was decidedly better as far as I was concerned. We anticipated that Selene hadn't been able to go far from the Ozarks, where we'd seen her last. She was toting an angry werecat, and Rourke would've put up quite a fight once he'd broken her spell. Goddesses could fly, but her time in the air would be limited. I was glad she'd headed north and not south.

"*Mademoiselle*, there will be nothing *easy* about this journey," Eamon snipped. "The Lunar Goddess is a powerful being. She is a fearsome warrior. We shall be lucky to escape with our lives."

I bristled. Gods, I hoped vampires weren't all this stuffy. "I wasn't talking about her being easy to defeat, *monsieur*. I was referring to being able to point the car in a northerly direction being something we could accomplish easily enough—and in fact, we can do so right now."

Both vamps stared at me with clueless expressions, which on a vampire was a face void of any emotion and so still it was eerie. They looked like they were carved out of stone.

Alrighty then. "Okay. Enough chatting. It's time to get moving." I broke away from the group and walked around the Humvee with purpose, my wolf yipping excitedly in my mind. We were finally leaving. I yanked the driver's side door open and jumped on the running board. No one had followed me. The wolves weren't willing to move until the vamps did. I stood, peering over the roof at the immobile group and cleared my throat. "The plan is to head due north," I said, wondering fleetingly where they were going to sleep during the day, and then the thought was gone. Not my problem. "If anything changes with you, give us a sign. If we have issues we'll pull over. Sound good?"

"That is acceptable," Eamon said. "When the road runs out, we will be waiting." Without warning, they both shot up into the air almost quicker than I could track. Almost.

"Well, that was a bit vague, wasn't it? *We'll be waiting* sounds like something out of a bad horror flick." Danny came around and pulled open the side door and climbed in next to a still unconscious Ray. "Creepy lot, vamps are. Though that female had a nice taper to her waist. Did you see her eyes when they flashed that bit of silver gray?"

"Leave it to you to find something endearing about a vamp." Tyler climbed into the passenger seat without protest. I wanted to drive. I was too restless to ride shotgun and was relieved he wasn't going to fight me for it. "I thought they looked even more hellish this time," he declared. "Their faces are the color of old, bleached bone, and they stink like decaying syrup. They can't possibly go out in public. If I were a human and I got a gander of the two of them, I'd run for my life."

"I don't think they get out much, hence their propensity to wear pantaloons and corsets when they're at home." I slammed my door, which took more effort than it should've, and turned the key. The monster revved up like an airplane prepping for takeoff. "I'm actually surprised the Queen was so willing to give us these two. Having us interact with each other so closely is bound to expose some of their most guarded secrets, and it's going to cost her. I've heard a rumor that they can mesmerize an entire room of humans without blinking. I wouldn't mind seeing if that one was true."

"They aren't required to blink anyway, are they?" Danny added. "Being dead, they've no use for wetting the eyes. Thus, no blinking necessary."

I arched my eyebrow in the rearview mirror, meeting Danny's sardonic grin. "Must you?"

"Yes. Of course."

I rolled down the window with the manual handle. James and Nick stood at the edge of the parking lot. "James, tell my father I will connect with him on the road," I called. "Nick, make sure you take the brunt of the office work until I get back. Marcy can't do it alone, and tell her that was a direct quote."

"I wouldn't dare." Nick smiled. "Don't get yourself killed, Jess. I mean it."

James stepped forward. "Take care and watch your back, Jessica. The Goddess will be hard to best." Wolves weren't a sentimental bunch, but I could scent their combined concern. "Use whatever means necessary to win this battle."

"I plan to," I said. "You and my father do the same. The South is not going to be any easier to subdue. I hope Redman

Martin cooperates and decides to join us, but if he doesn't, I hope you beat him into submission quickly."

Tyler leaned over my seat. "She won't be alone, Irish. We're not planning on failing. We're coming back. You still owe me a hundred bucks and I plan on collecting." My heart constricted and I had to stop for a second to catch my breath. The last time I'd heard James called "Irish" was by Rourke right before the barroom brawl where we'd met for the first time. I'd never heard Tyler use that nickname before.

James stepped back and gave us a salute as we pulled out. Nick stared ahead with a pensive gaze as he waved goodbye.

Once we were out on the road everything went smoothly.

Until Ray woke up.

"Shut the bloody hell up!" Danny yelled for the fourth time. "Or you'll end up worse than just rotting unconscious! I will sever your neck from your body if you continue to push me."

It was just after midnight and we were almost to the Canadian border. We'd chosen to take the interstate most of the way and I'd driven fast.

But it was more than time to exit off the main road.

Clearly, I hadn't considered the implications of bringing an angry American cop across the border. Ray wasn't going to play nice and it was unlikely the Canadian Border Service officers would be amused if they found an unconscious body in the backseat. Taking a few human guards down wouldn't be an issue, but the surveillance would put a damper on the events. The border was heavily monitored. I slapped my hands on the steering wheel in frustration, but not hard enough to break anything. I was learning how to deal with my new strength.

Not popping holes or breaking things every five minutes was becoming an art form.

Upon waking an hour ago, Ray had immediately started ranting and raving. He'd kicked the back of my seat repeatedly until Danny had threatened to saw off his legs with a hunting knife. When Ray hadn't acquiesced, Danny had brandished said knife in front of him and started picking his nails with it. Ray had stopped thrashing, but he hadn't stopped yelling. He was gagged, but it didn't matter. It was driving us all insane, and nothing short of knocking him out again was going to stop it.

My regret for bringing him along with us pounded behind my temples, throbbing in a dull ache. I'd clearly been out of my frigging mind thinking I could kidnap someone like Ray, even if it was only to save his sorry life.

The Humvee had a state-of-the-art GPS hardwired into the front console. I glanced at it and took a turn, following a small logging road off the main highway.

"One wrong move once we get out of this car and he dies, Jess," my brother murmured from the seat next to me. "I have no idea why he's here, but there's no way his life is worth more than ours. If he compromises this mission, he's out. Are we clear?"

Ray raged from the backseat. "Goow dan mo fut ba—"

"Clear." I was driving fast and hit the brakes, cranking the wheel hard to the right. We shot through a small break in the trees. The back end of the monster swerved in what seemed like a slow arc, the tires finally finding purchase in the dirt. I straightened it out and gunned it through the brush, careening over an old, weed-covered road like we were on a motocross circuit. All the crap in the back crashed around, making it sound like the truck was rending apart at the seams.

Tyler grabbed on to the side handhold above his head. "What the *fuck* are you doing? Did I miss something?" he shouted. "Where are we *going*?"

There were no streetlights and it was pitch dark. The truck bobbed over a small knoll and we skidded into a clearing, just missing a group of pine trees. I punctuated my mood by stomping on the brakes at the last second, sending us all flying forward in our seats. Then I jammed it into park. "Nope, you didn't miss anything," I said, turning toward my brother. "Just fixing the issue before it gets out of hand."

"I should've driven," Tyler muttered. "Girls are emotional drivers."

"Emotional, huh?" I chuckled. "Guess who finally shut up in the backseat? I did that." I tapped a finger against my chest. Before Tyler could comment, there was a whooshing sound outside and two shapes struck ground directly in front of the truck. The high beams of the headlights bounced off their faces, making them look like a couple of ghostly specters.

"They don't waste any time, do they?" Danny angled his body toward the front seat. "Were they just hanging in the sky, then? Waiting around for us to stop and ask for directions?"

I had no idea how the vamps were traveling with us, but zooming above our truck on the highway hadn't really crossed my mind. I figured they'd fly to the mysterious "end of the road" destination and be irritated we were taking so long. If we had an issue, like now, they would figure it out eventually. I hadn't expected them so soon.

But now that they were here, a plan began to formulate. I could use them.

A slow smile spread across my lips as I slid around in my seat.

Ray was finally blessedly quiet, but the look on his face as he absorbed the shapes standing before us in the headlights was priceless. I'd never seen Ray stymied over anything, but getting his first glimpse of vampires in all their glory had achieved it. I could almost see the wheels of disbelief turning. "Guess what, Ray?"

His eyes narrowed as they shot to mine.

"I just found you a ride."

7

"You brought a human with you?" Eamon's voice was part superiority, part curiosity. We were definitely coming off like a bunch of hillbillies in front of the überrefined vampires.

I had a gagged Ray, still tied with a dish towel, by the scruff of the neck. We stood just outside the Humvee. Even though the high beams were illuminating the darkness, I swear the yellow paint on the car doors would've sufficed as a lantern. I shook my head sadly.

Danny and Tyler had taken up behind us, looking as tough and bold in their jeans as the vamps did. They were at least a foot taller than the twins, with more muscle and fiercer snarls. "That's what I just said." My patience with Eamon waned with every single word out of his mouth. "What I want to know is if you can fly him over the border without snacking on him or dropping him for sport?" Ray tensed at my words, but stayed silent. Ray's utter shock made me certain that vamps could glamour themselves when they felt like it; otherwise they could never leave the confines of their home and go out in public, and I knew they had to go out. There was no way all those vampires stayed inside all night. But it was obvious they weren't cloaking themselves now because Ray was just short of babbling like a baby. They screamed otherworldly. "He's traveling with us and he goes unmolested unless I say so."

Eamon curled his top lip, like munching on humans wasn't what he did for a living. "We have already sipped tonight. We have no need of more."

Sipped? From what I gathered of the Queen's decorative chamber ceiling and walls during my last visit, when vamps ate, they ripped, tore, feasted, gulped, and sucked. I saw no evidence of *sipping* depicted anywhere.

"Great." I yanked Ray around to face me, hillbilly style. "Listen, Ray. This is your last chance to get this right. You absolutely lucked out tonight. Do you hear me? These nice vampires are going to fly you over the border. We'll meet you on the other side. Seeing that my original plan when I veered off the road involved a shovel and some digging, consider yourself spared. Vamp transportation is a much better alternative than a shallow grave." He stared at me unblinking like I was speaking gibberish. "And when we pick you up on the other side, you will come with us *willingly*." That was the key word. "If you don't get yourself figured out by then and finally buy into what we're selling, they get to eat you, or sip you to death, or whatever it is they do. Understand? This is *it*, Ray. End of the road. I've had enough."

Honestly, if flying through the air with vamps wasn't enough to convince Ray everything we'd said so far was true, nothing was going to do the trick and he was a lost cause. Introducing him to demons was not an option and anything else would take too long.

I hoped a little shock therapy would go a long way.

I ripped Ray's gag off and tossed it to the ground. Then I spun him around to undo his ties, which turned out to be an artfully tied three-foot extension cord. Jesus. "Hannon, this won't work," Ray sputtered as soon as he could find the words. "I know what you're trying to do. You're trying to scare me, but it won't—"

Naomi shot toward us in a blur, stopping a few feet in front of Ray, effectively cutting his tirade short. Her striking visage was even more startling this close. I could smell the fear instantly pool along Ray's skin.

"Of course it will work," I replied, acting like nothing unusual had just happened and a spooky vampire wasn't invading his personal space. "After you've flown with vamps, there won't be anything left to explain. You'll come to your senses, believe what we're telling you to be the truth, agree to our demands, and save your own damn life. We all win. I'm going to look forward to the pats on the back in Pack for being such a trailblazer when it comes to preserving human life. Who knew all it was going to take was a little solo flying with vampires?"

"I don't care wh-what you say," Ray stammered. "Vampires and werewolves *can't* possibly exist. It's not natural. I want no part of this fuc—"

Naomi leaned in quickly, her ivory fangs snapping down in an instant. She bared her incisors as her face began to do that slide-downward thing I'd seen Valdov and the Queen do when they were angry. Her skin appeared to melt off her face like hot wax. How in the hell did they do that? I wasn't about to ask and ruin the show. "We exist, human," she hissed. "You would do well to fear us."

Ray stumbled backward so quickly he fell. I let him go and he landed flat on his back.

I left him there as I peered at Naomi, watching as her face glided back to normal. She glanced over at me once everything was back in its rightful place, seeming proud of herself for providing the trick to terrify the human.

"I think I'm beginning to like you," I told her honestly. Nothing like a supe with a plucky attitude. She'd caught on to the situation fast, no tutorials needed. Unlike her brother, who stood off to the side brooding, with his arms crossed like a petulant child. "He's all yours." I nodded to Naomi. "We'll cross the border up the main highway and pick him up five miles on the other side. I'll look for an outlet."

Eamon paced forward like he'd sipped a lemon.

"We will take the human," Naomi agreed. "And we will make sure he's frightened."

Sweet. "Sounds like a plan."

Crossing the border took longer than it should have. The guards didn't pull us over to search the truck, but they held us in front of the window for a substantial amount of time, quizzing us about how we'd obtained our lovely vehicle. Tyler had all the pertinent paperwork in the glove box, but even so they kept asking. After the thirteenth question about our wonderful military Humvee, I arched a look at my brother and muttered, "You couldn't have gotten us a nice Buick instead of artillery Big Bird?"

Tyler scowled. "Nice and Buick don't run in the same sentence."

Nick's gift of persuasion would've been extremely useful right about now. It figured Nick would get a good gift like molding human minds to his liking, and I'd get stuck with supernatural domination, which was a totally useless skill to have if I planned on living to a ripe old age.

"So what do you think vampires eat, then?" Danny asked conversationally when they finally waved us through. "Do you think they only drink blood, or do you think they enjoy the occasional bit of raw meat or a nice swig of wine now and again? Must be frightfully boring just guzzling blood all day. It wouldn't suit me in the least."

"I couldn't care less what they eat," Tyler said as he sealed all the paperwork back in the glove box. "Just as long as they stay away from me. There's not another supernatural Sect out there worse than vamps. Being dead and still functioning is like reanimating a corpse. It goes against all the laws of nature."

"You know that's what necromancers do, right?" I said, giving him a sidelong glance. "They reanimate corpses for a living. To me, that's a million times worse than a vamp, with all the peeling skin and no eyeballs walking around like *Night of the Living Dead.*" I'd never actually seen a reanimated corpse, but my vision couldn't be that far off. We were lucky necromancers were few and far between. My father had told me long ago it was an old magic, seldom used these days. "Vamps just have a different magic than we do. No better, no worse. They're alive in their own way."

Danny ignored both of our comments completely and continued, "Do you think all their plumbing works properly, you know, after they become undead?" Danny leaned forward. "That'd be worse than all the blood guzzling. Not a life without being able to have a good shag."

I spotted a good place to turn after we'd gone five miles. "I have no idea if they can have sex, Danny, nor do I care." I angled the Humvee down a small road, paved this time. "Let's focus on picking up Ray and figuring out the next plan. You can ask the vamps anything you want later, but when you do, just make sure you watch yourself. Be prepared for them to fly into a rage if you start prying into their personal life. Eamon looks like he'd rather suck you dry than divulge one single detail about himself." I turned to my brother. "Roll down your window and see if you can scent them."

Tyler cracked the window and inhaled as we moved slowly down the road. "They're out there. I can smell them, but from the moving car I can't figure out which way the wind is blowing."

"That's good enough for me." I picked a wide berth on the shoulder and pulled over.

The second we stepped onto the road, a single shape landed ten feet in front of us. Up this close, the whooshing sounded like straight-line winds whistling through trees.

"Good trick, flying," Danny said jovially from behind me. "One of the pros to vampirism in my book."

Naomi held on to a limp Ray. He hung loosely from the front like she'd just given him the Heimlich maneuver but he'd choked anyway. I strode forward and she released him without preamble. He toppled onto the road, out cold. "Scaring him seems to have worked," I said. I knew he was alive because I could hear him breathing. Not that I'd thought she'd killed him, but rapport with the vamps was something I hadn't expected. Eamon was difficult, but Naomi was almost pleasant.

"Humans are weak." Naomi shrugged, a glint of silver piercing deeply inside her irises, flashing outward in the dark like a spark. "I made sure he was aware of what was happening, and then for good measure, I dropped him." When I appeared startled, she smiled. "But only for the briefest of moments. In human time it was only a few seconds at most. When I caught him, he had already fainted." She glanced down at Ray's lifeless body impassively. "I have no idea why you would go to great lengths for a human such as this. But this one stayed awake longer than most." There was a hint of grudging respect in her soft, French lilt.

"Ray is a guinea pig of sorts." I moved closer to them. "Vamps might have a greater disregard for human life, but my ultimate plan is to try and preserve it when and if I can." I had to be honest with myself and admit that wanting Ray to live was something I felt deep down, almost like an urge that was out of my control. The Prophecy pinged in my mind for a quick second, but I didn't have time to analyze my feelings on the matter.

"Humans are of small consequence to us." She shrugged her petite shoulders, her long chestnut hair swaying in the night air. The gesture and the breeze made her appear a teensy bit more normal and less supernatural horror. "We have little need to kill them. If we don't wish it, they would never know we were there. But if an occasional human life gets lost, so be it."

Under different circumstances, I might have been tempted to remind Naomi that she'd been human once. But now wasn't the time, and I knew too many years had passed since she'd been one for it to register with any kind of meaning. Add in the fact I had no idea how I would feel about humans when I was that old and it was almost a moot point. Maybe I'd forget what being human was like so much, they'd barely be a blip on my radar too.

Ray moaned.

"Well," I finally replied. "This one's life is not up for grabs yet." I pushed a toe into his thigh. "Hey, Ray, it's time to wake up." I wiggled my foot back and forth, shaking him. "Come on. We need to get a move on."

His eyes blinked open with a start, his body and fists instantly tensing for a fight.

I crouched down beside him. "Are you ready to come quietly now? Or do the vamps need to take you for another ride?"

"Hannon." His voice came out creaky and raspy, like his throat had been damaged from screaming. "I have no idea how they achieved that, but that was some of the craziest shit I've ever seen."

"You didn't answer my question. Does that mean you're ready to come without a fuss?" I peered at him closely. I could almost see the cogs rotating in his brain, his logical detective side warring with his whimsical side, likely a side of his brain he hadn't utilized since he was a child, if that. Children were much more inclined to believe in the unreal, their brains tailored to accept all things. I knew Ray desperately didn't want to believe in the unexplained, but we were beyond that now. "Your time is up. We can't keep going like this and you know it. Make up your mind." I stood. "Are you ready to accept or not?"

He sat up slowly, glancing around, his gaze landing on Naomi and then back to me. "Fine. I'm coming," he said, rubbing the road out of his hair. "It feels like my brain is skewered open, but a human being able to fly is no magic trick I've ever seen." He looked at me for a quick second and then dropped his eyes. "But if anyone comes after me, I will not hesitate to fight. Just because you crazies exist, doesn't mean I'm signing on the dotted line."

"Ray," I hissed on the end of a frustrated breath. "You exhaust me. You can fight all you want, but you're not going to *win*. That's been your biggest obstacle all along—thinking you actually have a chance against us." I motioned for him to stand. "Once you get that through your impenetrable skull, your brain will thank you for it. And you will indeed sign on the dotted line, either that or you'll be dead."

"A well-fought battle isn't a loss, Hannon. Only a loser doesn't try."

"Ray, my name is Jessica. No need to refer to me as Hannon anymore." It seemed another lifetime ago that I'd gone by that name.

He stood, but Eamon swooshed down in front of the group before he could answer. It was kind of incredible to see him land from full speed. It should have been a train wreck, but instead he looked like an Olympic gymnast sticking a perfect landing. The pavement didn't even wiggle. It seemed as if the velocity stopped right as his feet came in contact with the ground.

It was pretty cool. I could grudge him that much.

"The Goddess is close," Eamon proclaimed with stuffy arrogance. "I can feel her strength. When she detects us, as she will, she will not stand idly by and let us attack. We must move now."

I focused on Naomi, choosing to deal with the more rational of the two. "It will be daybreak soon. Can you travel during daylight hours?" My guess was no, but I had to ask. Maybe she and her brother had gifts I didn't know about.

"*Non*," Naomi said. Her accent was more pronounced than Eamon's, plus she used French words, which might be one of the reasons she seemed somewhat more agreeable. "We will sleep during the daylight hours. The oldest of us can tolerate sunlight, because as our bodies age we become stronger, but we are still too young for that." They had to be well over five hundred years old, judging by the level of power they emitted. The stronger the supe, the more power flowed, manifesting itself like tiny pressure points on the skin. The closer you were to the source, the more it needled you. Rourke's energy was the strongest I'd ever felt, but his power felt delicious against my skin, like a surge of tingles flooding my body continuously. The vamps' energy felt tight and concentrated, built to intimidate. If five hundred was considered young, how old did one need to be to withstand light?

Instead of asking, I replied, "To keep up the pace, we will continue on during the day. You can catch up to us when you wake."

"The mountains you are looking for are a great distance northwest of here." Naomi moved forward, stopping in front of me. "They border a large body of water, a lake five times the size of all the others surrounding it. The area she resides in is remote; its rocky passes are impregnable to humans without flight. You must drive until the dirt road dead-ends into the west side of the lake and wait until nightfall. It will not take us long to find you once we wake. Do not venture any farther than the road if you value your life. The pathway to her lair is littered with lethal obstacles." She was obviously the tracker, Eamon the sensor. "Selene has protected herself well from harm."

"You've scouted the entrance already?" I asked, somewhat surprised. I knew the two of them had spent the previous day locating Selene's trail, or we wouldn't have had any direction to follow, but pinpointing her fortress so quickly was more than I'd hoped for. "I guess when you fly, you can cover a lot more ground."

Flying was definitely a skill we lacked, but having the vamps fly us there would've been impossible. We outnumbered them four to two, plus we had all our gear. Even if it had been an option, there was no way on earth any wolf would willingly let a vampire carry them. It wasn't something I was willing to risk either, even though Naomi appeared to be somewhat trustworthy. There was too much dissention between Sects, and even though they likely couldn't kill us outright because of the oath their Queen swore to me, there were sneaky ways around that. They could easily have an "accident" and still be within the parameters of the oath. Dropping us or slamming us into the nearest mountain would be the quickest way to try and kill us for good, something I was certain Eamon would love to do. They could also take us anywhere without our consent. It was too risky. Traveling close to the ground was the only way to ensure our survival.

Naomi answered, "We did not go to the entrance of her lair. We went only as far as the perimeter. Eamon can sense many different magics, and a fresh imprint of her was all over the mountains. Though Eamon can detect magic is present across her boundary, we will not know what it is until we arrive. There is no doubt that Selene has anticipated your arrival. She is likely taking her time with her prisoner until you arrive. You will be the crudités to her final encore, which will be ending his life." My wolf snarled and flashed a picture of a bloodied Selene. *Yep.*

"There is another reason we did not go closer," Eamon added. "There is a chance if she senses too much danger she will flee. She will not risk harm, even when she is caught up in her games. She will kill him and disappear if she believes she will be overpowered."

"How do you know that?" I asked curiously. "From my experience, her vanity would fool her into thinking she's infallible to just about anything. She surely wouldn't think two young vamps and a newborn werewolf and her cohorts would be anything too strenuous to overcome. The thought of us *over-powering* her would make her laugh."

He looked uncomfortable for a moment; then he straightened, donning his usual persnickety face. "We have...dallied before and I understand her ways."

Danny coughed. "Dallied? That sounds a bit interesting, mate." Humor lined his voice. "From what I've been told, Selene packs quite a punch in those delicate fingers of hers. Can you attest to that then?"

"She's a warrior without rival," Eamon snapped. "She will strike you down as an afterthought and leave your body to rot if you're not vigilant."

This conversation was going nowhere. I hadn't expected Eamon to know Selene, which was curious at best. It was useful information to store away for later. From the passion in his voice I could tell it had been a close relationship, and from his pinched expression I knew there were zero odds he would talk about it. I turned toward Naomi for an answer, but she was looking away.

I faced the group. "We'll drive the rest of tonight and all day tomorrow. We regroup at the edge of the lake by sunset tomorrow." If we made good time, that seemed like a doable distance to get to the Rockies, according to the maps. "We can formulate another plan once we get there, depending on what we find."

"Aye, aye, Captain." Danny saluted.

"Hardy-har-har," I said.

He winked in response. Smart-ass.

Tyler headed back to the Humvee.

"Ray," I said. "Let's go. It's time to prove how ready and willing you are."

Ray followed, but peered warily back at the two vamps as

he trailed after me. He came around the passenger side and yanked open the side door on his own. Finally a step in the right direction. "Hannon," he grumbled. "What kind of crazy mess are you in? Where exactly are we going?"

"We're going up against the nastiest goddess you've ever seen. You'd better buckle your seat belt."

8

It took us all day and several failed attempts to find the mysterious dirt road that dead-ended into the lake. It'd been easy to find the lake, which was a gigantic crater fed by a few small glaciers surrounding the area. But every single road leading toward the west side of the lake was impenetrable.

We finally zeroed in on the least treacherous, most passable road we could find. It gained the most altitude according to our state-of-the-art GPS, so we followed it to the end.

It was damn lucky there had been no snow on the ground. Even in the gargantuan Humvee, chains wouldn't have been enough. The ruts we had to maneuver around were five feet deep in places, and a few times we had to move trees out of the road to get by.

Strength came in handy.

The road stopped abruptly at the end of what appeared to be a solid wall of old-growth pine forest. The trees towered above us, swaying and rocking in the high altitude. The sun edged toward the horizon, the sky changing to a pale orange above the treetops as we pulled to a stop.

I was absolutely starving. It'd been a long day with little breaks. "Well, it appears we've finally reached the mysterious end of the road." I killed the ignition. We'd volleyed driving during the day, but I'd taken the wheel when the boys had gotten out to remove obstacles. "I hope this is the right road, or we're pretty much screwed. Getting out of here and recharting our course will take too much time and we'd lose nighttime tracking hours with the vamps."

"It has to be the right one." Tyler opened his door. "This was the only logical choice."

"I'm glad you're so very confident," I said. "The fourth time must be the charm. Let's get out and stock the packs with food and water before the vamps arrive; then we can try to check in with Dad on the sat phone." It seemed we were out of range from our minds. Neither of us knew how the brain thing actually worked, but apparently it had a range if we weren't in our wolf form. The connection to our Alpha in our true form was instant, but neither of us had time to shift right now. If the sat phone didn't work, we'd have to reevaluate.

I jumped off the running board, went around to the back, and popped open the hatch—meaning I manhandled the door open.

Tyler strode up beside me. "Packs and supplies are in the green bins." He reached over and hoisted a huge container out of the back like it weighed nothing and set it on the ground.

My stomach growled. I slid the cooler into the empty space he'd just created. It was huge and metal, likely industrial-strength U.S. military grade, capable of keeping things cold for a year. I opened the top and glanced inside. It was full of specialized high-protein meals and shakes made for our high metabolisms. The meals were settled on a thick bed of dry ice. They spoiled quickly once they were opened, so the ice was necessary, but the food was nasty as hell at any temperature. Through the clear packaging, they resembled lumps of canned dog food and unfortunately smelled just as bad. I'd sampled them for fun growing up, but back then I hadn't needed to eat them in order to survive. Now was another story. And since my hunger was insatiable, I had to suck it up. The meals were designed to break down very slowly and curb hunger for a substantial amount of time, but I fished around for a protein shake instead, which was nice and cold because of the dry ice. I'd work my way into the meals.

I plucked out a shake and popped the lid.

Danny walked over. "If you don't fancy the protein mush, I've brought along some other samplings." He reached in and grabbed a large navy duffel and unzipped the top.

Inside, filled to the absolute brim, were packages of beef jerky, candy bars, and sunflower seeds.

"You've always been my favorite wolf." I grabbed a few candy bars and tossed one to Ray, who was coming around the side. "Eat up, Ray. You're going to need to keep up your strength. We've got a lot of hiking to do and some of it will be extremely difficult."

He snatched it out of the air. "What kind of a meal is a Milky Way?" He looked down at the candy bar in his hand. "Aren't we going to make camp?"

"This is not a camping trip," I said. "We keep moving until we find our destination. As far as the candy bar is concerned, consider yourself lucky I didn't offer you a dead rabbit to eat raw. The boys can't shift to hunt, so our meals have to be strategic. A wolf, even in human form, burns up to ten times as many calories as you do just breathing." I pointed to the cooler. "You're welcome to eat the mush, but I doubt you'll be able to keep it down. It's dense and meant to sit like a rock in your belly. But consider yourself lucky that Danny was thinking like a champ and brought a bagful of goodies, and there are protein shakes in the cooler. You're not going to starve."

Without meeting my eye Ray tore off the candy bar wrapper and took a bite. He chewed for a second and then glanced at me. "You guys turning into animals doesn't make sense to me," he grumbled. "If you've been running around for eons, why isn't there any evidence? I've been a police officer for eighteen years and there has never been so much as a whisper of a supernatural being. Now that I know, you guys seem to be all over the place. How in the hell do you keep it quiet?"

"There's evidence if you look in the right spots, mate. Most humans just don't want to see what's right smack in front of them. Didn't you read any fairy tales when you were a lad?" Danny asked. "Back in the day, those fairy tales were our oral recountings, not myth and legend. Populations were sparse and people lived in small villages. If you had a troll living under your bridge, everyone in the community knew about it—and stayed away from the bloody bridge so they didn't get eaten. But when the villages grew by leaps and bounds, and the humans began to outnumber us a hundred to one, many supernaturals were forced to go to ground. It takes only a few well-placed pitchforks and one angry mob to get the point well across. Eventually we were all officially ordered underground. It was the only option left shy of an all-out war with the humans. That was hundreds of years ago. Now the only ones who remember the old days are us, and the only thing marking history are in your children's books. But if you're still on the fence about our existence, I'd be happy to show you a thing or two." Danny grinned. "I'm pretty good at regulated fur growth."

Ray grimaced. "I'm going to take a leak." He turned abruptly toward the trees and wandered away without looking back.

I bent over and opened the bin on the ground. "Let's get this stuff packed," I said. "The vamps should be here soon."

Tyler, Danny, and I stuffed our backpacks with as much as they would hold: food, water, clothes, and essentials. The truck would be home base if it took longer to find Selene. If we wanted to, we could each strap a cooler on our backs. Weight wasn't an issue, but you can't defend against an attack with a cooler strapped to your back.

The sky darkened around us, the sun dipping below the horizon. Tyler went into the woods to sample the air and scout the path. Ray perched on a dead log wrapped in his own thoughts. I stood from where I'd been sitting on the edge of the bumper as the last of the daylight flooded from the sky, expecting the vamps' imminent arrival. "Danny, are you—"

The pack I'd been holding in my hands slid from my grasp.

I collapsed to my knees in the next breath.

My wolf snarled, barking fiercely in my mind.

It's ... another spell attack, I said to her. *Like the one we had last night.* But she already knew. The red lines amassed quickly in my mind as my wolf snapped and ripped at them as fast as she could.

My body began to lock up, and I watched in horror as my hands and fingers became engulfed in red. The spell spread like scarlet vines up my arms. This time it was happening much quicker. *Fuckity, fuck, fuck.* I couldn't breathe. My lungs were shutting down. Danny's shocked face hovered above mine.

Was I lying on my back?

"What the bloody hell is going on?" Danny yelled, but it sounded like he was under water.

I closed my eyes.

Someone shook me. "Hannon, wake the fuck up. You're turning red."

"Hold on to her arms," Tyler barked, but he sounded muffled and far away.

I convulsed. I felt it, but I was only vaguely aware. My wolf howled. I tried to hold on to consciousness, but I was losing focus fast. My wolf ripped at more of the lines, snarling wildly. *We have to share power and attack it together, or we can't win.* Without coupling our strength, we wouldn't make it. She growled at me, still attacking the sea of red in front of her with single-minded intent.

The entire spell meshed together like a honeycomb of lines, and I knew once it coated my mind completely there would be no way out. I pried open my eyes, but my field of vision was completely scarlet. *We have to combine our strength.* My wolf stopped biting and focused on me. A slow pulse tingled through my fingertips. *No, you have to blast me! Like when we shift to Lycan form.* She peered at me through the haze of my mind, tilting her head like she was trying to understand. Her eyes were unfocused and she faltered slightly. That's why I hadn't gotten any power from her. This time the spell had affected her, as well as my physical body. It was adapting, getting stronger. *If we don't snap out of it, we die here.*

In a single moment, I made a decision.

With the last of my strength, I blew open the opaque barrier between us. In an instant my wolf and I snapped together as one. My fingernails shot to sharp points and my canines dropped within the span of a heartbeat. Power shot through my senses like a lightning bolt as my muscles coalesced and fur sprang to the surface.

"What is she doing?" Ray yelled, dropping one of my arms.

"She's fighting it; that's what she's doing," Danny said. "Stand back. This could get ugly before it gets any better."

On a thread of consciousness I put my wolf in control. As the energy shifted to her completely, she let out a fierce snarl, and as she did it, my mouth opened and I could hear the sound reverberate in my eardrums. It was terrifying.

"Holy shit." I barely heard Tyler's voice over the rushing in my ears.

Instead of snapping at the lines, my wolf closed her eyes, gathering as much power as she could to her. I understood what she was doing and, as my muscles pulsed and grew, I threaded all the energy to her as fast as I could. *You have to hurry. I can't keep it up. It's too much.* Her eyes snapped open and she lifted her muzzle to let out another grating howl. The power streamed out of her mouth in one huge mass of energy and exploded through my senses like a fireball. My body jumped like it'd been defibrillated. The power manifested itself in a shock of white and annihilated the red lines like a nuclear blast, racing through my veins, wiping everything clean in a single sweep. As the energy wound its way through every cell in my body, I felt exhilarated.

My eyes flashed open.

It was dark and I was on my back.

The red haze was completely gone. I sat up in my Lycan form, half wolf, half human.

"Jesus Christ, Hannon," Ray breathed. His voice held both awe and revulsion. "What *are* you?"

"I'm a Lycan, Ray." My voice sounded like rocks bouncing around a garbage disposal as air grated over my distorted throat.

Danny stepped forward first. "You turned completely red this time. That was too close for comfort."

There was movement in the tree line. My head shot to the noise, my senses still on high alert.

My wolf growled and it came out of my throat, loud and scratchy. We were still connected, like two eyes peering out of the same body.

Naomi stepped out of the woods first. She stood in a weak pool of moonlight. I must have been out for longer than it'd felt, because it had gone from twilight to full night. Her steps were tentative as she came near. Eamon approached behind her. From their expressions, it was clear they had both witnessed my episode from the forest. They must have landed right as the spell took me over.

"You were fighting Selene's death spell. I could tell by the red lines. It's highly potent," Eamon said with slight accusation in his voice. "By all rights you should be dead."

I glanced down at my hands, no longer red but full of claws and smoky gray fur. "I'm clearly not dead." I stood to my full height, which was considerable. Beating Selene felt fantastic. "And, just so you know, the spell won't be coming back."

"She is the strongest of her kind, possibly in the world. You should not be able to rebuff her mastery so easily." Eamon glanced around, seeming confused. "That spell is made out of her essence, not just conjured. There is no cure."

"Eamon," I said patiently. "It's very apparent you know a lot about this Goddess, but you just witnessed firsthand what happened. It doesn't matter if it was her 'essence' or not. It's clearly not impossible to 'cure' the spell, because I just did it." I knew without a doubt the spell was gone. My blood hummed with clarity.

"What my brother is trying to say," Naomi cut in, "is that

if one of us was hit with the same spell, we would surely die. It does not make sense to us why you still live. It should not be so."

I shrugged my shoulders. "I have no idea why I'm alive," I ground out, my vocal cords straining to be precise. "But I'm not going to argue with the results." It was time to let this conversation go and regroup. I turned away, taking in several deep breaths, trying to ease myself out of my half form and calm down my stressed wolf. *Okay. The crisis has been averted. Let's get back to normal.* My wolf growled, hesitating. *We can't stay in Lycan form and hike up a cliff; plus our clothes are falling off. It's time to shift back and change.* My Lycan form did not support skinny jeans. They were still on, but completely split up both legs. From here it looked like I'd survived the zombie apocalypse, but just barely. My shirt had fared a little better, because it was stretchy, but it had still split up the seams. It was time to switch to spandex.

As we both calmed, I realized my wolf and I were still sharing a common space in my mind. The barrier had been completely obliterated. I checked my mind further, but there was nothing opaque for her to stay behind. If she didn't listen to me, it would be a fight to erect a new blockade and I was tired. *We should stay merged, because it feels stronger when we're united. But you have to agree on the parameters or it won't work. I make the human decisions and you take the dicey fights. It's an easy choice if you think about it.* I felt a moment of hesitation, but then she eased back willingly. Our features shifted back. *Perfect.*

Once I was fully in my human form, I had to hold on to my jeans so they wouldn't drop to my ankles. I looked up to see everyone staring at me. "What?" I asked. "What's the problem?"

My brother tried to contain himself, but worry leaked

around the edges. "It's just...it's a little strange to see you like that. I've never witnessed anything like it before. Being part wolf is sort of...incredible. Does it hurt?"

"It doesn't hurt at all. In fact, it's exhilarating. But it's nothing I can help," I reminded him. "Thank goodness I can do it, since I'm pretty sure it just saved my life."

Danny swung a full pack onto his back as he came forward. "The power strumming from your body as you fought the spell was off the charts. When you ripped out that howl, every hair in my body jumped to attention. I had to hug myself not to change. Whatever you are, the Goddess will have her hands full trying to best you. It's the first time I've felt like we might have a bloody shot of winning this." He grinned. "Let's get on with it then, shall we?" He directed his gaze to Naomi, who was still openly assessing me, her shrewd eyes missing nothing. No detail of my form or my fight with the spell had escaped her.

It was clear the vamps hadn't known I was a Lycan. Or even what a Lycan was.

Their Queen likely didn't even know for sure.

But they did now.

I had no idea how educated the vamps were about werewolves, but as sharp and as old as Naomi was, it was likely she knew enough to piece together what I was from what she just witnessed.

A buzzing noise echoed loudly in the air.

It sounded like an annoying car honk and was coming from the pack Tyler had just picked up.

He glanced at me. "You know who it is. He's going to want a detailed report of what just happened, so feel free to explain it in *full* this time."

I walked toward him, reaching down to grab my own pack, which was still by the bumper of the truck, slinging it over my shoulder. Tyler held his backpack out to me and I unzipped the main compartment with one hand to grab the sat phone, which was sitting on top.

As I plucked it out, it honked in my grasp.

I depressed the large red on button and maneuvered the long antenna away from my ear as I paced into the forest. I needed to talk and change in relative privacy. "Hi, Dad, I'm here."

"Jessica? What's going on?" My father's voice was full of concern. "Your wolf called to mine briefly, and then, once again, the line snapped. I need to be able to communicate with you when you're in danger. I'm getting tired of this," he growled.

"I know," I said as I entered the cover of the trees and found a downed tree. I set my pack down and sat. Everyone could hear me, but it gave me the illusion of privacy. "I never hear or feel anything from you when I'm in my Lycan form. I have no explanation. But I'm fine. I was fighting"—I paused for a moment, because I hadn't told him about the spell, which was why Tyler was perturbed with me—"a residual spell from Selene. But it's gone now." I held my breath. I'd kept this information from him on purpose, fearing he would never have let me go had he known I was harboring a death spell. It was hard to admit, and I knew he was going to be angry.

Tyler grunted, yanking the side door of the truck open loudly in the distance. I'd made him swear not to tell our father what had happened the night before, and it'd taken everything I had to convince him I had it under control. After what everyone just witnessed, "control" had been an illusion on my part. I'd put Tyler in a precarious position with his Alpha.

"What you talking about? What spell?" The phone crackled and broke across the line, but his anger came through loud and clear. "Answer me."

"Selene hit me with more than one spell when she took me down in the clearing."

"And you knew about this other spell before you left?"

"Yes."

"And how exactly were you planning on getting rid of it?"

"I was hoping I could reach her and kill her before it struck again." The theory with witches and spells was that if you killed the witch, the spell died. No fuel, no fire. Before Selene achieved her "goddess" status, she'd been a witch. Most goddesses started that way.

"I'm assuming that didn't happen, because you've barely been gone twenty-four hours and you've already been forced into your Lycan form." The phone buzzed in my ear, the connection worsening.

I sighed. "I was hit again with the spell without warning when you felt the change. We're right outside her boundary and it might have been triggered by the proximity, but I have no real clue. It could also be time release. But the good news is I handled it and it's gone. I know you're not happy with me, but nothing was going to keep me home. We both knew that. It would've been too much to tell you in the short time we had left and it was better to go without a fight."

"Jessica, I can't keep you safe if I don't know what's going on," he argued. "We could've had another witch examine you. There could've been some sort of counterattack. Going off on your own is not going to work. This is *Pack*. It's not a one-man operation. It infuriates me that you have the ability to block me. Keeping things from me in the future will not be tolerated."

"I hear you. I won't let it happen again and I promise to tell you everything from now on. But, in my defense, I couldn't risk Rourke's life like that. If you had ordered me to stay home, it would've been worse. We could've had a fracture between us. You would've forced me to leave Pack."

He was quiet for a few beats. "Jessica, I understand why you did it, but it stops now. I need to know everything, and from there we make the decisions…together. Your life is going to change very quickly from now on. I get it. But I'm still your Alpha." A fierce growl spread across the line. "I don't give a goddamn if my commands don't stick. You will follow my rules or you will find yourself on the outside. Are we clear?" His voice was stony and a few faint ripples of his emotion flowed through me, our blood connection barely triggering this far away. But it was there.

"Clear."

"I just arrived in Redman's territory. We meet with him first thing in the morning. I want you to check in with me again as soon as you can. If I feel any more issues from you, I'll call. If I can't get a hold of you or Tyler, I will drop what I'm doing and come after you."

"Got it."

"Jessica." My father's voice dipped low. "Please stay safe."

"I'm doing my best."

I clicked off the phone and reached down to grab a pair of pants out of my bag. Once I was dressed, I rejoined the group, strapping my pack on my back. Naomi stood silently next to the truck. She hadn't moved since I'd taken the call. Eamon paced off to the side.

"You are strong," she said as I came to a stop. "Stronger than most like you."

Was I strong or was I different? "I'm not going to argue with you, Naomi. But now's not the time to talk about my genetic makeup. We've lost enough time. Which way are we headed? Lead the way."

"We are one pass away from the correct entrance," Naomi said. Her voice rang with tension. "We will have to climb to the top of this peak and down to the next gorge. Once we cross the river at the bottom, we will pass into Selene's territory. It will take longer than if you had found the correct entrance, but we have no choice now. Follow us." Eamon was already moving through the trees.

"How did we miss it?" I asked, falling in step behind her. "This was the only road that made any sense on the GPS." Danny trailed behind me, followed by Tyler, who had just locked the truck. Ray took up the rear. "Can Selene mess with GPS signals?" I guessed a goddess could do what she wanted if she was clever enough.

"Whether she can or cannot is not our concern," Naomi said. "We do not need *GPS*. The road you were looking for had flood damage and the entrance has since been wiped away." She arched an eyebrow over her shoulder at me like a pro. "You are a supernatural, are you not? I will be more precise in the future. I told you the road you wanted dead-ended into the lake. This"—she gestured around her—"does not."

Touché. Another demerit for the hillbillies.

Tyler came up next to me, grumbling, "We can't shift, so it makes it a little harder to find the right coordinates. Especially if they're not on any map."

"Yes, but direction isn't our strong suit, is it?" Danny interjected. "Remember that time in the Everglades, tracking those alligators? It took us a week to get out of that bloody hellhole." Danny chuckled to himself.

"You're not helping," Tyler growled.

9

We hiked straight up. The incline was steep, but the vamps seemed to glide over every stump and rock like it wasn't even there. During the walk Danny had sidled up next to a patient Naomi and filled our walk with light banter. Eamon had taken the lead, and the rest of us trailed after them.

"So what do you eat when you're traveling, then?" Danny asked. "Not many humans out here to nibble on. Except for the one we've brought along, of course. We can loan him to you for the right price." Danny laughed good-naturedly. He was pouring on the charm, and even though Naomi was keeping herself close, I could tell she was having a teensy bit of fun.

She indulged his curiosity pleasantly. "We don't need to feed often. Our bodies are well preserved, requiring a fuel source only every few weeks or so. If we find ourselves out longer than necessary, we can take the blood of an animal. It's not as nutritious, and has a terrible aftertaste, but it will suffice. We will not starve."

"Where are you going to sleep when dawn breaks?" Danny asked. "Not a lot of spooky manors or crypts around here."

She gave him a patient look, paired with a slight smile. "My brother and I have scouted this area. There are caves and cool places for us to stay during the daylight hours. They will do."

I cleared my throat, coming up behind the two of them. "Will we arrive at the next pass before the sun rises?" As we'd climbed, I'd become more and more agitated. My body sensed Rourke was near. His essence was inside me and his blood sang directly to mine.

My wolf prowled in my mind like a caged animal, sensing constantly for danger as the air grew thicker with Selene's signature. Much like the immediate power a supe gave off, but more widespread. It brushed against my skin like an angry breeze.

"We will reach the peak in a few moments," Naomi answered. "Then we will start our descent. Likely we will arrive at the bottom of the gorge by daybreak. From there my brother and I will escort you to her direct perimeter line, which starts after the stream at the bottom. We have been forbidden to take you farther. Eamon will sense the area and try to prepare you for what you will encounter, but once we reach the edge of her lands, you will face her obstacles on your own."

"Of course," I said. My agreement with the Vamp Queen had been for tracking to Selene's boundary and nothing more.

Eamon stopped abruptly at the head of the line and we all slowed.

"What is it?" Tyler asked, edging his way to the front. The altitude was very thin here; the trees were less dense and scattered. We were just about to crest through the trees to the rocky edge of the summit, but we still stood within the forest. Ten feet in front of us the tree line stopped completely. Rolling granite covered the top before the cliff sheered off on one side and led down to what I assumed was a stream.

I heard the water bubbling below.

"I sense something." Eamon turned in a slow circle. "But Selene's lands do not extend this far, so it should not be so. The signature is here, yet it's different somehow. Changed."

Tyler immediately put his nose to the sky and inhaled. "I smell something slightly acidic in the air. It smells like guano, but with a sharper twang."

"Bat guano?" I asked. "Maybe we're by a cave and the bats just came out to feed?"

"No," Eamon said. "The smell is layered with a taste of Otherness, but one I've never sampled before. It's bitter. Bitter always means bad."

"I'm getting a trace of Otherness too." Tyler opened his mouth to take the air over his tongue. "It's almost undetectable, like it was supposed to be veiled, but the scent trickled out anyway."

"I can't detect anything," Danny said. "But smelling is not my strong suit. Much like directions. I just don't have the knack. Now, knocking someone out cold or handing them their teeth after a brawl, I'm your man."

I inhaled, forcing the air in slowly. My wolf twitched her ears. I noticed something too. After a few breaths it became stronger as it settled over my taste buds. It was faint, but definitely bitter. "I'm not exactly surprised we're coming up against something before we hit her 'official' territory," I said. "She'd be foolish to let us draw too close without a fight. Plus, she loves games. Putting up some puzzling roadblock sounds like something she'd do. We need to tread very carefully from here."

"I will investigate a bit farther." Naomi strode for a large opening past the trees. A bright moon and a bevy of stars kept the night sky luminous. The stars ran in an almost continuous swath of white. With my newly enhanced vision, I could see so much more. Stars that had been undetectable before now flickered in the sky. It was breathtaking. The only person who had an issue finding his way in the dark was Ray. He'd stumbled along behind us at less than half the pace, swearing up a blue streak as he went. But since he was following us on his own, I wasn't complaining.

"Be wary out there," I called. "It could be a trap."

Naomi reached the clearing. "Once I pass out of these trees I'll take to the sky and see what I can find—"

The instant she crossed the tree line she was swarmed.

Small, black creatures coated her, flapping their wings in furious motion. I ran toward her shouting, "Are those bats?"

If they were, they weren't ordinary bats.

Before I could process what was happening, Danny dropped his pack and ran. "Get the bloody hell off of her, you beasts!" Once he got to her, he tore them from her body. As they came off, so did bits of her clothing and skin.

"What are they?" I yelled to Eamon, coming up short of the trees and dropping my gear by the edge of the clearing. We had to know what they were in order to fight them. They hadn't attacked her until she passed through the trees, so that had to mean there was a delineation of some kind. Eamon was frozen in place, staring at his sister. "Eamon!" I shouted. "What are they?"

"Winged devils." He said it so quietly I had to strain to hear him.

"What?"

"Their proper name is *Camazotz,* which translates into 'Death Bat of the Underworld.'"

Underworld? These were from the *Underworld*? "How do we stop them?" I urged.

He didn't answer, so I shouted behind me, "Ray, head back into the forest. Find a log or something to hide under. When this is over, we'll find you." I turned to my brother, who hovered next to me at the edge of the trees, equally helpless. The bats had fully engulfed Danny. If we went out there now, we'd be swarmed too. "Tyler, we have to stop them! What do we do?"

We watched as Danny struggled to pull them off his own body. Naomi fell to the ground and Danny collapsed to his knees beside her.

I took an unconscious step forward and my brother's arm shot out to stop me. "We can't go out there." He grabbed on to my forearm to keep me in place. "They covered Danny instantly. If we go out there, they'll swarm us too."

"What are you talking about? We can't let them die out there," I insisted. "Selene must have them contained. They aren't coming after us here, so this tree line must be the cutoff. If we can drag Danny and Naomi back here, maybe they will disappear."

"Jess, there are too many." Tyler dropped my arm and started pacing back and forth agitatedly along the tree line. "I can make a run for it, but there's no guarantee I can grab them both before the suckers bring me down. They look like they're multiplying too. Every time Danny kills one, another one pops up in its place." It did look like there were twice as many as before, and every time one died, another popped up. They couldn't get ahead.

"Eamon!" I turned and ran over to his still immobile form. "You have to help us save your sister. *Eamon!*"

He stared stoically forward. "There is no way to help them. The *Camazotz* are summoned from the Underworld for protection. Selene has paid for them with a piece of her soul. Their claws are like razor blades, their teeth venomous. They are things feared even in the Underworld. We cannot stop them."

"Bullshit!" I yelled in frustration, throwing my hands in the air. "If they exist, there's a way to defeat them. They have to have a weakness." My voice was frantic. "Think, Eamon. My friend is dying and I'm going to help him, even if I have to run out there on my own. If you know Selene, and know where they came from, they have a flaw. Think!"

"A witch's spell," Eamon said with hesitation. "It might have an effect on them, but only temporarily. It won't kill them. The *Camazotz* are born of demons, and demon magic is born of the blood. Witches have an innate protection against blood magic. Their spells are crafted of the earth. But no witch is strong enough to kill them completely."

"A spell?" The darts from Tally. Tallulah Talbot was a powerful witch. If her magic wasn't strong enough to knock these things out for a few precious seconds, then no spell was. "I have spell darts in my pack." I dove to my backpack and tore open the zipper. I snatched the darts off the top and unrolled the fabric, careful not to shred it in my haste. I had no idea which one to pick. They were color coded, but there were no helpful labels or instructions. Two blue, two green, one orange, and one yellow. They were different hues than any of Marcy's. "Which one do we use?" I looked up at my brother, who stood beside me.

He knelt down. "There aren't enough darts in there to hit every devil."

Danny howled, and both Tyler and I wrenched our heads in his direction. He crawled toward Naomi, ripping the beasts off his body as he went. "Get the bloody hell off of me!" he roared. "You will not be the end of me. Naomi, stay with us! Naomi!"

He reached her and started to yank them off her, only to have them reappear a second later.

"We have no choice." I jumped up with the spell case in my hand. "We have to start throwing them or they're going to die." I gritted my teeth as I watched Danny continue to struggle. "Tyler, we have to act!"

"Aim the darts at their bodies instead," Eamon said, walking toward me. "When the spell explodes into their bloodstream, it will instantly contaminate all the winged devils. The *Camazotz* are consuming their flesh and drinking their blood; they will absorb it by proxy."

I met my brother's eye as I held the darts. "Which color? We have freezers, sleepers, and two others, no kills. Choose."

"Blue," he said. "Try blue."

I plucked out the two blues, rolled the case back up, and set it down on my pack. Then I walked as close as I could to the last tree before the clearing. I wedged the outside edge of my shoe against the bark for support and drew back my arm to take aim. Then I faltered. We had only a few precious spells and I couldn't risk missing my target. If I threw it at Danny and it bounced off one of those stupid blood-sucking rodents, we lost. New plan.

"Danny! Danny!" I called. He turned toward me, hearing my voice. "I have two spells." I waved my hand in the air. "I'm going to throw them to you and you're going to pierce Naomi and then yourself. Do you understand what I'm telling you?"

His face was bloody and ravaged. One of his eyelids looked like it was completely gone. Most of his face was covered so I couldn't see his expression. I couldn't tell if he understood me or not.

"Danny!" I shouted as I held up the potions again and waved them. "Do you see me? I'm going to throw these to you." I mimicked tossing them underhand. "You have to catch them and inject Naomi and then yourself!" If he injected himself first, he would be spelled and out cold, so he had to hit Naomi first.

After a moment, he seemed to understand. He turned to Naomi, but instead of turning back to me, he started mindlessly pulling more off her, ignoring me completely.

"Tyler, he's not listening," I cried. "Or he can't understand me anymore. I have to go out there and do it myself. We're running out of time. Naomi hasn't moved in too long. I can't let them die. I'll run out fast. We know what to expect. I'll drag them as close as I can back to you before the bastards eat me and I'll spell them. Then you can shoot me with another dart."

Tyler hooked me around the waist as I took a step forward. "You are not going out there, Jess. Do you hear me? They will eat you alive, Lycan or not," he growled. "If Danny's not listening, *make* him listen. If that doesn't work, I'll go out there."

"How do I make him listen? I just yelled at him and he ignored me."

"Your wolf is above his and he's submitted to you already. I'd do it, but Danny might not listen to me. Command him. Force him to hear you."

Danny's wolf had recognized and submitted to me the first time he'd seen me in my Lycan form. "Are you sure it will work?"

"Fuck no!" Tyler shouted. "But it's the only thing we have left. Do it!"

I gathered as much power as I could and shoved it into my voice. "Daniel Walker! Listen to me!" The sound echoed out of my body in a strong, steady current. I wasn't sure how much to use, so I threw everything I had at him. "*Stop!*"

Danny froze, his stunned gaze turning to meet mine.

It worked.

"I'm going to throw something to you. You will catch it," I told him, strength vibrating my vocal cords. "Insert one dart into Naomi and then one dart into yourself. Do it immediately! Do you understand me?"

He nodded slowly. As he stood, he batted the devils away from his face so he could see.

I was at the very edge of the boundary. A pulse of energy hit me as my foot strayed past the tree. A shock of warning. How could Naomi have missed it? It raced through me like an alarm, running up my leg and back down my spine. I yanked my foot back. The magic had a menacing undertone. I'd never felt anything like it.

Danny opened his arms to ready himself and I lobbed a single dart underhanded. He stumbled forward to catch it. It hit his open palm and he curled his fingers around it, capturing it without breaking it. Then I threw the next one. Once he held both, I yelled, "Go! Pierce Naomi first and then yourself. Do it now!"

He jerked around and fell to his knees next to her. There was a mass of devils on her chest. He ripped them off, their mouths saturated with blood, and plunged the dart deeply into her stomach.

She convulsed once and went still.

Then he turned the second dart on himself, stabbing it right through one of the screeching devils high on his thigh. Danny froze in place for a millisecond before he toppled onto Naomi, none of his body parts moving.

Blue meant freezer.

Almost immediately the devils started to fall off. Each of them twitching once before freezing in place on the ground.

"*Ohmygod*, it's working! Come on. We have to go get them

now," I yelled, tugging Tyler's arm. "Eamon said it won't last long."

I moved forward only to be yanked back once again. "Tyler! You have to stop doing that." I turned, angry. My irises sparking. "I'm not a child and you're wasting valuable time."

"The hell I'm letting you out there," he snarled. "My *job* here is to protect you. It's what you hired me to do and that's what I'm damn well going to do. Get another spell primed for me. I'll bring them back, and if those little fuckers get me, stab me with it once I cross the line."

He took off before I could argue. I hadn't technically hired him—my father had. But he was right; it was why he was here—that and he loved me. As he ran, the winged devils that hadn't succumbed to the spell swarmed him. "Tyler!" I screamed. "Keep moving!" I tried to infuse as much power as I could into my voice. I had no idea if it would work on my brother, but it was worth a try.

He raced to Naomi and flung her over his shoulder. She landed stiffly, which made it hard. Then he turned and grabbed Danny by the arm. Instead of lifting him, he dragged him behind. I fumbled for another spell, this time yellow. I fisted it right as Tyler barreled back through the trees.

He tossed Naomi at a stunned Eamon, who caught her with ease. At the same time he let go of Danny and dropped to the forest floor on his knees. The few of the devils that had clung to him fell off and seemed discombobulated, opening their red-stained maws, gasping for breath. None of them had bitten him. "Why didn't they bite you?" I asked.

"I think they all had a taste of the spell, even if it wasn't a lot, and I think they're confused." He grabbed one off the ground where it had fallen. The thing tried to latch unsuccessfully on to his finger. Its eyes blazed a feral orange and its skin was both scaled and leathery. Tyler gave it a squeeze. Its chest imploded and it went limp. Before he could toss it back over the boundary line, it disappeared right out of his hand with a little *pop*.

"*Okay*. That was strange." I took a step closer and one of the devils on the ground flew halfheartedly at me. It wobbled like it was drunk, but its intentions were clear—it wanted my flesh and blood. "Oh, no you don't." It zoomed at me lopsided. I angled my arm back. When it was within a foot of me, I pounded my fist into it. It connected hard, and the thing exploded with a shriek and sailed outside of the boundary line and blinked out of existence.

Tyler started picking up a few errant ones. "Help me toss them out there." He gestured to the clearing. "You need to kill them first so they go away. Then chuck them past the trees."

"Wait," I said after he'd killed two and threw them back. "We should keep one."

He glanced at me with a question. "Why would we *keep* one?"

"The ones that aren't frozen are dazed in here. Look at that one." I pointed to one on the ground that wobbled in a circle. "We have to find a way to defeat them or we can't go any farther, so let's keep one."

Tyler shrugged. "Okay. Fair enough."

"Alive."

He grimaced. "How are we going to keep it from attacking us? What if it decides to wake up?"

"We can tie it down somehow. How about nailing it to a tree?"

"That might work."

"But we don't have a hammer, do we?"

Tyler grinned. "I don't need one. I can pound anything into a tree with this." He lifted up his fist. "I'll find a sharp rock."

Now that the devils were figured out, I knelt by Danny's side. He was lying facedown, so I gently rolled him over. It wasn't easy because he was still frozen.

His face was almost unrecognizable.

Pieces of his flesh were missing and his clothes were shredded and bloody. There were gashes all over his arms and legs shaped in small, angry circles. Thank goodness the spell not only froze him—but knocked him out. He was a supe; he'd heal. I took his hand gently in mine.

Eamon had laid Naomi down a few feet away.

She was equally damaged. It was hard to look at her. The healing process would take time. I hoped it didn't hurt too much and that they both stayed unconscious throughout the process.

"They will not recover from this," Eamon stated, his voice remorseful as he gazed down at his sister. "They have been too gravely injured."

I glanced sharply at him. "What did you say?"

Eamon shook his head. "The wounds might close some, but they will never heal over completely. They will fester and bleed until the venom finally kills them."

"That can't be true. They're supernaturals." I ran a gaze over Danny's body.

Eamon was right; none of the wounds were closing.

"Naomi will need the blood of an immortal for any chance of survival, and she cannot drink mine. We are too closely bonded. It will not give her the healing properties she needs. Blood is her only chance, but even with it, she might not recover. *Camazotz* venom is powerful."

"What about Danny!" I cried. "How does he heal? He doesn't drink blood."

"I do not know."

Tyler knelt down next to me. "Nobody's feeding a vampire, Jessica, so don't even think about it."

"Tyler," I argued—it wasn't worth pretending he didn't know my thoughts exactly—"we have to be reasonable here. If we have a chance to save a life, we save one."

"Jess," Tyler said between clenched teeth, "our races don't mix. We've *never* mixed. Naomi was ordered by her Queen to do a *job*. It's not our problem if she dies. That's the risk her Queen took—"

"I'll do it." Danny's voice broke as he gasped for air. "Give her my blood then. I've lost a hell of a lot of it, but if there's anything left, she is welcome to it."

10

My brother and I stared down at him, slack jawed. "Danny, please don't be awake right now," I pleaded. "Are you in pain?" I reached my hands out to touch his body, to console him, but pulled them back. I couldn't risk hurting him.

Nothing was healing. The wounds were a festering mess.

Tyler bent closer, his voice filled with pain. "Danny, you don't know what you're saying. You're hallucinating. Go back to sleep." He glanced at me. "We have to knock him out again. We can't let him suffer like this."

"No," Danny breathed, his lips almost unmoving. "Give her my...blood. Now."

I turned to Eamon. His face was grim. He didn't like the idea any better than I did. I smoothed Danny's hair back carefully. "Danny, you're too damaged and you've lost too much blood. I can't let you do it."

"She needs it."

I glanced at Naomi. He was right. Neither of them appeared

able to survive this on their own. Danny looked horrible, but Naomi had been hit harder. She was smaller and had been out there longer. Her body was mangled and shredded beyond recognition. "I can't argue with you there, buddy, but you can't be the one to do it," I said.

Tyler glared at me. "Don't even think about it, Jess."

"Why not?" I snapped. "The wolves will never accept me anyway. I've been an outcast since the day I was born." My body tensed with emotion. "Why wouldn't I choose to save a life? It's the right thing to do!"

"Because it's not the *right* thing to do!" Tyler shouted, jumping to his feet. "We are sworn enemies of the vampires. If they had their way, they would've annihilated our race long ago. They've always wanted supreme power over all the Sects. Their Queen will not expect you to save this girl!" He gestured angrily at Naomi. "And the wolves will never accept it."

"What he says is correct," Eamon interrupted.

I narrowed my eyes at them both. "I don't care what the Queen *expects*—or doesn't—or anyone else for that matter. If I can save Naomi, I'm going to do it. She's already proven herself loyal on this journey. And Danny was willing to give it to her, even in the shape he's in." I indicated to his bleeding body. "There's no reason for me not to try." I yanked up my shirtsleeve to prove my point. I stared at my brother, both of our eyes sparking, each of us growling. "You can leave if you can't take it, but I'm not going to stand by and let her die when I have a chance to save her. And after I'm done, I'm saving Danny, even if I have to give him a blood transfusion. Do you hear me? Neither of them is going to *die* if I can help it." My voice came out in a wash of power all on its own, my wolf chiming in with a ferocious snarl.

Tyler took an inadvertent step back, frustration and anger

creasing his brows. "If you think I'm going to stay here and see you sacrifice yourself to save a vamp, think again." He turned and stormed off into the forest. I knew he wouldn't go far. He wouldn't leave Danny for very long.

Once he was gone, I scooted next to Naomi. She was so broken. I swallowed. "Okay, what do I do?" I turned to Eamon, who seemed as stunned as Tyler that I was actually going to go through with it. "Eamon." I snapped my fingers in front of his face. "Let's get moving. What do I do now?"

Eamon physically shook himself. "Bring your wrist up to her mouth. I do not know if the venom has rendered her senses deadened or not, but once she has the taste of your blood on her lips, she should latch on by herself. When you feel she's taken enough, you will need to sever the contact by ripping your wrist away. She will not let go on her own. If you do not, she will drink you dry."

Well . . . *hmm*.

I had a throwing knife sheathed on my waist. I drew it out and positioned it above my wrist. My wolf snarled a warning, making me falter for a moment. *What? You don't want to save a life? You were behind me just a moment ago.* She snapped her jaws twice, showing me a picture of wolves—only wolves—surrounding us. *A life is a life, even an undead one. Naomi was forced to help us by her Queen and she doesn't deserve to end like this—I don't care if she's not our kind.* She lifted her head once, brought it back down, and sat, resigned.

I exhaled the breath I'd held and sliced the knife cleanly across my wrist. Blood flowed out in a rush, but I had to move quickly because it wouldn't run for long.

I angled my wrist down toward Naomi's mangled lips, dripping blood onto them and into her mouth. She stirred after a moment, moaning faintly.

Eamon's breath hitched as he watched my blood flow into his sister's mouth. Vampires didn't need to breathe, but in order to talk they had to take in air. "I must leave now." He rose quickly. "Thank you...for helping her. It is a debt we will repay as required by our laws, decided by our Queen." He shot up into the air.

Right then Naomi latched on to my wrist. Her sharp teeth punctured it deeply, hitting bone. "*Jesus!*" I yelled, grabbing on to my forearm with my other hand to keep it in place, resisting the urge to pull back as she began sucking ravenously. My wolf let out a howl in my mind. *It's okay. We'll pull back soon.*

"Jessica," Danny whispered, turning his head slightly. "I'd like to point out that you have always been my favorite." He smiled grimly, obviously in pain. "You have something in spades that we wolves sorely lack. Compassion. Please don't ever forget it."

"Danny"—my voice full of sorrow—"I know for a fact beef jerky has always been your favorite. And I'm telling you right now, I'm going to fix this. Promise me you'll stay with me. We're going to find a way to make this better as soon as I'm done here."

As Naomi sucked, I wondered how long was long enough. I peered at her body as she took my blood. Her skin looked a little better, almost like it was *thinking* of knitting back together.

"*Ahhhh.*" Without warning her eyes shot open and her mouth detached, surprising me. She blinked twice, focusing on me as I leaned above her. "What are you doing?" she accused, my blood streaming down the side of her mouth, her eyes looking crazed and wide, oscillating from flecks of mercury to jet black, and back again.

"Um." I sat back on my haunches and wrapped my ripped wrist tightly with my other hand to stanch the flow. The bleeding stopped almost immediately. "We thought you were dying, so I gave you my blood. I also thought you weren't going to let go of me on your own. So that was a shocker."

She sat up slowly, *Dracula*-style, bending smoothly at the waist. She was still mangled, but her face was starting to repair itself at a rapid pace. "What did you say?" she asked, her eyes still eerie and unfocused.

"I said I gave you my blood."

"Why would you do such a thing?"

"I just covered this—you would've died otherwise. The venom was going to kill you. I didn't know what else to do. Eamon said this would work and that drinking the blood of an immortal was your only hope."

She glanced down her body, startled, her eyes easing back to their normal hazel color. "What has happened to me? I do not remember." She spread her arms out, taking in her injuries, her lips curling in distaste—a look I was used to seeing on her brother's face, not hers.

"You were attacked by winged devils, *Cozmos* or something, from the Underworld. Apparently they have poisonous venom that impedes supernatural healing. You don't remember anything at all? That must be powerful poison." Naomi turned, noticing Danny for the first time, lying, thankfully, out cold a few feet away.

"Quickly. We need to wake him." She sprang forward, crawling on her hands and knees, her voice trembling.

"Whoa. What are you talking about? You just woke up. You need to heal first." I reached an arm out to stop her.

She brushed me off. "*Non, non*," she muttered in French. "You don't understand. If we do not get the venom from his system he will die within moments."

"*What!*" I said, completely alarmed. I moved quickly next to her, crawling toward Danny, because it was the easiest way to get there. "That's not what your brother told me. He said the wounds would fester, but not that his life was in immediate jeopardy, like dying in the next few minutes kind of jeopardy."

"My brother is foolish," she mumbled in annoyance. "He thought to save me, but he was careless about your wolf friend. Come. Help me wake him and do as I say. I will show you what to do." She carefully rose up on her knees and reached into the pocket of her mangled jeans. There was material left, but not much. It wasn't a jeans kind of day. "You need to insert this into his body." She cradled something carefully in her palm. It was a small scarlet bag with a front flap, decorated in gold thread. Using the edges of the flap to protect her fingers, she pulled out a small cross and set it on top of the bag. It was beautifully detailed, the craftsmanship exquisite. It was carved with symbols and flowing decorations so small and intricate it must've taken years, and huge magnifying glasses, to complete.

"Is that silver?" I asked.

"*Oui*, yes, and it is spelled. It will destroy the venom and anything else in his bloodstream."

"But silver can kill a wolf," I said, my tone firm. "I'm not putting that inside his body. If it gets into his heart, it could stop it for good. I can't take that chance. He's too weak." Tyler's distrust rang through my mind as I put my hand out to push it away.

What if it was the vamps' agenda to kill us all from the beginning and I'd been wrong? What if this had all been a ploy to get me to give her blood?

"*Non*," Naomi tsked. "The cross is specially made; the silver will react only with the blood to kill the danger, not the body. Just do as I say. We are running out of time! You are stronger than I am now. It must be inserted deeply. Go!" She shoved it toward me again.

Something in her face, and the urgency of her voice, made me take notice. I had just saved her life. Surely she wouldn't repay that debt by killing my friend? Reluctantly I took hold of the cloth by the edges, grasping the cross through the soft fabric. Silver was highly conductive to supernatural magic, the very essence that fueled us, and would burn me if my fingers touched it.

I bent over Danny and shook his shoulder. Maybe he wasn't dying and I wouldn't have to use this thing. "Danny, Danny, wake up!"

He moaned and mumbled incoherently, his cracked, blood-ied lips turned down in a painful grimace.

"Insert it near the heart. Find a wound that is already open," Naomi urged. "You must do it now."

"Near the heart? You've got to be kidding!" I balked, feeling panicked. "Look. He's waking. Maybe he's not as dire as you think. He could heal on his own. Eamon might be wrong."

"Do you want your friend to live or die?" Naomi snarled, her voice fierce. "Now stop wasting time!" I glanced at her to argue my point, and gasped. She was nearly healed. "You're almost fully—"

She ripped the cross out of my hands and elbowed me out of the way, plunging it deeply into Danny's chest.

It was inserted at an angle, only the top of it visible. As she drew her hand away, I could see the imprint of the cross left in her palm. I didn't have time to do anything else, because Danny's back arched beneath him and he let out a strangled howl. The hairs on my arms rose.

"Quickly, grab on to his arms and legs," Naomi ordered.

This was a werewolf we were talking about, not a toddler. "Tyler," I screamed. "We need help!" Nothing else but to trust her now, because Danny was bucking beneath us. The cross was clearly doing something. I just prayed it wasn't killing him.

I chose to believe her.

Tyler raced through the trees toward us. "What are you doing to him?" he shouted.

"Naomi put some kind of charmed silver cross in Danny's chest. She says it will cure him. Without it he dies from the venom."

Tyler roared and lunged for the cross. Before he could reach it, I jumped up and knocked him out of the way. "Tyler, stop!"

He stumbled backward, but recovered himself in an instant, coming at me. "What do you think you're doing, Jess?" he raged. "This is insanity! I can't watch this vamp kill my best friend without doing anything to stop it. Wake up and take a look around. They have the full advantage here, and putting silver into a werewolf this weak means *death*. Danny's as good as gone, and this was probably their plan all along. Don't you see? You're playing right into it!"

"Tyler," I ground. "I don't have time to argue with you now, but I've chosen to trust Naomi on this. Time is wasting and we need your help. Like I told you before, not everyone is out to *kill* everyone else. I want Danny to *live*, and if you do too, grab his goddamn legs so that thing stays in!"

"And what if he dies?" Tyler demanded, his irises swirling amber. "What then?"

"Then I will KILL HER MYSELF," I bellowed with as much power as I could infuse into the words.

Tyler dove to the ground and snatched up Danny's bucking legs. I wasn't sure if I had manipulated him with power or if he'd gotten it on his own, and I didn't really want to know. Tyler kept his head down. I knelt and grabbed Danny's shoulder and torso on one side. Naomi had the other.

"I am not murdering your friend," Naomi whispered as we all did our best to keep him still. Danny groaned and snarled in our grasps. "My memory is slowly returning. Your friend was selfless to come to my aid when he was not forced to do so. I will return the favor, as is common among our kind. This was his only chance. It was the cross or his certain death. There is no other way to exorcise the venom."

Tyler did not respond. Danny continued to twist and yell. I glanced down the length of his body. His wounds were starting to fester in earnest. Yellow muck began to bubble out.

"What the hell is that stuff?" Tyler growled.

"That is the poison," Naomi answered. "Stay away from it. The venom is born of the Underworld and still very potent. The silver is reacting to it and forcing it to flee his system."

"Why didn't we see it come out of your body then?" I questioned, running my eyes over Naomi's almost fully healed body. There'd been no hint of yellow anywhere.

Naomi wouldn't meet my eyes for a moment. When she did, she looked slightly abashed. "I believe your blood neutralized the venom on its own."

"What? How can you be sure?" I asked. "Does that mean that my blood is immune to the little bastards?"

"I do not know for sure if you are immune." She shook her head. "But I do know that vampires are very sensitive to blood types of all kinds. We can detect even the most subtle textures and tastes. Without a shadow of a doubt, your blood has cleansed me. As I drank, it was like nothing I'd ever tasted before, even in my unconscious state. It was dangerous and wild, sweet and powerful. I believe your blood seared the poison inside me, eradicating it the instant it mingled with the venom."

I grimaced. Just talking about drinking blood gave me the willies. Plus, she just reminded me I'd broken every code and rule the wolves had about sharing anything with a different Sect—especially giving my *blood*. My father would be furious with me when he found out. There would be repercussions, there was no doubt. "If that means I'm immune, can I give my blood to Danny? Will it work the same way?"

"It won't be necessary," Naomi said. "He is almost clean. Look for yourself."

The yellow had finished festering out. Now only bright red blood leaked from wounds, which thankfully were starting to close on their own. Danny had stopped thrashing once the poison had finished ejecting, but he was still out cold.

There was a noise in the woods to my left. Ray was coming through the trees. It seemed he'd found his way back from wherever he'd hidden himself when the devils had attacked. I'm not sure how much he'd seen of them in the dark, but thankfully it had been enough to keep him away. "Ray, the threat might not be fully gone," I called. "But for now I think it's okay to stay. Just make sure you don't step out past the trees to my right. Unless, of course, you want to be eaten alive by supernatural devil bats."

"I'm not going anywhere near there," Ray grumbled. "I saw those things. I just spent the last hour huddled under a downed tree convincing myself I wasn't dreaming. Every time I turn around there's another freaking creature coming out of the woodwork. When does it end?"

"To be fair, I've never seen anything like them either. There are a lot of supernaturals on this earth that I've never heard about."

Witches might know about demons—and horrid demon pets—because they were natural enemies, but wolves had never bothered with the Underworld to my knowledge. The standing philosophy was: we stayed away from them and they stayed away from us. Demons could raise seventy-five different types of killer bats and we would be none the wiser. "Ray, as long as you're back, make yourself useful. Can you be a sport and get us some water?"

I'd been hoping for Eamon to return, but this would have to do.

"How am I supposed to find water in the dark, Hannon?" Ray said. "I could barely find my way back here in one piece. My eyes don't spark up every time I need to see."

I smiled. "Our eyes don't spark so we can see. They light because of the magic manifesting behind them. Eyes really are a portal into the soul, Ray. As for the water, it can be found in any of the packs."

"Fine," Ray grumbled, as he shuffled his way around the area.

"Water will be good," Naomi agreed.

"Do you think the venom will rinse off his skin?"

She nodded. "I believe so."

Tyler still had a grip on Danny's legs, but remained silent. We were all ready to spring if Danny started thrashing again.

Ray tripped over something and let out a string of curses. "Jesus, what's in this? Lead bricks? I can barely lift it."

"Just drag it over here," I said impatiently. "Hurry. We have to rinse this stuff completely off Danny." The yellow residue was now smoking where it lay on his skin. It was beyond nasty.

Ray toted the pack along the ground. "Here." He set the pack by my leg and leaned over my shoulder to squint at Danny. "Gods."

The cross was still embedded in Danny's chest. I didn't know when we were supposed to get it out. "Is it time to take the cross out?" I asked.

"*Non*. It needs more time. I will keep holding him in case there is a reaction. Run the water over him," Naomi ordered. "Once he is free of all the venom, he should come back to us on his own. After his wounds heal over, we will remove the cross."

I let go of Danny and unzipped the pack. There was a big canteen sitting right on top. I unscrewed the top and doused the liquid slowly over his body. His clothes were shredded or had been eaten away, so it was easy to see his flesh. I handed the canteen to Tyler when I was half done, and he ran the rest over his legs. We were careful not to let the yellow crap touch us as it washed away.

Once the water rinsed away the last of the venom, Danny started to moan in earnest.

There was relief all around when his eyes blinked open. "What...?" He brought a bloodied hand up to his forehead. "...Happened? It feels like a lorry ran over my face and crushed my legs in the process." He tried to sit up, but Naomi set a restraining hand on his chest.

"Take it easy there," Tyler murmured. "One thing at a time, tough guy."

"You must try to sleep," Naomi said. "It will take time to heal all your wounds."

"Sleep, my arse," Danny growled, glancing from her to me for an explanation. "My body feels like it's been shredded by a weed whacker. Sleep is the last thing on my mind. And can anyone tell me why I have a bloody chunk of silver lodged in my chest?" Before we could answer, he plucked out the cross and tossed it into the forest with one defiant flick of his wrist.

"No!" Naomi yelled as she jumped up and went to search for it.

"You just threw away your cure, buddy," I told him. "That was a little ungrateful of you, but we will forgive you given the circumstances."

"A cure?" Danny replied, a little bewildered. "How can that be a cure? It hurt."

"It's some kind of spelled cross of Naomi's that magically rids the bearer of all the bad stuff, but won't kill you. It must have cost her a fortune."

"Well, then, I am indeed very ungrateful. I thank you kindly, Naomi," Danny called. His body was healing extremely quickly now that all the gunk was gone.

Tyler stood as Naomi came back. His voice carefully measured. "How did you know we were going to need that thing?" He pointed to the cross, now wrapped in the shreds of her shirt so it wouldn't burn her skin. "Did your Queen know we were going to encounter something from the Underworld?" Tyler's voice rang with tension. "So you just happened to have a cure-all in your pocket for just such an emergency?"

Naomi stared back at Tyler, her eyes defiant. They held a glint of challenge. "I carry this with me always. It never leaves my sight." Naomi bent over and picked up the bag it belonged in off the forest floor and carefully wrapped the cross back up, placing it in her pocket.

"It's pretty handy you had the only thing in the world that could've saved him," Tyler egged, pushing for a fight. "Without it, he would've died."

"I earned this healing cross with the blood of my servitude," she retorted, a steel edge lacing her normally lithe accent. "Selene would take it back from me if she was given the chance, but it's mine now. I won it from her fairly."

"The cross was the Lunar Goddess's trinket?" I asked. No wonder it worked on the devil venom. It had been made for a goddess.

Naomi nodded slowly. "It was...yes."

"See," Tyler accused, pointing at Naomi. "This proves my point exactly. Naomi and Selene know each other personally. Did you know that?" He turned to me, his eyes blazing. "We can't keep trusting them blindly, Jess! If we do, we'll all end up dead. The Queen gave us two vamps who have a *connection* to the very Goddess we're trying to kill. This isn't an even game; it's rigged."

I ignored Tyler's tirade for the moment and instead narrowed my eyes on Naomi, assessing. There was pain and some guilt in her expression before she finally glanced away. I ventured a guess. "You said you earned that cross with the blood of your servitude." I pointed to her pocket. "You served Selene?"

"*Oui*," Naomi said thinly, turning back to face me.

"Willingly?"

She hesitated for a few beats. "*Oui.*"

"Your Queen is very shrewd. I'll give her that." Sending two of her best, knowing they knew the enemy better than we did put us in a challenging position. "Did your Queen order you not to divulge this connection to us?" I asked.

"We were to give you the minimum assistance, as always. It is so for any duty. She needn't have ordered us to keep quiet specifically; it would be expected of us."

"Now that we know you're connected to Selene, what happens next?" I asked. "If you served the Goddess, you have inside information, things that will make defeating her easier. Now that we know, what are you going to do about it?"

Tyler stood next to me, silent, his anger vibrating around us in waves.

A slow smile spread across Naomi's features, making her appear both sweet and gruesome at the same time. She was still covered in dried blood, the white of her cheekbones standing out in bright contrast against the red. "Now that this information is out it seems the rules have changed."

There was a gust of air and Eamon dropped beside her. "Naomi, you must keep your mouth shut. Our Queen will not tolerate anything more. We are almost to the boundary. That was our only duty. We will see them to the edge and leave— nothing more."

Naomi uttered a single word in response. *"Non."*

11

"That is not what we are doing, brother." Naomi put a hand on his arm, silencing him before he could form a rebuttal. He must have been lurking in the trees listening to us. My distaste for him heightened to new levels. "Have you forgotten what just happened here? Our duty was to take them to the entrance and to warn them of the dangers—*all* of the dangers. The winged devils were unexpected and much too far outside of her domain. Something is wrong here, different than it should be, and we will do our best to figure it out before it ends us all. The boundary lines have changed, and we will change accordingly."

"That is not our job," Eamon insisted. "Our duty is to fulfill the Queen's orders, not to divulge unnecessary information or battle what waits for us inside those lines. The Queen will not suffer us if we do not follow her wishes."

"You would choose to not repay a life debt?" Naomi quirked her head to the side. "You would choose instead to run with your tail between your legs yet again?"

"Of course we will repay the debt," Eamon sputtered. "But we need to do it according to *our* laws. We report back to our Queen and await her wishes. She will decide who owes and how much we pay. That has always been our way."

"My life was saved by one thing only: the blood of an immortal. To not repay such a gift immediately is *unthinkable*. We will repay the need, which means we will bring them to her door and give them the information they need to survive."

"The Queen will be angry."

"The Queen is diplomatic." Naomi crossed her arms. "If I were to leave when the bearer of my debt is in need, we risk war with the wolves, do we not?" She shifted her gaze to me and raised an eyebrow.

"Um...yes. Absolutely," I answered, following her lead. "Eamon, you can't desert us now. Your Queen wouldn't want a war on her hands. As a rule, wolves must pay up immediately if they can. Nobody wants a life debt hanging over their heads. If you don't pay it now as needed, I could demand something bigger from your Queen once we return. Then where would you be? There's not a doghouse big enough, especially with what I'm going to ask for."

Naomi smiled, covering it up delicately with the back of her hand as she replied, "And once we arrive at Selene's door, we will stay and help you defeat her. If we make it out alive, my life debt to you will be paid in full." She inclined her head. "Agreed?"

"Agreed," I said quickly.

Eamon gasped. "We will do no such thing! The venom has gone to your brain and made you rash. It's too dangerous. I will not willingly return to that place and suffer at her hands agai—"

"We will do it," Naomi snapped. "You are my blood-kin

first; my debts are yours to fulfill by *honor*. The Goddess will not harm us this time. We are smarter and stronger; we are not the children we once were."

Eamon raged, his hands balled into tight fists. It looked like steam could possibly pour from his ears.

"If you don't mind my asking," I interrupted, trying to defuse the situation. "How long did you...serve Selene? And why?"

Naomi turned to me, her eyes stark for a moment before she answered. "One hundred and fifty years," she replied softly. "We did not understand the gravity of our decision at the time. We were fledglings recently turned by a low-level master. Once it was known our special gifts in tracking and sensing were"— she cleared her throat—"rare, we became a bartering tool to make our master wealthy. He offered us to the highest bidder, which was the Lunar Goddess, but the Vampire Queen stepped in and gave us a choice—we could choose her or Selene. We were foolish. We thought being in the company of a powerful goddess would give us great power and ultimate status, that she could protect us better than our own *Queen*," she scoffed. "But we were chained and treated like slaves for over a century. Unleashed only when she required us to do her bidding."

"How did you finally escape?" I asked. I was both curious and appalled.

"She became lazy and began to leave us unattended for small periods. Then I happened across this." She patted her pocket. "The cross can do more than just heal an immortal. It is a powerful weapon. While it was buried in Danny's body, burning the poison of the Underworld, he was temporarily void of all his power."

"Pardon?" Danny interrupted. "I hadn't any power? That's funny, because I didn't feel any different. Though I was unconscious through most of it." He was still on the ground, sitting upright now, but not ready to stand. We were all following the conversation closely. Ray had taken a seat on a nearby log, and Tyler stood stoically with his arms crossed, patient for now to hear her out.

"If it is used against Selene," Naomi continued, "it will absorb her powers the same way, rendering her useless for the time it remains in her body. It will not kill her outright, but it will incapacitate her. Once she found out that the cross could work against her, she sought to destroy it...but it was already lost."

"And once she misplaced it—it was your property to find," I finished.

"*Oui.*" Naomi smiled like a shrew. "It was not my fault my jailer became careless and trusting in my company, that she mistook my placation for devotion and faithful servitude."

Keeping Naomi on my side was an absolute must from now on. She was proving to be a very smart, very powerful supernatural. Behind those petite shoulders and tiny waist was a cold-blooded killer.

"If that cross can cure a supernatural, how come your brother didn't use it on you? Why use my sister to get blood?" Tyler growled as he joined the conversation. He had calmed down, but not by much.

Naomi turned to Tyler and addressed him directly. "There is a caveat to having ownership of the cross. Once it is yours, it will not work against you, nor will it aid you. The spell is dead to me, though the silver still leaves a mark on my flesh. Selene paid a great deal for its creation, to use against powerful enemies, and had the insurance policy built in that the cross would never be able to harm her. But the crafters of this trinket were very powerful in their own rights, and they played a little game. If the trinket was lost, whoever found it became its rightful owner. Once out of her hands and claimed by another, it could work against her. So in essence she had crafted the only means in the world to render her own powers useless."

"I'm sure whoever crafted it didn't advertise their prank and risk her wrath, so how did you find out?" I asked. "Whoever did this played a dangerous game with a very powerful goddess."

Naomi shrugged. "I didn't know until I pierced it into her flesh. It worked. Of course, I had a feeling, as I often do with such things, but nothing more."

"You engaged a goddess on a *feeling*."

Naomi started to pace along the tree line. Eamon was still angry, but he held himself silent while she talked. It was clear he didn't have the power to stop her, or he would've used it by now. "Our lives were no longer worth living," she stated evenly. "I had reached a breaking point and had made peace with a true death. At that point I would've been happy to die."

"But you still have the cross?" I asked, confused. "And Selene's still alive. How did you get it back once you pierced her? She had to have been pissed off. You had her cross and you stabbed her with it. It must have been Clash of the Titans when she went after you."

Naomi stopped. "She did not have time to attack. After the cross absorbed her powers, I beheaded her."

"Geez," I exclaimed on a low breath. I hadn't been expecting that.

Danny whistled and Tyler exhaled loudly.

"How could she survive a beheading and still be alive now?" I asked. Beheading was the one thing that could kill a supe, even a powerful one. No head meant no communication with the vital parts that kept you alive.

"She is a goddess." Naomi shrugged. "I learned too late that in order to kill such a being you have to kill the *immortality* in her blood, along with the body. I left her to rot, but it was not enough." She sighed.

"How do you kill immortality?" I asked. I'd never even heard of such a thing, but I was young. The amount of things I didn't know would fill an ocean. I had some serious catching up to do. I guess that was the hundred-million-dollar question. Not being able to kill Selene in any of the normal ways was going to complicate things to an incredible degree—possibly even make it impossible to give her a true death.

Naomi shrugged again. "I know not how. I have the capability of stripping her of power with this. That is all." She patted her pocket. "The killing of the immortality will be up to you."

Now it was my turn to sigh. "I thought Rourke was the only one who had bested her and lived." And I hoped he was doing it again right now. He was alive. I knew it. But he didn't have a lot of time left. We had to keep moving. "That's what your Queen told me anyway. She said nothing about there being another who had escaped her wrath. Why would she lie about that?"

"Our Queen has always been very skeptical of us after all those years spent with Selene," Naomi replied. "She still wanted our talents, but distrusted our reasons for coming back to her. I divulged what had happened and showed her the cross, begging her for protection. She demanded I turn it over to her. But she'd made a grave mistake. We had not yet pledged ourselves to her and I was not yet hers to control. A vampire needs to swear fealty and exchange blood with their master before they can *manage* them. I threatened to leave and she swore an oath that she would never take it from me while

I *lived*. Eamon and I were desperate to belong to a powerful Coven, one that would protect us from Selene if she ever rose again, so we accepted."

"And Selene lived. She knew you took the cross with you. When she woke up…or grew her head back or whatever she did, why didn't she come after you?" I asked. Revenge would be logical. "That's a powerful weapon to walk away from."

"She did come and the Queen lied to her and said it was now in her possession, which it was, through me. But to pacify Selene, she agreed to never reveal its existence or what had happened between us. If the power of the cross became known, others would seek to steal it, and in turn it could wind up being used against Selene once again. She has many enemies, so she backed off."

"How long ago was all this?"

"Three hundred and fifty years ago."

"And you've waited patiently all this time for a chance to give her a true death?" I concluded. Getting even was high on the bucket list for supernaturals. When you lived an eternity, no slight was too small.

"*Oui*." Naomi smiled. "I've yearned for it."

"That's a long time to wait." I walked toward the tree where Tyler had staked the winged devil. "Now all we have to do is figure out how to get past these evil things. If Selene knows you're leading us, which she undoubtedly does"—every Sect had well-placed spies, and if Selene knew the Queen had her trinket, she would have people she bribed on the inside—"she will anticipate you've brought her prized possession and she will be awaiting her own revenge. It could have been her motivation to sell part of her soul for more protection and increase her boundary line, which will cost her in both energy and power reserves. She wants what you have."

Naomi followed me to the tree, while Eamon stayed rooted where he was, still glowering. "This place in the mountains is new to us," she said. "We have never visited here before. But her habits will be hard ones to break. We will expect some of her favorite defenses. Her mind is twisted, but she has likely convinced herself you are not stronger than she is, yet she is betting you will succeed in making it to her lair. She is always at war with herself. Killing your mate, however, will not be as *satisfactory* if you are not there to witness it."

I gave Naomi an appraising look. "Cocky, deranged, overly self-assured, and masochistic all make her weak, and give us a definite advantage. But there's no way we can get to her if we don't get rid of these little freaks." I peered at the squirming devil. Tyler had pinned it by the wings. It struggled sluggishly, its beady eyes glowing like a banked fire. But the worst was its gaping snout, filled with hundreds of needlelike teeth, which were currently dripping yellow goo all over the ground. Very slowly it lifted its talons and flexed them at me. It had one long thumb and one larger appendage, like the last three fingers of a hand, only melded together. Each of the fingery things boasted long nasty-looking blades. Like Eamon had said, they resembled thin razors for easy slicing. "How did Eamon know they had razor blades for fingers?"

"Selene has always coveted them," Naomi answered. "She had statues and carvings of them adorning her walls. She called them her pets, all while lamenting the cost of ownership was too high. She vowed she would own them someday."

"No pet I know costs a chunk of your soul."

"True," Naomi said. "But when you are as powerful as she, one covets what they can't have. Selene convinced herself if she could raise an army of them, she would rule the supernatural world. There are not many things that can bring us down as easily or as quickly as these." She shuddered, rubbing her arms. "They are vile creatures."

"They multiplied," Tyler said, coming over to join us. His tone was even, the fight gone. "When Danny killed a few, more popped up in their place." I smiled at my brother as he ran a tired hand over his face. I knew it took a lot for him to back off, and I was grateful he was willing.

Naomi nodded gamely. "Only the amount negotiated can be summoned from the Underworld at one time. When one is killed in this world, another materializes to take its place. It goes back to the Underworld to regenerate. They cannot find true death on this plane."

"If Selene wanted to amass a huge army of these things"—I stifled a gag thinking about how awful that would be—"how much would she have to pay?"

"She would belong to the Underworld for all eternity. If she did that, she would control an untold amount of them and the world would be a very bleak place."

I blew out a frustrated breath. "It's a good thing she's too narcissistic to give up her life in total. What do you think her payment is for this many?" I asked curiously.

"I would expect it to be a millennium of servitude; nothing less," Naomi said. "Payable once she perishes on this plane."

"So if we can kill her body long enough, the demons will come pick her up? It's not a perfect plan, but it makes her disappear for a mighty long time."

Naomi bit her lip. Her fangs were retracted so all that showed were straight, white teeth. "Yes, true death would be optimal, of course, but I would be satisfied seeing her in the demons' hands for a millennia. They will undoubtedly torture her repeatedly and painfully, as she will do nothing for them willingly. It would be just punishment."

"So how do we get by the devils?" I asked. We needed to start moving or nobody was going to get to do anything to Selene. My wolf gnashed her teeth. I agreed. This was taking too long.

Naomi shook her head. "It will be difficult."

"Can they attack during daylight?" Tyler asked.

She shrugged. "I would assume so."

"It seems they work properly only inside Selene's boundary," Tyler said. "Here they seem . . . off. This one is still moving slowly and it can't possibly be affected by the spell any longer."

"Boundaries would be in their agreement." Naomi nodded. "Demons have very strict rules they must abide by on this plane, and a group such as this could kill a human town in a blink of an eye. They need bite a human only once to make them die in unspeakable ways. There would be precautions put in place." Naomi peered closely at the devil. "I am surprised she did not save these until last, but likely she has trouble controlling them." The thing hissed at her, its eyes flaming violent orange for a moment.

"But once we get by these things, we're in for more surprises, right?" Danny said, coming up behind us. "This can't be her only line of defense."

I glanced over my shoulder at him, happy to see he was almost healed. All the gashes had closed and were on their way to fully mending. "Glad to see you're up, Danny. If you can heal from these things, then we can find a way to defeat them. We just have to put our brains together and figure it out."

Tyler stood next to me, but Eamon had refused to join the conversation. He was still angry. I was surprised he hadn't just flown off, but risking his sister's ire for the second time today must not be worth it.

"If the witch's spells worked even temporarily," Tyler said, "we could try and mix up the spells and find a way to blanket them across the group."

"Yes, but a temporary fix will only send them after us once they wake," I said. "That would trap us in her boundary with no shelter. We need to find a way to corral them, if not kill them permanently. Once we end Selene, they should pop back to the Underworld for good, since they can only reside in a domain she controls, correct?"

Naomi nodded.

"Why don't you freeze them?" a voice said from behind us. I turned slowly to see Ray, still perched on a log, looking tired. His face was drawn, but he looked determined.

"What did you say?" I asked.

"Use the cooler. You have enough dry ice to freeze a herd of cattle, and they don't seem to work here in the trees. Lure them in here and freeze the bastards."

"That has possibilities." I pondered. "I see you're still thinking like a detective, despite all the brain trauma you think you've endured. I'm impressed, Ray."

"They are diminished here for some reason," Tyler agreed. "The cooler might hold them if they stay alive. If they pop back to the Underworld once they freeze solid, we're out of luck. It will be a tricky balance to keep them alive but contained. But it's a possibility."

"The reason they are over here has been puzzling me," Naomi said. "They should not be able to exist at all once they cross over Selene's boundary. Once across they should be immediately forced back to the Underworld. They are not in her control here. Yet they are alive, but cannot truly function. It should not be so."

"I did sense a strange power signature by the boundary," I said, heading to the separation point of the trees and the clearing. "I was surprised you crossed it, Naomi. It felt menacing and it was definitely not Selene's magic."

"I felt no foreign power signature. If I had, I would have stepped back." Naomi followed me, her face pulled down in a frown. "Eamon is the sensor. I am the tracker." She turned to her brother. "Did you sense other magics here?"

Eamon walked briskly to us, unclenching and reclenching his fists. He had let Naomi say her piece, but he was clearly beyond his limits of tolerance. "No. There is nothing here. She is mistaken. I can sense nothing, even now."

"I feel it. Right here." I placed my hand near the bark of the closest tree and wiggled my fingers. "It's a small pulse of some kind and it's buzzing a warning. It jumps like a heartbeat in my veins. I have to be right next to it to get a current, but it's here." I glanced at Danny and Tyler. "Come over here and see if you can feel it."

They moved to where I stood. Danny reached his hand into the space. "I can't sense anything, but I can smell those little shites. Not everyone can feel residual power. I am someone who needs the beast in front of me to get a good read, but I trust you."

"You are mistaken," Eamon huffed. "Sensing is my gift and there is nothing here." He put both hands up to the clearing and moved them around like a mime.

I narrowed my eyes. "Are you certain you don't feel it, Eamon? You're not just pretending you don't because you missed it and sent your sister out to face her death? It's strong enough to send the hairs on my arms up when I'm this close. It's making my wolf agitated and wary as we speak." My wolf had growled a warning the moment we had gotten close.

Eamon glared at me and took a bold step though the tree line. I read his reaction the moment he felt it.

The winged devils popped up immediately in front of him and he stepped back quickly, almost in a daze. "Yes," he said. "I feel it, but only once my whole body absorbed it. It's so faint you should not be able to sense it so clearly. This is not Selene's signature." He retreated back into the shelter of the trees, his mind clearly processing. "It's a leftover current of the Underworld."

"From the winged devils, or something stronger?" I asked impatiently, following him.

"Not from them at all. Some being from the Underworld was summoned here, or was powerful enough to come on its own. Its magic still lingers. That's why the *Camazotz* can survive here. The power left here mimics the magic they have in their own realm. It's not strong enough to fuel them, only enough to keep them breathing. Whatever came here, came purposefully to the precise edge of Selene's border. What you're feeling is not a spelled line, or a boundary line, but residual magic left by something extremely powerful."

"Why would something so powerful sneak up to Selene's boundary?" I asked. "I thought she was in cahoots with the demons? Why would they tiptoe around?"

"Who knows why demons do anything? Maybe it wanted to check up on its pets." Eamon sniffed. "It was very careful to come just to the edge. But its magic is not only here." He turned, his eyes searching through the forest. "When something this powerful comes into our world, it comes in a huge circle of power." When we clearly weren't following what he was saying, he looked at us like we were the dumbest kids in class. "You *are* familiar with Circles of Power, correct?"

I glanced at Tyler and Danny. "I know witches use circles when they perform certain magic," I ventured. "And circular shapes have significance and can enhance power. The Circle of the Earth is the witches' sacred symbol." That's what Marcy had told me anyway. Beyond that, I had no clue. The only circle wolves cared about was the moon, and Eamon wasn't talking about the goddamn moon.

"This was no witches' circle," Eamon snapped. "This is a demon Circle of Power. Not only a demon, but most likely a *Lord*. It took a huge magnitude of power to leave this much residual magic—enough for the *Camazotz* to survive in it. This line here"—he pointed to the boundary he had just crossed—"is only part of a much larger circle. You must have driven through the other side—the metal in your car absorbing the brunt of it without your knowledge. It could be as large as fifty miles in diameter. We've been inside it since we've been on the mountain. But its edge rings with the strongest concentration of power, like the shock waves of an H-bomb pushing its entire energy straight outward. And even now the edges are only faint with it. You should not have been able to detect it without passing through."

"It's not faint to me," I said, meeting his accusing glare with a glare of my own. "It pulses and sends my hackles up, even now. You can't tell me that Selene doesn't know it came to visit. If she poked her head out of her hidey-hole, she should be able to sense it. She's a goddess. It can't be that undercover."

Eamon appeared put out that he had to explain so much. "Demon Lords rarely venture into our realm if they don't have to. They have adequate minions to fetch what they need. This one was careful not to alert Selene, but I agree, if she came close to the signature she would detect it. I'd say it was betting she wouldn't take the time to notice."

"Eamon," Naomi scolded. "It is your job to sense magic and Otherness. Without that skill we stand no chance. You must be more diligent as we move forward or we will all die."

Eamon had the decency to look a little abashed.

"Well," I said. "At least we know why the winged beasties don't pop out of existence once they crossed the boundary line. And we know there's a finite number. Now all we have to do is trap them. Ray might have a nugget of a plan. If we can contain them in something, freeze them, and add one of Tally's spells, we might have a chance to keep them out of our way long enough to fight Selene. So the question remains, how do we get them all over here to this side without dying in the process?"

Tyler ran a hand along the back of his neck. "The cooler is made of steel. I can go back and bring it here. Let's try and see if the ice will freeze this one." He nodded toward the one on the tree. "If that bugger can't get out, we'll go ahead with the plan. It's not going to be easy, and the sun will be up in a few hours. We're going to have to work fast."

I gazed out into the clearing. There were no signs of them, but that meant nothing. The moment Eamon had put a toe out there, they'd come back. "Okay. Go get the cooler," I agreed. Tyler took off immediately. I faced the rest of the group. "We're likely going to have to stay here through the daylight hours anyway. Danny needs to recover, and I'm not going forward until we have a concrete plan in place. If this is what Selene has to offer from the beginning, we have to be ready."

"Don't worry about me." Danny grinned. "I'm as good as new already."

I snorted. "You just had your face ripped off. We can take a break. At the very least you need a change of clothes and a nap." I glanced at the two vamps. "Let's take this time to figure out what Selene might be using against us. I want to know what her favorite toys are and what magic she specializes in.

If we can anticipate what's to come, we'll have a much better chance of fighting our way through her obstacles."

"That may be true," Naomi pondered. "But as you said before, Selene is not foolish and will know we are accompanying you. She will try to confuse us."

"Old habits die hard," I said. "In the end she'll likely go back to her favorites. I want to narrow them down one by one. We've seen she likes her pets. What else does she like?"

Naomi bit her lip. "She loves fire and her beloved whip. She is a brutal being, beyond anything you can imagine. Her lair is filled with hideous devices meant to torture and deliver lasting harm. She will desperately want to finish you off herself, or she will consider it a failure. But I believe you will be able to best whatever awaits."

I raised my eyebrows. "So are you saying if I wanted to, I could best these Underworld beasties myself?"

"Whoa, whoa," Danny interjected, sensing my mood. I wanted to get out of here, and speeding things up sounded like a good plan. "It's my job to keep you safe, and I will chain you to a tree if you even entertain the thought of going out there."

"*Non.*" Naomi shook her head. "He is right. They are something different. I am referring to her magic alone. I am over five hundred years old and have been through many trials in my long life, but I've never been incapacitated by anything before this day." Her eyes grew angry. "She has sold her soul for power, but I will not allow Selene to win." Naomi's features started to give that telltale vampire shake, which could only lead to the wet putty look of horror.

I was not a fan of the vamp-out.

"Okay, then." I clapped my hands together, trying to alleviate the emotional tension each of us was now carrying from the long ordeal with the devils. "Let's focus on something else. Eamon, what's Selene's go-to spell?"

Eamon paled, which was a tough thing to do when your features were the color of ivory and bone. His lips thinned as he likely remembered something terrible. It was clear he didn't want to answer, but finally managed, "The death spell is one of her favorites, meant to inflict as much pain as possible before it finally kills you. It has taken her many years to perfect it. But she has another. A spell that can play tricks on your mind, convincing you that you've killed and tortured the ones most dear to you. It drives you slowly insane as she watches."

Jesus.

Right as Eamon finished his sentence, a huge boulder flew from beyond the cliff face and into the trees, taking out everything in its path, slamming into the dirt ten feet from where we stood.

12

"Where did that come from?" I yelled. The force of the impact had flung us all backward, but being supernaturals, we recovered in an instant. I stood over a dazed Ray, my legs splayed across his body, eyes searching for the next attack. "Boulders don't just shoot themselves up in the air!" I scented the air, but the only thing I could detect was the bitter scent of the winged devils.

Naomi took flight in a blur. Eamon had disappeared sometime between the boulder's impact and the recovery.

Danny rushed over to Ray and me, scattering pine needles out of his hair. Tyler had gone to retrieve the cooler and had yet to return, thank goodness. "Whatever flung that rock over the crest was no small being," Danny said. "Either the boulder was spelled or something massive tossed it. Either way, not a great scenario."

A large groan rent the air as a hand the size of an armchair reached over the rock face and grabbed on to a lone tree. It bent the small trunk to the ground as it started hoisting itself over the top.

Before we could see what the head looked like, Naomi and Eamon simultaneously landed in front of us. "What the hell is it?" I asked. "Hurry up!"

"We could not go past the tree line because of the devils, but we did go straight above as far as we could," Naomi said. "It is our belief it's some kind of mountain troll, based on its size."

"A troll?" My voice held stunned surprise. "Selene has a troll? How do you even control one? I thought they were confined to Eastern Europe. What's it going to do when it's done smashing us with rocks? Eat us?"

"No," Eamon said with irritation. "You're talking about a bridge troll. A mountain troll is used to defend a mountain. It's deft at throwing anything and hitting its target with accuracy. If we linger in the sky, it could take us out by knocking us to the ground with a boulder, and then crush our bodies beneath its feet before we could recover. Do not underestimate a mountain troll."

"But it doesn't smell like anything," Danny complained. "I would assume a troll would have a scent. I've smelled many a bridge troll and they have a nasty, fishy stink."

"It doesn't matter. We're about to find out exactly what it is," I said. "It's cresting the top now."

All eyes focused on the dark edge of the mountain. Behind me, Ray staggered into an upright position. "I can't see a thing," Ray complained. "Are you telling me we're about to be attacked by a giant creature who carries a club with spikes on it and eats people?"

"That sounds about right," I said. My eyes were riveted on the other gigantic hand as it sailed over the edge in a loud crash, sending pieces of the mountain flying down into the gorge.

There was noise behind us as Tyler burst into the trees, the cooler hoisted strategically above his head. "I heard an explosion. What happened?" He set the metal box down with enough force to bury the bottom. "I ran all the way back here. It sounded like part of the mountain sheared off—"

A huge body emerged over the edge, ending all discussion.

Its dark stony eyes arched in our direction. It wasn't a troll. It appeared to be made up completely of rocks. My wolf let out a long howl. *What is it?* She barked in rough staccatos.

"No," Naomi whispered. "It cannot be."

"I take it that's not a troll," I said impatiently. I hated being a newborn. Everything was new to me. "Whatever. I don't care what it is. We just have to find a way to defeat it."

"I believe it's a Mahrac," Eamon said with a touch of awe in his voice. "They are very rare and very strong. It is much worse than a troll. A troll bleeds and breathes and has a heart that beats, making it possible to bring down. A Mahrac is the stuff of nightmares. A spirit being. Impossible for us to kill. We will not be able to best it." He made a move to leave. "We must turn back."

I grabbed ahold of his arm before he could go anywhere. "We aren't going back," I said, my voice just short of full-on rage. "I am not leaving." My wolf snarled her agreement, teeth flashing. "Tell me what a Mahrac is and then we'll figure out how to defeat it." As I spoke, the thing hoisted itself to its full height. It towered at least fifteen feet high and six feet across, completely massive. Its whole upper body was made up of a series of rocks hanging together in space. "The rocks don't look connected. What's holding it together? If we can disconnect the parts, it falls apart. Correct?"

"Wrong," Eamon snapped. "It's a spirit being made entirely of the rocks from its environment. If it loses one, it pulls another. It is not sentient. I told you, there is no way we can defeat it. We do not have the right skills," Eamon said with confidence. "We must clear the area. It can sense us better than a troll."

The thing let out a deafening howl from someplace other than its mouth, because it didn't have one. Then it leaned over and grabbed hunks of stone from the ground, like a child scooping sand from a sandbox. It started to pace toward us, the mountain shaking under its weight in a seismic vibration. "We have to split up," I yelled. The thing arched a stony arm and launched its booty. Rocks and boulders crashed into the trees, breaking them perfectly in half like some sort of cartoon. A huge boulder raced straight toward Danny. "Danny," I screamed. "Move!"

"Already a step ahead of you," Danny called. Using his preternatural speed, he dodged it no problem. "No need to worry about me. Get yourself under cover."

I turned to Ray, who appeared to be in shock. "Ray! Wake up! We might recover from a crushing blow, but you have zero chance. Run back to the Humvee and wait for us there. Crawl under the damn thing if you hear it coming down the hill."

Ray didn't move. The spirit monster turned and lumbered toward my voice. "There's no getting away from that thing," Ray said quietly. "Its parts aren't even fully connected. How is it moving?"

"It's enchanted in some way," I heard myself yell as I grabbed on to Ray and ran. "Selene is using it to do her bidding, like a golem. If there's a way to break her mind control over it, it might fall apart or lose interest in us." I shoved Ray behind a big tree, pinning his back to the bark, and ordered, with a finger up, "Stay here. If one of those rocks hits you, you're dead."

I didn't wait for him to answer. I slipped out from behind the trunk and sped for Tyler. The Mahrac turned slightly when it noticed me running through the trees. It didn't seem overly hurried in its assault on us.

I reached Tyler, leaping behind a mass of earth to land next to him. Danny darted through the trees toward us. Naomi started doing a little jig in front of it to keep its attention.

"She's going to distract it as long as she can," Danny said, joining us. "Anyone know how these things operate?" There was another deafening sound as a boulder exploded into the trees. "I've never even heard of a bloody Mahrac before. Golem, yes; Mahrac, no. It must be regional to some faraway land. Where does she come up with these things?"

I looked around. "We need Eamon," I said. "None of us knows what it's capable of besides him. Eamon!" I yelled, glancing around me. "Where did he go?"

There was wind in my ear one second before he landed in front of me. "I'm here, but I will not stay for long."

"Does Selene have mastery over it completely?" I asked. "Or does it have its own soul?"

Eamon's lips curled. An expression I wanted to slap off his face. Hard. With an open palm. My fingers twitched. "I do not know. I have already told you, I don't know how to best this monster. Mahracs live deep in the Altai Mountains. They were created by Mongolian shamans centuries ago to protect their people. They defend what is theirs, to the end. I know this only because Selene bragged about learning spells as a young witch from a very powerful shaman. The technique shamans use is very different from a witch's magic. It took her years to perfect it."

"It's like brain control, then," Danny urged. "The shamans control the monsters that way and now Selene can too."

"It takes trained power to manipulate them," Eamon said in an exasperated tone.

"How do they do it?" I asked. "Come on, Eamon. You know more about this than anyone else. Think!"

"I know of a sorcerer who wrested control of a golem," Eamon finally said. "I witnessed him dip his hand into the clay body and physically grasp its mind. But none of us is a witch or a sorcerer. It's doubtful the Vampire Queen could even achieve it. We cannot defeat this being. We must leave here."

And go where? The only option was to go back down the mountain. But there was no guarantee the Mahrac wouldn't follow us. Likely, now that he had us in his sights, we wouldn't shake him. We had to stay and fight.

My wolf brayed in my mind and showed me a picture of us glowing. *I know we have power. I can feel it—especially since we came together—but nothing like what Eamon is talking about. Even if we could put our hands inside, how would we know what to do once we had it? We aren't skilled in wielding magic.* She barked and then scratched at the ground. Slowly something appeared in my mind. It was a box of some kind. It had a lacquered top, inlaid with some kind of script. I didn't have time to see what it was because the Mahrac turned and bellowed, done with Naomi's dance.

The thing flung a huge piece of earth the size of a couch at us.

It took out everything in its path. I dove to the side, my wolf fueling me with a big dose of adrenaline. My claws extended as I flew through the air, my canines dropping to points. *We're going to need more if we're going to defeat this thing.* I rolled once and was on my feet. I turned to see where Tyler and Danny had gone right as the Mahrac let out a cry of joy.

A prone figure lay on the ground.

Tyler.

The Mahrac headed toward him gleefully, each step sounding like a trash compactor crushing everything in its path. If it reached Tyler, it would step on him, pulverizing his spinal column.

Before I could react, Danny shouted, "Come here you pansy-arsed piece of shit! Why don't you come and get me? Don't bother with that one; he's already dead. I'm still alive and ready to nail you to the wall." Danny launched the canteen we'd used to douse the venom at the Mahrac. It hit the side of its head with enough force to knock a small piece out. The canteen had no physical, weakening effect on it, but it was enough to gain its attention.

But instead of using rocks and earth as its weapon of choice, it grabbed on to a huge fir tree with its massive fist and plucked it straight out of the ground, roots and all. In the next motion it swung the tree at Danny. Even though Danny was already running, the top branches caught him, knocking him deep into the woods.

Naomi landed in front of me. "I'll catch its attention once again. You need to jump on its back."

"And what do I do once I'm there? I can try to tear its head off, but won't it just find another one?"

She looked at me with exasperation. "I heard everything Eamon just told you about the sorcerer. If there's enough power in your blood to disintegrate venom from the Underworld then there is enough to control this beast. Now go!" She launched herself into the sky.

The monster gave a howl and turned. Naomi put herself right in front of it, waving her hands, but the thing ignored her. It turned back toward my brother. It had a single-minded intention. And its intention was to kill Tyler.

No more time.

Here we go. I took a running leap, infusing myself with power, absorbing it greedily from my wolf. She howled along in a rush. My muscles coalesced quickly, fusing together under my skin, growing three times their size in a single heartbeat. Fur erupted along my arms and I let out a fierce snarl. I flew through the air and caught the thing squarely in the back, digging my claws deeply into the stone. My nails penetrated easily, providing me with a good grip. The thing bucked immediately, trying to shake me off, but I scrambled up like I was rock climbing—which technically I was. It wasn't particularly flexible, which worked in my favor, and as it tried to bat at me with its clumsy rock fists, it succeeded only in smashing the surrounding trees to pieces.

"Go for its head," Naomi shouted.

"Then what?" I muttered. "That's the real question."

I wrapped my hands around its neck, which was a wide, square stone, with both hands, digging my nails in again. I gave an experimental squeeze to see if I could wrest the block out and hopefully dislocate the head from the body. It didn't move. Not even a millimeter. It was stuck in place with some kind of crazy supernatural cement.

The Mahrac continued to twist us in a circle. It wouldn't be long until it smashed me into a tree. *There's nothing for me to grab. What do I do?* My wolf barked and began to uncover the box she'd showed me before, right as the monster started spinning quicker, trying to dislodge me. If it was smart enough to do that, it had a brain. "You're not getting rid of me," I hissed at the back of its head. "This ride isn't over until you are."

It slowed, almost like it'd understood me.

"That's right. You heard me," I growled. "I'm not getting off until you agree to stop all this. Care to give me any insight?"

The thing let out a gravelly howl and spun in a slow circle, like it was pondering its options. Then it took off through the trees. For a moment I wasn't sure which direction it was heading in, and then it burst through the tree line, making its way straight to the edge of the mountain it had just climbed up.

The Mahrac was going to take me over the side.

Like hell it was.

"Jess, it's going over!" Danny yelled behind me. "You have to jump. *Jump!*"

Naomi was in the air at the edge of my peripheral vision, coming at me quickly, covered in winged devils. For some reason they hadn't gotten to me yet. "Naomi," I screamed. "Get back! I've got this."

I had no more time to think. We were almost to the end of the road. In one solid motion, I arched my arm back and struck my fist into the back of its head. A portion at the base exploded into pieces, leaving a gaping hole. The thing didn't slow for a second. I rocked my fist back one more time, using supernatural speed, and plunged it into the opening with a snarl. This time I lodged it in there. The Mahrac faltered for a moment as I opened my hand inside the hole, feeling and searching for what made this thing tick. The monster slid to a stop, shaking its head, and it took everything I had to keep my hand inside.

My wolf started to bark frantically. *What? What do I do now?* She gave an impatient growl. *Show me! I don't get it.* She leaned down and nosed the box open. The lid fell back and a blinding light rushed out, racing through all my senses like someone had plugged me in. My first instinct was to shut my eyes against it—it was too much. But I knew I had to absorb it as fast as I could. As I took it in, my consciousness flooded totally white. Power flushed through me like someone had finally pulled the master switch.

My hand started to tingle inside the Mahrac.

A low pulse in the middle of my fist wound up my arm. I could almost taste the essence of the Mahrac. It tasted of sorrow. I shivered. The monster slid to a stop right at the precipice of the cliff. One false move and we would go over. I closed my eyes and focused on its Otherness. It was dense and heavy, and extremely strong.

I edged a single finger in farther, prodding its essence with my nail. It cried out.

Then I felt something else.

It was layered on top like a thick coat of sticky slime. In my mind it manifested as dark red, throbbing with menace. It was choking the Mahrac, forcing it to do its bidding. *Selene.* Her power was here, inserted like a sickness where it didn't belong.

Something reared up in my psyche so strongly I almost let go. Everything in me wanted to crush the evil thing inside this being. It made me angry beyond measure—beyond any words. Going only on instinct, I twisted my hand quickly, scooping up as much of its essence as I could in my palm. And with everything I had, I threw all the blinding power I'd gathered from inside the box and sent it hurling at the ball of life in my hands.

I needed to purify it. To set it free.

The monster arched its back and flung its rocky arms out, letting out a sound of echoing thunder. My light encapsulated it completely. Then a shock wave of power ran though my body like a tremor, ending with a huge burst of power that snapped my head back and forced my eyes and jaw to snap shut.

Everything went still.

The light in my mind broke apart and dissipated.

Without any warning, the Mahrac tossed me backward, catching me by surprise. I let go, releasing my hold on it. I landed on the ground hard, not thinking to right myself, just thankful I was off the beast.

The Mahrac gave me one look before it turned and launched itself off the cliff.

I didn't have time to be relieved or exhilarated. I was drenched in sweat and completely spent.

And covered in winged devils.

13

They tore at my flesh, their greedy mouths lapping at my blood. My limbs felt heavy and I was so tired. I shook myself, but none of them dislodged. My wolf snarled and barked, trying to force me to move. *I know. I know.* Adrenaline hit my system in a rush, exiting my nerve endings, and I managed to stand.

I was still in my Lycan form, and surprisingly I didn't feel much pain from their bites. From what Danny and Naomi had gone through, I'd thought there'd be more agony. *Why doesn't it hurt?*

One of the devils feasting on my arm suddenly fell to the ground.

In the next moment it disintegrated, leaving a thick smear in its place.

Did you see that?

A few more dropped. They each made a sizzling sound as they died.

"Jessica!" Tyler screamed. "If you don't get out of there right now, I'm coming in after you."

I glanced up, startled. He took a step into the clearing. I was happy to see he was up, but I didn't want him coming after me. "No!" I yelled. "Tyler, stop! Don't you see what's happening? They're dying." I pointed to the ground as another one fell. This one rolled a few times and gave a little primal shriek before it died. "My blood must be toxic to them. I have to let them keep feeding. If I can kill them all, we can move forward. If not, we're trapped here." Another one took a nosedive off my shoulder. Once it was on the ground it stumbled in a circle before falling over with a high-pitched squeal. It sounded like a mini pterodactyl.

Tyler stopped advancing, his eyes blazing amber. "Holy shit," he said. "You're right. It's working." The side of his face was caked with dried blood, his hair matted with it. The boulder the Mahrac had thrown had hit him hard, and because of that trauma he might not survive a venom attack from these things. I had to make sure he didn't come near me.

"Don't come any closer," I ordered. "You either, Daniel Walker."

Danny grinned from where he stood next to my brother. "Wouldn't dream of it. You're doing a bang-up job all on your own." He waved his hand in the air so I could see what he was holding. "Just in case you need it, I have a spell dart loaded at the ready." He flipped the dart in his hands. "If you're in too much pain, I'll stab you with it and put you out of your misery for a few hours."

"Save it. We'll need it later," I called as I took a slow step forward. My body fought the venom from the beasties efficiently, but all the effort it took made me stiff and drowsy. "I have to make sure they all get their fill, but it's exhausting me. I'm going to walk toward the boundary, but if I lose consciousness, don't you dare come out here until they're all dead and gone. My body will heal from this. I can feel it." I took another step closer and my wolf flooded me with more endorphins. Power tingled through me in a delicious current.

I took another step.

With each movement, more of the devils dropped, shrieking as they died. The ground was littered with thick, black smears.

My brother growled from the trees, "They're not dropping fast enough."

"Don't you dare come out here, Tyler. This is working," I answered. The strum of my brother's anxiety hit me in waves. He was on the verge of charging out here.

"Yeah, it looks like it's working perfectly," Tyler said, his voice laced in bitter undertones. "They're gobbling you up, and when they're done there's going to be nothing left."

"I'm going to be fine," I replied as a group of them plummeted to their deaths, leaving a patch of my arm free for the first time. I glanced down and finally understood why their bites weren't hurting me. "Look at my arm!" I waved it around and more beasties flew off me, leaving it completely clear. "I'm healing instantly from their bites." My blood seared the poison as my body closed the wounds the moment their teeth left my skin. I was fixing myself.

But it was sapping too much energy.

Some of the devils started disintegrating on me, leaving black goo stuck to my body. That was lovely. *I can't really complain, because gone is gone.* My wolf barked in agreement and sent more adrenaline racing through my system, but I was sleepy even with the extra dose. *It's taking too much from us.*

I'm tapped out, especially after the Mahrac. I feel like I could sleep for a week. My wolf laid down in my mind. She was tired too. *When was the last time we slept?*

"Jess, wake up! Your eyes just slid shut," Tyler yelled. "You need to come closer. It's almost over." I heard him moving. "Fuck it. I'm coming to get you."

"No," I mumbled as I snapped my eyes back open and took a few more steps. "I got this. I'm just sleepy. I don't want you to be hurt—" The motion of falling downward jolted my senses awake and my eyes opened. But I didn't hit the ground. Instead I was being lifted.

"I have you." Tyler smiled down on me, his dimples showing in earnest. "It's all over, Jess. Those bastards are all dead."

"Good," I said. "Now we can get moving." I rested my head on my brother's shoulder and everything went dark.

I woke with a start, running my hands over my body before I was fully awake. "*Wha?*" I shot up and glanced around. But there was no danger. The air was calm and stable. It was twilight, the sun gone, black creeping along the sky. My gaze landed on the only person around. "How long have I been asleep?"

Ray sat on the metal cooler staring at me. "I thought you might be dead," he retorted. "Even though they told me you were alive, I didn't believe them. You haven't moved a muscle all day. You've been out maybe fifteen hours."

"My body must have been in healing mode," I answered. At least I think that was the reason I'd been out. "All my available energy went to fixing the damage." I hadn't even dreamed. I checked down the length of my body just to make sure I was, in fact, healed, and this wasn't some cruel joke and Ray and I were actually having this particular chat in hell and I just didn't know it yet. I lifted my hands in front of me and wiggled my fingers. Very pale, slim pink scars covered my skin everywhere and I was wearing a new outfit. I was glad they'd picked spandex again. I looked around. "Where is everyone?" Danny and Tyler wouldn't leave me unguarded unless we'd been attacked again and they had no choice. "Did the Mahrac come back?" I dusted myself off and strode forward.

"Nope," Ray answered. "The wolf boys ran down to the truck to get more supplies. They said the vampires would be here within a few minutes because the sun just set. Seems we might have to stay here for a bit, depending on what the blood-suckers have to say." He paused for a moment. "What exactly are you, Hannon?" His voice echoed a wary tone, but it'd been delivered in a resigned cadence I'd never heard before. "You're not like them. If supernaturals, like the wolves and the vamps, are considered normal in your world, you don't fit in. You're not the same."

I paced closer to him, crossing my arms in front of my body. "How can you possibly know something like that? You can't even begin to imagine the scope of what's out there, Ray. You've known about us for exactly three days. We should all look equally scary to you." There was no way Ray knew anything about the Prophecy or what skill level any supe should or shouldn't have.

His lips formed a thin line. "I know, because I have two eyes in my head and I still think like a cop. You screamed 'different' to me on the police force and it's the same here," he said in a smug tone. "You don't fit in."

"I'm a supernatural just like everyone else."

"Bullshit."

I arched an eyebrow at him.

"You cured the girl vampire, right? Then you changed something in the monster's brain so it left us alone rather than crushing us to dust. You're the only one who figured out why the varmints could cross over, except that asshole vamp after he tried for an hour. Then you annihilated the bats from hell with your blood. According to what I see, you're at the top of the food chain."

"You know, he's right," Naomi said, coming silently through the trees in front of me. "Your blood is completely different from any I've ever sampled. And I've tasted a good many, both human and some very powerful supernaturals. But that doesn't matter, because killing all the winged devils would have been impossible for any other supernatural. You have a gift that marks you different."

"Well," I said, clearing my throat. I couldn't exactly argue, because all those things had happened. But going into the Prophecy with a human and a vamp wasn't an option. "It seems I do have some power, but since I've been a supe for only a few weeks, I'm still figuring out... all the logistics. I don't know what my special gift is yet, but there's a good chance it has something to do with my blood."

Before Naomi could form a rebuttal there was a loud buzz coming from the top of an old tree stump.

"That's been going off on the hour, every hour, since you came across the boundary," Ray said.

I knew why. I walked over and powered it on as I brought it to my ear. "I'm here," I said.

"Jessica." My father blew out a relieved breath. "Thank gods you're finally awake. Tyler has been keeping me informed. Are you fully healed now?"

I brought my arm up and examined the back of my hand.

"Yes. But things seem to be changing quickly. Did Tyler tell you everything?" My father obviously knew about the devils, but explaining to him that I'd fed a vamp and cured her wasn't top on my list. If Tyler hadn't shared, I was going to wait on that one.

"Tyler told me about the rock spirit and the *Camazotz*, which I have only vague knowledge of, but they shouldn't be on this plane at all. As in, there isn't anything powerful enough to get them here except a Demon Lord, which spells trouble for your journey on the highest possible level."

I paused and held my breath. I knew that tone and I knew what was coming.

"Jessica, if Selene is wrapped up in the Underworld, this is too big for you to handle on your own. You need to leave there now. I will conclude my business here in a few days. We will leave the fracture group alone for now and I will amass wolves and meet you in Canada. In light of the Prophecy and the current events involving the Underworld, this is no longer a journey to obtain your mate. This is a war."

I closed my eyes and brought my fingers to the bridge of my nose. "Dad, I can't wait that long. I'm sorry." I tensed, knowing that once again I was defying my father and my Pack Alpha. I hated every second of it, but I had no choice. "Please listen. I can't wait because Rourke doesn't have that kind of time. I'm a hundred percent certain Selene knows we're here. We just battled two of her best defenses. She's not going to wait much longer to play her games. She wants us now. If I leave and abandon the journey, Rourke dies. I can't let that happen. There is no time left."

He quieted. I could feel him processing. There was nothing ideal about this situation. Having Selene working with the Underworld was dire on every level; we both knew it. I had to keep explaining until he understood. "Dad, something happened inside me just before I set the rock monster free." It was difficult to describe, because I barely understood it myself. "Something opened up. My wolf showed it to me in a way I could finally grasp. I'm fairly certain it's been there since my shift, but it seems I'm not as quick on the uptake as she is, which, from my viewpoint, is completely understandable. But whatever power I unlocked allowed me to break Selene's hold over the monster, and when I came across the line with the devils on me... I killed them with power from my blood alone." I glanced over at Ray and Naomi, who were both watching me. I walked away. "If what we read on the computer is the truth, my powers are manifesting and they are... significant. It's going to have to be enough to defeat Selene on my own. Whatever's inside me has to be enough to save Rourke."

"Jessica—"

I cut him off before he could forbid it, because if he did, I was out of Pack before I even had a chance to start. "Dad!" My voice held a plea. "There's no other way. You have to understand. I have to go on. I can't leave him. We're connected on a level I can't explain. There's no way to sever that bond. If he dies... I don't think I will be able to function."

The line went quiet for a long minute.

"Okay." His voice was resigned. "But you may continue under *one* condition. And one condition only."

"Anything," I said as relief flooded over me. "I will do anything you ask."

"Tyler and Danny have to submit to you as their Alpha."

"*What?*" I held the phone away from my ear and looked at it like it had sprouted fur and fangs. I slowly brought it back to my ear. "I don't think I heard you correctly. I'm not an Alpha. We've already covered this. I don't even feel Alpha-inclined.

I don't understand what you're saying. It won't work." Panic welled in my throat as my wolf growled and paced, her eyes sparking violet in my mind.

"It's only a temporary Alpha placement," he said calmly. "I need you to relax. It will be remedied once you all return home." *If* we returned home is what he really meant. This decision to make me acting Alpha meant he wasn't giving us good odds. "In the Old Country, wolves built their own hierarchy on extended journeys. There was always a lead wolf, and he functioned as the working Alpha. He could talk to the other wolves internally when they were in their true forms and unite them and infuse power when needed. It was a necessary precaution to ensure survival of our race. We had many of them back then. A temporary Alpha doesn't have to be the most dominant wolf in the entire Pack. He just has to be the most dominant in the *group*." He exhaled. "Jessica, I'm unable to get through to you in your Lycan form. I can't help you, and I can't give you my power. I've tried. This is the only way. It's also the only way around the oath Tyler and Danny swore as Selectives. As of now, if they don't submit, they can't shift to protect you." Or to save themselves. "If they swear to you, all their previous oaths will be broken. This is the only way I will give this journey my blessing. If you intend to face creatures of the Underworld, you need an army. Two wolves is all I have to give."

My stomach thundered and I felt dizzy. This was too much. "Um, that might work for Danny"—he'd already submitted to me in rank—"but not Tyler." I swallowed. Hierarchy and Pack status was all a wolf cared about. "He's not...I can't ask him to do it. Tyler should be the working Alpha, not me. I've been a wolf for only a week. His status is clearly above mine in Pack."

"It's not that cut-and-dried," my father said firmly, growling in my ear. "Tyler's wolf might have status above yours in a working Pack, but you and he share a bond that goes beyond anything I've ever seen in siblings—something unexplainable and utterly unique. If you are the one the Prophecy speaks of, it's you who has the power. Tyler will know. He should feel it too. This isn't about status or ruling wolves; it's about something we don't completely understand. I'm certain this will work and once it happens they will be bound to you."

My voice quavered. I could defeat Underworld beasties, but asking my brother to submit to me made me queasy. "How... do I do it?" I knew there was a ritual and once it was done it was binding—until the wolf swore a new one.

"It's similar to a Blood Oath. Tyler will help you."

"They have to take my blood?" Interference started in earnest on the line. I talked loudly over the buzzing. "Dad, I don't think that's a good idea. Listen, my blood is unpredictable. Remember the Blood Oath for us didn't work and I think there might be a problem—"

"Jessica, I've made my decision," he shouted through the static. "This is the only way. It's the only chance you have to succeed. Once it's over I will know. My connection to Danny and Tyler will be severed. We will not speak until then."

"But I still don't think—"

The line went dead.

I had no idea if he'd hung up on me or if the phone had stopped working.

"Dad?"

There was nothing but dead air.

14

I threw the phone down in frustration right as Danny and Tyler trotted back into the area carrying more supplies. My father had known that if he'd stayed on the line he risked my complete cooperation. I'd somehow talk him out of it. So he'd left me no room for further discussion, which had been his sole intent. If I tried to call him back he wouldn't answer.

Shit. My wolf growled and showed us as the Alpha. *That's not helping! We aren't the Alpha. I don't even feel like an Alpha.* She flashed me the box and showed us glowing with power. *I know. I get it. I felt it.* She barked and showed me the picture again. I squinted in my mind's eye, but what she showed me wasn't the Alpha; it was something else. I could feel what she was projecting, but there were no words behind it. Before I had a chance to examine it better, Tyler rushed up to me.

He grasped me by the shoulders. "Glad to see you're awake. That was crazy and awesome at the same time. But don't scare me like that again. Seeing you in those situations is like watching someone murder a puppy. I don't think I'll ever get used to it."

I stared at him intently, unable to talk just yet. He wasn't going to be happy and I didn't want to ruin our relationship. I loved my brother.

"What?" He glanced at me, reading my face, and then noticed the phone lying in the dirt. "Did you talk to Dad?" He dropped his hands. When I didn't answer, he asked in my mind, *What is it? Are you hurt? Are there complications with the venom? Is it still in your body? They were all over you. I wasn't sure you were going to make it even though you said you had it handled.*

I'm fine. There's no venom, but we have a situation. I couldn't beat around the bush with this one. It was too big. I cleared my throat and addressed both Danny and Tyler out loud. "It seems, in order to move forward with the blessing of our father, and in light of the added Underworld component, Dad has issued a new order for us."

"What is it then?" Danny asked. "I'm all for scouting ahead without you. If we encounter any other beasts, as we surely will, we can have at them first. Even if we don't make it, we will have cleared the road a little better for you."

"No." I shook my head. "That's not it."

"Spill it," Tyler said, narrowing his gaze. He knew he wasn't going to like it. "The anticipation isn't necessary."

"Um, apparently"—I cleared my throat. It felt like I had a grapefruit lodged in there—"he wants you . . . to be able to shift and have your full powers back. He thinks it's necessary if we're going to try and win a combined battle with the Underworld and Selene."

"That makes sense," Tyler agreed. "But how do we do that? The oath we swore as Selectives is binding. We can't shift."

I squared my shoulders and took a deep breath. "We're...
going to break it," I said with more confidence than I felt.

Tyler peered at me hard, his face going from animated to
drawn. "How *exactly* did he tell you we were going to achieve
that? He's not here to *break* our oath." Tyler knew Pack Law
to the letter. Only an Alpha could physically release you from
your vow. There was likely blood exchanged.

"He wants you to swear a vow to me instead," I said quickly,
"and by doing so, the old vows you swore become void."

"Swear a vow to you?" Danny asked with a puzzled expression. "What vow can supplant one given directly from the
Alpha? Unless...unless you're talking about an Alpha Troth?"
He read my grimace clearly. "Gods, you are! Your dad wants us
to swear a pledge of fealty to you, bonded by blood, and if we
do that, you become our Alpha." He smiled like a shrew. "I'm
in then."

"Danny," I said, exhaling on a long sigh, "you could at least
let this news marinate for a half a second before you throw all
in. This is a big deal! I have no idea what will happen. You saw
what my blood is capable of doing."

"There's no need to marinate," he said with a surety I didn't
share. "The way I see it, above all else I want to save my arse
and protect yours in the process. This is the only logical way
to achieve both goals. When we get home, your dear old Dad
takes our Troth again and we just had a bloody grand adventure,
didn't we? No harm, no foul."

"The vow will work only if your wolf is superior in status to
ours." Tyler was clearly warring with an order he knew came
from his Alpha and how badly this news sucked. Submit-
ting to a female was a low he'd never experienced until now.
And he was trying to handle it like a champ. "Your wolf is above
Danny's, but not mine. Wolves sense power. Status swirls around

us all the time. Just like what we talked about before we left—even if you *were* more superior in status, you still don't *smell* like an Alpha. This won't work."

That was exactly Dad's point, I said to him privately. *He doesn't think it's about status. He thinks it will work because of the Prophecy, my Lycan-ness, and our sibling connection. This vow is not about "my balls are bigger than yours." It's purely a survival tactic to make us stronger as a unit. He said you'd feel it and know what he was talking about. He said we have a unique connection. Can you please try to feel it? Or do something so we can move this forward? We lost another day because of me.*

We didn't lose a day. The vamps had to sleep and I don't know how to feel what you're talking about. You feel like my inferior-status sister. Your power doesn't threaten me. If it did, I'd feel an urge to fight you or submit. I'd feel some kind of pull, but instead I feel nothing from you.

Maybe that's what he's talking about! The fact you don't feel anything. Isn't it strange you don't get any signals from me? Maybe our sibling bond makes the status thing between us immaterial. Which would be such a blessed-ass relief.

He studied me for a moment, clearly upset. *I don't know. It's a possibility. I never thought of it like that before. It is kind of strange I don't feel like fighting you.*

Can you at least try to smell me again? You've always said I smell funny. Maybe that funny has something to do with this entire thing.

He inhaled, pulling it across his tongue and tasting. He shook his head. *You smell strange, as always, but I don't know what it is or what it means. I've never smelled a female like you before. Your scent has a thin layer of ozone or something attached to it.*

Ozone? Not what I was expecting. I tried a new tactic. *You don't have to stay, you know. Dad can't force you to do this if you want to leave. I know Selectives can be excused of their duties at any time. I knew this was going to be a hard journey and I never wanted to put you or Danny in any jeopardy. It makes me sick thinking you could die here because of me.*

He sputtered out loud and looked horrified. "I'm not leaving you!"

"Then we don't have another choice," I challenged. "Dad said if we all continue on—it's this or nothing. He won't support it any other way, and I agree with you needing your full power if you're going to have a chance to survive."

Danny clapped Tyler on the back. "It's okay, mate. It'll be like this for only a quick bit, and when we get back things will go back to normal in no time. No one can fault you for trying to protect your sister. She's your blood-kin after all. If the Alpha orders you to swear to her, you do it."

Tyler stared at me, his irises churning. "Fine. I'll do it, but I'm sticking by my original theory. I don't think it will work. Blood binding is not something tangible—it's full of magic. When you choose your Alpha and make that pledge, the blood you swear to *has* to be stronger. The magic will know. It won't bind unless it's true."

"Frankly, if we try and it doesn't work, I'll be relieved," I said. "At least then we can move forward in good faith." If my father ordered it done and it didn't take, there was no risk of breaking the rules. "Okay, how do we do this?"

Tyler dropped the pack on his back and reached for his belt. "It's a relatively easy oath—like I said, the blood does all the work. The words are spoken and they mix with the blood and it either takes or it doesn't. That's why you don't see alpha wolves rounding up followers. You have to be *Alpha*. There are very few who qualify in a Pack." Naomi and Ray moved forward but kept quiet. I wondered briefly what was going through their minds. For the first time I realized Naomi had come without Eamon. Maybe he had finally abandoned us after all his threatening.

Danny and Tyler formed a loose circle around me.

Tyler brought a knife up from its sheath on his waist. "Just repeat the words I say—"

"No. Stop!" I grabbed on to his wrist as a bolt of fear shot through me. My wolf howled. Something was about to change. I didn't know what, but it felt major. "Tyler," I said a little desperately. "You have to promise me you're doing this of your own free will. If it doesn't take, fine, but none of us knows for sure what my blood will do to either of you. We all have to swear to live with the consequences. I don't want it to tear us apart."

Tyler's irises shot to amber, emotion churning deeply in their depths. "I get it, Jess. You don't have to worry. I don't think you're Alpha, but I can honestly say I don't know what you are, so I'm willing to give it a try. Whatever happens, happens. But I'm not leaving you, and Dad's right—we can't do this without changing the game. The stakes went through the roof when the Underworld joined the party. This is of my own free will and I'm willing to deal with the consequences."

"If you're not really Alpha," Danny said, "I, for one, am curious to see what you are. Honestly, I haven't had this much fun since I broke into the palace at Whitehall to give Queen Elizabeth a cheeky surprise. She'd been tied up with that Dudley sot, but as soon as he'd left she'd been putty in my hands. We had quite a romance after that. I'd like to think it's why she never married." He winked and inclined his head in the direction of his waist.

"Danny, you never cease to amaze me. The Queen of England?" I shook my head. Danny could defuse a situation like no other and I was grateful. "Okay," I said, getting back to business. "Let's go." I dropped my hand from Tyler's wrist.

Tyler lifted the knife again and said, "I'll feed you the words while I cut Danny's palm. He can go first."

"We don't need to do anything more formal?" I asked. "This seems too easy."

"Nope," Tyler said. "It's all about the words and the blood. Ready?"

"Yes," I said. As ready as I could be. My wolf paced back and forth in my mind, patiently waiting. *Do you know what's going to happen?* She snapped her muzzle at me and lifted her head. I took that as a maybe.

Tyler said, "Of my mind and body, I ask thee."

He sliced Danny's palm open and I repeated the words. "Of my mind and body, I ask thee."

"Do you Pledge of me freely?"

"Do you Pledge of me freely?" I asked Danny, looking into his eyes.

Danny answered, "I pledge to you freely with body and soul." His eyes flicked down in submission.

I held out my palm and Tyler sliced it cleanly. I winced a little.

"With the blood that mixes, it binds us together," I repeated after Tyler. Then reached out to grab Danny's palm.

Tyler finished with, "You are my Pack and I am your Alpha."

"You are my Pack and I am your Alpha," I intoned.

The second our palms met there was a shot of power so strong it blocked everything out of my mind. It jolted from my body into Danny's and back again.

"Bloody hell!" Danny yelled. The force of the connection bucked us both backward, separating us very quickly. I leaned over, panting.

Danny was on the ground.

I turned my hand over. It was completely healed. I angled my head toward Tyler. "Was that normal?"

"Fuck no!" Tyler said, his voice stricken. "Danny, what happened? What does it feel like?"

Danny pulled himself up from the ground with ease, dusting the dirt from his mended hand. He looked at me, his mouth quirking at the sides. "That was off the charts. Like nothing I've ever felt. Even now your blood is singeing my insides. But it's not like your father's at all." He turned toward a waiting Tyler. "You were right. The bond is different."

"What is she?" Tyler asked.

"I dunno, mate, but I feel electrified. Like I could take on the world. If you give me a minute, I might even want to fight you." He clenched and unclenched his fists.

Tyler looked startled. "You want to fight me? *For status?*"

"My wolf senses your power, and right now I'm above yours." Danny chuckled. "There's a first time for everything, right?"

Tyler's expression changed as his wolf sensed Danny's power for the first time. "Holy hell," he breathed.

"Once you take her blood, we'll see where we lie," Danny ribbed. "And even if she's not Alpha, she's clearly my leader now. My connection to your father vanished the moment her blood seared my palm."

I straightened and looked directly at Tyler. "We're not doing this. You can't take my blood."

Tyler still seemed shell-shocked.

"Tyler," I said, waving my hand in front of his face. "We're calling Dad back to tell him what happened. He won't make us do it. It's too risky."

Tyler glanced at me, blinking a few times, and replied, "So he says no. Then what? There's no way to break my Selective bond without doing this. I already told you I'm not leaving you." His lips pursed together stubbornly. "We're doing this."

My mouth opened in surprise. "You can't be serious. I just shot Danny to the ground with a few drops of my blood. We're not doing it." If I could've stamped my foot like a five-year-old child I would have.

"Jess," Tyler said, his voice low. "I think I get it now. The thing Dad was talking about."

"What do you mean 'you get it now'? We've been at this for exactly three minutes," I said. "What can you possibly have learned in that short amount of time—other than my blood is toxic and I should wear a sign around my chest telling people to back the hell away?"

"Danny's smell just changed." He gestured to Danny. "He's giving off a hint of ozone now. But it's just a fraction of yours— almost undetectable—but it's your same signature." I took a gratuitous sniff, but I didn't even smell ozone on me, so there was no chance I was getting it off Danny. "When you bond with your Alpha, you don't smell like your Alpha."

"So?" I said. "What does that mean?"

"It means you're different than an Alpha, just like I thought. Danny took a piece of you with him. I also think it means we don't need to exchange the vow for this to work between us."

"Come again?" I asked, with my hands on my hips. "How are you figuring this out? I'm still as confused as I was when this all started."

"I know it, because I know genetics. DNA compatibility for normal siblings is fifty percent. We're twins with an unusual connection; my guess is we share more than fifty percent. Possibly much more. Because we're so closely bonded, your blood isn't going to change me as much as it did Danny, and because you're not technically an Alpha, there's no need for the vow."

"But once the words of the vow were spoken, Danny exploded. Nothing happened before then," I helpfully pointed out.

"I didn't technically 'explode' per se." Danny chuckled. "It was more like a force of supreme magnitude toppled me over for a mere second. But as you saw, I recovered fully and feel better than ever."

"Danny is not blood-bonded to you already," Tyler said. "What I'm saying, Jess, is we are too closely related and share too much DNA for you to be above or below me in status. You were right. The absence of any feeling was the key. Once we're connected on this last level"—his irises sparked amber—"it will change the last of my DNA enough to sever my Alpha bond with Dad."

"How do you *know* that?"

"Because you're not tied to Dad the way I am. He can't reach you or control you when you're in your Lycan form." Tyler ran a hand through his hair and exhaled a long frustrated breath. "I don't know why I didn't figure this out before. You must have something in your system that inhibits the Alpha bond. And when we exchange blood, you're going to give it to me."

"That sounds way too risky," I said. "What if you're never able to get the bond back with Dad?"

Tyler shrugged. "There's a chance that could happen, but this feels right to me, something we've been missing all these years. I'm never going to take over Pack while Dad is alive anyway. And I'm still his son, with his DNA inside me. That will never change. Honestly, Jess, the protective instinct I have when you're around almost paralyzes me with its intensity; it has ever since we were young. It's made me crazy with worry all these years. If I have to choose Dad or you right now, I pick you."

My heart thudded in my chest. "Tyler," I stammered. I

didn't know what to say. "It feels like too much. Like you're giving away too much. I don't want to be responsible for your break in status." But he was right. Something about it seemed to fit, the final connection that had been missing between us all these years.

Before I could say anything else, he sliced his palm. I extended my hand without looking down. He sliced it cleanly.

"Here we go," he said, grasping my hand.

He closed his eyes and I followed.

The moment our blood connected, his emotions flared inside me, bright and clear. Everything we had shared as children ran through my mind at lightning speed. All the fights, the battles, the love, and the protection. He was right. This was different from Danny. Danny's bonding felt possessive.

This felt like home.

"Jess," Tyler said. "I feel Dad's emotions in your blood too. He can feel this. I'm sure of it."

My blood had just connected the three of us.

"It's all so vivid," I murmured. His blood seared through my veins, bringing a piece of him with it, just as mine was doing to him.

We both stumbled backward after a minute.

I panted again, bracing my hands against my thighs to catch my breath. Tyler looked up from where he stood a few feet away, his irises blazing full yellow. "The Alpha bond is severed with Dad," Tyler said. "But I can still feel him from whatever was in your blood."

I nodded. "When Dad and I took our Blood Oath, I connected with him on a different level. I can feel his emotions through the bond, like I'm feeling yours right now. I can feel Danny too, but it's very faint." I glanced at Danny and tried to speak to him inside my head. *Danny, can you hear me?*

No response, so I tried my brother. *What happens now?*

I'm not sure, but I feel stronger, just like Danny said. Everything feels a little more enhanced. I was relieved to hear him in my brain. I would've been sad if that connection had changed. *I'm glad I can still feel Dad, even if it's in a new way. When we get home we deal with the bond and all the complications. But now we can protect you. It feels right, Jess. I don't regret it.* He turned to Danny and grinned. "So do you want to fight me for status now?" he asked. He put up his fists in the classic fight pose.

"Nope," Danny responded, his tone mockingly remorseful. "My station above yours, it seems, was short-lived. But no matter; it was still brilliant while it lasted. Maybe when we arrive home, you can go along back to your dad and I'll just stick around here with Jessica. It suits me just fine."

I walked over to pick up my pack. Naomi had moved to the edge of the tree line. We'd delayed our journey too long. "Do you see any winged devils out there?" I asked her. Who knows if the Underworld would send new ones.

She turned around, looking pensive. "*Non*," she said. "I believe they are gone."

I hoisted the pack on my back and turned to Ray, who had been sitting on the cooler the entire time. Who knew what was going through his mind, and frankly, I didn't want to know. I didn't have the energy to answer any of his questions. Mostly because I had no answers.

He stood up. "So what other fun surprises are in store for us on this mountain, Hannon?"

"I have no idea, Ray, but we're about to find out."

15

The mountain was blessedly quiet on the way down. The winged devils were indeed all gone. Danny had used my blood on the one we'd captured while I was out in a fit of good thinking. The climb was going fairly slowly because we had a human in tow, which I tried not to bemoan too badly, since it was my own damn fault. Eamon had shown up right as we'd left, but had refused to hike. I had no idea if he'd witnessed the blood swap or not, and I wasn't about to ask. Naomi walked with us, even though she could've flown. Everyone was quiet and pensive, thinking about what had happened and what the implications would be when we got home.

"Once we hit the gorge and cross over, we'll be in Selene's direct territory?" I asked Naomi, who was behind me.

"*Oui*," Naomi said. "She controls the next mountain range."

"I wonder why it's so quiet. After the winged devils and Mahrac, I thought we'd be encountering something every second."

"My guess is she cannot afford to control so many at one

time," Naomi said. "It takes massive power to keep such crea-tures in check. She has to pick and choose her best arsenal. We will encounter more of her roadblocks, but under the laws of the supernatural world, which even Selene isn't above, she cannot risk unleashing a powerful supernatural on the human race. It's different from what happened with the devils, which are bound by rules of the Underworld. Selene must tightly con-tain things of this world. She is allowed to defend what is hers, but if whatever she employs brings disaster, the Coalition will come down on her fiercely, as they always have. After all these years she has learned to respect them."

The Coalition was our oldest supernatural law Council.

From what I knew, it was made up of freakishly old, freak-ishly powerful supernaturals who determined things like whether we went into hiding or came out in the open. If you went against High Law, there was swift retribution. As far as I'd ever known, there hadn't been a change of Old Law in cen-turies and the Coalition's identities were never revealed. Not even my father knew who sat on the Coalition. In their view, he was considered a young leader, barely above their notice. If my father upheld the High Laws, he could go his entire lifetime and never come in contact with them.

In the last hundred years, it was also rumored they'd gone into "Stasis," and they would remain that way until they felt—or were warned of—a major magical "disturbance" of some kind.

Waking them meant you were in deep shit.

The Coalition made me think of Rourke and how long he'd been alive. It was possible he knew who sat on the Council. "When Rourke bested Selene to escape," I asked curiously, "were you there?" My wolf growled and clacked her jaws at the mention of our mate. *I know. I want him too. We're going as fast as we can.* She flashed me a picture. Magnificent, strong, tall, blond, and tattooed. He was a warrior of old and he was *mine*. I missed his body and craved his mouth. *He will be okay. We have to trust that. She won't kill him until we are there to witness. She's too sure of herself.*

Naomi leapt over several large boulders, landing effortlessly. "No. We were gone by then. But details of that event did trickle into the vampire court. Over the years our Queen has hired your mercenary many times to do her bidding. She even tried to keep him under her control, but it proved impossible. He is too strong for anyone to manage. When Selene took a liking to him, it quickly turned into an obsession." She gave me a half smile. "No one would come out and admit such a thing, but there is a grudging respect given to him by all vampires. They also fear him. The power he wields comes from a deep source. There are whispers that he might be a god or close to godhood now."

A god? Achieving godhood was much different from how humans perceived it to be. In our world it was something earned. As supes aged, they gained great power. Over time their immortality became intertwined with every fiber of their being, making them truly immortal. Thus godlike and unstoppable, able to avoid a true death altogether.

But Rourke a god? I shook my head. Surely that would be something I would've picked up on. His power was immense, but being a god was an entirely new level. "I wonder why he allowed Selene to live instead of killing her while he had the chance?" I asked in a hollow voice, forcing my mind in a different direction as quickly as possible. Picturing them together made my nails morph into sharp points and a growl to creep up my diaphragm. "He must've had a very good reason for not finishing her off."

"I'm sure he thought he had killed her, just as I had," Naomi said in a firm tone. "She cannot be killed so easily, as we have all learned the hard way. But now that Rourke is mated, it must be like an ocean of salt in the wounds Selene has been licking all this time. She will make him pay in ways you had not thought possible."

A fine coating of fur sprouted along my arms as I pictured Selene harming him. She was going to be so dead when I was done with her. "That woman is beyond deranged. The world will be a better place without her."

"There's no doubt." Naomi snorted. "I've been waiting to rid the world of her for over three hundred years."

"Did you just snort?" I glanced back, laughing.

Naomi looked sheepish for a moment. "We are not allowed to be so...flippant at court. I have not left court, except to fulfill missions, in too many years to count. It feels...nice to be free."

"Can vamps go rogue if they want to?" I asked. "A wolf can."

"No, not really. There is no safe place for a rogue vampire. The Queen controls all the Masters around the world. If we turn our backs on our Queen, we will spend the rest of our days avoiding death by her hand or the hands of her followers. There are smaller courts, ruled by less powerful vampires, all Masters, but Eudoxia is the supreme leader. She has won the right of power. A vampire can swear allegiance to a greater court, but there is none greater than our Queen's court. If we had sworn first to a smaller court, we could have moved up to the Queen's court, but you can't...What's the word?" She appeared flustered.

"Demote yourself?"

"*Oui*, you cannot demote yourself to a lesser court. And because of our usefulness to her, she would be enraged at our desertion and stop at nothing to bring us true death. A vampire does not do well alone. It is in our nature to ... cohabitate with others."

"I'm surprised you can share this all with me so freely," I said. "Don't get me wrong. I'm happy to glean this information. I find it fascinating. But I think we're coming close to the line. I don't want you to get in trouble for crossing it because I'm too nosy." I smiled. "I never thought I'd be friendly with a vamp, but you're turning out to be okay, Naomi. Vamps aren't as stuffy as I thought, barring your brother, of course. Is he a typical vamp? That's how I pictured them all to act."

Naomi stopped in her tracks.

"What?" I slowed when she didn't follow me. "Did I say something that's going to make your face slide? You don't have to answer anything else if you don't want to. I didn't mean to be so intrusive. I know it's important for each Sect to keep their secrets."

She hesitated for a moment, shuffling the rocks in front of her. "It's just ... I could not be so free," she said finally, "if it wasn't for one thing."

I waited a few beats for her to answer, but she remained quiet. "What?" I prodded. "Now that we're closer to Selene's territory your Queen has less reach over you? Are you too far away? Is there interference here?" I looked around the rocks, trying to spot the reason.

"*Non.*"

After another small moment, I said, "What is it then?" Her face was a mask of intensity and it was starting to make me itch. "What's wrong? You're killing me here."

"Your blood," she said quietly, "seems to have severed my bond."

"Excuse me?" I gaped, stumbling over rocks, catching my

footing right before I tumbled ass over end down the steep slope. "I don't think I heard you correctly." My fingernails dug deeply into the stone wall next to me, steadying me. I prayed I hadn't heard her correctly. "Did you say my blood broke the bond with your *Queen*?"

There was a flurry of motion and Eamon landed next to us, scattering rocks and dust in his hurry. "We agreed you would not divulge that information," Eamon raged. He'd obviously been eavesdropping, and likely Naomi knew it, which was why she had taken so long to answer my questions. "No one would have known. We would have figured out what to do with our Queen. You play with fire, sister, and I will not be part of this any longer." He shot up into the sky.

We'd been stopped for so long, Danny and Tyler had tracked their way back up to us and it was clear they'd heard the entire back-and-forth.

It was also apparent Naomi had just made a major decision to come clean. She clenched her fists by her sides. "Eamon forbade me to share this knowledge, but he does not rule me," Naomi stated, her voice stony. Her calm demeanor belied her eyes, which twitched side to side like a bird's.

My blood was powerful enough to sever a Queen's bond with her underling? *Holy crap.* Being able to break that kind of a bond was much different than swapping blood with another wolf. Naomi had likely been warring with herself whether or not to tell me, and by Eamon's reaction, she'd finally decided to choose me over her brother's wishes. With her bond being severed, she would either be killed or forced to rebind herself once her Queen found out.

I was stunned into silence.

"Your blood has freed me from a bond I no longer desired," she continued, her voice gaining strength and confidence as she spoke. "My relationship with my Queen has always been strained. Because of my time spent with Selene, I was never able to carry myself as a normal vampire, even after so many years at court. When a vampire is first turned, we lose some of our humanity for a time. The Queen, or the Master, takes on the job of reshaping us once again. Normally, for that grace, we become enraptured with whoever it is, for they give us food and protect us, like a true parent. But it was never that way for us. Selene did not nurture us, so I did not form any bonds. Now you have granted me a kind of freedom I never thought possible. I will be in your debt for the rest of my life."

"Um," I stammered. How did I respond to that? "Okay." I waved my hand around in a circle, because I had no idea what else to do. "The first thing we have to do is promise to keep this knowledge between us for now." My voice hummed with stress. "If your Queen, or any of the other vamps, find out what my blood can do there will be a bounty on my head immediately. Do you understand?"

"Of course," Naomi said simply. "My allegiance is now yours, as I told you. I will be paying you back a debt of honor until the day I find true death." She started to bend on one knee.

"Wait, *wait* a minute," I said, panicking. She stopped midmotion and sought my brother for help. *Tyler, what do I do here? This can't be happening*, I pleaded. *We need to fix this. If I can free vampires and they decide to pledge themselves to me, I've started a heinous war that will stop only once I'm wiped cleanly off the earth.*

Jess. Tyler sounded calm. I needed calm. *Listen to her words. She says she owes you a debt. Debts in our world are fully binding. She won't betray you. We can keep this close and figure out what to do when we get home. Your power seems to be . . . incredibly vast. A lot stronger than any of us thought. We just have to figure out what the hell you're capable of as quickly as we can and harness it into something so powerful nobody wants to fuck with you, no matter what happens.*

While we spoke, Naomi had gone fully to her knees and was murmuring something under her breath. "...I pledge to you my honor and my faith. May my words bind us together forever." Then she brought up her sacred cross and slashed it across her palm. The wound hissed as the silver cauterized as it cut. A slow dribble of blood flowed out of her palm.

"Naomi!" I sputtered. "Get up! There's no need to pledge in blood. I believe you're being truthful. I don't need any more proof."

"Spilling blood is the way of the vampire," Naomi said as she stood. "I have given you an Oath of Honor, of my own free will. It's the strongest oath I can pledge, and by giving it without constraint, it holds the most power. By spilling my blood, I give you my fealty. If you were a vampire, you would drink to show you accept." She smiled. "But I don't expect you to do so. In return, in our world, you would offer to give me your protection, but I waive that right. For you are no vampire and should not be bound to me as such. I refuse to be a burden to you."

I took in a big breath to steady myself. "Naomi." I had to think of what to do next and how to respond. She'd just pledged herself to me like she had to her Vamp Queen. "I accept your pledge"—I paused, trying to find the right words—"because right now I don't know what else to do. What's done is done and we can't go back. My only concern is what to do about your brother. He will never drink my blood—not that I'm offering—but what will keep him from betraying us to your Queen?" Former Queen? "This puts both of us in a very dangerous position. It will spark a war between our Sects, and

I cannot launch my Pack into a war by my own stupidity. I should've been more careful. I have no real idea what I am." But, honestly, would I have let Naomi die if I'd known? I didn't want to ask myself such a thing, because there was no way to undo my mistake.

I was going to have to be extremely diligent with my choices in the future.

"My brother will not betray me. He is very angry now, but our kin-bond is more powerful than his allegiance to our Queen. We were both damaged by our time with Selene. He will come around in time." She paused and tilted her head inquisitively. "It is very clear to me that you do not realize how much power you wield. You have proven, in the short amount of time I've been in your presence, you are a fair leader, generous and worthy of following. I am over five hundred years old, and I do not give my fealty to anyone lightly or without thought. It is my belief you might be one of the most powerful supernaturals to ever be created. I have put my faith into you because I believe the side you choose will win."

"Win what?" I tried not to act too surprised, but I wasn't sure it worked.

"The war, of course."

"What war? I just told you I didn't want to start a war with your Sect." My voice grated as my neck started morphing. I was too emotional to stop it. My wolf was right along with me, yipping and growling in frustration.

"It is not a war with the vampires I am referring to. The Sects have grown restless these last hundred years. As proof, my own Queen has accepted a pledge from your rogue wolves. The Sorcerers are on edge and the witches have been stirring. Demon Lords are coming to the surface. All of this points to a major uprising. There will be much fighting in our future until all can be settled again. I believe you will be the one to settle it."

"What?" I gasped. "How do I settle a war between Sects? That's impossible! I'm strong, but I'm not that strong."

"*Non*," Naomi said with confidence. "Your presence here is to keep it fair, to make sure all sides are forced to play by the same rules. It would be happening anyway, with or without you, because the supernatural races grow too large and there is too much power. We cannot be contained and live among the humans much longer without a major catastrophe. We will fight. The Coalition will wake. And a new order will be formed. It is time."

A new order?

"*How* do you know all this?" I asked. "You can't anticipate that much, even if you had some of the information ahead of time."

"I know, because I have read the Prophecy for myself."

I sat down on a large boulder with a thump.

Everyone shifted uneasily, but stayed quiet. Ray had picked his way down sometime during this revelation and was perched quietly on the end of the ledge. Fur lined my arms and my canines had extended. Emotion roiled inside me. I didn't have to ask her what Prophecy she was referring to. "It exists in written form then?" I said quietly.

"*Oui*," Naomi said. "It seemed to be very old when I saw it, which was merely by accident. Selene had sent me to capture one of the Three Hags. The Lunar Goddess desired knowledge of her fate and she thought this job would be as easy as plucking an apple from a tree."

"I take it that was not the case."

"I almost lost my life. But before the Hag set me free, she showed me the Prophecy, giving me a potion to drink so I could decipher the ancient language it was written in. Then she told me there would come a pivotal time in my life when I would finally be *set free*. From this freedom I would be given a choice. I could either take the life for myself or I could pledge it to another. If I gave my pledge, I would live to see the wrongs of the world righted. If I did not, I would spend my days looking for something I might never find. I believed, up until this very day"—she bowed her head—"that my freedom came from my escape from Selene and the pledge I gave freely was to my Vampire Queen. I see now that I have made a grave mistake. I know now that you are that pledge. I am certain, body and soul, and I give it to you freely, without reservation."

The world had just thrown me a gigantic curveball.

I took a deep breath and forced some calm back into my system with tremendous effort. The Prophecy was true. And I couldn't change my fate, no matter how much I wanted to. My features shifted back, almost reluctantly, as I shed some of the emotion gnawing at me. There was nothing I could do, except move forward the best way I knew how. There was no time to bemoan my life. I had a mate to free and a goddess to kill.

I stood and brushed dust off my legs. "Naomi," I said, meeting her gaze fully, "I accept your pledge, but I honestly have no idea what to do with it. I will offer you my protection, as freely as you've given me your loyalty. When your Queen finds out you've defected willingly, and eventually she will, it's going to be like dropping an atomic bomb on your court. We will need to put our heads together and play this as smart as we can. Once we get back, I'm hopeful we can come up with something plausible—something that doesn't include any mention of my blood. I owe your Queen a debt, which I am required to pay in a very short period of time, and if she finds out while I'm at court my blood is even more powerful than she realizes, she'll do everything in her power to kill me—or siphon me dry. Either scenario is unacceptable."

A slow smile spread across Naomi's lips. "The Queen will not win." Her features shifted down ever so slowly.

"If the Vamp Queen learns this information ahead of my scheduled arrival it will put us in even greater peril. Your brother is going to be a problem." I glanced up in the sky. He'd left, but I was certain he was close enough to hear us. He wanted the information; he just didn't want to accept what was happening. "How do we force him to cooperate?" Thinking of ways to convince Eamon not to expose us made my head ache. "He will not come on his own. I can guarantee that. He reviles me."

"I will deal with my brother," she said, her voice brisk. "He will not be so quick to turn against me. Our kin-bond has held for all these years; it will prevail. He knows he will sign my death warrant if he dares breathe a word of our secret."

"And if he does it anyway?"

Naomi's face became grim, hard as ivory. "Then I will sign his."

My eyebrows shot up my forehead. "You could kill your brother so easily?"

"*Non*," Naomi said. "But I know ways to incapacitate a vampire. He would not be able to move until I set him free." She paused. "And that would be long after our side wins."

16

We made it to the bottom of the canyon unscathed by any more of Selene's traps. A large stream cut through the gorge at the base. Selene's fortress was on the other side and up the steep mountain face, according to the vamps. My eyes shot to the water as something bubbled in the center. "There's something in the water," I yelled. "Everyone step back!"

Naomi took flight as I turned to my brother. "Let's try to find a place to cross before whatever it is breaks the surface."

He shook his head. "No. We have to see what it is so we know what we're up against. It might be a fucking siren or a serpent with ten arms. We can't risk it without knowing."

"No way. Once that thing emerges it will be much harder to defeat. Let's cross while we can. Most likely it's something Selene has to conjure, so it might take some time to arrive. My guess is it was triggered once our feet hit the bottom of the basin." I grabbed on to his arm. "It's still not here yet. We have time. Come on."

"I'm with you," Danny called over his shoulder, trotting downstream. "Once that thing rears its ugly head we're likely in for it. Best to get to the other side while we still can, and once we're there we can fight it or just bloody run."

"Ray, stay close to me," I called as I started to jog. "If you can't keep up, Naomi can fly you over."

"Like hell she can," Ray said, charging after me. "I'm not going into the sky again while there's still breath left in my body. I'll take my chance in the water."

I snorted while I ran. "Yeah, like those are better odds."

We jogged down the stream away from the bubbles. Danny called from ahead, "This part here looks shallow enough to cross and there are some rocks."

"Go," I yelled, motioning with my hands. "We'll see you on the other side."

Tyler trailed behind us reluctantly, eyeing the water. "I still think this is too risky," he said. "We should wait and assess the threat."

"Too late, mate," Danny shouted as he flung himself from shore to the first rock. It was solid and he continued quickly, not wasting any time. He was over in less than ten seconds. From the shore he bounced up and down. "Come on, then! It was a piece of cake. We can scale the hill behind here and hurry away from the swamp monster without having to dirty our hands at all."

I was almost to the third rock when a rotting smell hit the air, followed by a stifled scream. I twisted my body in one motion and tried to reach him, but it was too late. Ray was under the water before I had a chance to see what grabbed him. "What took him?" I yelled to my brother, who was charging up quickly behind me. "What was it?" I searched frantically in the water.

Tyler's face was grim, almost sallow in the moonlight. "Jess, we can't worry about it. The thing is occupied for now. Ray gave us a chance. Let's not make his sacrifice in vain. *Go!*" He shoved me forward with two hands, but I held my ground, my feet locked in place. "Jess," he said in an exasperated tone, "you can't help him. He's human, and this is our chance to escape. Whatever that thing was, it will kill him quickly. Now stop wasting time!"

Tyler was right, but I didn't want to listen.

I turned and took a flying leap onto the next rock. "*Dammit!*" Once I reached the shore, I ran to where Danny, and now Naomi, stood, their faces set. The water hadn't moved, not even a ripple. "Did you see what took him?" I asked. "If there's a chance to save him, we have to try."

"It was a Naiad," Naomi said in a shallow voice. "One of Selene's favorites, though I have never seen one on this continent. They guard her fortresses in Italy and Greece. The Naiad comes from the depths quickly to steal her prize with her long arms and cannot last out of the water for more than a blink of an eye. She will have already embraced him and taken his last breath. A Naiad steals life with greed. We will not see your friend again." She shook her head sadly.

"I don't know what a bloody Naiad is, but the thing I saw was hideous." Danny shuddered. "It was seven feet tall with slimy seaweed hair. Its skin was gray and dead-looking and peeling off. Its arms were twice as long as its body. If that thing touched me, I would've gone to wolf instantly and snapped its head off."

"Out of the water it's a hideous monster," Naomi agreed. "Under the water it's breathtakingly beautiful, a gorgeous nymph with long flowing hair and angelic features, except for her arms. They remain twice as long as her body. Naiads hunt their prey from under the waters, entrancing those who look upon them, convincing the innocent they are drowning and in need of saving. All of Selene's servants stayed clear of them and the waters."

"If it can last only a few precious moments out of water, it dies if we can get it to shore?" I said. No one said anything. "Right?"

Naomi worried her lip, a gesture so human it looked odd. "Yes. Technically that is true, but a Naiad is a powerful being and will not be easy to wrest from its habitat. What you say is not simple, and believe me, your friend is already gone. We need not engage her now if she does not come for us. If we best Selene, then all of her spells, and those in her control, as this Naiad must be, will become null or will be freed. If we are forced to pass back this way, she will be uninterested in us if we stay out of her domain."

The water began to bubble in front of us and there was thrashing beneath the surface. "Look. The water is moving," I yelled. "Ray must still be alive." I took off before I knew what was happening. My wolf snarled for me to stop. *No. We don't leave him behind. He deserves to live just as much as we do.*

"Jessica!" my brother yelled, racing toward me. "Don't do it!"

I dove headfirst into the stream.

It hadn't looked that deep, but as soon as I hit the water I understood. This wasn't an ordinary stream. It was an underground lake. What appeared to be a small river actually deepened into a big cavern underneath.

The water glowed.

A strange light issued from under one of the lips in the shoreline, but I had no idea why. The glow was tinted green, so possibly something phosphorescent. I swam down farther and spotted the Naiad with Ray. She had him around the neck and she was diving quickly. He struggled against her, forcing them to sink deeper. He had used his fists in some capacity, because the Naiad was leaking something green from an eye and appeared to be furious. As I took a stroke closer, she wrenched her head toward me and opened a mouth full of sharp teeth like a giant fish.

I had no idea how long I could hold my breath, but I knew I wouldn't die of asphyxiation. Passing out from loss of oxygen now, however, would not be a good idea.

I followed, and the Naiad bared her teeth again in a sound-less hiss. She stopped and brought Ray around. Her face was beautiful, just as Naomi had described, but her teeth were wretched—needle-sharp tips running in several rows like a shark. Her long arms looked grotesque, bending at multiple joints. They held Ray close, trying to contain his struggling.

I maneuvered myself into a position to tread water vertically, facing them. "Come and get me, you freak," I screamed into the water. I heard my voice, but I had no idea if I'd made any coherent sounds.

She paused and then swam closer to me to investigate, with Ray in tow, one arm still firmly locked around his neck. Her feet were webbed like flippers, even though they sported toes. That was creepy.

"What's the matter? Too scared?" I said on my very last ration of air. I had to breathe, or risk passing out, so as she swam closer, rage and menace etched in her perfect features, I headed toward the surface with a big kick. I hoped she'd fol-low, because if she didn't I was out of luck. My head crested the top of the water and I opened my mouth in a big gasp, taking in as much air as I could. Now that I was supernatural, my lung capacity was much bigger than the last time I'd dallied in the water, which was a relief.

"Jess," Tyler screamed. "Swim over here and I'll pull you out!"

I turned my head to face the embankment and saw the three of them standing on the very edge. Worry strained Tyler's features, Danny looked horrified, and Naomi appeared calm, as always. "I think the Naiad is following me. Once she gets here, I'm going to engage her," I gasped. "She'll let go of Ray to fight me. Grab him and pul—" My mouth filled with water as I was hauled under. The Naiad had my ankle and was tugging me quickly as she dove.

I reared my body against the current, using all my strength, and latched on to the slimy hand that was clasped around my ankle. It was hard to see in the murky water, but it appeared she still had Ray. I wanted her to fight me and let him go. My hand snaked up her forearm, which felt oddly rubbery, and once I got to the elbow, I pulled backward, giving it a snap. She immediately let go of me and howled, which sounded like a screech that would shatter ears above water. Our momentum stopped and my ears gave a defiant pop. I tilted my head upward, but it was impossible to tell how deep we were because it was dark above and the strange green light down here was muted.

The Naiad recovered herself quickly, throwing Ray to the side like a limp doll as she came at me. *We have to get to him*, I told my wolf. Air was already an issue. *We need to get angry or we're not going to make it.* As the Naiad came at me, raging, my claws elongated and adrenaline poured through my system. Everything enlarged in an instant, including my arms. As she swam into my space, I brought my forearm up and sliced my claws cleanly across her face. I knew my actions were fast, but underwater they felt slow.

My nails went through her flesh like razors to pudding.

It hardly felt like I'd connected, but her face broke open and deep lines of green slime oozed out. She arched back away from me, grabbing her face, her shrieks echoing through the water like a dog whistle. I didn't hesitate; I dove down to Ray, who was floating a few yards below. I gripped him around the waist and kicked for the surface. I'd gained only a few feet when something latched on to my ankle again. One beat later sharp pain zinged up my leg. *Did she just bite us?* I asked my wolf. She'd either bitten me or pulled some kind of knife out of her seaweed dress. Blood started to flow from the wound in earnest. *It would be just our luck if she had killer venom.* My wolf snarled as the adrenaline we both channeled through our system spiked with a rush of power.

The Naiad had me around the leg and tried to tug me down again. With all the force I could muster, I tossed Ray upward. I had no idea if he would make it to the surface, and if he did, if they could grab him or not. I didn't even know if he was still alive.

His body rose right as splashes came from above and three figures arrowed down into the water around us. Naomi took hold of Ray and bolted upward like a shot. Danny and Tyler moved toward us quickly, taking big strokes.

They can't swim very well, I told my wolf. *We have to get out of here before the Naiad takes an interest in them too.* I twisted my body around in the water and grabbed the Naiad's hair. It looked blond and normal, but when I touched it, it had the texture of kelp. Her head was full of nasty, slimy seaweed. I wrapped it up in my fists and wrenched her off my leg, where she'd been gnawing. "Get *off* of me," I yelled into the water.

Tyler and Danny reached us, and without hesitation, each of them grabbed on to one of her arms and pulled. She shrieked and turned, trying to escape.

Danny twisted his body to the side hard, yanking off one of her arms in the process. He made a face as he tossed it away.

Her insides were green and putrid as they oozed out of the gaping wound.

Tyler and Danny both stopped, letting go of the underwater ghoul simultaneously. She floated unmoving, appearing dazed. I kicked toward her, grabbed her good arm, and tugged her behind me as I started swimming. I motioned up and we all kicked toward the surface, me with the Naiad in tow.

I couldn't leave her down here to regenerate, no matter what Naomi said about Selene's powers. This could be the Naiad's natural habitat and that's why Selene chose to have her hidey-hole in this location. I, for one, did not want to worry about getting back in the water.

We were almost to the surface.

I could see the stars blinking through the last of the water when Danny punched my arm frantically. I turned and followed his gaze.

"*Holy shit,*" I mouthed. There, coming up from the depths, were a swarm of Naiads, looking like a united underwater Barbie doll army. "*Go! Go!*" I yelled, a mass of bubbles erupting out of my mouth, releasing the Naiad I held. She immediately sank toward the oncoming troops. I hoped she warranted needing help. And lots of it. There was no reason to keep her now.

Tyler and Danny were ahead of me.

I saw the rocky shelf and kicked toward it frantically. If we didn't get out in the next thirty seconds, we'd be Naiad dinner. Tyler and Danny climbed out, and right as I braced my hands on the shelf, two sets of strong arms yanked me out of the water in one quick motion. They tossed me onto the embankment with enough gusto to leave me reeling. Tyler turned, still standing ankle deep in the water on the shallow shelf. "What the fuck were you thinking? Huh? You could've die—"

He crashed down, sliding across the stone, his nails digging in hard to slow himself.

"Tyler!" I lunged toward him. Danny beat me to it, taking hold of his wrist. Tyler was almost completely underwater. Danny kept him just above the surface, straining against the pull of the Naiads. I joined Danny and grabbed his other hand. "Kick your legs!" I shouted. "They aren't as strong as we are." I scrambled into a good position, using the shore to brace myself.

Tyler thrashed in earnest and all around us the water started bubbling and moving. Green kelp strands, as thick as Christmas ribbons, broke the surface, betraying the monsters beneath.

I readjusted and slid my hand down farther, dipping under the water to grasp Tyler's biceps. I pulled with all my strength, my wolf snarling in my mind, my muscles flexing tightly. All at once Tyler soared out of the water in a rush. Danny and I staggered backward, not missing a beat, backing up onto the shore as fast as we could, dragging Tyler along with us.

As we watched, hundreds of heads broke the surface, only to duck down again in the blink of an eye.

It was only a matter of time before one streaked out to grab us.

Or more than one.

I bared my teeth at them and snarled, "We're not going easily." I growled to the masses. "Do you hear me? Did you get a good look at Goldilocks? Do you want to end up like her?" I had no idea if they could understand me. So far none of them seemed to be coming after us. How could Selene control, or conjure—or whatever it was she did—an army of Naiads? It seemed impossible.

"Hurry," Naomi urged from somewhere above us. I turned

and saw her on a high ledge halfway up the hill. "They cannot risk their lives by coming out of the water this far. You will be safe if you can reach us."

Tyler gained his footing and we all started to run.

"How many supernaturals exist that we have no knowledge about?" Danny cried. "How can we best things we know nothing about? It's a bloody minefield."

I heartily agreed. "If this is the beginning of a war, the wolves are going to need an extensive education in all things supernatural."

Wolves were too confident about their place at the top of the food chain. A Naiad who occupied a remote part of the world didn't constitute any alarm whatsoever. But it certainly did now.

"Did you see the size of the ones that surfaced?" Danny said as we continued to climb upward. "I think the one we bested was a wee one."

"You mean a *baby*?" I craned my neck around to look back at the stream, but there was no trace of them. "No wonder all she knew how to do was bite me and scream. If that was the baby, there's no way we're going head-to-head with a grown-up."

"Come. Just a little farther over this rise," Naomi urged. "We will be safe here."

Naomi stood on a shallow ledge just above us, a limp Ray laid out next to her. It was the second time I'd seen him passed out at her feet. Had only one day come and gone? It felt like a lifetime. "Is he alive?"

"There is a faint heartbeat." Naomi nodded. "He seems to be a strong-minded human."

"He's a pigheaded sonofabitch," I said as I pulled myself onto the rocks. "But it looks like it's working in his favor this time."

17

Once we were all on the ledge, I gazed down at the stream. It seemed innocuous, the water calm, nothing disrupting the smooth surface. I knelt next to Ray and ripped the front of his shirt open, putting my head to his chest. I could hear the faint beat without physical contact, but I wanted to be sure.

Tyler stood next to us, his legs covered in dried blood where the Naiads had bitten and clawed him. Since neither of us had reacted to their evil bites, they must not be too detrimental. Tyler was just short of shifting, fur sprouting along his wounds, he was so angry. "Why would you risk your life—scratch that, *all* our lives—for this human?" Tyler's jaw clenched, tension radiated outward. It rang through our new blood connection, making me edgy. "It doesn't make any sense. Why would you do such a thing? If you keep taking chances like that, there's no way any of us will make it out of here alive."

I glanced up at him. "Nobody asked you to join me. And this human has as much right to live as you or I, and while we're on the topic, who made you lord and superior over the entire world? Human or supernatural? You don't get to choose. A life is a life."

Tyler sputtered, "We've always been above humans. We're stronger, faster, and smarter"—he searched for more—"and we can't die like they can!"

"So what?" I snipped. "That's like saying humans should kill all *inferior* species on the planet because they can't keep up with them physically or mentally." I eased Ray onto his side. I had to drain the water out of his lungs. "Tyler, I suggest you go take your anger out somewhere else while I try and save this inferior human's life. I'm not in the mood to go around and around with you on who's a better species." Tyler spun away as I started rapping on Ray's back, careful not to break any ribs. As I pounded, water jutted from Ray's mouth like a hydrant. When Ray finally coughed and quit spitting water, I rolled him back over.

Danny crouched next to us. "I have no idea what you're doing or what your motivations are in the long run," he said. "But you can count me in. Ray is a bloody pain in the ass, but he seems to have one hell of a strong soul. By all rights he should've been dead many times over." Danny reached over and took Ray by the shoulders and I let go.

"I know." I shook my head. "I don't get it." Ray was now sputtering and groaning, as well as hacking up a lung. I put my ear down to his chest again. "His heart is beating stronger, but I'm not sure how clear his lungs are."

"He seems to be taking care of that himself, isn't he," Danny said.

Ray groaned. "Goddammit, Hannon," he rasped. "Did that slimy thing eat me? Am I in hell?" He cracked his eyes open. "Or have I been here all along?"

"That's not very optimistic of you, Ray," I said, a ghost of a smile on my lips. "I'd think a guy like you would have his eyes on the Pearly Gates, thinking he'd done his time for the good guys."

"I think it's hell because of that giant spider creeping toward us." He coughed hard, losing his breath for a moment as he ejected more water. "Spiders that big can only be created by Satan."

Danny and I sprang up at the same time. It was stupid to think we would be free and clear on this side of the river. If anything, the worst was yet to come.

"That's not a bloody spider!" Danny shouted. "It's a freak of nature. Do you see all those eyes?"

I bent down and snatched Ray under his armpits, pulling him backward as quickly as I could. "Yep, and look, he has friends." Dozens began to flood out of cracks around us, almost simultaneously, like they'd been summoned, which was likely the case. Danny was right. They weren't spiders; they were some kind of scorpion spider mix. They were totally black, had eight legs, huge glossy spider eyes, thick, coarse hair, and a killer spiny tail that curled above their backs loaded with barbs as thick as my fingers.

They were as big as lobsters.

"They look venomous as hell," I said, glancing down the ledge, but Tyler and Naomi were nowhere to be seen. "We have to get out of here. If Ray gets stung, it's all over, and I didn't just fight a baby Naiad for him to die from a spider bite now. Where are Naomi and Tyler?" I whipped my head around. "She has to get Ray out of here and we have to jump."

Instead of Naomi, there was a whoosh and Eamon landed in front of us, right as Tyler came bounding around the far corner into view. It seemed the ledge curved around the mountain.

Tyler was within inches of one of the killer arachnids. It rattled and scurried back and forth. "Tyler, hold still!" I yelled. He froze instantly. I took a breath in, wondering why we couldn't scent them. I smelled only rocks. "Eamon," I said, "where's your sister?" He glanced at the bugs impassively and didn't answer. "Eamon! If you're here, you might as well help us. You can get Ray out of here." I started guiding Ray toward him.

He turned. "I will not handle the human. I care not if he survives."

"Then why are you here?" I stopped midstride. "Just so you can be unhelpful?" He stood between us and the Scorpers. I had no idea what they were called, so I gave them the name they deserved. I was willing to give Eamon a smidgen more time to answer the question since he was in between us and the bugs. I glanced over my shoulder at Danny. "Is there someplace to go behind you?" I started shuffling backward, holding on to Ray, who was still coughing intermittently.

"They're not interested in me," Tyler called from across the ledge. "They're focused on you. I'm going to climb higher and see if I can make a rock slide to knock them off."

"To answer your question, I came back," Eamon snapped, "because I still owe you a debt for saving my sister's life, and after helping you get rid of these"—he gestured to the Scorpers—"I will consider my duties repaid in full."

"Fine. Fulfill your debt by getting these things off of here and we're good." My back was pressed up against the side of the mountain. Danny stood beside me. The ledge had narrowed down to no place left to go. "Where is your sister?"

"I am here," Naomi said as she landed gracefully in front of us, just behind her brother. "We are very close to Selene's lair. This seems to be her last big defense. There was nothing else I could see, but my sensing skills are not as strong as yours." She looked accusingly at her brother's back. He hadn't moved an inch.

"Naomi, I need you to take Ray out of here. Preferably not close to any water. We can't take him any farther. Maybe put him up a tree so he can live for more than a few minutes while we tackle the next task."

"I'm not a monkey, Hannon," Ray half sputtered, half coughed. "I don't want to be left in a goddamn tree!"

"I will take him and deposit him safely," Naomi agreed. She reached for him and he stumbled back against me. She scolded Ray with a finger wag and glanced at me. "I will take him and then come back for you." Her eyes narrowed, begging me to argue.

I wasn't going to argue. Now that she had pledged herself to me, I had to trust her or our bond was worthless.

"I'm not going with you." Ray shrank back even more. "I can take care of myself just fine. Leave me be."

"Ray, you have no choice." I pushed him outward. "If one of these suckers stings you, there's no waking up again. That can't be your choice. Not after all this."

Before Ray could answer, Naomi locked on to him. His scream rent the air as she bolted upward. I chuckled, thinking about how pissed he was going to be when we picked him up. Then I turned my focus on Eamon, who had become a blur of movement as he swept the Scorpers closest to us off the ledge in big arcs toward the riverbed, kicking them with his legs. I heard one of them plunk into the water. Scorpers and Naiads? You couldn't pay me to go swimming again. There was no guarantee Eamon wouldn't get stung, which was why we weren't joining him, but his persnickety demeanor was likely helping him—either that, or he was familiar with these, another of Selene's pets, and he wasn't letting on how much he knew.

That would be a better guess.

"They keep oozing out of the cracks," Danny muttered next to me. "It doesn't matter how fast he can sweep them away. We'll have to cover the openings."

There was a loud grating noise and several rocks rained down above us. "It appears Tyler's already on it."

Tyler shouted from above, "Get out of the way! I'm going to plug the holes."

We glanced up in time to see him shove a large boulder over the side. It crashed down the hill, jumping and bouncing along the wall, shifting rocks loose as it went. I pressed my back as far as I could against the mountain as rocks poured down on our heads. The boulder had triggered a small avalanche and when it slammed onto the ledge where we stood, the entire platform sheared off, tossing us forward. I spun in midair, trying in vain to dig my nails into the cliff face, my claws ripping out of my fingertips to help me latch on.

It was too late.

My wolf howled in my mind as my body fell forward, tumbling into the rock slide.

"Jessica," Danny yelled. "Hold on!"

To *what*? I crashed down hard, joining the melee of rocks and boulders, tumbling head over ass. There was nothing to hold on to. The sharp stones bashed into me at every turn. I just prayed my body didn't get jammed under the big boulder. If it crushed my neck, it would be all over. My wolf snarled and barked in my mind. *Nothing we can do; just hold on.* My muscles hardened together as adrenaline rushed through me, my body needing the natural protection of my Lycan form. I took it greedily, fortifying myself as best I could as I continued to tumble down the embankment. Once I leveled out, I threw my arms to the sides and clawed the earth to slow my final descent. The tumble felt like it lasted an eternity. I hadn't realized we had climbed that high.

I slid to a stop among a heap of rocks and debris, only a few feet from the river. *Fuck.* I spit dust and pebbles out of my mouth. My face was bloody and my hair was matted around my shoulders and I was covered with gravel. "Jesus," I muttered. "Great idea, Tyler. Let's bring the mountain down on top of us. It's the perfect way to get rid of the Scorpers."

As soon as the words left my mouth, I heard a rattling noise. It was close.

I lifted my head slowly. Was it too much to ask that they'd all be crushed to death? I spotted four of them creeping over the mess of boulders, only ten feet from my face. They appeared to be completely unharmed. My wolf snapped her jaws at me urging us to get up and get moving. No argument there. I jumped to my feet and took a step backward. My body was bruised and dried blood caked my arms. I was regenerating, but it would take a minute.

The water splashed behind me.

I whipped my head around and there were so many Naiads disturbing the surface it looked like a breeding ground for angry eels. Their seaweed tresses danced back and forth in a jumble of mossy green. I'd already done the Naiad thing; there would be no repeat performance.

Naiads behind, Scorpers in front.

Channeling my wolf, I showed my teeth and snarled toward the stream. "Do not mess with me. Do you hear me!" I yelled to the rippling water. "You will not like what you find."

"Hold on," Danny said from somewhere close. My gaze landed to my left on a group of small river birch nestled right next to the stream. Danny rolled out of a pile of rocks. He sat up and brushed himself off. "That was quite a ride, wasn't it? Wasn't expecting that—"

"Danny, look out!" I yelled right as a green blur darted from the water.

I leapt into the air.

The Naiad had shot out of the water quickly, but I tracked it as I moved. In my Lycan form, I was just as fast. Its long arms reached for Danny, its body already shriveling out of its environment. I screamed as we collided. Danny rolled out of the way. The Naiad's horrid face met mine, its eyes putrid in their moldy sliminess. The thing barely weighed anything. My canines were down, my claws slid into the soft, squishy flesh of its shoulders, poking though the other side.

I had to stifle a wave of nausea as we hit the ground. It struggled beneath me, its gaping mouth snapping its rows of sharp teeth open and closed, its tongue like a giant green worm wiggling back and forth.

I snarled through my raspy throat. "If you tell your people to back off, I will let you go. We don't mean to harm you, but I will do what is necessary."

The thing continued to thrash beneath me. I had no idea if it understood me. We were right next to the water and waves started churning in earnest on the surface, the angry Naiads wanting their comrade back. I gazed down into its face, watching as its eyes shriveled in its sockets. This one was an adult for sure. It was twice the size as the one I'd fought in the water. Pieces of its flesh were deteriorating at an alarming rate. They were flaking off and falling to the ground. "I don't want to kill you," I snarled. "Give me a sign you will not attack and I will toss you back in the water! Do you hear me?"

The thing stilled.

I knew I had only moments to decide. I shifted myself off of it to see if it would fight, but it didn't move. It was too weak. Its hideous arms resembled shriveled raisin skin. I bent down without thinking, scooped it up, and carried it to the edge of the shoreline. It was long and gangly, but it weighed nothing. "We want no war with you," I yelled, my vocal cords straining. I tossed the shriveled Naiad back into the water. I had no idea if it would live or die. Once it hit the surface it was pulled under immediately and the water calmed.

But in less than a few seconds, heads popped up again, almost like a choreographed ballet.

I backed up.

The water swished like a wave pool, and at the exact same moment hundreds of gaping mouths opened up to face the starlit sky.

Shit, this doesn't look good. My wolf agreed with a howl.

I took a few more steps backward as one solid chord of sound pierced the air. A single shrill note, beautiful in its intensity. Like a high note in a choral number, perfectly pitched. It went on for three beats and ended abruptly as every single head slipped below the surface at once.

Not even a ripple remained.

There was no evidence there had just been an army of super-natural beings beneath the surface. *What was that? Did they leave?* My wolf growled, as unsure as I was about what had just happened.

"Thanks," Danny panted, coming up to me, his body still healing from the damage from the fall. "In my shape that thing might have been able to take me and gobble me up."

"You would've had it handled," I said. "They're like jelly out of the water. Come on. We have to get out of here." I slowly morphed back into my human form as I took a step forward. "We have to start climbing."

"Jessica," Danny yelled. "Watch out!" His hands reached me an instant too late.

The Scorper had wound itself around my foot, all its barbs digging in, easily piercing deeply into my ankle. The sting burned like molten lava, blinding me with the intensity. Scorching-hot coals raced up my leg, infesting my body with its poison spell in an instant.

I fell to the ground.

Then the thing was miraculously off my leg. Someone was lifting me. There was yelling and screaming.

"It's going to be okay. Do you hear me?"

Tyler?

Danny's calm murmurs floated over me, but were replaced by a horrid screeching inside my brain. My whole head ached, quickly filling with a thick, orange haze. It enveloped my wolf. She was fighting, working hard to clear it, but it wasn't easing. The haze just kept getting thicker.

I was transferred into a new pair of arms. "You must stay strong." Naomi's voice echoed in my ears like thunder, her mouth right next to my ear. I latched on to it like a lifeline. "I am taking you up the mountain. You have had Selene inside you already, *Ma Reine*. Use it to your advantage. She will have left antibodies in her spells, and if these spiders are her creations, you can fight them using her essence. The same essence that ran through your veins a short time ago. *Find it.*"

My human side had trouble processing her words, but my wolf started to howl, clawing at the ground in my mind, trying to uncover something we had buried deeply. I saw the glimmer of red as she kept digging, her paws moving quickly, the orange so thick I almost couldn't see her. Then like a fountain, red sprang forth again, its tendrils sprouting in the air like a vicious web. My wolf jumped back, letting it flow outward.

My back arched, my spine bowed backward. The intensity of the reaction was forcing me to change. I embraced it.

Anything to stop the howling pain.

The red veins of Selene's essence hit the orange poison, and where they met, it burned clear, making a *pssst* sound as each tendril seared a little more. My muscles danced under my skin.

"That's it," Naomi murmured. "Fight this. You must fight. Use your power."

My body arched again, my full change coming on fast. My legs bucked, shifting, my clothes tore, and my jaw lengthened. I tried to calm myself to make it easier, but that was impossible. I knew if I couldn't clear my body of her vile spell, I wouldn't wake up.

This was it.

"That's it, *Ma Reine*. Let it come," Naomi spoke softly.

Tyler's voice echoed in the background. "Step back," he instructed. "Give her room."

"It is within you, *Ma Reine*," Naomi said, her voice getting thin and hard to hear. "Selene is not stronger than you are. These things are a child's plaything compared to your power. Eradicate the spell they carry from your being, using what Selene has left in you, and you will be free of her forever."

Ma Reine.

I finally understood.

My Queen.

18

"Jess! Jess!" Tyler yelled straight into my ear canal.

His voice was so loud it shocked me.

"Wake the *hell* up. Do you hear me?" he continued. "Jessica! I'm not going to let you leave now, not after all of this." I felt his hands on me, but they felt odd, like he was pressing on me from outside a bubble.

"She hasn't moved in ages, not even a twitch," Danny said, his voice filled with something that sounded close to remorse. "Even if she's not dead, she won't be the same. Did you feel that power? She blew herself up trying to fight off that spell."

"If she was dead, we would feel it. I can still feel her energy. Can't you sense it? Plus, she would've changed back into her human form. She's still a wolf," Tyler argued. *I was still a wolf?* I didn't feel like I was in my true form. In fact, I felt insubstantial, like I was hovering. Our bodies changed back to human when we died. It's an insurance policy so humans don't come across a dead werewolf. "She's alive. She just has to *wake the fuck up,*" he yelled right next to my ear. I cringed inwardly, but I still couldn't move.

"Well, that might be true. I do feel her," Danny said. "But she hasn't taken a bloody breath in hours! How many wolves do you know who don't have to *breathe*?"

I wasn't breathing?

How was that possible? My wolf twitched in my mind and I noticed for the first time she was lying on her side, facing away from me. *Can you hear me? Can you move?*

No response.

"Go check the entrance for those insects and do a sweep," Tyler said. "I'm not taking any chances letting one in here. If she gets stung again, she'll never wake up."

"Fine," Danny murmured. "But when the vamps come back, we have to make a decision."

"I already told you, we go for the cat as planned," Tyler said. "Then we kill the bitch who did this to my sister. I'm going whether you join me or not."

"We don't stand a chance against a goddess on our own. It would be suicide to go in there," Danny argued. "We can get Jessica home and have her figured out, and then come back with reinforcements later."

"We go, Selene dies, and we save the cat." My brother's tone brooked no argument. "When we're finished, we come back, Jessica wakes up because Selene is dead, and we go home."

"I don't give two shites about the bloody *cat*!" Danny shouted in frustration. His voice echoed, bouncing back to my ears. *We must be in a cave*, I told my wolf. No response. "What happens in that scenario is we go in there and die. Selene lives and Jessica rots here because she can't wake up."

Tyler jumped to his feet. His anger pressed down on me. His emotions swirled through my blood, pummeling me with intensity. Pain, sorrow, and rage. "The cat is my sister's *mate*. Whether she lives or dies doesn't change that. We kill the Goddess and he *lives*. We are strong enough to do this ourselves."

"You have a bloody thick skull, you know that? If we go in there, we all perish—including the *cat*." Danny's footfalls faded as he left the cave.

Why couldn't I wake up?

I reached out to my wolf again, probing my mind for any clues. She was still lying on her side. *Wake up!* I shouted. *Can you hear me?* Her front paw twitched, but nothing more.

I gave a mental push.

My power flowed out, but then flexed back at me when it hit something. *I think we're trapped in some kind of power bubble.* If that was the case, I just had to figure out how to break it open. *That sounds easy enough, right?* Zero response from my wolf. It seemed that for some reason my human side had woken up, but my wolf side was still asleep. I wasn't going to argue. I was happy to be awake, but now I had to fix it.

Come on, Jess, Tyler pleaded. *Just wake up.* His hand hit my fur at the same time he pushed into my mind.

A crackle of power ran between us at the contact, like a jolt from a car battery.

He gasped and I knew he felt it too.

He knelt down immediately, both his hands plunging deeply into my fur. The weight of him calmed me. *What's going on? Tell me what to do. Are you trapped?*

I pushed out to him with my mind, but I had to force it with all my strength. *I'm here. Can you hear me?*

He stilled. *Yes.* His voice was excited. *But you sound far away. If I couldn't feel you in my blood right now, I almost wouldn't believe it was you talking.*

My wolf is unconscious and I'm in some kind of suspended state.

Your heart isn't beating, Jess, Tyler said quietly. *And you're not breathing. You should be dead.*

Clearly I'm not dead, but honestly, I'm not sure I would've woken up had you not been here. Did you touch me before?

Yes, just a few minutes ago.

I think our blood connection is what woke me up. It feels amplified now with your hands on me. You're bleeding some of your energy into me.

That's the best fucking news I've ever heard. But why aren't you shaking this off?

I don't know. I think I have to pop the cocoon somehow, but my wolf is still out cold.

I can push more energy toward you, like a direct hit. Do you think that will help?

Give it a try. I must be in a state of limbo of some kind. I wasn't breathing and my heart wasn't beating. I tried to gather some of my own power to me, but when I opened myself up, it felt completely empty. I couldn't find anything to draw from. I pulled anyway, and as I did the bubble bowed, sucking back at me.

The totality of my power was being used to protect me. It had all shifted outward.

Tyler, all my power is on the outside. It's keeping me safe in this enclosure.

I'm going to give you some of mine. A current of raw power hit my senses immediately, igniting me. My wolf stirred for a second, shaking her legs and growling. It wasn't enough to wake her, but we'd both felt it. Supernaturals, especially the older ones, could focus their power like Tyler was doing now. Witches were especially gifted at doing this with their familiars, who stored the extra power until the witch needed a boost. Tyler wasn't that old, but the new connection between us made it seem like a natural thing to do.

I absorbed it greedily. *It's working. It's easier to communicate with you now. Once I accumulate enough, I'm going to aim it outward. If I can break whatever's holding me in with enough energy, I think I'll be free.*

Be careful, Jess. I've never seen a wolf in this state. Are you sure if you pop it you won't die? What if the cocoon is the only thing keeping you alive?

I paused. I had no idea. *I have to go with my gut on this one. It feels right to burst it open. Honestly, what other option do I have?*

Fine, Tyler grumbled. *But if you die, I'm going to kill you.* He continued siphoning power toward me, taking me at my word.

How long have I been out?

A couple hours.

I was relieved we hadn't lost another day. *By the way, you're my hero. I heard what you said to Danny about saving Rourke. It would've been the stupidest, most foolhardy thing to do, but noble and awesome at the same time.*

Saving the cat would've been a by-product of killing Selene, Tyler groused. *Don't get too excited.*

Keep telling yourself that, little brother, and maybe you'll start to believe it. I'd been born seven minutes before him, but it was the gift that kept on giving.

Harrumph.

His energy filled me quickly. *Am I taking too much?* I asked. I hadn't thought of what it could do to my brother.

No, he said between clenched teeth. *Take as much as you need.*

I quieted, concentrating on what he gave me, making sure I placed it optimally. I could feel his strength wavering, despite his arguments. If I depleted everything from him it would be a hardship when he needed to shift. Changing took massive amounts of energy. *Okay. I think I have enough. Back off.*

Reluctantly he slid his hands away.

I need you to leave wherever we are, I said. *I have no idea what's going to happen. I don't want you caught up in anything.*

Okay. His voice held more than reluctance.

Tyler, I mean it. If something happens, I don't want to blow you up. Plus, you need to be able to help me if something goes wrong, and you can't if you're in pieces.

I waited until I heard his footsteps retreating.

My wolf rolled back and forth, but she still wasn't fully awake. I closed off my mind from her and gathered Tyler's energy as best I could, trying to harness it. It felt like a mass of slippery oil, foreign yet powerful.

Are you awake? I could use help containing this. My wolf lifted her head at my voice, searching for me, but her eyes were still closed. She wasn't in any shape to help me yet, but I didn't want to waste another minute. *Brace yourself if you can, I'm going to try to do this on my own.*

All at once, I released the energy. It shot out in a straight line and collided hard against the protective wall around me, shaking the inside of my mind like a sledgehammer. I tried to steady myself, but the intensity threatened to pull me under again.

I grappled to stay conscious.

As the power rebounded back again, I used the momentum and turned it around and shoved it back at the walls, harder this time.

This has to work, dammit! It crashed into the bubble the second time, piercing it like the tip of an arrow. For a moment nothing happened. Then a shallow gust of air blew by my ears, seconds before a huge explosion ripped my subconsciousness apart.

Power raced back into my body like a shock from a defibrillator. My eardrums exploded on impact and my jaws crashed together. My body bucked and I gasped in a huge breath at the same moment my wolf sprang onto all fours in my mind, snarling fiercely.

Then my heart gave a single quavering beat.

Without pause, my body began to shift back to my human form so rapidly I almost couldn't process what was happening. In the next blink I was panting and naked on all fours.

"Well, thank goodness that worked," Tyler said, ducking his head as he walked into the small cavern. He went to my pack, which was lined up next to the others along the wall, and dug around, tossing me some clothes. I caught them with one hand. I was thankful my outfits were easy to pack and took up little space. "I guess we can chalk that up to a success. You appear to be your normal self."

"Normal is up for debate." I pulled on the shirt and leggings. "What time is it?"

"It's three a.m.," he said right as Danny strode in.

He stopped in his tracks, his face comical in its surprise. "You woke up! I thought I felt something different. Clearly I'm going to have to get better at reading these blood connections between us. But, blimey, I didn't think it was possible. You hadn't taken a bloody breath in ages."

"I couldn't have done it without Tyler." I nodded in his direction. "It was all him. He woke me up."

"Well, it's good to see you're speaking in full sentences." Danny grinned. "I'm assuming this means you're not brain damaged then?"

"No. There aren't any lingering effects as far as I can tell." I chuckled. "Can I ask where we are?" I glanced around the shallow cave. Nothing but dusty rocks and a damp smell.

"Naomi flew you up the mountain and found this cave and

we followed with the gear," Tyler said. "The vamps say we're very close to the entrance to Selene's lair, which is apparently camouflaged somewhere above us."

"Where's Ray?"

They both stared at me blankly.

"You know," I prompted. "The irritating, inconsequential human who keeps making our lives harder? Did Naomi bring him back after you found this hideout?"

"The vamps are out scouting now," Tyler hedged. "Naomi was upset about your condition and Eamon paced outside the entrance egging her on to leave. Ray's name didn't come up. I know you think I'm crass and unfeeling, but I'll say it again— he doesn't register on my radar. He never even enters my mind."

"What time are the vamps due back?" I asked. I couldn't blame Tyler for being who he was, even if I didn't agree. Naomi was the only one who knew where Ray was anyway, so there was no use arguing. "We need to start moving. No more distractions. We need to reach Selene by morning." A niggling feeling of loss crept into my psyche. Rourke had a very short time left. I could feel it. I needed to reach him. No exceptions.

"They should be back soon. We have about three hours until sunup," Danny replied.

"Let's refuel quickly," I said. "I hope you have food, because my stomach just ate its own lining."

Tyler dug in his bag as Danny sat down. He pulled out several bags of protein mush and tossed them to both of us. I caught one right as the sat phone buzzed.

Danny plucked it off the floor and handed it to me.

I glanced at Tyler. "How many times has he called?"

"Twice."

I pressed the receiver on. "Hello."

"James has gone rogue."

19

"I'm sorry, what?" My head snapped to my brother and Danny, who had clearly heard the missive. Both of their faces were stark. I'd been expecting another tirade from my father about our lack of communication. Not this.

He cleared his voice once. "James is missing."

"What do you mean *missing*?" I jumped up, my breath hitching. "Was he taken? James would never leave willingly on his own."

My father growled, "He left Pack of his own volition."

"*What?*" Going rogue was as serious as it could get. You did not leave your Pack. "That's not possible. He's dedicated to this Pack."

"He vanished last night, no trace, no note, no whereabouts. He hasn't shifted, so I haven't talked to him. But we are in the middle of a war, Jessica. He gets no leeway from me—"

"Dad," I reasoned, trying to slow this conversation down. "This is James you're talking about. If he's gone, there's a damn good reason. Just hold off on any action until we know what's going on. He could be coming up here to help us. Nick could be in trouble. It could be anything."

"I'm about to take on an enemy, a Pack of rogue wolves whose agenda is to kill my only daughter. I need all my wolves. My second-in-command does not get to *defect* whenever it's convenient for him." His voice was cold as stone. "Whatever his reasons are, they are not good enough."

I glanced at Tyler and Danny. Tyler shook his head and stalked out of the cave. Danny gave a low whistle. There was nothing we could do.

"Dad," I argued. "James is loyal. He's always been loyal. Please don't jump to conclusions. What if he was taken?"

"Taken?" my father huffed. "Not a possibility. But he will answer when he is found."

Shit. "When we get back, I'm on it. I will find him. We're leaving to get Rourke within moments and after that James will be our first priority."

"Jessica." My father's voice softened. "You have to be smart. Arm yourself and let the boys shift first. Go in strong. Don't worry about defeating her. Incapacitate her and free Rourke. We can deal with her and any fallout as a Pack when you all get home."

"I'll give it my best shot."

My father growled into the phone, "Tyler said a giant scorpion spider, one of Selene's creatures, stung you and forced you to change. But when you were in your true form, I couldn't reach you."

"I think the spell put me into a...coma of some kind. I'm not exactly sure."

"Tyler said you weren't breathing and your heart wasn't beating, but you were still alive. He felt your connection. I did too. I knew you weren't dead."

"I'm glad you weren't worried. It seems I was in rough shape, but I feel fine now. I don't have any residual effects."

"Jessica." My father's voice became quiet in its intensity. "I believe your body went into Stasis."

"Stasis?" I said. "Like the Coalition? I thought only gods could do that?"

"They can. Or a god can put you in one. Stasis acts like a protective cocoon of power, but it has to be incredibly strong, because it feeds you and protects you for the length of time you're under. I cannot put myself into Stasis."

I gulped. "What exactly does that mean?"

"It means your body wields an incredible amount of power." There was strain in his voice. "And you're going to have to figure out how to manage and control it better from now on. Having any kind of ability like that is extremely dangerous. The power takes over and you lose control." He was right. Without Tyler I might not have awoken on my own.

"Do you think it's a special gift?" I'd never heard of a supe having "Stasis" as a special gift, but I couldn't rule it out. "Or something to do with the Prophecy?"

"I don't know, Jessica." He sighed. "There's so much we don't know."

"Did you feel the break when Danny and Tyler took my blood?"

"Yes," he said. "Danny left my control immediately, but Tyler's connection shifted to something else." He sounded satisfied. "I can still sense him, even though he's no longer under my immediate control."

"Is that what you thought would happen?"

"I had no idea what would happen," he admitted. "But my son is bonded to me genetically, unlike Daniel Walker. It was enough to sever the Selective's vow and that's what it was intended to do, so that pleases me."

I couldn't bring myself to discuss Naomi or the possibility my blood had something in it that would affect Danny adversely later. My head spun trying to process this information, but overall my mind kept slipping back to Rourke. I had to move.

I needed to find him.

My wolf growled to accentuate her feelings on the matter. *I know. We're going. I can feel it. We will see him shortly.*

"We've run into trouble with the Southern Pack," my father continued. "There've been a number of defectors that have gone missing this morning. Redman's Pack is a mess. He's rounding up what's left of his loyal wolves right now and we will be tracking the rogues this evening. I expect there to be infighting. I don't know when I'll be back at this rate." His voice held an odd note at the end. I picked up on it immediately.

"What's wrong?"

"Something feels...off."

"I feel it too," I said. "The female vampire thinks a war between all Sects is beginning."

"She might be right." He pulled the phone away from his ear and answered a question someone asked him. "Jessica, I'm glad you're safe. I need to go. Call me once you're out."

"I will."

He was betting on me.

I was too.

The vamps arrived five minutes later. Naomi strode into the cave first. "*Ma Reine*, it is good to see you are awake and well. I did not know if it would be so."

"I'm happy to be awake," I replied. "But before we start

moving we need to set one thing straight. I'm not your *Queen*. There's absolutely no need to address me as such. It makes me uncomfortable. I'm not your ruler. We're in this together. I have accepted your fealty, but I'm not your mob boss. You must come freely into this merger or not at all."

"*Ma Reine* is a term used for affection only." Naomi smiled. "I have never addressed Eudoxia as such. If you are uncomfortable with the title, I will come up with another."

"You can just call me Jessica," I stated. "That works fine for me."

"In my world, a superior cannot be addressed by their given name. A name holds too much power to be used carelessly. I will not endanger your life in that way. Please do not ask it of me. But I will come up with a suitable title if it pleases you."

"Um, okay." I couldn't argue with her if that's how she felt. I knew witches held formal names sacred. That's why they all had nicknames. I didn't even know Marcy's full given name and she was my best friend. But wolves had no issues with names. Using your full title was a sign of respect. Movement caught the corner of my eye. Eamon lurked at the cave entrance. He looked put out, as usual. I was surprised he was here. "Is your brother coming with us?"

Naomi turned her head, her face showing signs of fatigue. Having a brother myself, I knew what that face meant. "Yes. He seems to believe his debt for my life has been paid to you in full. I disagreed. As my blood-kin, my debts are his to fulfill and vice versa. It has always been that way. He has agreed, with some resistance, to accompany us to the entrance. Then it will be his choice after that to stay or leave. He is deeply troubled by all that has transpired. If our Queen discovers my secret, she will want our blood and souls as payment. My brother will not survive without a court. His choices are limited. He can join us, drink your blood, and pledge himself to you, or he can flee and spend his life running." She shrugged her petite shoulders.

"That's not exactly a compelling argument to sway him to our side. What if we pretend you were killed in the battle here?" Assuming we all got out alive in the end. "And Eamon goes back to court with the story of your death? Could we get away with that?"

Eamon stormed into the cave. "And what happens when my sister is found alive and well? Her bond to her Queen mysteriously broken forever? I would only be buying myself time. Months at most."

"Eamon, if there's a question," I said, "there's almost always a solution. You just have to believe we can find one." I turned to Naomi. "Has he always been this way, or was it an aftereffect of becoming undead?"

"He has always been strong-willed," she answered, stifling a smile. "It is his nature."

I turned back to an angry Eamon. "To avoid fallout, you can tell your beloved Queen you *believed* your sister to be dead at the hands of Selene and you fled. Naomi broke your Queen's order to help us, you tried to stop her, she was killed, and you left. The Queen has likely felt the loss of connection to Naomi and will assume it's the truth. Anything that 'miraculously' happens after that is not your issue. Then, when Naomi is found alive, we can blame her short 'death' for the severed bond with your Queen." My gaze landed back on Naomi. "Has a vampire ever come back from a true death before?"

"*Non.*" Naomi shook her head. "Not to my knowledge."

"Great," I said. "Problem solved. Once you're found, people

will wonder, but it won't matter if it's never happened before. Your Queen will have no reason to believe my blood was the true culprit of the severed bond, and not death."

Eamon sputtered. "It is not as easy as that!"

Naomi waved her hand, effectively cutting him off. "Enough of this. We waste time. Eamon, it is of little consequence now. We do not even know if I will emerge alive from our battle with Selene. Once we have an outcome, we will forge something reasonable."

"That's one way to look at it," I mused. "But I'm actually hoping we all make it out alive."

Tyler strode up beside me. "We need to move now. We're wasting time."

I nodded. "Let's go."

"I feel something strange," I told Danny, who stood next to me. "The game with Selene has shifted. She wants me and I'm taking too long." Shivers ran up my spine as the energy in the air seemed to move on its own. We stood on the shallow ledge outside the cave we'd just emerged from, waiting for Naomi to come back. I'd sent her to check on Ray and drop off all but one of the packs with him, since we wouldn't need them until we were done anyway. Tyler had gone with Eamon to scout the climb.

Danny shook his head. "I don't feel anything, except for the new massive strength running through my veins thanks to you. I feel like I could take on a goddess and win." He flexed his muscles and grinned. "It's a rather nice feeling."

I smiled. "That's a good thing, I hope." I kicked some rocks out of my way and glanced around for any ugly bugs that might be wandering around. No Scorpers in sight. Danny had kept a good vigil while I was out. Some had come out of the cracks below us, but it looked like we were up too high for them. "The vamps say it's a short, steep climb up and to the right," I said. "Once we get there, we stick to the plan."

Naomi had agreed to come in after us carrying the spell darts, but Eamon refused to commit to helping us in any way. Tyler and Danny were going to shift outside and follow me in. It was the best plan we had.

My mind raced to Rourke. His blond stubble, his ridiculously clear green eyes, him laughing, fighting, his arms on my waist. My wolf sat up and whined. *We will get him out alive.* She barked and flashed me a scene of her own, him in the creek, shirtless, the sun glinting off his body, dark tattoos snaking up his forearms, beautiful and bold. Then she did something she hadn't done in a long time. She echoed his voice in my ears. *"Don't worry, sweetheart. It's all going to be okay."*

I stumbled forward, my breath catching in my throat, producing a strangled mew before I could stop myself.

Danny whipped his hand out and yanked me back from the edge. "I don't think now would be a good time to head down the hill," Danny chastised. "Plus, that would be quite a setback having to dig your broken body out of the rocks below. We are up quite high, you know."

"I can see that. I'm sorry," I stammered. "I just...something caught me off guard. Thank you for catching me. Where's Naomi?" I scanned the sky. "She should've been back by now. It should've taken her five minutes. There must've been a problem with Ray."

That was unfair, I scolded my wolf. Hearing Rourke's voice had overwhelmed me and triggered a new flood of emotion

I hadn't realized had been lingering right under the surface, waiting for just the right moment to erupt and swallow me whole. My wolf lifted her muzzle, curling her lips, showing me her teeth—almost a snarl, but more like a warning. *I get it. I might be actively suppressing my emotions, but it's only to protect myself so I don't go insane. It's a human coping mechanism, and I happen to need it. You can't expect me to think like you do this quickly.* She chomped her muzzle down twice, her eyes flecked with violet. *Okay, but ask yourself this—what if we're too late?* The thought of losing Rourke forever sent emotional needles prickling through me, causing me actual, physical pain.

I rubbed my arms.

My wolf turned her back on me, her fur bristling. *Fine. You don't want to talk about it. But maybe my not dwelling on it has some merit. It will be devastating enough to see him hurt. Selene will not go easy on him.* My wolf slowly turned to look at me and a scene shot into my mind, clear and bright like a movie playing out in front of me. Two children. A boy and a girl. One blond, like her father, one dark like his mother.

A child ran toward me, his arms open.

What are you doing? I cried out in my mind. *Stop!*

I was too horrified to shut her down; instead I watched as I stepped into the frame, happy and laughing as the child raced toward me. I bent down to embrace him, and right as he bounded into my grasp the images evaporated before me, leaving total grief in its wake. Shocking, awful misery pounded against my heart, threatening to suffocate me completely. *That was totally uncalled for!* I yelled, rage churning inside me. *What can you possibly gain by torturing me with something like that?* My wolf shifted her head to the side. She quieted completely, as if she was waiting for me. It took me a minute, but then I understood. She wasn't trying to hurt me. She was showing me something. *What happens if this doesn't become a reality? What are you trying to tell me?* She lay down and rested her head on her paws and whined. *You have to tell—*

"Jess," Tyler called, charging around the corner. "Naomi and Eamon have vanished."

20

"What do you mean *vanished*? How do you know?" My fingers traced to my temples and I pressed hard. *We are not done here*, I told my wolf. Her eyes were already closed on the subject. I actually wasn't sure if there *were* words for what she has just tried to show me. The sense of loss still flowing through me was unfathomable. I knew without a doubt if my children were never born, something would change or be broken. I wasn't sure if I wanted to find out what that something was, because whatever it was it was big and horrible.

"I know she's gone because I just found Ray," my brother informed me. "I climbed straight up from here. There's a shallow butte at the top. He's there and pissed as hell at being left. Naomi never showed. No packs, no supplies. She's disappeared."

"Well, she wouldn't desert us—just like James wouldn't leave the Pack without a damn good reason," I said. "Something must be wrong."

"No shit. This whole situation is wrong."

"Tyler—"

"We don't have time to argue about the merits of a vampire's loyalty; we need to move. I'm done waiting." His face was set. "And I know you are too."

He was right. We were out of time. "Did Eamon happen to show either of you the path we need to take?" I asked. "Or give you a directional point before he took off?"

"He gestured to a vague area someplace to the right," Tyler said. "He also said the entrance was masked to look like something else."

"Like rocks?" I asked. "Or something completely different?"

"He didn't specify, but if it was rocks, it wouldn't look like something else; it would look the same," Tyler replied. "My guess is it's a tree or something that sticks out. That way if Selene invited some sadist over, they'd have a marker to go by. Everything around here looks the same."

"Yeah, I'm sure she hosts a lot of get-togethers up here," I said. "More than likely she's too lazy to bother with trying to find it every time she comes back, so she made it easy on herself."

"Ah, I have a little question," Danny interrupted as he squatted down and unzipped the one pack we'd kept. "Did we already hand the spells over to Naomi? Or do we still have them?" He stared at us. "Honestly, I'm not sure I want to know the answer to that question, as they were practically our only advantage, but let's have it, then." He did a cursory check, but we all knew the answer.

Tyler's face was stony. "She has them. I gave them to her before she left." He swore and kicked a flurry of rocks over the side.

"Okay. We need to regroup," I rallied. "Naomi didn't leave

of her own free will. Eamon must have done something to her or she's trying to talk some sense into him. That means she still might be able to reach us, and if she does, which I'm betting on, she'll meet us as quickly as she can. Not having the spells is not ideal, but we can't let it stop us. We'll find the entrance ourselves and go from there."

"Fine with me." Tyler immediately started for the end of the ledge. I followed and Danny picked up the pack and stepped behind me.

"There has to be some sort of power current marking the entrance," I said as we walked. "We'll probably feel it when we're closer. Breaking through it will be the hardest part. Once we smash past her wards, she'll be waiting and ready." Tyler swung himself to the next outcropping of rocks and deftly started climbing. I grabbed on behind him and hoisted myself up. "I'll go in first, as planned; you two bring up the rear. We separate once we're inside and try to surround her as quickly as possible. The key will be to keep her mouth shut and her hands down. If she can't speak, she can't spell us." Spells had to be physically uttered. The words had to connect with the air to trigger the spell. A powerful goddess had only to whisper or mouth them, but they still had to have substance of some kind. And from our last meeting, I knew silencing Selene needed to be our top priority.

"I'm in, of course, but without the spells our odds diminish a bit," Danny said, climbing behind me. "But I quite like the challenge. We can't make it too easy on ourselves, right?"

Ever the optimist. "Tally's spells were only going to provide a minor deterrent, if at all," I said, latching on to another rock and pulling myself up easily. "They might have had zero effect on her. We can't worry about it. With you guys in wolf form and me as a Lycan, we can take her down physically. If we hit her hard enough it will take her time to regenerate. Then we free Rourke and kill her if we can." I had no idea how to kill a goddess who'd come back from being decapitated. We were going to have to sever all her limbs. Then what? Could she regenerate? I had no idea, but I was going to do everything I could to end her and her immortality permanently.

Climbing wasn't hard. The problem was we weren't sure if we were heading in the right direction. We'd kept to the right, which led us up a very steep, very high incline. When we came to a small rocky ledge well above the tree line, we stopped to reevaluate. I stared out, looking for any signs of life, but saw none. Tyler had told Ray to sit tight, which I'm sure had made him insane. I couldn't see the butte he was on as I scanned the area around us, because we were climbing in a different direction, and it had led us away from it.

I angled my head to gaze up the mountain. We were about a thousand feet from the nearest peak. "What do you think Eamon meant about the entrance being camouflaged to look like something else? Are there any trees up there?" I asked. I scanned the scenery, but all I saw for miles were rocks. We were above any vegetation line. We'd been climbing for about an hour and Naomi still had not returned. The sky was brightening with the dawn. I hoped she was safe. "I can't believe Eamon snatched Naomi," I muttered. "He probably tried to take her home and I bet she's putting up a fight right this minute." I glanced at Tyler out of the corner of my eye. If he'd been about to die for someone else's cause, I might have done the same thing. I gave Eamon a grudging appreciation for trying to keep his sister safe. Very grudging. "How are we supposed to find it without the vamps?"

Tyler scanned the horizon along with me. "We just have to keep looking."

"Let's do it as we move. The mountain splits into two directions about five hundred feet above us. Which way do you want to go?" I asked. The peak closest to us was higher than the peak on the right.

"Let's stay right. It's the only information Eamon has ever given us." Tyler took a handhold and hoisted himself up. "Are you sure you can't feel anything yet? Any energy or some other mysterious mojo? Selene's power should be in abundance here. I don't get it."

Other than the feeling of dread, like we were taking too long, I didn't feel any centered energy. "She's probably masking it so it feels like something else." I closed my eyes. I had no idea if I could project feelers out or not, but it was worth a try. *Do you know how to do this?* I asked my wolf. She lifted her snout and scented the air above her, tracing her head back and forth slowly. I copied her movements, pulling the air in over my tongue, tasting and sampling as I went. *Can you taste or smell power?* She yipped and stilled, cocking her head to the right. I sensed a strangeness. "I can taste something different. It's not Selene, but the air is different over there," I said, pointing along the rock face to the right. "I'm not sure if it's power or something else, but it's very faint. I also smell animals and the scents are mixing. Does anyone smell wild sheep or goat and something like that?"

Danny took in a deep breath. "I can scent them. They must be mountain goats of some kind. They smell ragged and dusty, but I don't smell anything else."

Tyler tilted his head upward. "I scent animals all the time, but I parcel them away without giving them any thought. Let me see." He inhaled, nostrils flaring. His eyes sparked yellow for a moment, triggered by something that had caught his attention.

"What?" I asked. "What'd you find?" I took another breath in to see if I could figure it out myself.

"There's something odd wrapped in the animal smell," Tyler said. "Almost a warning of some kind." He took more air in. "Decay."

"I thought so too," I said. "But I don't understand all the animal markers. They mix for me." I inhaled to full capacity and blew it slowly out my nose.

Tyler was right. Something was wrong with the goats.

I tasted it this time. Their earthy smell was mixed with something that shouldn't be there, something sharp. "Can you see where they are?" I backed up on the tiny ledge, careful not to step off, and craned my neck upward.

"There they are." Danny pointed. "Look there, to the right."

"I see them. Are they moving?" Tyler said.

"They're not moving, as far as I can tell," I said. The goats all stood, but none were animated. "That's strange. Maybe goats sleep standing up? Are they nocturnal? They still smell like they're alive. If they were dead they wouldn't be upright, correct?"

"Just our luck. Bloody possessed goats," Danny groused. "Killer bats, spiders as big as cats, and sea wraiths weren't enough of a sampling of the animal kingdom? She had to add *goats*?"

"Wait a second." I paused. "Eamon said the entrance appeared as something else. Selene wouldn't want to announce it to the world, so what better way than to disguise the *actual* entrance with a bunch of goats? A natural piece of the landscape. The smell of power is very faint, so she's obviously trying to mask her magic through the goats. As beings, they can absorb some of her power. It's not like the Scorpers, which she created with a spell. The goats aren't coming after us; they are our ticket inside."

"We have to go through a *goat* to get to her?" Tyler asked. "You're kidding me."

I chuckled. "It's petty ingenious. I bet there's a gatekeeper goat. There have to be at least twenty of them up there." Tyler started his ascent.

I shrugged and followed my brother toward the tricked-out goats.

"When we reach them, they'll attack. Make no mistake," Danny muttered as he came from behind. "I hope they're not weregoats. Does such a thing even exist?"

"I've never heard of one," Tyler called. "But that doesn't mean much. I had no idea wereweasels existed before one attacked you."

"That was a wicked little thing," Danny replied. "I hope the Goddess doesn't have a cache of them at her beck and call. Their teeth are like shards of broken glass."

"Werewolves are so damn egocentric," I complained as I climbed. "If you guys paid attention to the world around you once in a while, you'd be better versed and better prepared to battle what might come your way."

"Nobody is stronger than us," Tyler answered from his point twenty feet above me. "Not even your *cat*. There is no need for us to worry about what's on the bottom of the food chain. It's like a shark worrying about the small fish. Why bother?"

I snorted. "Yeah, that works until that guppy grows fur, a pair of wicked incisors, and comes after the shark with a million of his little pals. One wolf is no match for an army of *anything*."

"You have a point, of course," Danny added. "But guppies don't ever come around, so it's easy to forget they exist altogether. I haven't encountered anything to give me pause in more than a century. A hundred years is a long time to get comfortable with your life. No wars, no enemies, no issues. It's been grand."

"Then I'm christening this the 'Dawn of the Guppy' because I have a feeling the small things are going to throw the biggest punches." We all pulled ourselves steadily closer to the statuesque goats. None of them had moved during our entire climb. Danny had edged farther right and had positioned himself directly under them, while Tyler and I had stayed more left.

"I'm pushing ahead of you both," Danny called. "One of us has to investigate the bloody beasts and I pick myself to be the lucky winner."

Tyler and I stopped climbing and watched Danny steadily close the gap between himself and the goats. We were all waiting to see what was going to happen. When he was within ten feet, he placed a single foot on the ledge directly below them and a decisive power shift flowed over me in a hot, prickly wave. "Danny!" I yelled. "Be careful. Something just happened. You must have triggered a boundary line."

A single bleat echoed in the air.

"Bloody hell, did you see that?" Danny yelled back. A snowy white male with long ragged hair and two sharp-looking horns moved its head.

Then it took a single step forward.

"I see it," I answered.

As we watched, it angled its head toward Danny, blinking once as a slow fire ignited in the center of its eyes.

It bleated again.

Then, one by one, they all turned their heads slowly, like possessed animatronic fiends.

All of their eyes blazed a fiery red.

21

"This doesn't look good," Tyler said. "We can't fight off twenty two-hundred-pound possessed mountain goats in our human form and there's no place to change safely. There's barely a foot clearance in any direction."

"Wait. Maybe we don't need to fight all twenty," I said. "They're all starting to move except one. Look."

The red-eyed monsters started to pace agitatedly as fierce angry sounds erupted out of their snouts. They milled back and forth like army sentinels, except for one who was pushed up tightly against the rocks.

"I see it. That one's different. It's bigger," Danny called as he pointed where we were all looking. "And from here its eyes aren't lit and it hasn't come alive quite yet like the others."

"That's because I'm pretty sure it can't. Tyler, can you isolate the scents?" I asked. "And pinpoint which goat smells exactly like what?"

Tyler eased himself onto a small rock that jutted out above

my head. The mountain angled steeply from where we were positioned, so we had a good view of the goats. Tyler shifted his head back and opened his mouth. I did the same. As the air crossed over my tongue, there was a startling difference. Now that the goats had become animated, power zapped over my tongue and sizzled my taste buds. There was no doubt we were in the right place. Selene's magic signature was all over.

I took in a deeper breath, trying to catch the specific scent of the stationary goat. It was hard to do. Smells in general still overpowered me with their complexities and notes, because of all the layers. All the scent information flooded into me and I had trouble sorting. "Are you having any luck?" I asked my brother. "Everything just tastes awful and powerful at the same time."

"Yes," Tyler said. "I can't taste the power like you can, but I can smell the differences in the air. The goats have a rancid undertone, almost undetectable. The stationary one smells clean, almost artificial."

"I smelled the stink too," I said. "It's definitely carrying on the air now that they're moving around. But is it some of their kill and not their actual smell?" I curled my nose.

"Goats don't kill for meat," Danny called, hearing me perfectly. "They're vegetarians, as far as I know. They forage around, eating shrubs and roots and things."

Of course *regular* goats were herbivores—but I could see rabid, possessed goats with red eyes eating meat, preferably while it was still alive and struggling. They probably required fresh blood on the hour. "They aren't vegetarians if they're weregoats, right? These aren't normal goats; these are—"

"Dead goats," Tyler said grimly. "They have been reanimated somehow. Selene must be able to wield some sort of necromancer enchantment. They wake when they detect a threat, and stay stationary the rest of the time."

"Well, that explains why their eyes are red," I said. Red was Selene's spell color. "But they can't last that way forever. Goats are living things, so even with a strong enchantment they will fully decay over time."

Tyler inhaled. "This must be a relatively new batch, because I'm picking up only a little decay. They must get really nasty over time."

"Great." I climbed closer to my brother's perch. "So we're dealing with necromanced goats. The bonus is they can't be that smart. I think the artificial one is the gatekeeper. I'm suggesting one of us makes a racket at one end to lure the goats away from this immediate area, and the other two tackle the gatekeeper. I'm volunteering for gatekeeper duty."

"Fine," Danny answered. "I knew handling the goats would be my job the moment we laid eyes on them. I'll make my way over to the very right edge of their ledge." He motioned to the far side of the rocky face we were on. "When the diversion comes, you'll know it." As he moved, all the goats eyed him. Every so often one of them would stomp a foot and give a scary bleat. It sounded like an old woman being murdered.

"We need to climb closer so we're ready," Tyler said as he started up the wall.

"Don't get too close," I said. "We don't want them to take an interest in us if we can help it."

"It's too late for that, sis," Tyler grunted as he hoisted himself higher. "Selene isn't stupid. If a threat makes it this close to her lair, she'll be ready for multiple attacks at one time. I just hope Danny can herd most of them to his side so we only have to deal with a few."

Right as Tyler finished talking a giant goat shambled over to us, angling its head down to bellow a warning. This one sounded ten times as loud, its eyes blazing a wicked red. It was massive. I wondered for a moment if coming back from the dead meant you put on extra pounds. Surely goats weren't this big in the wild.

"I wonder if it can shoot lasers out of its eyes," I said half kidding, half not. "Selene can shoot red lines out of her fingers— if her spells manifest themselves here in a tangible state, why couldn't she make it work in the goats?"

"Jesus," Tyler sputtered. "Quit talking crazy. If she could make something like that happen, powerful witches all over the world would be holding up banks with dead animals."

"Well," I chuckled. "It's just a thought." The goat bleated at us again and I cringed. "Not every witch is as powerful as Selene. I'm pretty sure a young witch can't shoot physical spells out of her fingers. I'm certain Marcy can't do it, but I don't know about Tally. I've never laid eyes on her."

"Witches are tricky," Tyler answered. "I bet some of them can, but don't want the supernatural community to know. It would make them seem like a bigger threat. Selene prances around like she doesn't give a crap about anyone else in the world. But that's about to change." Tyler's eyes shot amber. "I've had enough of this and I'm ready to go home."

"Amen," I replied. The angry goat stomped its hoof at us, like it knew what we were saying. This one wasn't going anywhere, no matter how much noise Danny made on the other side.

There was more bleating to the right. "Come on, you bloody beasts. Come and get me." A huge crash exploded against the mountainside. "Huh? You don't like that, do you? But I don't care. Here's another." There was a loud *thunk* and one of the goats toppled over the edge, emitting a scary yowl on the way down.

"Is he trying to stone them to death?" I asked. My head was down because I was climbing quickly, but it sounded like rock on rock with an occasional rock on putrid flesh. "Come on," I urged, catching up to Tyler. "Hurry."

"Ow!" Danny yelled. "The bloody horns are sharper than a blade." Another goat flew over the edge. His diversion was certainly a ruckus, but as we climbed closer, less than half had followed the noise. Another third were focused on us, and the rest stood by the artificial one, defending what I was sure was the entrance. There was a strangled howl and my head shot to Danny. "Their horns have some kind of spell on them," Danny gurgled in pain. "Don't touch them. My arm is losing feeling quickly." He clutched his arm right above the elbow.

"Dammit," Tyler muttered. "Stay away from their horns, Jess. I have to get Danny before they gore him to death." Before I could voice my concern, Tyler vaulted onto the goat ledge, immediately shouldering two large beasts over the side. He stayed low, using his preternatural speed.

Tyler, in his wolf form, was faster than any other. It was his extra gift. He was also incredibly fast in human form. Three others went over the side. Remarkably, all the remaining goats started to follow him, snorting and bleating their rage. They were slow, so they were easy to dodge. Tyler made his way to Danny, who was still busy trying to stone them with rocks thrown with one arm.

Was this really Selene's last defense? We had to be missing something. The goats were scary enough, but not crazy deadly. This would have been the right place for a winged devil attack. We would've been picked over like carrion.

We have to stay vigilant. This can't be all she has. My wolf growled in agreement, her eyes darting around, taking in everything around us.

I pulled myself onto the ledge carefully. Not wasting any time, I beelined for the stationary goat. It still hadn't moved an inch, but all its guardians had followed Tyler. As I moved closer I could see it wasn't alive in any form.

It'd never been a real goat.

Now the question—was it a mirage or something I had to defeat to get inside? *What do you think it is?* My wolf barked and scratched at the ground. I sampled the air again. The smell of decay was stronger on the ledge, but there was also a hint of warning in the air. It made my stomach churn, like I'd ingested something nasty. *What do we do with it?* I asked my wolf. She was up at attention, ears back, teeth bared. She didn't like it either. She flashed a picture of the goat morphing into something else when I put my hands on it. *I need to touch it?* She batted the empty wooden box into view. I understood. We would gather power to ourselves and try and break whatever magic was inside the goat. Selene's last ward. Once it was gone, the opening to her lair should be clear. It wasn't an excellent plan, but it was enough. *Okay. Here it goes.*

We both concentrated on channeling the power inside us, the same power we'd reabsorbed after the bubble broke. I finally understood that my power was never in the box; it lived somewhere inside me, situated deeply. In the future I had to learn to call it up quicker, but for now I closed my eyes and focused on grabbing it with everything I had, like sucking on a gigantic straw.

Power began to materialize in my psyche.

I could see it. It manifested like bright gold ribbons floating in my mind. I realized as I saw it that my power signature must be gold. The power swirled until all I could see was bright golden sunlight in my mind. Fur sprouted along my arms; my muscles shifted under my skin. My Lycan form was strong, as strong as it could be. *I think we're ready.*

An angry bleat sounded from right behind me.

Shit! We've got company. Its breath hit the back of my neck like stinky swamp ass. I'd been too preoccupied to notice one had ambled over.

"Jess, look out!" Tyler yelled.

"I got it," I called, my voice gravelly once again as my neck morphed. Power swirled around me, inside and out. I didn't wait to see what the goat was going to do. I bent at the waist and locked one hand into the ground. I dug my claws into the rocky floor and pivoted on my arm, bringing my body and legs around in a blur. My feet connected with the side of the mangy freak of nature hard, sending it flying backward. Straight off the cliff. It bleated its anger and surprise, its red eyes sparking evilly right before it dipped over the side. It was a massive animal, but its weight didn't even register in this form.

This is too easy, I said to my brother in my mind. *Selene wants us here. She's got the death goats on a level two danger attack, not a level ten. If they were level ten they could probably spit venom.*

We still have to watch it, Jess, my brother replied. *It looks like she wants us in there, but these goats could be masking something else lurking just behind. A stupid diversion.*

Is Danny okay? I asked.

I think so, but I'm not sure. The spell seems to be moving slowly.

Right then I heard Danny swear and yell, "You aren't going to keep me down, you bloody bastard!"

I turned my attention back to the inert goat. My brother was right. This gatekeeper could be a ticking time bomb. *We have to move fast*, I said to Tyler. *Once I insert my power into this thing, all hell could break loose.* Which was likely inevitable. The final showstopper. I just hoped the calamity would be contained to me and not destroy the entire mountainside.

I extended my arm slowly.

Get ready, I told my wolf and my brother at the same time. My wolf gave a bark ending on a snarl. She had no idea if this would work either, but it was the best we had. My fingers brushed the side of the goat and once they came in contact with it power rushed up my arm. There was nothing solid about it, only massive energy. The goat was a figment. A mirage. *There's nothing here but power, and it feels like it's seriously contained*, I told Tyler. *Get ready to jump.*

I took a step closer to the figment; nothing impeded me.

Instead Selene's signature began to envelope me, covering me completely. It poked and prodded me, trying to burrow under my skin, but my golden strands of power held like a shield locked around me. I heard a faint yell behind me.

"Jess!" Tyler's voice held more than stress. "Don't go any farther. You're fucking disappearing!"

Disappearing?

I gazed outward. Everything outside looked normal. Danny and Tyler started toward me, Danny's arm clutched to his side, blood running down his sleeve. *You can't follow me in here*, I called to my brother. *Selene's power is trying to insert itself into my flesh. You won't get through. Her power will eat you alive. I have to destroy it. When it goes there's going to be a massive explosion.* My wolf gave a yip of agreement. Tyler kept coming. *Tyler, I said back off!* I inserted power into my voice.

He skidded to a stop, grabbing Danny by his shirtsleeve.

Jess, it's too dangerous, he pleaded. *There has to be another way in.*

I don't have time to find another entrance. When I throw my power into this goat, energy will ignite. You and Danny have to get off this ledge right now. After I'm in, find a way in.

Jess, he said, *it's too risky. We can climb to the top and see if there's another entrance. She has to have more than one entry point.*

I refuse to waste any more time, I replied. *I need to find Rourke and this is it. Do you understand me? This is my last chance. I can feel it. He needs me and nothing is going to turn me back now. I want you to get off this ledge.* Tyler struggled against me, but I was issuing a command and our blood connection rang with it. *Tyler, go now. I'll give you thirty seconds. After that, Selene's power will find a way into my body. I'm running out of time.*

Tyler pushed Danny to the edge. Danny understood what was happening and gave me a salute with his good arm. "Godspeed, Jessica."

Tyler glanced over his shoulder at me and moved his lips one last time. "See you on the inside."

I'll see you there. I knew Tyler would find a way in. Or he'd die trying.

Then they were gone.

Okay, this is it, I told my wolf. *We throw our power out. If we break this ward, we're in.* She gnashed her teeth, her eyes sparking violet, which mirrored my own. She was ready.

One, two...*three*...Power ejected out of me in a sudden rush, staggering me to the side. My hands shot out to brace myself, but there was nothing to hold on to. Gold strands leapt out of me on all sides, and as they collided with the fog of power, they sizzled and sparked, hitting Selene's magic with claustrophobic intensity. The pressure rose inside whatever was covering me, accumulating quickly, pressing down on my chest like an anvil trying to crush the life out of me.

It was hard to breathe. I gaped like a fish, trying to draw in air. At the same time I continued to push energy out of me in concentrated waves. This goat was going to blow sky-high. A fraction of a second later there was a loud sizzle in the air, and the last of my accumulated energy shot out of me like a hydrant.

It hit the walls of the ward, shattering them in an ear-piercing explosion.

I fell through the air, the ward and the ledge gone, my arms lashing out instinctively as my sharp claws dug into the side of the mountain as I dropped. I managed to stop myself, my foot catching a small rocky outcropping. My ears rang with the residual effects of the sonic boom, healing quickly. After the ward had shattered, my power, the millions of gold threads, had snapped back into my body all at once, shaking me to the core. I glanced down and saw the drop below me, my fingers bloodied as they anchored us in place. "*Holy shit*," I hissed as the power surged through me for a few more seconds before it finally calmed, my wolf howling along in distress.

I panted for a minute and shook my head, trying to clear the last of the impact.

Then I angled my neck upward and then back down. I dangled off the edge of the mountain. Everything that had just been there was gone.

Demolished.

I could see nothing but a rock slide of fresh rubble in the valley beneath me. I tried to spot Tyler and Danny, but I couldn't see them. *Tyler?* I called.

Here, he answered, sounding tired and out of breath. *We're down and to the left of you. I can see your legs, but I don't think you can see us. That was a hell of a charge. The entire mountain quivered. Did you take care of the ward? Can you get in?*

Yes. I think so.

Danny is trying to fight the spell and he needs to change. We found a space big enough. We'll follow you up as soon as we can.

You're right. She wouldn't leave herself only one escape. The mountain is sheared off here. Find another way in. There has to be one on top.

We'll be right behind you. Just be careful, Jess.

I will.

I looked skyward. Twenty feet above me was a small opening, dark like an entrance to a deep cave. *She knows we're alive*, I told my wolf. She snapped her muzzle in agreement, urging me up the rock face. My Lycan form was strong and now that the power had settled fully back into my body I could focus again.

I dug my claws into a handhold and pulled.

Here we go.

22

I paused at the mouth of the opening. It resembled a regular tunnel, nothing but a long rocky hallway set in the mountainside, but the darkness felt icy and dangerous on my skin. A second later the smell of blood hit me.

Lots and lots of blood.

The fur covering my arms jumped to attention and anxiety crawled across my neck and shoulders like an army of ants hellbent on destruction. My hackles rose even higher. I was tall for a woman to begin with, but in this form I was well over six feet. It made me feel like a monster, but being imposing worked in my favor. I ducked carefully into the opening. Once inside, the tunnel enlarged after a few steps. Magic swirled around me, sharp and pungent, testing my skin but not threatening me directly. *She wants us*, I said to my wolf.

I picked up the pace and trotted down the short tunnel.

The walls on both sides narrowed as I ran and the cave made an abrupt ninety-degree turn to the left. Once I made the turn, the darkness became absolute. I used my hands to guide me, as well as my eyes. I could see in the dark, but when it was this dark, only hazy, grainy outlines were clear. *Once we get there, it isn't going to be pleasant*, I said. *We have to be on high alert or we die.* My wolf snarled. She was already at attention.

I just had to make sure I was too.

I gathered more power to me before I turned the corner, pulling hard on my inner resources. I'd used a lot of energy on the goat, but it was replenishing quickly. I made one more turn and candlelight flickered onto the cave wall, coming from what must be a bigger cavern.

I slid along the edge of the cave, stopping short of entering the cavern beyond. I inhaled. *Rourke.* The scent of my mate hit me. My hands clenched as a tornado of emotion washed over me. *I can smell his blood everywhere. There's too much of it.* My wolf gnashed her teeth, pushing me forward. *Get ready.*

I listened for a second and then poked my head around the corner. Nothing jumped out at me, which was both a relief and a disappointment. The first thing that caught my eye were the thousands of candles lining the walls of what was indeed a huge dome-shaped cavern, easily a hundred feet across. The candles hung in metal hangers secured somehow into the rock, as well as perched on various outcroppings and ledges. It figured she was into candles.

I scanned the rest of the room quickly.

There was a short natural rock wall cutting off my full view, but from what I could see, there was a raised dais in the middle of the room.

Of course there was a fucking dais.

The Vamp Queen had a throne on hers, but it seemed Selene, the Lunar Goddess, had a bed. A huge, ornate mahogany bed, which appeared to be covered with hand-carved celestial beings—small, chubby cherubs with feathery wings and cruel expressions. The scarlet covers were mussed and appeared to be very well slept in. My ire spiked, right as my wolf let out a terrifying snarl. I hadn't realized the snarl came out of my mouth until I heard a tinkle of laugher.

"What's the matter, darling?" Selene's voice echoed around the cave, impossible for me to pinpoint directly, which I'm certain was her intent. "I can't help it if your mate *loves* to bed me. It's hard to keep up with his stamina, you know. He requires sex so often and is so lusty, it's a full-time job. But I do try my very best."

I ignored her, which was a feat, and instead scanned the room, trying to locate where her voice was coming from. Continuing to stay quiet, I ducked a little farther into the room, sticking to the wall, my eyes tracing their way back to the dais and raised bed against my will. *It's going to be a great joy to tear her to pieces.* My wolf snarled her agreement. The silky sheets were illuminated by a huge chandelier glowing with flickering candles. A low orange cast spread downward, creating dancing shadows on the rumpled sheets.

I growled out loud again. I couldn't help it.

My wolf threw graphic images of us ripping Selene apart with blood and bits flying everywhere. *I know. We're going to do it, but we can't fall for her taunts. She's only playing with us. Rourke is incapacitated, or we would've heard him by now.* Large stationary boulders still stood in my way, so I couldn't see what else was inside the room unless I broke away from my position by the wall and slipped into the open space. It was tricky and I didn't have a good plan.

Once I was in the open, things would happen fast.

My hands ran along stone as I made my way forward, keeping all my senses alert. I took in breath after breath, testing for smells. I didn't smell anything other than Rourke's blood. She must have it masked all the other scents and was taking glee in knowing I could smell only him.

"Come in, by all means. What's keeping you?" Selene's voice betrayed its practiced calm. "Not backing out now, are you? The gifts I've labored and toiled over, in your honor, have almost been spoiled by your tardiness."

Gifts? I asked my wolf. My nose worked overtime.

"No need to be overly frightened. You will die, of course, but I promise to take my time with you." She laughed again. Her voice still echoed around the cave, but this time I could tell it was coming from above. I lifted my head up and scanned the walls. When I didn't respond to her, she snapped, "What's the matter, little wench? Don't you want to come claim your prizes?"

I knew refusing to acknowledge her would only piss her off more. I wanted her angry and sloppy. My movements were slow and methodical as I crept forward, still scanning the shadows. There were several ledges and cutouts in the cavern above, but I couldn't see all of them from my vantage point. I slowed my heartbeat with effort, taking only quiet, shallow breaths. The smell of Rourke in the cavern, which I tried my best to ignore, was assaulting me on every level. His scent sang to my wolf, who was now beside herself, trying to urge me on faster. *We're going. The wall ends in ten paces.* I parceled his scent away as fast as I could. *If we go out on emotion, we lose. Keep it together.*

"Fine, if you don't want your gifts, I'll just take them back. It will take only a moment of my time. Your loss."

It was time to play.

I slid forward. "Of course I want to claim my prizes, Selene. That's what I came here for." I drawled in a lazy tone, "But first

I'd like to remove your head from your body. After that, I'm sure I'll have enough time to free my lover and whatever else you have in store for me. Where do you keep the clean sheets, by the way? Your bed looks so wonderfully inviting. It will be a nice release after a very long day."

Hatred reverberated around the room in waves as she snarled, "Your mate will be hard-pressed to fulfill his duties as a lover before he takes his last breath. Why don't you step into the room and see for yourself? It's such a shame you never got to taste him or feel his hardness rock you to climax. He is *divine* and such a very skilled lover."

My wolf surged so quickly I dug my claws into the wall so we wouldn't gallop into the room in a blind rage. *She's playing with us! Calm down!*

I cleared my voice. "There will be plenty of time for me to feel all of him as soon as you're dead and gone, Selene. We'll start the minute you die. No need to worry yourself needlessly. Your bed will be well used."

"He's a lover worthy of a *goddess*—not," she spat, "a mongrel such as yourself. If he were to live, he would bore of you within a week. He would be back in my bed where he belongs, his cock firmly embedded inside me for all eternity."

"Unfortunately for you," I answered as I took a step forward, "I'm extremely talented in the bedroom. Boredom won't be an option."

"Show yourself," she raged. "I've had enough of these games."

"Selene," I taunted, "you sound a little stressed."

"I am not *stressed*," she yelled. My head snapped to her location. She was in the upper-left corner, just out of my sight. Keeping her enraged was working. Her spell was wavering. "I am a *goddess*. I have immense powers; nothing stresses me—"

"Having to tell people you have immense powers defeats

the purpose entirely." I shifted closer. I was almost ready to spring. "Maybe you've lost some of your mojo with all your beheadings—"

"Enough!" Selene raged. "Show yourself!" A shock wave hit the boulder in front of me and it exploded. I dove to the right, rolling into a shallow recess. "Come forward, wench, and we'll see who is stronger and has more stamina."

I crouched, waiting. I wanted Selene lost to her anger. *No matter what we see once we clear this wall, we go straight for Selene. Understood? Keeping her from spelling us is our top priority.* My wolf whipped her nose down, but I didn't trust her not to react to Rourke. His scent still rocked us, making us distracted. My wolf's instinct would be to go to him, to save him above all else. *He's going to look bad. There's no way around it. If we don't defeat the witch, we all die.* She was barely listening. I inhaled, at her urging, and scented for trouble. *Stop trying to figure out the smells. We can't be distracted—*

Naomi.

Selene had the vamps.

The traces were faint. Selene's masking spell was breaking down because of her rage. She hadn't wanted me to know she had the vamps yet.

"You are too late, coward," Selene called. "She dies now." Power filled the room. It was time to act. I needed Selene focused on me, not Naomi.

I sprang, bounding out into the open.

This was exactly what Selene wanted, but there was no other choice. Once I cleared the barrier, the scene in front of me was almost too much. I stumbled for a single moment as I took in the whips and sinister devices lining every inch of the vast cavern, each alcove adorned with shackles, implements of torture, spikes, and chains.

Blood, old and new, drenched the walls and ground like a thick carpet of red paint.

This woman was deranged.

A huge blast of power hit the side of the cavern above my head as I ran. *Good. She's aiming it at us.* From the angle of the explosion, I knew she was behind me. I blocked the revulsion that had erupted in my gut as quickly as I could. *Don't look at the walls!* I instructed my wolf as we ran. Once I hit the middle, I leapt over the dais in a single lunge. I spun in midair, so I faced her, landing on the balls of my feet. I crouched low, protected by the angle of the stairs. I tilted my head toward the ceiling, following my wolf's lead. I glanced upward, past all the candles, into the deep shadows and recesses. My eyesight was excellent. Selene must have made herself invisible. *Can she do that?* "What's the matter, Selene?" I called. "Too worried I'll take you down if I can see you? Come and show me your *immense* powers."

"You think to hide from me?" Selene laughed. "There is no place to hide." Another huge ball of energy raced through the cavern.

I spotted a warped, wooden table covered in matted tissue and leftover parts. I jumped at supernatural speed, and with a running start, slid under it like I was stealing a base. Selene's red lines hit the ground two feet behind me in a rush, rocking the cave floor, leaving a deep, rutted crater in its wake as rocks rained down from the ceiling, thumping and cracking onto the big wooden top.

The table wasn't going to protect me from the next spell.

I poked my head out, my eyes darting around the room for the next cover. I couldn't fight something I couldn't see and I couldn't throw a spell. Dammit. *Do you see Rourke or Naomi?* His smell was still everywhere, but I couldn't see him. "Who's the coward now, Selene?" I taunted. "Glamouring yourself is such a pansy way out. You think I'm a weakling compared to you. You must really be scared to take such precautions." I eyed my next cover, a cranny ten paces away. It might hold one strike if I was lucky.

"I do not fear you, wench," Selene spat. "I'm just not foolish enough to put myself within an *animal's* reach." Her voice tinkled around the room. "Come and look up. See what nice gifts I have waiting for you here."

Don't look.

I looked.

My breath hitched inside my diaphragm, threatening to never leave my body again. *No, no, no, no, no,* I cried. My wolf echoed her painful howl right along with mine.

Selene's glamour slowly evaporated, like a fog lifting from a mire, exposing Rourke for the first time. He hung from the ceiling upside down thirty feet in the air. From what I could see, his chest was eviscerated by a long, jagged incision. All his organs had tumbled out, masking his torso completely. *My gods.* His beautifully tattooed arms were bound with silver chains. They swung listlessly below his head, as thick, coagulated blood covered them. Most of it had congealed, but a few slow, fat drops hit the ground as I stared in horror.

Selene had done this unspeakable thing recently. She had cut him open and bled him dry, wanting me to witness his agonizing death personally. If she'd done it before, there would be no fresh blood.

A sorrowful sound came out of my mouth as I willed his skin to knit back together with my mind. *Please, baby, please start healing. Is his chest pinned back with something to keep it from mending?* I asked my wolf. She couldn't answer me, because her muzzle was foaming with rabid anger. I crawled from under the table, mesmerized by his pain, my heart shattering. Candle-light flickered and something glinted off his side. *It's silver. She's secured his skin back with silver. He can't heal!* My wolf stood motionless, her ears pinned back, a feral sound issuing from her throat. *We have to get to him quickly.* I started to run. *She hasn't severed his spine. We can save—*

"Do you like what you see?" Selene cackled. I didn't stop running. "He's a little busy dying right now, but do you see how wonderfully he glistens? *Ahhh*, and that smell! Death radi-ates a special kind of scent. Don't you agree?" I was almost to him. "Stop!" she screamed. "Or he dies now." An explosion hit the wall closest to me.

My head snapped to her voice and I slid to a stop.

She must have dropped her glamour at the same time she dropped her hold on Rourke, but I hadn't even noticed. There was a small alcove running along the cavern directly across from where Rourke hung. She was just outside it, swinging on something. *Is that some kind of trapeze?* My wolf didn't answer. She refused to tear her mind away from Rourke.

The thing Selene sat on was attached to the rocky cavern ceiling by thick chains and she swung idly, like she was bored, dressed in her ridiculous biker-chick outfit: all black leather, corsets, and spikes. Her long, red tresses flowed out behind her, her porcelain skin glowing in the candlelight. I focused my eyes harder. What she was on was too bulky and too thick to be a regular swing.

My stomach gave a wild lurch.

The only distinguishing human feature of the thing wrapped up in dark netting was the chestnut hair flowing through the holes. The body was drenched in blood and unrecognizable. But I knew who it was. *I'm coming for you, Naomi. We will avenge her together.*

Selene caught my eye, making sure I took in every ounce of her dramatic unveiling, and then tossed her head back. "Do you know how long I've waited to have my revenge on this hateful traitor? More than three hundred years. I gave this bitch *everything* and she threw it all in my face the first chance she got." She smiled, her pouty lips straightening into a grim line. "It was so deliciously wonderful that you led her right to my doorstep. You did something her brother failed to do for three centuries! I should reward you, but honestly it will be more fun to kill you. But, because of your generous gift, I'll save you for last."

Eamon had failed to bring her here? That means he's been working as Selene's spy the entire time. He never left her service. Things fell into place quickly. My wolf was still inconsolable, pushing me toward Rourke with all her might. Before I could get her full attention, there was a small noise behind me.

"Seize her!" Selene yelled, laughing. She was enjoying this way too much.

It was time to change things up.

I spun without looking. With incredible speed I collided with Eamon, shoving my foot into his rib cage, smashing him back into the nearest rock wall. The side of the cavern blew apart on impact. Eamon sprang out of the broken pieces immediately, seemingly unharmed, except for a line of blood lingering at the left corner of his mouth. His lips curled at the sides as his chin started to slide down, his cheekbones twisting ghoulishly.

His mouth opened to reveal long, sharp canines dripping with blood. "Finally," he hissed. "I get to witness your end. I've wanted to do this since the first time I laid eyes on you standing in front of my Queen, cocky and insolent, showing no respect to anyone. You deserve to die! You can bring nothing but madness to the supernatural race."

"You bastard," I raged. "You set your sister up. You knew you were bringing her to her death. Admit it! You broke a sacred blood-bond, and you're going to rot for it and I'm going to make sure you do." I lunged before he could give me one of his pissy retorts. I grabbed him around the neck before he knew I'd moved a muscle, infusing power into my arms as I went, my body reacting in pure fury. My hands pulsed, my nails sharpening to long razors, power flowing out of the points that bit deeply into his neck. Blood poured out of the wounds. My wolf gnashed her teeth at him, fully engaged with me now.

Eamon gurgled, scraping his hands against my forearms in an effort to loosen my hold. "You...will not...win..." He coughed.

"Oh, yeah," I snarled right next to his ear. "Do you know how many times I've heard that in the last few weeks? You picked the wrong side, asshole. And I hate traitors." I hauled him up like he weighed nothing, shook him hard, and brought my arms back, tossing him into the rock wall again. He smashed into it like a bullet, collapsing in another flurry of rocks.

Selene's voice grated into the air, her composure slipping by the minute. "Eamon is a fool, has always been a fool. As well as a weakling. I will enjoy watching him die." She tossed her head back with delight.

Eamon froze at his mistress's words, looking confused. "I have faithfully served you for over four hundred years." He gaped. "I have gone behind my Queen's back repeatedly and have betrayed my sister willingly. You said we'd finally be together forever, as we should be."

Eamon had fallen for his keeper.

Naomi had said they had forged no bonds, but it seemed Eamon had indeed forged a big one. Selene had obviously manipulated him for centuries, dangling her reward of eternal love. Only she never meant to make good on her deal, because she was a horrid sadomasochist who could only ever love herself.

"Eamon," I said, "I hate to break it to you, but your Goddess has never loved you. Not even a little bit. I don't think she's ever even *liked* you. You've been her messenger and slave for all these centuries for absolutely nothing. It's time to break the cycle. You can make amends to your sister if you help me defeat Selene now. It's your only chance for salvation."

Eamon's face went full vamp. His cheeks slid as his canines sprang from behind his thin lips. A vicious snarl hissed out of his elongated throat. "This is your fault," he accused. "If you die, things will go back to the way they once were."

I sidestepped him with ease, his confusion and emotions making him erratic. Even though Eamon was old, it was almost like he was a child, having never had the chance to grow up and be a man.

Selene cackled again, enjoying the show.

Time to mix things up.

Eamon turned and wheeled at me again. My body bent down in a crouch, concentrating on his movements. When he was within my grasp, I snatched him up around the middle, my body pivoting in a full circle, my feet anchoring me steadily. Once I gathered the momentum I needed, I tossed him as hard as I could. He flew through the air.

The moment he hit his target it was game on.

23

Selene's shriek was satisfying, but hearing her hit the ground with an *ooof* was priceless. I wasted no time. I headed straight for Rourke, my wolf pushing us forward fast. Selene hadn't expected Eamon to land in her lap, but I'd thrown him with more speed than even I knew I had. It would occupy her for a few precious seconds while I tried to free my mate.

"Get off of me," she snarled, tossing Eamon off her in one fierce kick. He smashed against a far wall.

I shimmied up the cavern wall in a blur, using my claws and speed. Once Selene was done with Eamon, she would track me, but I hoped I made myself a hard target. I neared the alcove at the top and ducked into it, running along the top. If I could lower him down and take the pins out, he could regenerate enough to heal those wounds. He had to. I eyed the chains as I ran. They were silver. It was going to burn like hell, but it didn't matter.

I launched myself in the air, leaping the distance onto the chains.

Rocks above my head exploded with incredible force. "Get away from him," Selene shouted. "You cannot save him! He's under my spell and the chains are enchanted. He will never wake for you." I kept moving. "*Stop!*" There was a delicious amount of desperation in her voice.

The moment the silver touched my fingertips the skin on my hand sizzled. I transferred my grip to the inside of my arm, blocked by my shirt, and slid down the length, leaving a trail of blood in my wake. My wolf channeled energy to me as I went. I barely felt the pain. "You never intended to kill him," I told Selene with confidence as I landed on the bottom of his boots. "Why would you kill him when you can keep him all to yourself once I'm gone?"

Her scream told me everything. "You know nothing, mongrel! I will kill you both! Just watch me." She fired a spell, but it went wild, hitting the rocks five feet to my left.

The moment my body had touched Rourke's, it responded on its own.

Mine.

Vibrations of need rang through me. My wolf had been so right. I'd kept this emotion from myself, trying to protect something inside so it didn't break. They'd been locked away in a private place in my mind, because emotions this intense were dangerous. Even now I had to block them, or they would overwhelm me completely.

She hadn't lied. The chains were heavily spelled. Her power lashed at my body. *We have to break the spell. Can you get a read on it?* My wolf snarled. The spell had begun to enter my skin. *We have to hurry.*

"You will both die." Instead of firing a new spell, Selene flew at us in a rage, her porcelain features taking on an edge, making her look like a devil doll. I worked overtime to hack at the spell in the chains, but it wasn't going to break that quickly. I grasped the chains with my hands to steady myself, my fingers bleeding, and kicked toward her as she came at us. But she spun upward, avoiding my strike.

She was behind me before I could register the direction change.

The only warning I had was a single scream just as a spell crashed into my back. I was on the ground before I knew I had fallen, breath completely gone from my body. My wolf was frantic, yipping and snapping at the red lines as they entered my mind, urging me to move and get back to Rourke. *I'm trying. Get the spell first.*

Selene's voice rang from above, and I cracked open an eye.

"Well, that was easy. I told you—you are no match for me." She stood on Rourke's boots, where I had just been. Fury surged through me. *Get away from him!*

She'd hit us with the same death spell, but she didn't know I'd already defeated it. My vision was momentarily red, but no lines etched across my mind. Golden light quickly formed a halo in my mind and all the red that had struck me was pushed outward before it could take hold.

"Are you dead yet, wench, or do you need more?" There was curiosity in her voice, likely because I hadn't started convulsing.

I lay still, my eyes slightly open, trying to play possum and figure out my next move. Rourke needed me now. There was movement up to the right. Eamon. He had quietly freed his sister from the netting, likely regretting his betrayal by now, especially in light of his lover wanting him dead. Selene was too focused on me and I needed to keep it that way. But before I could start pretending to convulse, another spell hit me fully in the chest.

"Why aren't you dead yet?" she snarled. "There is no way you can survive that spell."

I didn't have to fake anything. My body jumped, ringing with energy anew as red washed over me again, pushing and prodding into my shield, enough to make me quiver and moan. *It might be too much this time*, I gasped. My wolf chuffed at me, as my body vibrated and rocked with her spell. Once again, there was a haze of red, but no lines.

"Die, mongrel," Selene called as I moaned again. "Once you die your mate will grow to love me once more."

"*Never.*" His voice hadn't been above a whisper.

My body stilled.

My heart began to race like a greyhound. My mate's voice boiled through me, triggering more responses. *Mine.* My anger blasted a new stream of power into my golden shields and Selene's lingering red disintegrated around me like ash. My hands healed in an instant. My wolf snarled and spat, urging me to rise and rip the witch apart.

Instead of moving at her urging, I stayed motionless.

"You are mine!" Selene shook the chains holding Rourke. "Your mate is dying. Do you hear me? Once she is gone there will be no other standing in our way."

"Not...yours," Rourke ground out. "*Never* yours."

I tried to send Rourke a mental missive. I had no idea if mates were connected internally. *Rourke, please, you have to listen to me and play along. I'm not dead. I'm right here. Selene's spells don't work on me. Tell her you love her, for chrissake! Anything to make her cut you down.* My wolf sprang in my mind at that idea. I ignored her.

"You've always been delusional," he whispered to Selene. "Just kill me now. I won't live without her."

Stubborn man. *We move now*, I told my wolf. *Selene is focused on Rourke; it's time to act.*

But before I could spring, there was a breeze as Selene's black thigh-high boots landed on the ground beside me. "Can you see this, Cat?" She pulled the foot of her pointy boot back and kicked me high in the side. I bit my tongue, but acted like I was still in the throes of her spell. "See that? She's almost dead." Pain raced through my side. The bitch had broken my ribs. "There's nothing that can stop my death spell, not even your whore. She's never coming back—"

I lunged upward. "Wrong, Selene," I said as I grabbed hold of her legs and pulled. She went down. I rolled on top. "I'm not dead yet," I snarled. She struggled to wriggle out from under me, muttering a spell under her breath. My physical size was much bigger than hers. No wonder she always chose to vanish. "No more spells." I whipped my fist back and smashed it into her face. She screamed. I had effectively stopped her spell midsentence.

"You *biiiiitch*!" She squirmed under me. Her head was damaged from the blow, but her body was healing it at an alarming rate. *Damn, goddesses.*

"No, Selene, you're the bitch," I snarled. "And this is for harming my mate." I smashed my fist into the other side of her head, extremely satisfied when her eyes rolled back into their sockets and she did a little convulsion of her own. "And this is for hurting my new friend." I slashed my claws down the front of her chest, raking it open, leaving deep furrows in her creamy skin. "Do you hear me? Now you're the one who's going to die, Selene!"

"Jessica," Rourke moaned. His chains rattled as he rocked in agitation. "Please . . . get away from here."

At the sound of his voice I jumped off of Selene and ran without thought. I leapt, catching the wall, pivoting my foot off the rocks, and landed on his chains again. I slid down to him in half a second, the feel of him electrifying me. "I'm not leaving you," I growled. The pain he had to be enduring must be unfathomable. "I'm *never* leaving you, so get that through your thick skull. We leave this place together, or not at all." My wolf howled her agreement, clacking her jaws happily.

I forced myself to glance down the length of his abused body as I pushed my power into the spelled chains once again. It was hard to process how he was even functioning in this state. His lungs filled with air, quivering as they fought to keep working. "Hold on," I murmured as I scanned the domed roof for coupling hooks where the chains should be attached. There were none.

The chains hung in the air attached to nothing.

If we pour enough power into the spell, I think we can break it. Then we jump before he falls and catch him. It was risky because of the shape he was in, but I had nothing better.

I shot power into the connection as Selene gasped in a big breath and moaned on the ground. No more time.

"Jessica, please . . . go," Rourke said on a small breath. He was getting weaker, struggling to stay awake. He was fighting whatever Selene had done to him, but I could feel his power leaking out. *So strong.* He must have broken one of her spells when he'd heard my voice. "I want you to . . . *live*. Please . . . Jess . . ."

"Rourke, listen to me." I lined my voice with as much power as I could. "I'm staying here and we're going to make it through. I'm going to break this chain and catch you at the bottom."

Movement caught my eye. Eamon again. *We can use Eamon.*
He stood at the edge of the alcove, his sister's lifeless body in his
arms. She was free of the awful netting, but covered in dried
blood. "Eamon," I shouted frantically. "You have to help us! If
you do, you will be free of any vow you owe me or your sister,
even though you deserve death for your betrayal." As Naomi's
protector, I had the right to waive a debt. But if he complied I
would deal with that separately. I changed the tone of my voice
to appeal to him. "Please help us. We're running out of time."

Eamon spat, "I will never help you. I am grateful you will
meet your end here." His eyes cut to Selene on the ground. She
sputtered and moved her legs. *Goddammit.* "I never should
have come back here."

"Eamon." I pinpointed Selene's spell on the chains and my
wolf threw all the power she could into it. "Once your Queen
finds out you're a traitor, that you've spent the last few centuries helping Selene, your life is forfeit. Help me now and I will
make sure you live. I swear it on my life."

"I don't need anything from you," Eamon sneered. "We will
go far from here and my sister will be well again, away from
you, away from your dirty mind tricks. We will survive on our
own just as we have done before."

"I highly doubt it." Strands of my power snaked their way
into the chains. The spell weakened by the second. I was going
to have to jump soon. *Hold on, baby.* "Eamon," I called. "You're
forgetting your sister swore an oath to me and—unlike you—
she's someone who will honor it to her dying breath. How long
before she leaves you and comes back to avenge my death? She's
going to be furious with you. Fix it by helping me now. You
have a chance to make yourself worthy."

"I don't answer to you!" Eamon screamed, his emotions
ragged and raw. He moved to the precipice, still holding his

sister. Feelings were clearly not something he was used to dealing with. "I will never help you."

Selene rose to a sitting position, her face almost completely healed. "That's right, my darling," she purred, her head swiveling toward Eamon. "You won't help her, but you will help *me*. I was foolish before, remiss in not rewarding you for bringing your sister to me, *mon chéri*, please forgive me." She stood easily, her black leather corset flapping open where I'd slashed it with my claws. "Come here and remind me of our love. It's been too long and I have forgotten. Come, Eamon, remind me of our wedded bliss, the love we once shared together."

Wedded?

Eamon paused, confused once again, his face considering. His expression betrayed how badly he wanted what she was saying to be true. Pain and stark need etched across his features in a tide of longing. I so didn't want to feel any pity for him. *Shit.* He never had a chance. "Eamon, you have to be kidding me. Wake up!" I snarled. "She's going to eat you up and spit you out. Are you really that stupid?" He didn't so much as blink in my direction. I pushed more power into the chain, my wolf snapping and growling, flooding us with more adrenaline. She was laser-focused on the task of freeing our mate.

Eamon made his decision, glaring at me from across the cavern. The candlelight made his bone-white face flicker in the shadows ominously. Naomi hadn't twitched so much as a pinky finger. I prayed she'd wake up soon. I didn't think she was dead. Selene would want to play with her, making sure she endured multiple tortures, before she finally gave her true death. He turned and gently set Naomi down behind him, tucked into the corner.

Once he turned back, he stared at Selene, waiting for his orders. He'd made up his mind. Selene knew it too. He was hers. He'd always been hers in a twisted, tormented way. "That's right, *mon chéri*," she purred. "Come fight with me and I will reward you. We will go back to the beautiful place we had before, just you and I."

She was good.

And I was disgusted.

The chains quivered. My power had wrapped itself around the spell, smothering and choking it. *We're almost there.* My wolf barked. "Eamon!" I yelled, trying to snap his attention back to me. "You're a fool and I'm going to make sure you regret your choices. All of them."

Selene stalked across the floor, her fingers dancing with red. "Sic the bad wolf, Eamon," she said. "Do it for me and we will be lovers again."

Eamon lofted himself from the ledge, right at the same time the spell holding the chain snapped.

Rourke fell, but I was already in motion, one step ahead.

A split second before my mate landed in my arms, a voice hit my consciousness.

Jess, we're here. Sorry we took so long. My brother's voice flooded my mind like a Welcome Day parade. *We ran into complications getting though this maze and I had to change back to human.* One of the boulders near the far side of the room lurched forward as I wrapped my arms around my mate. The force pummeled us both to the ground.

Then another voice rang through the room, loud and angry.

"What the hell is going on in here, Hannon? Looks like you could use a little help."

24

What's Ray doing here? My brain boggled as I gently laid Rourke down. But before I had a chance to do anything more, Eamon rammed into me at high speed, the two of us smashing into the wall ten feet away with a booming crash.

Selene wheeled on her new intruder. "Human! How dare you enter my lair."

All conscious thought left me as I shoved control to my wolf. I was done. She wasted no time launching us at Eamon, who had rolled away from the impact. Rourke was hurt and we were going to finish this. Everything else vanished. Rage bubbled inside me as we flew through the air.

The world slowed, almost as if Eamon's movements came to a standstill.

He glanced up slowly, his faced vamped out and cruel. The hatred in his eyes paired with a cold sneer of satisfaction. I adjusted my trajectory slightly and slammed into him, my arms locking around his throat. I twisted without thought. He was no match for my strength; his resistance felt childlike. But he wasn't a child. He was a cruel, powerful supernatural who'd just made the wrong choice.

For the very last time.

His neck cracked and his body went limp beneath me. I dropped him like a bag of garbage.

"Jess." Tyler ran to me. "Holy Christ, what happened to the cat?" He gestured to Rourke, who was on the ground ten feet away.

I raced back to him, Tyler following. I swallowed. "She cut him open."

There was a scuffle and then a *thunk* from the other side of the room. "Did you just hit me?" Selene's rage tumbled around the cavern, making the room quake. "With a *rock*? What do you think I am? A fucking *squirrel*?"

"Lady, you're no squirrel, but you certainly have some anger issues. I heard you bellyaching from on top of the damn mountain," Ray stated evenly.

"I don't bellyache!" Selene screamed. Another rock hit its mark, *thunk*ing off flesh before it hit the ground. "You will die for that, *human*."

"I'm hoping someone will put me out of my misery soon," Ray groused. "But first you're going to have to go through a few wolves."

There was a ferocious howl and Danny bounded into the room in all his glory. He was huge and striking, with a dark brown coat. He skidded to a stop between Selene and Ray, snarling fiercely.

"Make no mistake, you will die, human, but first I will take this animal—" Danny lunged, hitting her shoulders. They went down in a snarling heap.

I jumped up, grabbing Tyler by the arm. "Selene will kill

the two of them without hesitation. She doesn't care about them. Go over and be a diversion, keep her attention. She heals quickly. After I pry these pins out of Rourke so he can start to mend, we'll take her down together."

He left without a word. I dropped to my knees, my hands working quickly to extract the silver needles embedded into his sides. They held open his chest cavity and were set deeply into flesh and bone. I had to yank hard. *Oh, baby. Sweet Jesus.* My heart lurched into my throat and I struggled to breathe.

Once the pins were removed, I threw them across the room and gathered his soft tissue and organs and placed them carefully back into his chest. *Ohmygod. Ohmygod.* I was close to hyperventilating. I tried to slow my breathing down. My wolf howled and gnashed her teeth. I took the battered skin and laid it together, trying to force the seams closed, but they didn't line up exactly right. *I hate her so much.*

Rourke was out cold again, thank goodness. Selene's spell, the one she likely gave him to keep him from struggling or getting loose, prickled my fingers as I worked. The spell was weak, since he'd managed to break it briefly, but it was there. I would have to break it to wake him up, but I wanted to see if his skin would start mending on its own first. "It's going to be okay, Rourke," I whispered, leaning over him. My fingers traced through his matted hair and down his face. My wolf stilled, both of us waiting to see what would happen.

He stirred beneath my touch as his skin began to knit itself. *He's healing!* My wolf barked happily. *He's too strong for her spells. Thank gods.* A normal supernatural may not have healed from these injuries, but Rourke wasn't a normal supernatural.

"Get off me," Selene raged. Danny flew backward, landing on the wooden table, exploding it on impact.

I glanced up and saw Selene's red fingertips swing around.

"Ray! Get out of the way," I yelled. Ray immediately dove for cover, his years of active police duty kicking in. When someone yelled duck, you ducked—or you died. He wasn't nearly as fast as a supe, but he made it just in time. Selene's spell smashed into the short boulder Ray had landed behind. It exploded, flinging stones and dust into the cavern. "Stay down, Ray. You've done your part. Now get out of here while you can!"

Selene spun around at the sound of my voice, forgetting her human diversion in a heartbeat, which was my plan. I lifted my hands from Rourke's healing chest, but not before I sent a flicker of power into him, crushing the last of Selene's spell.

He started to moan.

I stood, stepping over him, putting my body between us.

"Get away from him," Selene snarled at me, eyeing Rourke with bright lust. Her arms rose, red lines firing like sparks from her fingertips. She appeared to be a little worse for the wear, her clothes torn, her hair disheveled. "He's *mine*."

I was done bantering. I sprang, soaring into the air, landing on the first step of the dais on all fours. I needed to give Rourke as much time as I could to mend. Danny crouched to my left, still in wolf form, trying hard to shake the spell Selene had given him. Quickly, I tried to infuse my power through our bond. I could feel him, and I hoped he could feel me and take what I was sending. My father had said an Alpha could send power, but since I'd never done it, I wasn't sure. I glanced around briefly for Tyler, wondering where he'd gone, and hoped to hell Ray had the good judgment to stay hidden.

A spell hit the ground inches from my feet.

Selene marched toward me, taking her time. We weren't going anywhere, and she knew it. She had a captive audience in her cavern of death. Just like she had planned. "I will relish your death like none other." Another spell lit out of her hands, racing toward me. "I will look back on this day fondly."

I dodged it easily, bounding up the dais steps to the queenly bed, my nails raking the sheets, shredding them as I propelled myself over to the other side. I laid myself flat as another explosion hit above my head, narrowly missing the lit chandelier. The ceiling shook so hard wax flowed like rain, coating the ruined sheets. Not a great place for a chandelier if you weren't a sadist.

"You can run all you want, but I will find you," Selene declared as she stalked closer. "If I'm forced to, I'll blow this place sky high. This is my least favorite home." Disgust radiated from her voice. "It's primitive and unclean. I reserve it for prolonged tortures and punishments only. You will die and I will regenerate."

"You won't be regenerating, Selene," I called. "You're going to wake up in hell once I'm finished with you. Isn't that where leather-clad goddesses who sell their souls are thrown? The Underworld is itching for you to begin your work-study program and I'm here to make sure you fulfill your duties. I'm sure the demons are rubbing their greedy little hands together as we speak."

"I am not going anywhere near the Underworld," she sneered as she came to a standstill below the dais. "I owe the demons nothing. The winged devils failed to do their job, so the deal is void. The demons have gone back on their agreement, so I am free of my debt."

"I think you've overlooked a loophole in your contract, Selene. *Tsk-tsk.*" I lifted my head above the mattress. "You should've hired a good lawyer and paid attention to the fine print."

"There was no loophole!" she raged as another spell raced from her fingers. The mattress exploded as I leapt down the steps, rounding the back of the dais.

"I incinerated your pets with my blood as they fed on me," I taunted. "They turned to ash." It was more like thick resin, but ash sounded more dramatic. "They didn't pop back home to regenerate, they just ... *died*."

"Impossible." Her fury shook things. Equipment lining the walls and chairs rocked in place. Selene was finally showing her true rage. "What you say is *impossible*. Even I could not kill a beast from the Underworld on this plane."

"Do you see any around here?" I mocked, glancing around as I lifted my head above the dais. "You'd think, with the steep payment of your soul, they'd be here."

"*Bitch!*" she screamed, lunging for me, the rest of the bed exploding, sending cotton and splinters from the demolished headboard in every direction. I dodged the mess and ran, still heading away from Rourke. She turned, snarling, fingers waving again. "I will boil your body from the inside out." Her voice held more madness than I'd heard before. She was becoming unhinged. That could only help me. "I will deliver pain and agony unlike any you ever thought to imagine. You will *beg* me for mercy." Her porcelain features were harsh, making her look like the scary doll in the attic come to life.

My wolf snarled, readying for a fight. "You're the one who's going to beg, Selene," I replied, scanning the cave above me, searching for my next move.

I spotted what I was looking for and smiled.

I love you; you know that, I told my brother. *You get the hero award tonight.*

Feeding a vamp actually wasn't that bad, he said. *Once you get used to it.* I felt his emotions roil in my blood. He wasn't lying, but it had taken everything he had to do it and I loved him for it.

I'll get Selene to come this way. She's losing her mind. This hasn't gone according to her plan. You guys do the rest.

He nodded. Next to him Naomi stood, her face a mask of hate, all of it focused on Selene.

"After you die a painful, agonizing death, I'm going to take your mate to bed," Selene announced, all her energy focused on me, just where I wanted it. "I'll start by running my tongue over his chest—"

"That sounds lovely, but the party's over, Selene," I replied. "And the only one who will be licking Rourke's chest will be me."

I turned toward my brother and sprang, hitting the wall and bouncing off a large boulder. Selene turned toward me, coming forward just as I knew she would, her face contorted in a blind rage right as something whizzed through the air.

And pierced her right between the eyes.

25

One of Aunt Tally's darts, the orange one specifically, stuck straight out of Selene's forehead.

She had collapsed on impact. It was a sleeper. And it had worked.

Then Naomi was before me. "We need to work quickly. That spell won't hold her for long." Dried blood matted her face and hairline. Cuts and contusions covered her skin, mending quickly, along with a weird mark peeking out on her shoulder where her shirt had torn. "Come," Naomi urged. "We need to kill her once and for all. Let's disassemble her body to begin. It might not be enough, but we must try."

Tyler jumped, landing easily next to us. "I need to check on Danny," he said. "He was turning back to human last I saw."

"I'm right here, mate." Danny strode toward us. He had a remnant piece of one of Selene's sheets tied around his waist. He looked awful, pale and exhausted, but I was happy to see him alive. "Let's get on with taking her apart, then. I'm ready to be done with this. Not quite the adventure I had hoped for, but I'll take it as a win."

"Are you completely healed from her spell?" I asked, scanning his body to make sure.

"Only thanks to your power and my wolf," he said grimly. "Without it I would've been a goner. That Goddess packs a serious punch. It made the goat spell seem like a bloody tummy ache."

I nodded. I could feel his relief in my blood. I was relieved too. "Before we do this, I need to check on Rourke," I said. "He's healing, but he's too vulnerable. Then I will kill her personally. If for some reason we fail, I can't leave him"—*I won't leave him*—"at her mercy again."

Naomi's hand found my arm. "Go to him. I will start on Selene. I have waited years for my revenge and it starts now." Her face hardened as she turned to the boys. "We will take her head first." She glanced at me. "In the end we will need your power to kill her, no matter what we do here first."

My eyes met hers, flashing violet. "It won't take me long."

She nodded.

I ran to Rourke. He was still unconscious, but his chest had knit together more, which was a welcome sight. *Why isn't he awake?* My wolf growled and snapped her jaws. *We broke the spell and he was moving. He should be awake by now.*

Something was wrong.

"Wait!" I called over my shoulder. "He should've woken up by now. Something isn't right." Naomi met my stare across the room. She looked feral, her eyes a gleaming mercury in the pale candlelight. Whatever pain she endured once Eamon brought her here must have been immense. "I already crushed Selene's spell out of his body. Why isn't he awake?"

"I do not know," Naomi replied. "Search for another reason.

I will wait, but we have only a few minutes at most." Killing Selene before we knew what she'd done to Rourke could be dangerous. Most spells vanished once the maker was dead, but someone as powerful as Selene could find a way to do damage after her death. There was no question. She could have feasibly inserted something into his system only she could reverse and I wasn't willing to take that chance.

I crouched down, placing my fingers on his forearm. Electricity jumped between us and his arm twitched in response. I ran my hands up to his hair as I gathered power to me, pulling hard on my resources. Then I placed both my hands on his shoulders and threw my senses into his body, testing for another reason why he wasn't waking.

There it is! My wolf snapped her jaws.

It was barely detectable and it felt rough, like a prickly beard running along my mind. My head shot up quickly when I felt its ugly intent. "There's something vile here! But it's masked very well. It doesn't even feel like her signature. Whatever it is, I think it's preventing him from fully waking. I'm going to try and break it." Naomi stood up and reached for something in Tyler's outstretched hand.

"Be careful, Jess," Tyler said. "Her spells are tricky."

"We will wait to see if he wakes before we behead Selene," Naomi said. "But in the meantime, I will give her another reason to stay asleep." She crouched next to the Goddess, plunging another dart of Tally's into Selene's stomach. Selene's body gave a gigantic lurch, but she stayed immobile. "We will not take undue risks."

"Remind me not to get on your bad side," Danny muttered to Naomi, shaking his head. "I think that dart went all the way through and lodged in the rocks below."

"*Oui*," Naomi said. "And it did not give her the pain she

deserves, but it will have to do for now." She turned to me, urging, "Hurry. We must not let her wake."

There was no way I was arguing with Naomi. I worked fast. In one powerful thrust I shot my power into Rourke's body, the gold of my essence covering the spell I'd found. It floated along the lines in his body, coating it like glue, but these spell lines were curiously blue, not Selene's color at all. But they were definitely mingled with her essence. Tricky witch.

Once I coated the spell, I yanked my power back in a rush, pulling hard.

The spell snapped apart instantly, withering and evaporating like a flower dying on a vine.

Rourke shot awake instantly. "Jessica, Jessica," he cried, his hands grabbing on to my arms, sweet energy rushing through me. "You have to get out of here right now. You don't know what she's capable of now—"

"*Shh.*" I lowered my face to his, inhaling his rich scent. "I'm not leaving until you're fully healed, so you can forget that right now." His smell brought all the hairs on my body to a delicious peak. His body began to thrum with a current of power that hadn't been there a moment before. Whatever Selene had spelled him with had inhibited most of his power, but it was gleefully returning. "But first I need to take care of Selene." Before I could stand and go to Naomi, Rourke grabbed on to my face, pulling me down quickly, his lips hitting mine, hot and frantic. I didn't have time to register it until his tongue entered my mouth.

Emotion raced through me, the taste of him overpowering anything else in the room. I moaned into his lips, gripping his shoulders with both hands, pulling myself closer to him. He snarled into my mouth. Our bond rang through me, his body and soul pouring into mine. My arms and legs began to shake.

He broke away from me slowly and I stifled a cry. "Jessica," he said roughly. "Please tell me this is not a dream." His beautiful clear green eyes blazed as he ran his hands along my arms and face.

"It's me," I said. "I'm here and Selene is down, but only for a moment. I have to finish this before we can finally go home."

"No." He shook his head emphatically. "Listen to me: you have to ignore her and get out. Go now. There's no reasoning with her any longer." There was a time you could reason with her? "She's sold her soul. There's no stopping her. Nothing we can do can defeat her. You need to leave here as quickly as possible and I'll be right behind you." He angled his body upward, a grimace of pain on his face.

"We have to try." I rested my hands on his shoulders and tried to calm him. "I'm not leaving here unless I try. I refuse to look over my shoulder for her once we leave here. She will hound us to the death. She will never give up." I pressed him gently back to the ground, hovering over him with concern. "Naomi just hit her with another spell. If I can't kill her, we can at the very least incapacitate her for a very long time. I'm thinking fire might work if we disassemble her first."

"It won't work," he said urgently, his face intent, his hands closing tightly over my forearms. "Jessica, please, you have to listen to me." When he said my name it made my insides tingle. I pushed it out of my mind. I needed to stay focused. "She can't be killed or even be incapacitated for long. I've tried. Once I got here, I broke her spells and managed to hold her down until the demons came. They did something to her, and everything changed. She must've struck a deal, because her essence morphed. Once that happened, she was able to secure me easily. I want you to get out before she wakes. I will follow you as soon as I can."

"There's no way I'm leaving you," I said. "If she's as strong as you're saying, she'll be after us as soon as she heals. It won't matter where we run." I glanced at Selene's body, still inert. "If Tally's spell can knock her out, she's clearly not invincible. I'm betting we can do some damage."

Naomi murmured her agreement. "*Oui.* The only thing that can bring a demon down is a powerful witch. The spells of blood and earth are natural agents against each other. If this is true, what he is saying, and Selene's blood is now tainted with demon, this is likely the only reason she has been out this long. We've been lucky and nothing else."

"And that was the last bloody spell we had." Danny nodded toward the dart still lodged in her stomach. "If she's full of demon essence, once she slakes this bit off, it will be impossible to secure her for long."

I stood. "Then we take her apart now. There has to be a way." I walked over to Selene, laser focused. She would not win. "The demons want her soul as soon as they can get it, so there has to be a way for her to die on this plane or they never would've struck a bargain—as in, if she can't revive herself within minutes here they are free to pick her up." I didn't know much about demons, but I did know they collected on their debts immediately. A debt like Selene's had to be something to celebrate in the Underworld. It's not every day you landed a goddess. I glanced around to the group, my face hard. "Getting her a ticket to the Underworld will have to suffice. How long do you think she'll be bound there?" I asked Naomi.

"I think nothing short of a millennium," Naomi replied. "Selling a part of your soul is a steep payment."

"That sounds good to me," Tyler said as he grabbed a pickax off the wall. Who had a pickax handy, dangling on a wall?

A deranged goddess, that's who.

"Let's start with her hands," Danny said. "If she has no fingers, she can't shoot a spell. Right?" He looked around hopefully. His bare chest was massive in comparison to the tiny piece of fabric that covered him. He radiated strength, even though his brown hair was tousled, as usual, and this journey had clearly taken its toll on him.

Naomi stared at Danny, slightly openmouthed, but she averted her eyes quickly. Not before I noticed, however. "Um, *oui*, that might work. Let's start with her hands."

I bent over Selene's body. "Hand me a shovel instead."

Tyler went to retrieve the shovel, which hung next to the pickax, and brought it back. There was literally a plethora of torture devices lining the walls within easy reach. If the shovel tip didn't work for the job, we had other options.

"Jessica." Rourke's strong voice echoed around the cavern. "I beheaded Selene already since I've been here. This is not going to work. She slips back together like a ghost."

I glanced at Rourke, who stood, looking magnificent and almost fully healed. "You beheaded her here? Already?" I peered down at Selene. *Jesus.* If she could recover from a beheading that quickly we were in deep shit.

Rourke was naked from the waist up, but instead of a sheet he still had his jeans on. They were crusted in blood. "Of course I beheaded her," he growled as he paced forward. "And I took her heart out. She would never have been able to keep me had she not called the demons. She's never been as strong as I am. It required everything she had to keep me here, knowing you were in danger. She was losing, so she dialed up her new backup squad and spelled me with something different. It knocked me out until I heard your voice."

"That's what the blue lines were then," I said, contemplating. "Blue must be her demon essence." My eyes locked on him as he approached. My wolf growled, full of lust. I shook my head to clear her. I couldn't let anything distract me from my goal. "But I broke her demon spell in you, so maybe—"

He angled his head at me, his irises sparking. "You think you can break it in her," he finished.

"How would I do that?" I asked, glancing down at her body again. My only choice would be to throw my power in and hope it was enough. I looked up at him. "If it works, and I can break something inside of her, do you think it will be enough to send her to the Underworld?"

"I don't know," he said. "But it sounds like the best chance we've got, even though I don't like it." His voice held a growl. "But cutting her up will give us only a temporary fix, however satisfying it might be."

I turned to Naomi. "Where's your cross?" We were wasting time. "We can use it to null her while she's out and I can try to break the demon-bond or kill the essence inside her. Then we take her head off and hope it's enough to get her a ticket to the Underworld."

A dark look passed over Naomi's face. "Eamon took it from me as I tried to use it against Selene. I assume it is still in his possession. He's never understood its worth and thinks I am too partial to it, but I will kill him for the betrayal."

"He's over against the far end of the cavern." I nodded my head in that direction. I hated to break the news to her like this, but there was no good way. "I broke his neck before you were fully healed. I'm sorry, Naomi, but it needed to be done."

Naomi stood. "I am not sorry. He broke our kin-bond and he betrayed me in the worst way he could. This would have ensured his death at my hands. He chose his side and he lost." She flew off to find the cross.

I knelt down by Selene again. My brother and Danny came in

close, Rourke right behind me; his heat calmed me. It was good to feel it again. I didn't want to wait for Naomi, but I couldn't risk waking Selene without it. If I put my hands on her, there would be a reaction. It might be enough to trigger her to wake.

Naomi's voice echoed loudly a minute later. "Eamon is not here."

I jumped up. "What are you talking about? I killed him ten minutes ago." Had only ten minutes passed? It felt like a life-time ago.

She flew to the top of the dais, landing on the scattered debris. "He is not here."

"I broke his neck," I said, almost accusingly. "Severing the connection is enough for a wolf. He fell to the ground like he was dead."

"It's not always enough for a vampire." Naomi shook her head. "The spinal column must be separated fully from the body. Our bodies are already dead, while your body lives. You require communication to survive; we need no such thing. We can fuse it back together, but cannot live without a head. This information is not widely known, so it is not your fault, *Ma Reine*, but I must find him. There are tunnels here."

"Dammit all to hell." I realized I hadn't seen or heard from Ray in too long. My face dropped. "Naomi, he took Ray. He had to have taken him. He needed blood to heal."

Before she could answer, Selene gave a huge gasp and with one hand ripped the spell dart out of her body, her irises bright red. "Now you all will die."

Then she popped out of existence.

26

"Oh, my love, did you miss me?" Selene cackled from right behind Rourke, popping back into this plane again exactly like the winged devils had done. I wasn't familiar with how teleportation worked, but I knew it was extremely rare and usually connected with the Underworld. Something to do with having one foot in both worlds, because transferring your body mass like that was tricky.

I blinked once and Rourke and Selene were on the ground in front of me, locked in battle.

His body began to morph as I watched, golden fur sprouting along his powerful arms. "You will answer for your deeds," Rourke yelled, his voice full of malice. "Do you hear me? You will die a final death this time!" Blood poured from Selene's lips as she grinned up at him. He smashed his fist into her neck just as she dematerialized. Rourke stood, fuming. "She's going to be hard to catch," he snarled, "and all I want to do is crush the life out of her."

Now that we knew she could pop in and out, Selene was going to play with us like a kitten batting a ball.

Energy swirled around the cavern, bouncing off the walls. She was clearly enjoying her new lot in life as an Underworld whore. We all knew she couldn't die no matter what we did to her now, and I had a sinking feeling that her final encore had always been to blow the mountain up like she had threatened earlier. Even if she was lost to the explosion, she wouldn't die.

"We're going to have to surround her," I murmured to Rourke. "If we all come at her at the same time we might have a chance." Tyler and Danny had gone back-to-back, each of them on high alert. Tyler clutched the pickax once again. "I've beaten all her magic so far, so it won't hold me for long, if at all. If I can get her down without succumbing to her magic, I might be able to keep her in place long enough to do some damage."

"Jess," Tyler said. "Danny and I need to shift. There's no way we can do this without a wolf counterattack. You bring her down; we rip her up."

"Sounds good to me," I replied.

They both dropped immediately and began to change into their wolf forms. It wouldn't take them more than a minute.

"I can hear you," Selene snapped from above us in an alcove. "You think you can best me by cornering me? Think again." She twisted her wrist.

The spell hit me fully in the chest.

Her lines entered my body and left just as quickly, but the impact flung me backward. The only thing I registered before I hit the wall was Rourke's frustrated snarl.

Selene gave a wicked shriek and I watched in horror as she materialized right next to him. "Rourke! Look out!" I yelled as

I scrambled to stand. She touched a single glowing red finger to his torso and he spasmed once and crashed to the ground.

I had to get to her before she popped out of sight again.

This is all you. We sprang in a blur.

My wolf latched on to her neck and I snarled through the canines in my mouth, biting deeply into her, taking great joy in tearing her pristine flesh. She tried to pop away from me, her magic swirling around us, prodding my skin. I caught hold of it, my gold strands winding their way into her magic. I wove my power through her energy and cinched it tight like a noose. "How does it feel now?" I roared, releasing her neck, blood dripping down my chin.

"You are not stronger than I am," Selene spat, her mouth already moving; magic quivered at her fingertips. "I will always have my spells."

"No, you really won't." I smashed my fist into Selene's mouth. Her jaw cracked, stopping her spell in its tracks, blood racing down the side of her face. "You are not going to win this time. Your reign is over. Do you hear me?"

She spit blood out of her mouth, her jaw completely healed. "Is that so, mongrel?"

The room shook with power.

Sulfur began to seep into the cavern from every corner. I couldn't pinpoint exactly where it came from. My wolf howled, changing her focus from Selene to the new threat. I kept my hold firmly on Selene, my magic still keeping us intertwined. "You really did it, didn't you?" I sneered at her in disgust. "You sold your entire soul to the Underworld. Not just part of it. You were banking on me being stronger than you, that I was going to win, so you sold yourself to the Underworld for *help*." My hands slid up and clamped around her neck. "You're nothing but a fraud, Selene. You deserve to die and go straight to hell. Lucky for you, it's a very tangible place. I'm sure the Demon Lords have something special in store for you. It's a shame we won't be able to witness it."

Selene twisted in my hold, her face hateful. "I *win*, you wench. Don't you get it? The price of my soul makes me impossible to defeat. I made the deal of the millennium. Ultimate immortality. Nothing can best me now, so I can never truly die. The Underworld can't take me if I can't die, so they will never have me."

Incredible power enveloped me. It was dark and smelled like thick, rancid eggs. It pulled at me, tearing my skin. "What—" I was flung backward, like a giant hand had swiped me off my feet. My wolf snapped at the blackness that began to infiltrate our golden protection. I hit the wall and slid to the ground. "*No.*" I uttered the single word with all the power I had inside me and the blackness danced back. It came at me again. "I said, NO!" I interlaced the word with the color inside my mind, bonding my golden strands to my words.

The blackness shrank back and stayed away.

I stood.

Selene staggered back a step. "Impossible!" she screeched. "My power combined with the Underworld is no match for you. It can't be—" Rourke took hold of her from behind, grabbing her by the hair, and slammed her into the wall. She crumpled, momentarily stunned. The sulfur smell wavered.

"I'm glad to see you," I told Rourke, who had shaken off her spell this time on his own.

He growled menacingly. "Nothing is going to keep me from you again while there's breath still left in my body."

Shivers raced up my spine.

Selene moved, ruining the moment, and I paced toward her.

"Looks like your Underworld bargaining skills need a little work, Selene. You should've asked for more. Maybe a basilisk or a Demon Lord sidekick? Something more than immortality, which you already had. Do you really think the demons are that stupid? Do you honestly think they'd offer you something so great without a single hitch?" I stopped in front of her. "I'd like to introduce myself as the hitch in your well-designed plans."

"I'm not out of the running yet, mongrel." Selene stood. But before she could pop out of sight, I lunged. My magic intertwined with hers immediately.

We tumbled to the ground.

"You were out of the running before you even started," I whispered.

Selene snarled. Her body reverberated like a gong, and blackness enveloped me again. This time it shot into my nose and mouth.

I gagged.

"Looks like you just needed a bigger dose—" Selene broke my hold and flew away from me.

Rourke had her by the neck, snarling savagely. "You will not hurt what's mine again. Do you hear me?"

I grasped at my throat.

Get it out. My wolf tore into it. She pulled on our resources as adrenaline shot through us. The black wavered, but continued its assault. I rolled onto the ground, trying to breathe. I looked up and saw Tyler and Danny, in their wolf forms, standing by my side, each of them snarling. I turned over, raging at the blackness. "Get out of my *body*!" I yelled, my power shooting outward, electrifying the darkness in one single blaze of light. The black mass retreated like a smoke machine plugged into a vacuum. I coughed and stood up, catching my breath.

Selene twisted in Rourke's grasp and popped out of sight. That was getting old.

Tyler put his big muzzle in the air, scenting, and then took off to the right. The moment she materialized he had his teeth around her throat, bringing her easily to the ground. Danny charged after them, circling, waiting for an opportunity to get in the mix and snapping his jaws. I met Tyler's eyes for an instant before Selene reached up and took him by the neck. "Bye-bye, wolf boy."

Red lines engulfed him.

"No!" I ran hard, colliding with Tyler, knocking him out of the way with my body. Before Selene could stand, I fisted her shredded leather bustier with one hand and forced her back to the ground. Her neck was torn—Tyler's canines had bit deeply—but it was healing quickly.

She laughed up at me, trying in vain to dematerialize. "Can't you see you won't win? No matter what you do, I am stronger. I will keep defeating you until you are all on your knees, begging for your lives."

"That's not how this is going to work." I punched my other hand deeply into her chest cavity. She gasped, her body spasming, surprise lining her features. I was going for the kill. I just had no idea how I was going to do it. Her heart sounded like the best idea. There was no way I was doing another run around with her. One of us would win; I just hoped like hell it would be me.

"You little *bitch*," Selene shrieked, trying to get away. Magic twisted around us, black and gold, each fighting to conquer the other. I had to find a way to kill her immortality quickly. If I did that, she would belong to the Underworld. I believed her when she said she couldn't die—physically. But if one part of her died, it might be enough for them to come and retrieve her.

I held her down as she struggled, my hand closing around her heart. Everything inside of her bucked. Danny growled and barked, agitated as he paced around Tyler, who was in the process of changing back to human. He was no longer red.

"I think this is what you are looking for now, *Ma Reine*," Naomi called as she flung something into the air.

Before I could catch it, there was a tremendous roar and Rourke's fist shot out. Claiming the prize, he fell to his knees beside me. "Let me help you with that." He reared up and plunged Naomi's cross into Selene's body, right into the hollow of her neck.

Selene gurgled, still fighting. "Never...going...to win." Her body convulsed once and went completely still. All her power evaporated.

The room stilled completely as the sulfur smell leaked away.

"Jesus," I breathed, wiping the back of my free hand along my forehead to get rid of the sweat. "I guess that is what we needed." I didn't relax my other hand for an instant. Her heart beat around my fist, blood pouring from her wounds in earnest now that her powers were null.

She was still awake, but just barely. "Get that thing out of me," she moaned. "It will not kill me. Once I'm free, my powers will come back and I will finish you for good."

Rourke had her arms pinned down at her sides and Naomi hovered over us. "*Ma Reine*," she said. "You need to kill her now. Completely. We cannot keep the cross in her forever, and she is right: once we take it, she will heal within moments."

"Now that her powers are null I can feel something else in her body," I said. "There's a pulse of something alive in here." It was pushing her to heal, fighting off dying. I had to grasp hold of it and finish it for good. I glanced at Rourke, who was taking it all in with a frown. "Rourke, I need to take her immortality and try to shred it. I'm not sure what it will do to me, but if something happens, or if I look like I'm in some kind of a coma when I'm done, it's okay. Find my brother. He'll know how to wake me up."

"I don't like the sound of that," Rourke said. "Let's take her apart in pieces first and keep the cross in her there. If she doesn't have arms, she can't fish it out."

"*Non*," Naomi said. "Eventually the body will decompose and the cross will fall out. Once it's gone, I believe her body will begin to regenerate once again."

"If I don't try to kill what's inside of her," I added, "the demons won't come to get her. If I kill her essence, I think they will come to retrieve her. This feels right to me." My hand was still gruesomely stuck in her chest cavity, my magic testing her blood. My wolf paced, sensing all the magics, both hers and the new demon power. Both were null. The cross had done its job in full and it felt like a lucky break. Whoever had crafted it was a powerful supernatural in their own right. "Plus, I refuse to look over my shoulder every hundred years to see if she's back."

Selene's lips opened and there was a shallow cackle. "I will haunt you forever, make no mistake. My vengeance will preserve me." I had no doubt her revenge would be all consuming, but I had to hope the Underworld would put her under heavy guard and wouldn't risk losing their biggest catch.

Tyler snarled as he walked up to us, looking ragged but alive. He was naked as he bent to grab up a shredded pillow to cover himself. "I hope the demons hook you up to a whipping post for eternity, you sadist. No punishment they can mete out will be enough."

"The demons will have better uses for me, all of them involving my whip, I'm sure." Selene coughed. "I will be back for my revenge."

I met my brother's eyes as they sparked with emotion. "Jess," Tyler said. "Do what you have to do to get rid of her. That's my vote."

Rourke growled, but stayed silent.

Danny was still in his wolf form and I knew how Naomi would vote. I closed my eyes and focused inwardly. I'd made my decision.

Thin strings of gold poured out of me slowly. I directed them into Selene. Her body began to arch against the intrusion, her eyes rolling back in her head. *This isn't going to be easy*, I told my wolf. *But I know we're stronger.* I sent my power into her body in a constant stream. It built on itself, doubling the energy. Power swirled around us, leaking out of her, engulfing me. It sizzled in my veins. My body began to get physically hot as the intensity built.

For a single brief moment I felt completely alone.

My gold devoured Selene's entire body. In my mind I could see her immortality manifested in tiny red beacons. No surprise there. They bit at my energy, fighting my power. Underneath me, Selene bucked and moaned. I pushed back. *We're going to have to give her a blast of our power at the end, when everything is saturated.*

I wasn't sure when to do it, when it had covered her enough.

Selene made the decision for me.

Her body flexed beneath me and she began to fight back in earnest. Red sprang to life where it hadn't been a moment ago. Pressure built on its own. *This is it.* I threw more power at her. *Let's try to stay awake after this one*, I told my wolf. She didn't have time to agree with me.

I heard Rourke yell something, but I was lost to the fight.

Selene vibrated beneath me like a tuning fork. I held on. I tossed my head back, fairly sure I was screaming. I gave one last pull on my power. Once it was all concentrated, I yanked it back to me like a spring. Selene's immortal essence flexed once and began to break apart, shredding under the force of my power.

Selene's rage filled the cavern, finally getting through to my senses. "*No.* No!" she screamed, her back bowed to me. "I will not *die*!"

"Too late," I ground out of my rough vocal cords. I pulsed with energy as I gave one more internal squeeze. The remaining red exploded into nothing right as I squeezed her heart.

Selene's body went limp beneath me.

My eyes snapped open.

I fell forward, gasping for breath.

Rourke hovered behind me. Fur coated his arms as they wrapped around me, easing me back up. I leaned against the weight of his chest, exhausted. We both glanced down at Selene's immobile body. I spoke first. "Just to be sure, we should take her apart next. Leave the cross in. I just have to catch my breath."

"Anything," Rourke whispered into my ear. "I will do any goddamn thing you tell me to do. I thought I'd lost you for a second there. Your whole body glowed. I thought Selene was killing you with another spell. I tried to pull you back, but I couldn't move you. Not even an inch." He shook his head. "What happened?"

"I don't know," I said truthfully. "But in the future, if I look like I'm glowing, it's a safe bet not to mess with me." My body had already morphed back to normal. I was getting good at snapping back to my human form quickly. It was becoming second nature.

I took a deep breath and turned to face Rourke.

He grabbed on to my face, his eyes searching. "Are you sure you're okay?"

"Yes, but I'm exhausted."

His mouth covered mine deeply. I took him all in, my senses jumping for joy. I wanted to lick him, taste him, and feel him against me. My body burned for him. I pushed myself forward. He growled with pleasure, his blond stubble tickling my chin as he kissed me.

I wanted to lose myself in him forever, but I couldn't. I broke from him with supreme effort. "As much as I regret this, we have to get this over with."

Rourke let me go reluctantly. He knew what was needed and moved me over, immediately kneeling by Selene's head. "Do you want me to take it off? Her neck is damaged beyond repair, but her head is still attached."

"I don't know." Her chest was open, and her neck was shredded. She wasn't healing because the cross was still in her neck.

Rourke grabbed on to her head. "I'm not taking any chances. We take her head off and her heart out—whatever's left of it." But before he could do anything rocks began to shake from the walls. They rained down around us.

Instead of pulling Selene's head off, Rourke jumped up with a roar and came at me, grabbing me around the waist and pulling me backward against him.

"What is it?" I yelled.

Sulfur poured into the room, making us all gag.

"Something's coming," he said. "Let's go. The way Tyler came in is the back way. Head for the opening." He herded me along.

"Do you know what it is for sure?" With the scent of sulfur, we knew it was coming from the Underworld.

"Whatever it is, it's huge," he said grimly.

"Jess," Tyler said. "We're right behind you. Go, go."

Naomi gave a diminutive shriek as Danny wrapped his arm around her middle and picked her up. "You weren't moving fast enough." He'd changed back and was in his sheet once again. We all moved toward the opening. The only person who was missing was Ray. I had no idea what happened to him—if he had gotten out or if Eamon had indeed taken him.

The floor continued to shake, rocks tumbled, candles flickered, and the chandelier jumped. The power climbed quickly and it started to taste familiar. "Oh my God," I gasped. "This is the same signature from the forest."

An explosion ripped through the room, smashing Rourke and me into the wall, the others following, all of us tumbling into one another.

When the dust settled a single shape stood in front of us.

"Well, well, well. We finally meet." A voice laced with sarcasm floated through the room. "I've heard so very much about you."

27

"And yet I've heard nothing about you," I said as I picked myself off the ground as elegantly as I could manage. Rourke was already beside me, a low warning issuing from the back of his throat. I figured my best line of defense at the moment was to act like the sight of a Demon Lord in the flesh wasn't freaking me out completely. I wasn't sure I could pull it off, but it was worth a try. *Get a handle on the fear*, I told my wolf. *We don't want to emit any scent if we can help it.*

"Well, my reputation does precede me in certain *circles*," it said.

"I'm assuming you came to pick up your prize?"

"What? Are you referring to this?" It arched a well-manicured hand toward Selene's lifeless body like it was nothing. If imps were greasy and unkempt, Demon Lords were the exact opposite. This man-thing emitted enough power to choke all of us and was dressed like a news anchor in a perfectly tailored three-piece suit without a single fiber out of place. It must have been glamoured on him in some way. I'd always pictured demons wearing capes—*not* dressed to deliver the nightly news. What was most disturbing was its face. It was as precise as it was cruel, flawless and hawkish at the same time. Its hair arched away from its forehead in a poof that would be impossible to re-create, even on the Jersey Shore, no matter how much shellac. "Selene is not why I came. I came for you, of course."

"What do you mean you came for *me*?" I balked. So much for cool.

It took a step closer and the room erupted in growls. I glanced to the right. Both Tyler and Danny had their game faces on. "My sister is not up for adoption, Demon," my brother snarled. "You came to the wrong cave."

The demon stopped and opened its hands like it was going to give a sermon to a roomful of worshippers. "Let me correct myself. I came to assess your threat to my race and make an appropriate diagnosis. Once I make my judgment I will do what needs to be done. As always."

Rourke took a step forward, but before he could get a word out, I latched on to his forearm and stepped in front of him. He was not getting in the middle of this. I'd just gotten him back. "I am no threat to your race, I can assure you. I told your imp the same thing. I have no interest in demons, and that will never change."

"That's pleasant to hear, of course, but our oracle says otherwise. A female werewolf is no small thing, you see. The powers entrusted to you are unpredictable. They are said to *morph* as necessary and take on the attributes of those you fight, and because of this, you have been singled out as a threat to our race. I am here to erase that threat."

"How can I threaten your race if I have no interest in you? I haven't made a single move against you. Getting to the Underworld is no small thing, and you can believe me when I tell you I have no desire to visit."

"Ah, but you have. Made a move, that is." It put its fingers carefully in front in a mock bow. "Recently you have killed, not one, but two imps. They do count as ours, however distasteful. And please correct me if I'm wrong, but within the last day you have defeated a small army of our most precious pets, the *Camazotz*. Such a shame, as they are irreplaceable. Now, it seems, you have managed to kill a powerful goddess, who was also technically ours. The totality of that claim can be debated, of course, but once a soul is *entrusted* to us and we have distributed the agreed-upon power, we take full credit. Committing each of those crimes carries a debt of servitude in the Underworld, each indiscretion a different sentence. It seems, in just a very, very short time, you have amassed several centuries worth of debt to be meted out how we see fit."

"Several hundred years of hard labor in the Underworld for each crime? You've got to be joking." A giggle escaped my throat, because what else was I going to do but laugh? "And, just for the record, I didn't technically kill the second imp. When I brought him back to my father, he was alive. I only rang his bell a little. What my father chose to do with him after was none of my business." Why was I arguing stupid points? Because my brain was reeling. My wolf gnashed her teeth together and I had no better comebacks. This couldn't be right. I had nothing to do with demons. "In my world, if your imp buddies come after me, I have full rights to defend myself. It says so under *my* Pack Laws. I can't be in violation of an Underworld law for defending Pack Law. That goes against any kind of supernatural code and wouldn't hold up in any court.

I've heard you guys are big on courts." The rumors were always that demons operated in a very regimented world, by their own regimented rules.

"My *buddies*, as you refer to them," it said, "were not authorized to attack. It's my understanding that you—what's the human word?—*tailed* an imp who was minding his own business, and once confronted, that imp defended *himself* against you."

"Minding his own business?" My hands fisted. "You mean in the process of *raping* a sixteen-year-old girl? Endangering human lives can't be an acceptable Underworld practice. He had called attention to himself and had served jail time in a human prison. Those things have to count as some kind of an offense in your world."

The demon's mouth curved in distaste. "What an imp chooses to do on this plane is up to him. He had broken none of our laws." Its hand flipped upward. It was shiny and way too clean. "You were the pursuer"—the demon flipped the other one so they were both out—"therefore you must pay."

"Damn right I was the pursuer," I said as I took a step forward without realizing it. "And I would pursue again and again to stop *any* imp from harming another innocent."

"My point exactly." Its eyes narrowed, its meticulous mouth curving up on one side in a half grin. It was like an extremely refined Hannibal Lecter. There was something so creepy and unnatural about this demon. Chills raced along my spine. I'd just inadvertently put myself right in its snare. "You are a nuisance and you will answer for your crimes before we allow you to commit any others against us."

"I'm not going to answer for anything," I growled. "But if it gets you off my back, I will vow to you that I have no beef with the Underworld. My words should ring true enough to you."

"Your vows are not valid to us."

"Why not?"

"There are too many loopholes with the spoken word and it is too late for that anyway." It turned from us, clasping its hands behind its back, as it stalked away. "You have already violated our laws. You will pay for your crimes first, and then we will craft something that will bind you to your word, but it will take time to hone it to perfection, of course."

"I'm not paying for my crimes because I committed none."

Rourke, Tyler, and Danny were all a hairsbreadth away from dropping and changing. I had to make sure that didn't happen. If they attacked we would go to war with this Demon Lord, and I didn't like those odds.

"Are you challenging my authority? The Crown of Astaroth is mine, you see." It looked at me curiously. "Don't you know who I *am*?"

"Um." I paused. I was a twenty-six-year-old newborn were-wolf. I had no idea who this demon was. I'd just heard of the Crown of Astaroth for the first time from the imp. I had zero idea what it meant. "I don't know who you are and, to tell you the truth, I don't really care. I know you won't tell me your real name, because giving it to me would be too risky—even though I don't know how to summon anything. My disinter-est alone should prove I have no desire in your crown or your throne. Keep your imps and soul-selling goddesses on a tighter leash, and we shouldn't have any more problems in the future."

"That's not how this works." It turned back to face us. "I apologize for any miscommunication. Crimes were committed and payment is due. We do not barter." Before it could mask it, the demon's eyes blinked and its pupils flashed serpentine. The irises went completely oval. In the next blink they were back to normal, which was a true, solid black.

"I told you, I'm not going anywhere," I stated again,

throwing power into my words. I could use all the help I could get. "According to my Pack Laws, I perpetrated no crime. Supernatural Sect laws will prove my innocence, and I know you have to follow the rules on this plane to some extent, or you'd already have swept me away. You can't take me without my permission, right? I have to agree to something. Isn't that how it works? Did you really think I'd agree to go with you willingly?"

"I will not debate my laws with you." Its voice shook the cavern and sulfur permeated the air so quickly I coughed into the back of my hand. "I am a Demon Lord, a Prince of Thrones, the Lord Treasurer of *Hell*. I am not some low-level imp! If I say you are in offense of our laws, that is enough." It pointed its manicured hand at the ground and rocks jumped. "You *will* be tried for your crimes in the Underworld and you *will* be found guilty."

"*No.*" I threw as much power into the word as I could and I felt my power press up against the demon's energy. "That's not what's going to happen here. What's going to happen is you're going to go back to where you came from and be thankful I want nothing more to do with your race."

Its eyes flipped to full serpent and it made no move to correct them. "I can carry you to the Underworld without your consent. I do not need your permission. You have a court date with the High Court of Mephistopheles. It has already been written in the Book. It is a mandatory appointment. If you do not show up, you will die."

"You can't bind me without my consent."

"Your own blood has made the binding already."

I gasped. "What?"

"You left your blood on the imp. You shouldn't be so careless. In the future, I would advise against it."

"That's impossible," Rourke interjected for the first time. "I don't know a lot about your race, but I know words have power. She has to agree, verbally, to what you are saying. You can't sweep her off to the Underworld without verbal consent. A deal has to be brokered between the two of you."

"Not correct." It waved its finger at us, looking like a possessed anchorman with its snakelike eyes. It was a creature with very little humanness. This demon couldn't possibly function in our world without being noticed even though it was doing its best to glamour itself into what it thought was a proper human form. "When crimes are committed, the magic shifts. Our world has branded her a criminal. We have her blood and her full name. That is enough to place her in our Book. Once it is written there, her future is sealed."

I had to think fast. I wasn't a criminal and power was power. If this Demon Lord wanted to take me, and what it was saying was true, it could've already done so. Why hadn't it just whooshed me away? *Why is it sitting here debating me? Something is up.* I cleared my throat. "If I'm in your powerful Book, why didn't I just instantly materialize to your plane?" I paused. "It's because my court date isn't today. And you can't take me against my will ahead of time unless I agree to go with you," I said. "The only way you can is if you manage to trick me into agreeing, which is what demons live for."

Its façade glimmered for a second. Behind the human mask was more ugliness. Sharp, bony features shadowed by an exaggerated brow. I was pissing it off.

It energized me. "I'm right! You can't, can you?" I said. "You were allowed to cross over to get Selene and nothing more. Finding me still here was a bonus, and now you're trying to trick me into believing I will die if I don't go to your court. Well, it's not going happen. Even though I'm new, I wasn't born without a brain."

Its eyes flicked. *Did it just blink a clear eyelid?* "I will see that you pay for your indiscretions. If you had come with me of your own volition, things might have been easier for you." Its perfectly white teeth snapped tightly. "I will personally see that you suffer." Its mouth opened again, and instead of glamoured white, there was a row of sharp yellowed stubs. The Demon Lord was losing it fast. "You have earned an eternity of pain and agony, the likes of which you have never witnessed."

"That sounds lovely," I replied. "But for right now, I need to recover from a hard day of killing a goddess. So why don't you run along. And don't forget to take her with you. I'm sure the two of you can swap plans about my imminent demise over noon tea, but honestly, I'm not interested in hearing about it anymore."

The walls shook so hard, I thought the mountain was going to tumble down on top of our heads. Rocks and stones flew around the room as suffocating power shoved us all to our knees. The sulfur was so strong I wanted to rip my nose off my face so I could breathe again. I now knew why Rourke had used sulfur to cover our smell in the creek before. With the cloistering smell of rotten eggs in my nostrils, I couldn't even begin to scent anything else. It burned all the way down my esophagus.

The demon's voice boomed around the enclosed space, but we couldn't see him anymore. "You will answer for your crimes, *Jessica Ann McClain*. I look forward to our reunion."

"Um, can you give me a time frame for that?" I coughed, gagging on the putrescence. My wolf forced power into my vocal cords, trying to channel pure air into our lungs, and gold immediately wound through them like a protective netting. "I'd like to get it on the calendar. I've got a date with a Vampire Queen soon, so it will have to be sometime after that." A few days to them could mean months or years to us, if my limited understanding of the Underworld was correct. I'd bet money Aunt Tally knew the rules. I'd have to set up a meeting once we arrived home.

And the information wouldn't come cheap.

"Sooner than you think" was all it said before a ring of power echoed in the room.

Then everything fell blessedly quiet. The sulfur smell started to diffuse and we could all breathe again.

"So that's what a Demon Lord looks like up close. I thought they'd be taller." Danny coughed as he stood up, his sheet hanging at a precarious angle. His hair was disheveled, but he looked great, because he was *alive*. We were all alive.

"Selene's gone," my brother said, directing our attention to where she had just been. "She vanished with the demon."

I glanced over. The Demon Lord had indeed taken her, which was the real reason why he'd come. Likely a goddess warranted a Lord to pick her up. "She won't stay dead in the Underworld, but her new normal will be ugly. I hope we never meet up with her again."

"You're not going there if I can help it," Rourke growled, warm hands encircling me. "I know some about the Underworld, but we'll have to learn more. I believe they have to serve you papers of some kind. The Demon Sect is carefully controlled by the Coalition. You can see what happens when they're in this plane. It's an explosion of power." Rourke pulled me close. His touch electrified me. *Is that always going to happen?* I asked my wolf. She gave a happy bark. I licked my lips.

There were just a few more things we needed to do and we could leave this wretched cave forever. "Where's Ray?" I asked Naomi. She had retrieved the cross, which meant she'd found Eamon. I didn't really want to know the answer, but it was time.

Naomi walked over to the spot where Selene had just been. She bent over and picked up something by its edges, surprise on her features as she turned toward us. "The cross must not be able to travel to the Underworld or it would be gone." She placed it into her pocket. Then she turned to face me. "I did not see your human. I encountered Eamon coming back in one of the tunnels." Her voice was hard. "He did not survive our reunion."

I wasn't sad to hear that Eamon had found his end, but I was sad to know his sister had to be the one to mete it out. There was no way that had been any fun. I would never be able to kill Tyler. "Did he say anything about Ray?"

She shook her head. "He had no time to ... speak."

"Then there's a chance Ray might be alive." I know my face held hope, even though my heart didn't believe it. "Do you think Eamon drank him dry?"

Naomi bowed her head. "There is very little chance the human survived their encounter. Eamon was not in his right mind. It would've been ... a brutal feeding."

"I have to find him," I said. "Which way was the tunnel?" Sulfur still clung to the air, making it impossible for me to scent anything.

She pointed back behind the dais. "There is a small opening in the corner. Follow the tunnel for a few meters. You should be able to scent him there."

I looked at the group. Danny lowered his gaze and Tyler set himself onto an old wooden chair that had somehow survived the carnage of the room. I took a step forward and Rourke made a move to follow me. "No," I said, reaching back to place my hand on his warm chest. All I wanted to do was crawl into his arms. But that would have to wait. "I just need to say goodbye. He was a thorn in my side, but he was a decent guy in the end, however misguided."

I crossed the room and entered the tunnel.

It was no more than a crack in the wall at the beginning, easily missed from the wrong direction. I stepped over Eamon's bones at the entry point. The only thing left was a skeleton wrapped in his clothes. The bones were old and rotted looking. Vampires must degenerate to their actual age, because those bones looked five hundred years old.

"Ray?" I called. I knew he wouldn't answer, but it made me feel good to think he might. I moved through the tunnel slowly. As I walked, it opened up. There were boulders jutting out from each side, closing the circumference considerably in places and making it more like a maze than a tunnel. As I paced farther in, I began to scent blood. The sulfur smell was less concentrated in here, and my nose was clearing.

It was Ray's blood.

There was no mistaking it. I came along the edge of a shallow boulder and closed my eyes. He was behind it. His scent was all over the place. I didn't really want to see. He was human, and therefore his weakness had always been a liability. This was the probable outcome of the journey. I'd known it going in— not that he would be eaten by a vampire, but that his chances of surviving this were slim to none. I had no idea how he'd found his way in with Tyler and Danny. My best guess was that Naomi must have inadvertently dropped him by a backdoor entrance and they had met up in the maze of tunnels. This mountain clearly had many.

If he'd stayed on top of the mountain like we'd instructed him to, he'd be alive right now, complaining about how long it had taken us to get back. But, in the end, he'd done his best to help me. "Ray, can you hear me?" I called. There was no answer. Of course.

I stepped slowly around the boulder.

His broken body lay on the ground. His neck had been ripped open in several places, savaged and mutilated. Even his hands were bloody and torn. He'd tried to fight. Eamon's persuasion, a vampire's automatic defense, must not have worked. I didn't doubt it, because Eamon had become unhinged in the end. His love for a goddess who had tortured him had been his undoing.

But persuasion had never worked on Ray as long as he'd lived, and if Eamon had used it, Ray would've hated every minute of it. I grinned, enjoying the fact that it must've pissed Eamon off as this human fought for his life.

I drew closer and knelt. "Oh, Ray," I said on a small breath as I crouched down by his side. "I'm so sorry it had to end like this. If you can believe it, I was actually beginning to like you." I placed my hands carefully on his broken body and cocked my head. His heart had just given one single, strangled beat. "What are you doing? Trying to survive at all odds?" I smiled. "You are one stubborn mother. I'll give you that." I lowered my head to his sternum. There wasn't another beat for several long seconds. I lifted my head. "Ray, I can't fix this." I swallowed, angling my face up toward the ceiling in frustration, trying to clear the ball in my throat. "Even if you're holding on as hard as you can, I can't help you." I forced myself to look down at him again. He was ravaged beyond repair, the wounds deep and deadly. "You're human, and this kind of damage can't be fixed even by the most skilled doctor in the world, even one of our own. There is nothing I can do. I'm so sorry. I really am."

"I can fix it," a voice said behind me. "If you'll allow it, *Ma Reine*."

28

"What the—" Tyler slammed on the brakes. The ridiculous canary-yellow Humvee skidded to a stop right in front of my office building, tires jacked halfway up the curb, rocking us all on our seats.

It was three a.m.

Every light in my office building was ablaze.

My head shot off Rourke's lap, his growl of displeasure reverberating around the truck. I squinted out the window, rubbing my eyes. "Damn, what's going on? Did anyone call us?"

We'd left Selene's lair, tired and bedraggled, without Naomi or Ray. I had no idea if Ray would survive the transformation into a vamp or not, but there was nothing more I could do. We'd been in the truck for eighteen hours straight, stopping only for gas and a shower at a local YMCA at my insistence.

"My phone is dead," Danny said. "I didn't remember to pack the bloody charger."

I sat up straighter while Tyler evened out the beast. I reached for my cell phone in my backpack. I'd spoken briefly with my father on the sat phone once we'd emerged from the mountain, and told him we were on our way home. "I don't have any messages and nobody's called since I talked to Dad."

"This looks like it happened recently," Tyler said as he shut off the engine. "Likely no one knows what's happening yet. It's the middle of the night. I'm going to look around. Stay here." I was tired enough to let him figure it out.

"There are no other visual disturbances," Danny said, scanning the building. "Does Nick usually work this late?"

"No," I said. "Something's definitely happening. Every light is on. In the entire building. To do that, someone had to access the main housing. Or they spelled the entire thing. Looks like they were trying to find something. Or someone." Likely me— who was I kidding?

Rourke opened the door. "I'll go too." He followed my brother, who had gotten out already. He leaned over to kiss me first, lingering for a long moment.

"Bloody hell, do we have to stand witness to every single kiss?" Danny grumbled. "I'm surprised your lips haven't melded together yet with all that snogging."

I broke first, chuckling.

Rourke's eyes seared me, sparking emerald. He gave me a wicked grin before slamming the door. I was starved for him. As in, if-I-didn't-get-him-soon-I-might-die kind of starved. But we hadn't had two seconds of freedom since we'd all trudged out of the mountains. By the look in Rourke's eyes, if we didn't find some privacy soon things were going to happen whether anyone liked it or not. My wolf licked her lips. *We are ladies; we can wait.* She growled. In all honesty, I was with Jezebel on this one. My wolf wasn't the only one who wasn't going to care if anyone was around.

"Danny, if you'd had a chance, you would've ridden horizontal on top of the coolers in the back with Naomi. Don't even pretend you wouldn't have. I saw all the flirting going on. You don't offer to save a woman's life if you're not interested." Wolves had very little modesty when it came to sexuality. They liked sex. End of story.

"Damn right I would've, but that's not the blasted point." His tone held a note of remorse. A vamp and a wolf would be a hard pairing, even if their personalities seemed well suited for each other. "I still don't want to witness all your lovemaking. I'm of a delicate nature, and seeing it makes me cranky."

I chuckled as I turned back to the window and focused on Rourke, watching him move around my building wearing Tyler's T-shirt, which was stretched to a comical degree over his huge body. He moved gracefully, like a predator. My wolf growled. *Yes, we get to taste him soon.* "We're going to see Naomi soon, you know," I said, glancing at Danny. "Maybe you can ask her on a date."

Danny let out a strangled sound before he answered. "Yes, I just might do that."

I peered at him, curious about his reaction, but he had turned away from me.

We'd arranged to meet Naomi at Rourke's cabin in the Ozarks in a week's time, it being the only secluded place to rendezvous that we could come up with on short notice. If Ray survived the transition, Naomi said he would need space away from any humans. It might be risky to return there, but it's where they least expected us to be, so it was a unanimous decision.

I leaned forward in my seat. "Look, someone just walked into my office." My office was situated on the corner nearest to where we were parked. The figure started rummaging through my desk. "Hey! What is she doing?" I peered closer. "At least I think that's a woman." I edged up to the window. "Seems too delicate for a guy, right? Could be a kid." It was hard to tell because the figure was short, no more than five feet tall, and had a black skullcap pulled down low over their face. "There's Nick!" Before I knew it, I'd opened the door and shot out of the truck so fast I couldn't hear any protests. The brief thought skittered through my brain that I really shouldn't be racing through the night toward an obvious problem not knowing who or what this threat was, but my body didn't seem to care. That was my best friend in there. My wolf growled in agreement, urging me on.

I skidded to a stop just outside the building door, an arm catching me around the middle before I bounded inside. "Jess," Rourke purred into my ears. "Taking it a tiny bit slower might be a good idea. Wouldn't hurt to use a little more caution." I turned around in his arms. He was grinning and his scent washed over me for the millionth time. My wolf yipped in delight.

"Someone's in my office with Nick and we need to get in there," I argued, facing him. "Whoever's in there is having a party with my files. There can't be that much danger if Nick's up walking around and not tied up in the back room."

"Whoever's in there with him is extremely powerful. I smell witch and a very strong one at that."

"Witch?" I inhaled, forcing air over my tongue. It prickled with the residual power left in the air from a recent spell, likely the one that had opened all the locks and blasted on all the lights. I also scented heavy rosemary and herbs, similar to Marcy's signature, but not exact. I tilted my head up at him, since he was almost a foot taller than I was. "I think we might have a problem. Nothing feels very dangerous to me. I taste the power, but it doesn't seem to register. I feel no urgency and very little fear." My wolf yawned to accentuate the point. "I'm sure the witch in there is extremely powerful, but it's not sparking my warning bells."

Rourke growled. "It doesn't matter if you don't feel a threat. You still can't take risks that could get you killed. I rarely feel any real threat from any supe, but you learn to be cautious all the time no matter what. They can still be tricky."

Tyler and Danny rushed up behind us. "What's going on?" Tyler asked. "There's a big signature out here."

"I smell a witch," Danny said, turning in a circle. "And it smells a bit familiar."

"It smells like Marcy," I said grimly. "And that can mean only one thing."

"There's a blood relation inside," Rourke said, releasing his arm reluctantly from around my waist.

"I think that means something's happened to Marcy," I said. "I'm starting to get a very bad feeling. We need to get in there." I started to pull open the door.

Three fierce growls rent the air.

"I'm going first," Tyler said, grabbing the door and edging in front of me. "If this is a trap or we get cut off, head to the Safe House. We rendezvous there. Clear?"

"Clear," I said. I wasn't going to argue. "I'm right behind you."

In a line, with Rourke so close he was like a second skin, we all crept quietly into the building hallway and to our front door. Hannon & Michaels was painted on the front in block letters. The firm had been started under my alias, Molly Hannon, and had run successfully for the last five years.

"This is a bit ridiculous," Danny stage-whispered from the end of the line. "If there's a powerful witch inside, she's spelled everything and knows we're here, likely from the moment we drove up. We're acting like criminals in a bad police drama."

He was right. "That's true," I said. "But we don't want to go balls out and piss off whoever's in there either. Nick is with them. We have to act like we respect the power."

Tyler reached for the door handle, but the door sprang open on its own.

So much for respecting the power.

"Where is my *niece*?" A commanding voice rang out.

Standing with her hands on her hips in front of Marcy's desk was the tiniest woman I'd ever seen. She appeared to be in direct odds with everything Marcy was—where Marcy was tall, curvy, with gorgeous long red hair, this woman was short, had the body of a twelve-year-old boy, and the hair spilling out of her black knit cap, complete with an embroidered skull and crossbones, was white as snow.

Aunt Tally.

Tallulah Talbot, the undisputed supernatural heavy in this city, possibly in the country, stood with her hands on her hips, looking very put out. Her power was legendary and she was likely the only reason we'd slowed Selene down for those few brief moments.

I'd never come face-to-face with her until now.

I stepped forward cautiously. This woman was clearly pissed, and if something had happened to Marcy, I was going to hurt someone. "Hello. I'm Jessica McClain. This is my office and Marcy is my secretary."

"I know who you are." She gave me a dismissive look. "Do you honestly think I'd allow my niece to work here if I weren't well aware of the situation?"

"Um, I guess not." Had I ever been under the radar? "Why are you here?"

"My niece is missing; that's why I'm here."

"What do you mean missing?" I asked as I took a step farther into the room. On inspection, Tally's face was surprisingly young. If it weren't for the white hair and her small, frail stature, she would've looked somewhere in her late thirties. But with all the other accompaniments she looked late forties, early fifties.

Her eyes were a striking hazel, just like Marcy's, but it was truly all they had in common.

"Jess," Nick yelled as he came around the corner. "I thought I was hearing things."

"Nick!" I ran over and gave him a big hug. He picked me up and squeezed me back. "Why didn't you call me?" I asked as he put me at arm's length.

"Well, first, I didn't think you'd be back. But honestly, I would've called once I had more information." He smiled. "I just got the news that Marcy was gone an hour ago. I came here, at her request, but she was...er...already inside the building."

"My niece was taken from here this evening, against her will," Tally said. "At approximately seven p.m."

"How do you know for sure?" I looked around, but there was no sign of a struggle. I took a breath in, but didn't scent anything in the air, except for Tally. Massive amounts of powerful witch filled my senses. I turned to Nick. "Do you know what happened?"

He shook his head. "I'm just as confused as you. I got a call from"—he gestured to the small but commanding woman with her hands on her hips, not knowing how to address her—"about an hour ago. The last time I talked to Marcy, everything was fine. She was packing up to leave for the day."

"She was not fine," Tally said with authority. "She was worried.

She called me from here. That's the last time I heard from her. She had laced the perimeter of this building with a detection spell and it was going off. She thought it was something big, but she didn't know what it was. I ordered her to leave immediately and go home. She called me an hour later and told me everything was fine, she was sleepy, and was going to turn in for the night."

"That sounds normal."

"It wasn't normal! She called me from a strange number, and *The Impossible Date* is on tonight and she'd rather lose a spell finger than miss it. So I went to her house."

"She wasn't home."

"Damn right she wasn't home. So I came here. I knew immediately who had her. Their signature is all over this place like neon lights in a pig barn."

I glanced around the room and took in another breath. Nothing. "Who has her?"

"The sorcerers."

"Why would the sorcerers want Marcy?"

"Are you really that daft?" Tally strode over to me. Magic flowed around her, sizzling the air. "They want you, of course. They took my niece because you weren't available. Likely to extract information, but if we're lucky there's still time to ransom her back."

I looked down at this woman. She didn't have to prove anything—she just was. She was the opposite of Selene in every way. "I'd gladly trade myself for Marcy, but how do we know they won't kill her anyway once we arrange a swap? What we need to do is break her out before they see us coming."

Tally cocked her head, examining me, taking in my ragged appearance and my big talk. "You think you can defeat the entire Sect of Sorcerers on your own? With your ragtag crew"— she gazed over my shoulder—"and all your powerful combat spells?" She gestured at the boys. "These aren't games for children. This is big. The High Council of Sorcerers is heavily guarded and you can't just waltz in undetected." Her voice ended on an edge and things in the room vibrated with energy. I glanced down at her fingertips and they were sparking, manifesting physically, just like Selene's had. Tally's signature was purple.

"No, but you could," I said.

Surprise flashed over her features. "No. Even I couldn't walk in under the radar. My radar is too big. What I could do is blow the place up—and likely my niece in the process—but that's only if I could find it. These are wizards, not bunny rabbits. They are highly skilled and dangerous. I can break their wards, but that doesn't get me anywhere, because they would be waiting for me with more. They wouldn't just kidnap my niece willy-nilly. They know what I can do. This is a well-thought-out attack, and they've likely taken her to a place we won't be able to find in time. Only a ransom will work without killing everyone in the process."

"You might not be able to find them, but we can." I walked toward the door. "Our noses are perfectly suited for tracking."

"That's big talk coming from a newborn wolf." Tally took a step toward me and power crackled in the air. Rourke growled behind me. "I don't care if you're the only female born to your race, it doesn't mean you can automatically defeat an army of Sorcerers with no training."

"No, but together we can."

Her eyes narrowed. "What are you proposing?"

"We pick up her scent, find where they've taken her, and get her back."

"And what about the wolf who already went after her?" Tally said. "If it was that easy, he would have her back already."

"Huh?" I wasn't expecting that. "What wolf? What are you talking about?" I took a quick breath in to see if I could smell anything, but under Tally's large signature, my entire office smelled like a wolf den. The entire Pack had been here last week. Wolf scent lingered all over. How did Tally know who'd gone after her?

"He won't succeed, by the way, but he might have a lead," she said begrudgingly. "If you can get ahold of him, we might have a place to start."

"I'm sorry, but I still don't know who you're talking about exactly."

She reached out to grab my arm and three sets of snarls rent the air along with a very polite, "Ms. Tally, I'm sure we can work this all out. There's no need to get hostile."

She ignored every single snarl and addressed them all with a glare. "I'm not abducting her, you fools. I'm taking her outside. With your superior scent detection—things wolves love to brag about—are you all telling me that you missed the most important piece of this so far?"

She tugged me by the shirtsleeve out of the office. Everyone trailed after her. She was a remarkably strong woman for such a tiny person. I had no idea how old she was, and witches aged differently than shifters, but I was thinking *old*.

She yanked open the door to the parking lot, the one we'd all just tiptoed through, and marched us directly across the asphalt, coming to a stop by a large patch of bushes.

I walked a few paces closer, my fingers reaching out to touch the green leaves. I took a big breath in and exhaled, pulling the night air over my tongue. My eyebrows shot up into my hairline and I turned around, meeting a few more surprised faces. We'd all scented the same thing.

"James."

The End of Book Two.

The story continues in book three of
The Jessica McClain Series:

Cold Blooded

Acknowledgments

To my husband, Bill. You are amazing. There's no way I could embark on this journey without you. You've supported me at every turn, you pick up the slack at home with no complaint, and you keep me laughing. I love you.

To my kids, Paige, Nat, and Jane. Thanks for putting up with cheese and crackers for dinner and being patient with my deadlines. You guys are amazing. Someday you'll get to read my books. I promise.

To my agent, Nicole Resciniti. You are beyond wonderful. You cheer me on, put up with my stress, and believe in me like no other. You're so talented at what you do and have such a great heart. Thank you for all you do.

To Amanda Bonilla for keeping me sane all the time and without question. You are such a bright light on this journey and I'm so very thankful to have you in my life.

To my awesome early readers, as always, DeLane Corbin and Kathy Faircloth, for all your cheerleading, e-mails, notes, tweets, and support. I love you guys!

To my author pals at Magic & Mayhem, Shawntelle Madison, Sandy Williams, and Nadia Lee for including me in the fold. So happy to have joined the ranks.

To Cindi, for always being there. Without your awesomeness, the world would be a bleak place. To Mira Lyn Kelly and

Carolyn Crane for being my Minnesota rocks. Every time we get together and talk writing, I'm happy.

To Molly Winkels, for your unfaltering enthusiasm and support. I have the best family in the world.

To my agency mates Jules, Amanda, Lea, Melissa, Jen, Marianne, Marisa, Cecy, and everyone else at the Seymour Agency, for all their awesome shoulders, advice, help, and laughter. You guys rock.

To my editor, Devi, and the entire crew at Orbit—Tim, Anna, Susan, Lauren, Laura, Alex, and Ellen—for being so wonderful. I'm excited to write every day because of all of you. Thanks for making my dreams come true. To my awesome copy editor, Penina Lopez, for correcting all my "further"s and "farther"s and for help in making this manuscript the best it can be.

To all my new fans! It's been such a fun journey so far. I hope you enjoyed the book. To all the reviewers who have supported me. I'm blown away. Thank you for your willingness to spread the word and for giving an honest review.

And to my parents, to whom this book is dedicated. Your enthusiasm for my writing knows no bounds. You give your love freely and often. I'm beyond lucky to have you.

extras

orbit

www.orbitbooks.net

about the author

A Minnesota girl born and bred, **Amanda Carlson** graduated from the University of Minnesota with a double major in speech and hearing science and child development. After enjoying her time as a sign language interpreter, she decided to stay at home and write in earnest after her second child was born. She loves playing Scrabble, tropical beaches, and shopping trips to Ikea. She lives in Minneapolis with her husband and three kids. To find out more about the author, visit www.amandacarlson.com or on Twitter @AmandaCCarlson.

Find out more about Amanda Carlson and other Orbit authors by registering for the free monthly newsletter at www.orbitbooks.net

if you enjoyed
HOT BLOODED

look out for

THE SHAMBLING GUIDE TO NEW YORK CITY

by

Mur Lafferty

CHAPTER ONE

The bookstore was sandwiched between a dry cleaner's and a shifty-looking accounting office. Mannegishi's Tricks wasn't in the guidebook, but Zoë Norris knew enough about guidebooks to know they often missed the best places.

This clearly was not one of those places.

The store was, to put it bluntly, filthy. It reminded Zoë of an abandoned mechanic's garage, with grime and grease coating the walls and bookshelves. She pulled her arms in to avoid brushing against anything. Long strips of paint dotted with mold peeled away from the walls as if they could no longer stand to adhere to such filth. Zoë couldn't blame them. She felt a bizarre desire to wave to them as they bobbed lazily to herald her passing. Her shoes stuck slightly to the floor, making her trek through the store louder than she would have liked.

She always enjoyed looking at cities—even her hometown—through the eyes of a tourist. She owned guidebooks of every city she had visited and used them extensively. It made her usual urban exploration feel more thorough.

It also allowed her to look at the competition, or it had when she'd worked in travel book publishing.

The store didn't win her over with its stock, either. She'd never heard of most of the books; they had titles like *How to Make Love, Marry, Devour, and Inherit in Eight Weeks* in the Romance section and *When Your Hound from Hell Outgrows His House—and Yours* in the Pets section.

She picked the one about hounds and opened it to Chapter Four: "The Augean Stables: How to Pooper-Scoop Dung That Could Drown a Terrier." She frowned. *So, they're really assuming your dog gets bigger than a house? It's not tongue-in-cheek? If this is humor, it's failing.* Despite the humorous title, the front cover had a frightening drawing of a hulking white beast with red eyes. The cover was growing uncomfortably warm, and the leather had a sticky, alien feeling, not like cow or even snake leather. She switched the book to her left hand and wiped her right on her beige sweater. She immediately regretted it.

"One sweater ruined," she muttered, looking at the grainy black smear. "What *is* this stuff?"

The cashier's desk faced the door from the back of the store, and was staffed by an unsmiling teen girl in a dirty gray sundress. She had olive skin and big round eyes, and her head had the fuzz of the somewhat-recently shaved. Piercings dotted her face at her nose, eyebrow, lip, and cheek, and all the way up her ears. Despite her slouchy body language, she watched Zoë with a bright, sharp gaze that looked almost hungry.

Beside the desk was a bulletin board, blocked by a pudgy man hanging a flyer. He wore a T-shirt and jeans and looked to be in his mid-thirties. He looked completely out of place in this store; that is, he was clean.

"Can I help you?" the girl asked as Zoë approached the counter.

"Uh, you have a very interesting shop here," Zoë said, smiling. She put the hound book on the counter and tried not to grimace as it stuck to her hand briefly. "How much is this one?"

The clerk didn't return her smile. "We cater to a specific clientele."

"OK... but how much is the book?" Zoë asked again.

"It's not for sale. It's a collectible."

Zoë became aware of the man at the bulletin board turning and watching her. She began to sweat a little bit.

Jesus, calm down. Not everyone is out to get you.

"So it's not for sale, or it's a collectible. Which one?"

The girl reached over and took the book. "It's not for sale to you, only to collectors."

"How do you know I don't collect dog books?" Zoë asked, bristling. "And what does it matter? All I wanted to know was how much it costs. Do you care where it goes as long as it's paid for?"

"Are you a collector of rare books catering to the owners of... exotic pets?" the man interrupted, smiling. His voice was pleasant and mild, and she relaxed a little, despite his patronizing words. "Excuse me for butting in, but I know the owner of this shop and she considers these books her treasure. She is very particular about where they go when they leave her care."

"Why should she..." Zoë trailed off when she got a closer look at the bulletin board to the man's left. Several flyers stood out, many with phone numbers ripped from the bottom. One, advertising an exorcism service specializing in elemental demons, looked burned in a couple of places. The flyer that had caught her eye was pink, and the one the man had just secured with a thumbtack.

Underground Publishing
LOOKING FOR WRITERS

Underground Publishing is a new company writing travel guides for people like you. Since we're writing for people like you, we need people like you to write for us.

(continued)

Pluses: Experience in writing, publishing, or editing (in this life or any other), and knowledge of New York City.

Minuses: A life span shorter than an editorial cycle (in this case, nine months).

Call 212.555.1666 for more information or e-mail rand@undergroundpub.com for more information.

"Oh, hell yes," said Zoë, and with the weird, dirty hound book forgotten, she pulled a battered notebook from her satchel. She needed a job. She was refusing to adhere to the stereotype of running home to New York, admitting failure at her attempts to leave her hometown. Her goal was a simple office job. She wasn't waiting for her big break on Broadway and looking to wait tables or take on a leaflet-passing, taco-suit-wearing street-nuisance job in the meantime.

Office job. Simple. Uncomplicated.

As she scribbled down the information, the man looked her up and down and said, "Ah, I'm not sure if that's a good idea for you to pursue."

Zoë looked up sharply. "What are you talking about? First I can't buy the book, now I can't apply for a job? I know you guys have some sort of weird vibe going on, 'We're so goth and special, let's freak out the normals.' But for a business that caters to, you know, *customers*, you're certainly not welcoming."

"I just think that particular business may be looking for someone with experience you may not have," he said, his voice level and diplomatic. He held his hands out, placating her.

"But you don't even know me. You don't know my qualifications. I just left Misconceptions Publishing in Raleigh. You heard of them?" She hated name-dropping her old employer—

she would have preferred to forget it entirely—but the second-biggest travel book publisher in the USA was her strongest credential in the job hunt.

The man shifted his weight and touched his chin. "Really. What did you do for them?"

Zoë stood a little taller. "Head researcher and writer. I wrote most of *Raleigh Misconceptions*, and was picked to head the project *Tallahassee Misconceptions*."

He smiled a bit. "Impressive. But you do know Tallahassee is south of North Carolina, right? You went in the wrong direction entirely."

Zoë clenched her jaw. "I was laid off. It wasn't due to job performance. I took my severance and came back home to the city."

The man rubbed his smooth, pudgy cheek. "What happened to cause the layoff? I thought Misconceptions was doing well."

Zoë felt her cheeks get hot. Her boss, Godfrey, had happened. Then Godfrey's wife—whom he had failed to mention until Zoë was well and truly in "other woman" territory—had happened. She swallowed. "Economy. You know how it goes."

He stepped back and leaned against the wall, clearly not minding the cracked and peeling paint that broke off and stuck to his shirt. "Those are good credentials. However, you're still probably not what they're looking for."

Zoë looked at her notebook and continued writing. "Luckily it's not your decision, is it?"

"Actually, it is."

She groaned and looked back up at him. "All right. Who are you?"

He extended his hand. "Phillip Rand. Owner, president, and CEO of Underground Publishing."

She looked at his hand for a moment and shook it, her small fingers briefly engulfed in his grip. It was a cool handshake, but strong.

"Zoë Norris. And why, Mr. Phillip Rand, will you not let me even apply?"

"Well, Miss Zoë Norris, I don't think you'd fit in with the staff. And fitting in with the staff is key to this company's success."

A vision of future months dressed as a dancing cell phone on the wintry streets pummeled Zoë's psyche. She leaned forward in desperation. She was short, and used to looking up at people, but he was over six feet, and she was forced to crane her neck to look up at him. "Mr. Rand. How many other people experienced in researching and writing travel guides do you have with you?"

He considered for a moment. "With that specific qualification? I actually have none."

"So if you have a full staff of people who fit into some kind of mystery mold, but don't actually have experience writing travel books, how good do you think your books are going to be? You sound like you're a kid trying to fill a club, not a working publishing company. You need a managing editor with experience to supervise your writers and researchers. I'm smart, hardworking, creative, and a hell of a lot of fun in the times I'm not blatantly begging for a job—obviously you'll have to just take my word on that. I haven't found a work environment I don't fit in with. I don't care if Underground Publishing is catering to eastern Europeans, or transsexuals, or Eskimos, or even Republicans. Just because I don't fit in doesn't mean I can't be accepting as long as they accept me. Just give me a chance."

Phillip Rand was unmoved. "Trust me. You would not fit in. You're not our type."

She finally deflated and sighed. "Isn't this illegal?"

He actually had the audacity to laugh at that. "I'm not discriminating based on your gender or race or religion."

"Then what are you basing it on?"

He licked his lips and looked at her again, studying her. "Call it a gut reaction."

She deflated. "Oh well. It was worth a try. Have a good day."

On her way out, she ran through her options: there were the few publishing companies she hadn't yet applied to, the jobs that she had recently thought beneath her that she'd gladly take at this point. She paused a moment in the Self-Help section to see if anything there could help her better herself. She glanced at the covers for *Reborn and Loving It, Second Life: Not Just on the Internet,* and *Get the Salary You Deserve! Negotiating Hell Notes in a Time of Economic Downturn.* Nothing she could relate to, so she trudged out the door, contemplating a long bath when she got back to her apartment. Better than unpacking more boxes.

After the grimy door shut behind her, Zoë decided she had earned a tall caloric caffeine bomb to soothe her ego. She wasn't sure what she'd done to deserve this, but it didn't take much to make her leap for the comfort treats these days—which reminded her, she needed to recycle some wine bottles.

The Shambling Guide to New York City

THEATER DISTRICT:
Shops

Mannegishi's Tricks is the oldest bookstore in the Theater District. Established 1834 by Akilina, nicknamed "The Drakon Lady," after she immigrated from Russia, the store has a stock that is lovingly picked from collections all over the world. Currently managed by Akilina's great-grandaughter, Anastasiya, the store continues to offer some of the best finds for any book collector. Anastasiya upholds the old dragon lady's practice of knowing just which book should go to which customer, and refuses to sell a book to the "wrong" person. Don't try to argue with her; the drakon's teeth remain sharp.

Mannegishi's Tricks is one of the few shops that deliberately maintain a squalid appearance—dingy, smelly, with a strong "leave now" aura—in order to repel unwanted customers. In nearly 180 years, Akilina and her descendants have sold only three books to humans. She refuses to say to whom. ■